Copyright © 2003 by Victoria Welsh

ISBN 0-9755739-6-9
First Printing 2004
Cover art and design by Anne Clarkson

Published by:
Dare 2 Dream Publishing
A Division of Limitless Corporation
Lexington, South Carolina 29073

Find us on the World Wide Web
http://www.limitlessd2d.net

Printed in the United States and internationally by
Lightning Source, Inc.

Acknowledgements

We'd like to thank Arly, Lisa, Mary, Heather of Soul Food Café, and all of the folks at Xena Rules for their invaluable help. Your support and belief in us is appreciated beyond measure.

~~ Love and hugs, K. C. and Victoria

This story is dedicated to sleeping Amazons everywhere.

Prologue

650 AD
Central Arizona

The sun rides high in the sky, a blinding orb that overheats the air and sucks the moisture from our bodies. It sears the barren ground and reflects the heat upward through the soles of our worn sandals.

We are in bad shape. That last battle with the strange, dark skinned warriors hurt us and we were forced to leave the bodies of several of our own. Individually, we are demoralized, but as a group find renewed strength.

There are just five of us now, Leeja, Peli, Shanna, Solana, and myself, Marna. We are the sole survivors of a long and arduous march across some of the most inhospitable country we have ever encountered. It is my duty as our Queen's trusted companion to be true to her at all times and protect her from any evil that might befall her. I will lay my life down for her if necessary. Now, without question, I attempt to guide our small tribe toward the distant mountains, but it's hard to convey confidence when it appears that we are heading deeper into disaster.

Our choices are limited. We cannot go back for fear of meeting again with the same fierce warriors. While we are equally fierce and unafraid, we are only five and they are tens of five.

Leeja, my Queen, my partner on the battlefield and in my bed, is wounded. An arrow pierced her belly. My heart aches, for I have sworn to protect her forever. When she dies, and I know she soon will, my heart will die with her.

1

We gather enough tough, woody material from a dead prickly plant, the nearest thing to real trees we have found hereabouts, fashion a litter, and cover it with skins, worn and ragged from our long trek. Together we lift Leeja and place her gently upon it. She holds her breath and grunts in pain while we make her as comfortable as we can. I weave some thinner pieces into a cover, shading her from the glare of the sun and from its infernal heat.

Our progress with the litter is slow, but I will not leave Leeja behind despite her requests that we do so. Nor do my companions expect that I would.

The prickly plants do provide water, not a lot, but enough to keep us going if we use it sparingly.

Day after day, we trudge toward our destination, a distant range of mountains, but each morning when we start out, they appear as far away as they were yesterday, the day before, and the day before that. They shimmer, a ghostly mirage in the hot air, ever-beckoning, inviting.

Peli, Shanna, and Solana insist they take turns pulling the litter. I, keeping my eyes on the distant peaks, lead the way. It takes two to pull the loaded litter over the rough terrain. The other follows at a distance, frequently checking our backtrack. At night we take turns watching and listening, searching the darkness for marauders or wild animals hot on the scent of blood. I take my turn at watch, but when I am not so involved, I lie down beside the litter and hold my Leeja. When I look into her green eyes, they brighten a bit, but always they reflect the pain she is suffering.

"Leeja, my love, I curse the ancestors who so long ago started us on a journey that has brought us here, to this place that has been forsaken by the gods."

"Do not despair." Leeja's voice holds little strength. "The mountains ahead will be covered with lush forests," she says, focusing on some distant point. "There will be game to spare, fresh water gushing from grottos, and sparkling lakes in which to wash our bodies."

"Alas, woman of my life, I wish I could be as sure."

2

"Be sure, Marna, the mountains will welcome us. We will find peace there, a place where we can rest on our journey." She pauses to catch her breath. "Perhaps, Marna, my love, it will be the end of our journey, a place where we can start anew. There may even be young women who will join with us, make our tribe strong again. There may even be women with child who will add twofold to our number."

"Yes, love of my life, that may be so." I sigh, for I know in my heart that there is no land of plenty awaiting us, no lush forests like Leeja, in her fevered mind, envisions.

The litter moves again and I awaken. I see Marna close by and I am calmed by her presence. My pain is a constant companion. I do not remember where I am or what cycle of the moon it is, but I remember why I hurt.

I am gut-shot and will soon pass beyond this world to serve my Goddess in spirit form. I am called Leeja, Amazon Queen, soul partner of Marna. Never again in this world will I make love with my beloved Marna. I can see the agony in her eyes and feel the despair in her gentle touch. That is why I hurt.

The others keep me as comfortable as they can. They carry me on this litter and use leaves and bits of clothing to dress my wound. Peli cuts and chews the tough flesh of the spiny green plant, then places it in my mouth. It moistens my throat. The fierce sun burned and blistered my body before Marna made a canopy for the litter. Now, I have some relief from the heat, but I smell filthy from sweat and blood and this festering wound. We all are weak and weary from the constant search for food and water and a way out of our desperate situation.

Marna crouched beside my litter and stroked my face with her strong, tapered fingers. "I have appointed Solana as my lieutenant," I say, "only because you are too close to me and will act, perhaps foolishly, with your heart. You must follow her now and leave me here." I watched her eyes glisten like jewels. "I am only slowing you down."

"Never, my dearest one," she answered, her voice husky. "I will never leave you."

Then, she recounts my brave deeds in battle and tells of my prowess as a tribal hunter and leader. Alas, those days are gone forever. I feel a few tears threaten and swallow hard, amazed that there can be any moisture left in my body. My fingers clasp the Amazon Medal of Valor that I wear around my neck. I rub it between my forefinger and thumb. How proud I was to have earned it for valor in battle. Marna wears a similar one, but she was awarded hers many seasons ago, before I was so honored. I must give my medal to Marna. When I pass over, she will have it to remind her of our undying love. As for Solana, although she is young, she is experienced in the ways of the tribe. She will keep our band of lost souls together and see them safely home. I have faith in her leadership ability.

We halt for the night in a narrow canyon with a shallow cave. As the sun leaves the sky, I shiver. Shanna covers my nakedness with a bit of fur and Marna hugs me to her breast and whispers words of love.

I manage to sip a portion of broth that Solana has heated for us. "You all need this nourishment more than I." My protests are in vain.

"Do not speak this way," Marna scolds me. "Drink. It will make you stronger. You must fight on, my beloved. Do not give up on us...Do not give up on me."

It breaks my heart. I must pretend for her sake.

Dear, gentle Marna, so fierce a warrior, so stubborn and wise, but so gentle and patient with me. I long to tell her that the Goddess has visited me several times. I am prepared. I am not afraid. She has shown me visions of the lands beyond this infernal rock and sand, this barren place of oppressive heat. I can see great, lush, green valleys, flower-filled meadows, smooth, clear streams and lakes teeming with fish. I close my eyes and smile through the pain.

Someday, my sisters will live in beautiful huts and peace will be restored. Our daughters will know great happiness. The Amazon Nation will spread into many lands. My sisters will live and prosper far into the future, not as a nation perhaps, but as strong independent women, bringing courage and strength, wisdom and beauty to all they meet. At times, they will

4

recognize their fellow sisters and band together in pairs or groups. Sometimes, just one or two will work to bring harmony and peace to a village or country. They will be strong; they will have great power. The Goddess has promised. She has shown me the way. I must convince Marna that the Amazons will survive ... somehow.

May the Goddess give me the time and the strength.

Now, I place my hand in Marna's. She kisses my cracked lips and lets my head press against her breast. I hear the strong, familiar, rhythm of her heartbeat. It comforts me.

"Sleep, dear one," she murmurs. "I love you with all my heart. I will love you always."

"...And forever," I whisper.

Our camp overlooks the broad and barren valley so recently traversed, an uncompromising landscape of rock with a scattering of strange plants, a land thirsty for the healing properties of life giving water. The oppressive heat continues into the nights making it impossible to sleep. Our skin is dried and blistered ... we are dirty and short of temper, but we cling together for therein is our only salvation.

I see Leeja losing her grip on life; even her desire to continue is threadbare--the fabric tearing.

"Don't give up, my dearest one. Soon it will rain, the grass will green and flowers will blossom from the dirt and rock."

"It is hard, my Marna," she says. "The pain is relentless. My wounds refuse to heal and evil has entered my body."

"Don't speak that way." I hold her in my arms.

"It is too hot, even to embrace."

"I know, dearest one, but there will be time for that later when the land is lush again and the rain falls from the sky to renew our life and all life."

My words speak of hope when there isn't any. My arms speak of a love that will soon be taken from them, and already, I feel the shriveling of my heart. How will I go on without my Leeja? I have been a brave warrior, a wise counselor to the younger members of my tribe only because she was the woman who encouraged me. Now, even as I try to give her hope, I am losing mine. We have come to this ... this desolate mountain overlooking the valley of Tartarus from whence there can be no escape.

"Do you remember, Leeja, the stories our mothers told us when we were children?"

"I do."

Her fevered eyes brightened and I was able to again see the pride behind them.

"I will never forget the stories," Leeja said, her voice croaked with dryness, her lips cracked with fever, "though this cursed land threatens to wither everything including our memories."

I kissed Leeja's forehead and felt the heat of the evil thing that was consuming her. Keep talking, I told myself. As long as you keep her talking, she won't leave.

"What a time it was when our long-ago grandmothers built rafts of reeds and left their homeland to travel across the great water. Imagine, seeing the home land you had known forever fade into the distance and seeing nothing ahead of you except water, and not knowing if there was any land out there, on the other side of the setting sun."

"I'd rather it be endless water than this dirt and dust."

"Whatever they thought to find, Leeja, they must have felt it better that staying where they were."

"Why did they leave?"

"Hunger, drought." I thought about it for a minute and remembered another story I had heard when I was a small child. "There were evil men ... tribes who came from the North ... who came in such numbers that our people couldn't fend them off. They raped the women and made slaves of our children."

"How did our long-ago grandmothers find their way across the water without landmarks to guide them?"

Leeja had heard the stories, as had I. She knew the answers, so she was keeping me talking, too. She must feel as I do, that talking would shield against the death that threatened to separate us.

"The Gods sent the Water People to guide them, the finned ones who flew through the water like birds through the sky.

They would leap, these Water Beings, high into the air. Sometimes, they leapt over the raft and dropped fish food for our long-ago grandmothers to eat."

"Yes, Marna, and they stayed right with them until our long-ago grandmothers arrived safely on a new shore."

"We should have been there, Leeja, you and I."

"In a way we were and still are ...we're the end of a long line of Grandmothers who never gave up the search for a better life." Her smile relieved momentarily the pain that was etched into her features. "And what of Taceesha's band? I wonder how they are faring?"

"Ah yes, my headstrong, younger sister."

"How long, Marna, since they split from us ... three, four moons?"

"Longer. We have lost count of the seasons for this is the place the seasons forgot."

"Taceesha is young, Marna, but she's not headstrong. You only say that because she's your sister, and you worry about her. I saw the sadness in your eyes the day you and she drew sticks to decide which paths to follow." Leeja paused long enough to catch her breath. "We'll rendezvous with Taceesha and her band again ... when we get beyond this cursed land."

"I am sure, Leeja, that they are safe. After all, the young girls travel with them, those of age to bear daughters ... if they can find men worthy to plant the seeds. Our future lies with them. Taceesha knows that and she will lead them well." I had read the future though, even that day when she and I drew sticks ... I knew then, we were destined not to meet again but the strength of our grandmothers stayed with me so I never gave up hope ... until now, that is, as I watch my Leeja slipping away.

"Marna, hold me, take me this last time in your arms and let me feel the touch of your soft lips on mine."

I draw her to me and kiss her gently. "Stay with me, Leeja, for I will never leave you."

"I will not leave you either. Even though I will reside with the Great Goddess, the Mother of all Gods, I will be here with you." She pauses, catching her breath. I can see the light dimming in her eyes, as if a shadow is crossing her sun.

7

"I will always be with you, Marna, loving you and looking out for you. You will know that I am with you when the wind touches your cheek and when life-giving rain falls upon your body ... I will be there in the wind and in each raindrop, for I have seen the Goddess's Garden and I know what awaits me there. And when She calls for you, I will be waiting to greet you at the garden gate and we will walk, together again, through fields of flowers." She pauses, a long absent smile upon her face. "It is a place, Marna, where fruit trees grow in abundance and sunshine polishes the apples, where vegetables ripen on the vine and birds fill the morning with song."

"I love you so much, Leeja," I say, trying to contain the tears that dry before they are shed. I hold her to me, and kiss her crusted eyes, her dried and cracked lips. "I will love you always."

"And forever," she responds, before the rattle in her throat tells me that she has left quietly and peacefully like the sun setting over a distant ocean. The light that brightened my life has been extinguished.

I look up to see Peli, Shanna, and Solana standing, heads bowed, behind me. As they begin to keen, I sob dry tears.

We place Leeja's body in a shallow cave and pile rocks in front of the entrance. A few moments before we seal it completely, and while there is room enough for me to crawl inside, I turn to the others, "I want to say good bye one last time."

I wriggle through the almost sealed entrance and kneel beside Leeja. The others move away to allow me a moment of privacy.

I take the medallion she has worn so proudly and pull my own from my neck. The surfaces, now pressed together, create a heat that warms my hand and heart. "Oh, my Leeja, we have been so blessed, I doubt there can ever be another love as great as ours."

I lay the medallions on a recessed shelf along the wall behind Leeja's head, high above her. "May they guard you as you sleep, dear one. Perhaps, some day, another worthy couple will discover them and know the passion we possessed. I hope so."

I kiss Leeja's cooling checks and her lips that no longer respond.

Slowly and methodically, I draw my dagger. "Where you go, I go."

There is no pain. I do not feel the blade enter my chest. I am aware only momentarily of my blood pouring forth. I collapse on top of Leeja and allow the darkness to surround us.

Chapter One

September 1999
Arizona's Superstition Mountains

"Dammit all to hell! I'm an archaeologist not a babysitter!" I kicked a small stone and watched it rattle along the rocky slope in front of me until it settled at the base of a Prickly Pear Cactus. A Poor-Will whistled in the distance.

Pup, my five year old, half wolf companion, nuzzled his head against my hip. I leaned over and scratched behind his ears, noting a hint of sympathy in his bright yellow eyes.

" 'Kim, you're the best,' Curtis had said, as if flattery would sway me. 'Take her under your wing. Teach her the reality of what it means to be an accomplished archaeologist.' Can you believe that, Pup? The nerve of it."

He snorted and shook himself. I smiled in spite of my anger. *Sometimes, I swear that animal knows just what I'm saying.*

We stood on the ridge and breathed in the cool night air. I felt my initial anger subside in the presence of such peaceful surroundings. A full moon spread its eggshell white blanket over the mysterious Superstition Mountains of Arizona. Below us, in the Valley of the Sun, the city lights dimmed the stars as if trying in their own way to deny all that was not man made. Only a few, unidentifiable, rustles and squeaks, and the occasional cry of a coyote broke the silence.

These days my imagination invented strange shapes and I saw visions in the shadows. Perhaps I'd been an archaeologist too long. Searching for hidden answers in the dirt and dust of time is so much a part of who I am that there are times when I am

11

unable to define the moments of my own reality as distinctly separate from the ancient lives I seek.

Tomorrow is going to be a trying day. Frederick Lane Curtis is a wealthy, powerful man. As Chairman of the Curtis Foundation, he controls the grant money for my expedition.

"Why is my funding contingent upon making his daughter my assistant?" *Or is it? He didn't say that but...* I pulled the collar of my jean jacket up around my neck. I hadn't met Priscilla Josephine Curtis, but I was familiar with her reputation as a spoiled little rich girl. After earning her doctorate from Boston University, she had worked for four years at various sites on three continents, and had published several excellent papers. If she would focus, she could make a name for herself in archaeology. Unfortunately, she was a playgirl, a jet setter, whose idea of the good life was the party circuit.

I turned my back on the city lights and strolled back to my tent, a twelve by twelve foot room that I had purchased years ago from an old prospector. The lantern burning inside cast flickering shapes on the canvas walls. I had furnished the tent with the necessities; a couple of hard folding chairs, a folding table, a laptop computer with extra batteries, research documents, and maps.

My motor home, which served as both home and office, was parked in nearby Apache Junction, an untidy community at the foot of Superstition Mountain, but this night, like so many others of late, I was staying on site. Was it because I felt I was getting close to those I sought that I didn't want to leave? Or was it that, in my reflective mood, I just needed to surround myself with the mystery of the mountain, the quiet of the night, and the light of the full moon?

"What can I do, fella?" I sat on my hard camp cot and waited for Pup to join me. He sat with his chin on my thigh and huffed a weary sigh. "You understand, don't you? I'm dependent on the Curtis money to complete my work. And I'm so close ... so very close to finding them."

My fingers slipped through his thick ruff. We knew each other well, he and I. We each understood and loved the other without question or expectation.

12

I had worked alone all my professional life, especially during the last five years, except for my student assistants. Even when I was teaching I was my own person, but now ... being responsible for Curtis's playgirl daughter was going to seriously cramp my studies. How was this woman's presence going to affect my team of carefully chosen graduate students? Would she disrupt them, especially the young men? Would she claim their attention with her worldly art of seduction? Young men are so vulnerable when it comes to beautiful women and from what I had seen of Doctor Curtis in *People* and other publications, she was an attractive young woman.

I hoped that Doctor Curtis would understand my not taking time to meet her at Phoenix's Sky Harbor Airport. Even if she didn't, that would be her problem, not mine. She'd get no preferential treatment from me. Sandy, the most responsible of my students, would greet her and escort her to the inn. She'd appreciate a little breathing time before meeting me for dinner anyway. Sandy was a shy young man and I hoped that this quality would be an effective barrier to the advances of a woman whose questionable reputation preceded her. I had toyed with the idea of warning him about Doctor Curtis, but decided that he was an adult and could take care of himself.

After spreading my sleeping bag and air mattress on the ground under the stars, I boiled water for tea on my single burner Primus Stove. A few minutes later, I was sitting cross-legged on my inviting bed, cupping the warm mug in my hands. Pup stretched out in front of me, his head resting on his paws, eyes ever watchful.

This expedition was so important to me and I felt that, finally, I was closing in on my quarry, the mysterious Lost Tribe of the Amazons. Much of my life to this point focused on this one project. While most people, even some of my contemporaries, believed the Amazons were legend, I felt there was much more to their story. Even while working other expeditions, which I did from time to time, my mind seldom strayed from this small band of women warriors who had supposedly reached North America. According to legend, they built a raft and with the aid of wind and currents made their way across the vast ocean.

Francisco De Orellana, Spanish Adventurer and Explorer, allegedly fought a tribe of Amazon-like warrior women in the summer of 1542 near the Maranon River, later renamed the Amazon. Could those warriors be related to the tribe I sought? I had reason to believe my band had reached the New World and I was hot on their trail. Nothing would stop me or slow my progress, not the spoiled Doctor Curtis nor the local media who had been hounding me for a story. Frederick Curtis, at my urging, had seen to it that this site was concealed from public view with round the clock security.

Lying on my back, I began counting the stars in the Milky Way, letting the majesty of my surroundings relax my brain and my body until I was just one more soul at peace with Mother Earth.

I don't know how long I'd been asleep before I awakened in a sweat. My watch told me it was two-forty. I pulled my sleeping bag up around my shoulders and began to analyze for the umpteenth time the strange dreams and visions that had disturbed my sleep these past months. Had I spent too many years chasing this small tribe around the globe? Was I obsessed with the chase? I was pushing fifty. Not old by a long way, but what to do if this latest lead ended at a blank wall? Could I risk taking my career farther along this path? Would it be better for me to start over and forget this lifelong search for the lost tribe?

Unable to go back to sleep, I got up and walked the quarter mile or so to the mouth of the small canyon where we worked long hours each day. The beam from my flashlight played across the grid, the measured squares of promising dirt, then on, into the shadows. *Why here? Why am I so sure the answer is here?* I searched the low desert shrubbery illuminated by the moonlight. I marveled at the pure artistry; the feathery shadows cast by the Palo Verde Trees onto the canyon wall. Strata in the rock bent the shadows like sticks in a pail of water. Standing still and silent, I focused on my surroundings, hoping something there would speak to me ... a voice from the past would be nice.

14

Before crawling back into my sleeping bag, I swallowed a mild, across the counter sedative. Pup stretched his muscular body alongside me. Moments later, the howl of distant coyotes brought his head up. I stroked behind his ears. "Settle down, fella. There's nothing you need worry about." He gave me a wise look before laying his long muzzle on his outstretched paws. His ears twitched as another howl echoed across the ridges. A pair of coyotes spoke to each other across a draw below camp.

I closed my eyes with my fingers buried in the comforting warmth of Pup's ruff. Tomorrow was going to be a difficult day. Meeting Doctor Curtis for dinner was not something I contemplated with pleasure, but I intended to do what I could to make her feel welcome.

Victoria Welsh and K.C. West

16

Chapter Two

Mitch and Stacie secured my gear and settled me into one of the plush seats in my father's corporate jet. I buckled my seatbelt, opened a bottle of mineral water, and perused several articles written by Doctor Kimberly Blair.

"Sorry, Doctor Curtis, this was all I could find for snacking." Stacie dropped two packets of peanuts and cheese crackers on the table beside my seat and tucked a pillow behind my head.

"Damn, what happened to the cashews?"

"Your father has a fondness for them, too." She fussed a bit more with the pillow and dimmed the cabin lights the way I like them. "The blanket is just to your left. Is there anything else you need?"

"Besides cashews, you mean?" I said, half-seriously.

"Next flight, I promise."

With a final glance about the spacious blue and gray interior, she wiped a smudge from the polished teak table and moved through to the cockpit where Mitch prepared for takeoff.

Once we were airborne, I kicked off my running shoes and drew the blanket up around my shoulders, taking a last look at the photograph of Doctor Blair. The first thing I noticed were her piercing brown eyes. My stomach clenched at the thought of them boring into my soul on a regular basis. I'd call her face handsome rather than pretty. Threads of gray gave an air of distinction and maturity to her short, dark hair. Her lean body was a testament to many years of outdoor activity. I read further about her arduous and determined search for a tribe of lost Amazons, and experienced something akin to awe.

"You probably don't know me, Doctor Blair," I whispered to her picture, "but I worked my butt off to get this assignment. If you knew how difficult it is to communicate with my father these days, you'd appreciate that effort. He thinks all I do is screw up. He's never taken me seriously as an archaeologist ... nobody has, really. I guess I can't blame them. They read the tabloids, believe the rumors, and remember the photos. Damn it, I'm more than a blonde in a bikini on some beach. All I want is a chance to prove it. Father says you're the most dedicated archaeologist the Curtis Foundation has ever funded. I've read all of your papers and I agree with him. Help me, please. Teach me everything you know. Someday, I want to be just like you."

I snuggled down inside my fleecy jacket, letting its softness surround and comfort me. It had been cold and cloudy when we left Logan Airport. I knew Phoenix would be warm and sunny. Finding an outfit that transcended the climate and cultural change presented a challenge. The Polartec 300 fleece jacket would work, with shirts layered underneath. I could shed them as the temperature climbed. My khaki cargo pants, while lightweight for Boston, had proved serviceable on other digs above and below the equator.

I felt silly worrying about first impressions, but it was unlikely that my new boss needed me as her assistant director. If she had heard of me at all, it would be by my less than stellar reputation. I planned to change that image, if Doctor Blair would just give me the chance.

The cabin grew warmer. I must have fallen asleep because the warbling phone startled me. "PJ Curtis," I mumbled.

"You sound all fuzzy and soft around the edges, just the way I like you."

"Stephen? Where are you?"

"Still in Rio. I should be back in New York next week. They've taken my advice on reinforcing that wall with high-grade steel beams. The job's almost finished, though I must say; it's boring as hell, now, with you not here to amuse me. Do you really have to do this, Cilla?"

"Yes, Stephen. Soon, I'll be face to face with the legendary Doctor Kimberly Blair. Then, we're off to the Superstition Mountains to search for Amazons."

I heard him sigh and pictured his 'little boy' pout, but I wasn't falling for that act ... not this time.

You're a master at manipulating me, Stephen. The society pages predict marriage for us, but something is missing from our relationship. You're handsome and successful and I can't complain about the sex, though I rarely see fireworks. We share beds but we never manage to share our hearts. My father seems to love you. I don't know why I can't.

"Cilla, don't you think you'd have better luck finding Amazons here in South America?"

"Not these Amazons. Really, it's all very Top Secret right now. I promise to call you in a day or two. Are you still at the same hotel?"

"Until Friday. I just keep hoping you'll change your mind and come back to me. You left your toothbrush and some silky unmentionables in the bathroom."

"Oh shit! I knew I forgot something."

"You forgot to stay here with me."

"Stephen, we've been over this ground before. You know it's important for my career..."

"Gotta go, hon. I'm late for a meeting. God, I miss you. I can't believe you're doing this to me."

"You'll survive, Stephen, and I promise I'll call you." I replaced the phone and closed my eyes, picturing his curly, brown hair and brilliant blue eyes. With a little more effort, I could feel his body on top of me, and his possessive kisses on my throat, neck, and ... a couple of other places.

The phone rang again. I took a drink of mineral water before answering.

"Priscilla, I've just got a moment."

"Hello, Father. Is something wrong?"

"Should there be?" His laugh was somewhat brittle. "I just wanted to tell you that I leaned on the people at the University of Arizona and they'll let you folks use their labs."

"That's wonderful. They have all the latest equipment."

"Well, that's good then, Priscilla. Remember you begged for this assignment. Doctor Blair is a highly respected professional. Don't embarrass me."

Stacie poked her head into the cabin and drew her hand across her neck.

"I'll do my best Father. I've got to hang up now. Either we're about to land or Stacie wants to slit my throat."

"Probably both." This time there was no humor at all in his voice. "Call me if you need anything further." The line went dead.

I sighed. *How about a father who cares about me ... and some more cashews?*

It was warm and sunny in Phoenix. Sky Harbor teemed with travelers. I shed the fleece jacket, leaving a dark brown camp shirt unbuttoned over a white tank top. I pulled on my favorite pair of Oakley sunglasses and an old safari hat as a defense against the relentless sunshine. Mitch and Stacie took my bags and helped me through the gate and into the terminal before refueling for their return flight.

The air was filled with the aroma of southwestern cooking, reminding me that I was a long way from Boston and hadn't eaten since breakfast. I ignored my rumbling stomach and scanned faces in the crowd for the illustrious Doctor Blair. A rectangular cardboard sign with 'Doctor P. J. Curtis' in black marker caught my eye. Holding it over his head was a handsome, muscular young man with a dark tan and hair so bleached by the sun it appeared white. As I made my way through the crowd toward him, I got a glimpse of a silver belt buckle, slim hips encased in faded jeans, and a plaid shirt displaying well-defined biceps. His blue eyes twinkled and he favored me with a shy grin.

"I'm Doctor Curtis."

He tucked the sign in back of his sweat-stained straw cowboy hat and nodded, extending his right hand. "Peter Arnold, ma'am. Just call me Sandy. Doc Blair sent me to getcha."

As we shook hands his gaze hovered politely near my shoulders, not my chest. I was accustomed to getting the once-over by men, some brazenly overt in their perusal. Not that my breasts merited any great attention; they were adequate, but nothing spectacular. This chivalrous attention was incredibly refreshing.

Then, I absorbed his message and its implication.

"I see. And just where is Doctor Blair?"

"She uh ... well ... she's still out at the site. I'm to get you settled at the inn and she'll meet you 'bout six for dinner."

I felt a flush warm my cheeks. *There ya go PJ. I guess that says it all. You're just her second in command. Now, you know how much she values your ability.* "Well, Sandy, it seems I have all afternoon with nothing to do. Can you suggest how I might while away the hours until our boss manages to fit me into her schedule?"

He raised his sights to my face this time. "Ma'am, I'd be proud to show you around some, if you'd like."

I smiled. "I'd like that just fine." His grin widened. "And you know what else I'd like?" I grabbed my two bags, while he shouldered my duffel and suitcase.

"No ma'am."

"I'd like you to call me PJ. None of this ma'am stuff. That's for much older women."

I flashed one of my sexy, sweet smiles and he turned an adorable shade of pink.

"Yes, ma'... uh ... PJ."

It promised to be a fun-filled afternoon. I looked forward to getting more intimately acquainted with this handsome cowboy. We loaded my bags into his dusty Jeep and set off to see the sights of the cactus fields...or as the locals called it...the Valley of the Sun.

Chapter Three

The shower stall in the motor home was small, but adequate. Warm water cascading over my body felt like the touch of a lover massaging the stiffness from my shoulders, but did little for the weariness I felt after having had another night disturbed by strange dreams. Truth be known, I felt more like sleep than dinner.

As I towel dried my short hair, I wondered how I would hit it off with Doctor Curtis.

Would she take the job seriously? The last thing I needed was a playgirl whose interests would more likely focus on my male students than on the project. Would the young women on my team be affected by Curtis's overt attention to the men? Would she be a disruptive force on a team that had worked so well together?

I tucked a blue-checked, crisply pressed shirt into my lightweight slacks, threaded a leather belt through the loops, and secured the turquoise buckle, all the time wondering why Sandy hadn't returned to the site. Perhaps her plane was late. Unlikely though, since Frederick Curtis had mentioned she was to arrive on the company jet. I turned back the cuffs of my sleeves. One last look in the mirror and I was ready to meet the notorious Doctor P. J. Curtis.

I spoke briefly with the hostess, a pleasant, well-endowed woman in her late fifties. She showed me to my favorite corner table with a fine view of Superstition Mountain. Having eaten many times at the Casa Grande, I was welcomed by the staff and treated in a relaxed, friendly manner. I liked the Casa Grande mainly for its convenience, close to the mountain and my motor home headquarters.

"I'm expecting someone," I told the hostess.

I had the waitress bring me a pot of hot tea. While waiting for the tea to steep, I glanced about the dining room and its occupants. About half the tables were occupied. Later, when the snowbirds gathered for the winter, this place and others like it, would be overrun by seniors gathering in Arizona for the winter, but right now, the season had barely begun. I glanced at the old utensils displayed on the walls, along with prints of western scenes. Art appreciation is in the eye of the viewer, I thought to myself, and none of this appealed to my sense of decor.

I removed the teabag, wrapping the string tightly around the spoon and squeezing the liquid from the bag before setting it in the saucer. Glancing at my watch, I realized that Doctor Curtis was late, quite late. I didn't want her to arrive and catch me toe-tapping and drumming my fingers on the table, but I was feeling put out so I turned my attention to Superstition Mountain, framed as it was by the window. Now that is art, I thought.

Doctor Curtis arrived a half hour late. I did my best to conceal my displeasure. Her blonde hair was expertly styled and she wore just the right amount of makeup, making me conscious of my weathered complexion doctored only with moisturizer and a hint of lip color. I smiled at the differences between us. She wore white shorts and a body-hugging green tank top. A couple of lecherous old men followed her every move as the hostess led her to my table, their wives stared with distaste. Doctor Curtis could turn heads, no doubt about it.

"I apologize for keeping you waiting," she said. "The truth is I overslept." Without waiting for a response from me, she offered her hand. "We finally meet."

"Doctor Curtis." Her hand was soft and smooth. I wondered just how much actual digging she did or was willing to do. Was I saddled with a theoretical archaeologist?

"Call me PJ, this doctor stuff is such a drag, don't you think?"

"I'm proud of my doctorate." My tone was testy. "But, you may call me Kim. By the way, I ordered fruit cups for an appetizer. I hope that's ..."

"No problem." PJ picked up her spoon. She continued talking while concentrating on her fruit.

"What an exhausting afternoon. Sandy and I didn't plan on spending so much time together."

I shot her a stern look. Fortunately, she wasn't watching me.

"Gawd, I was so sore ... I just had to jump in the tub when I got back to the inn."

"Really, there's no need to explain." My imagination was filling in the blanks. Sandy was no match for this woman. She had been around the block more times than there were blocks to go around.

PJ, still playing with her fruit, continued. "The Jacuzzi made me sleepy. You know how that is. Anyway, I slipped into bed for a few minutes, long enough to rejuvenate before coming here, I thought, but the next thing I knew--"

"Doctor Curtis."

She looked up, surprised, I think, at my tone. "Yes?"

"Further explanations aren't necessary." I cleared my throat. "What you do on your own time is your business."

"Yes, of course, but I don't plan to make a habit of ..."

"I most certainly hope not."

"... being late for dinners and appointments."

"That, too." I was being disagreeable. While I had no love lost for Doctor Curtis, she was a fellow archaeologist and for that reason alone, I should treat her with the respect her credentials demanded. Besides, I was a civilized being, subject to polite interaction with others. All I knew of P. J. Curtis, the person, I gleaned from headlines scanned at supermarket checkout lines, hardly a fair evaluation of the woman behind the archaeologist.

"You know," she said, waving her spoon in the air, "I think Sandy was really impressed with my skill. He was amazed that I had so much experience in--"

"My gawd, woman!" I choked on a piece of bread.

"Doctor Blair?" PJ looked at me with some concern. "Are you okay?"

"I just swallowed wrong." I dug into my pocket for a tissue.

We finished our fruit cup in silence, each of us sizing up the other much like boxers stepping into the ring.

When the waitress came with the dinner menu, I ordered my usual, a steak medium well. I caught PJ's raised eyebrow.

"You were about to say?"

"You're not concerned about animal fat and cholesterol?"

"I rely on my work to keep me healthy." PJ bit her lower lip, then ordered a Grilled Chicken Salad with low fat dressing on the side.

I changed the subject. "I trust you had a comfortable flight."

"Well, there weren't any cashews."

"I beg your pardon?"

"Father had eaten all the cashews."

I shook my head.

"I like cashews. Stacie should have seen to it that the supply was replenished before my flight."

"Perhaps Stacie had more important things to do than worry about cashews."

"It's her job to make sure Father and I are comfortable when we travel."

Why, you spoiled little… I bit my tongue, afraid I would say something out loud that I would regret.

We paused when our entree arrived. I was hungry after a long day at the site. My steak looked good, as did the baked potato just waiting to be smothered with sour cream and chives. When I bit into the meat it was so tender it melted in my mouth. I watched as PJ drizzled a scant teaspoon or two of dressing onto her salad.

"Tell me, Doctor Curtis, PJ, why do you want to work here with me? Are you interested in the Lost Tribe?"

"Your work intrigues me."

"How familiar are you with what I'm doing?"

"I've read all you've written and published on the subject. You think the legend is based in fact and you want to prove it. I know your search has taken you from Greece to South America and now here." PJ paused to chew a mouthful of salad. "You must think you're on to something."

"What makes you think so?"

The waitress stopped at our table to make sure everything was okay. I complimented her on the steak and asked her to bring a fresh pot of tea.

"I think you're on to something because you've cloaked this part of your search in secrecy." PJ dabbed her mouth with her napkin. Her table manners were impeccable. "You're either on to something or you've recognized failure and you want to hide it from the world." Her smile was challenging.

"Doctor Curtis ..."

"It's PJ, remember, and I was kidding. I believe you're on to something big. I'd like to be part of it."

"You can be as long as you believe in the project and are willing to give your all to it." I took a deep breath. Was I making a big mistake by accepting the high and mighty Doctor Curtis as a member of my team? And what had she done to me personally to trigger such animosity toward her? Despite all the negative press she had received, I knew she was well versed in her chosen profession and she appeared to know enough about my project to speak about it intelligently.

"I read your paper on the use of forensics in archaeology. It was very good."

"Thank you." PJ smiled, pleased, I think, with the compliment. "I'm surprised you've read anything of mine."

"I admire good work no matter whose it is." *That was uncalled for.*

"You do know that Sandy was supposed to return to the site after meeting you today."

"You were supposed to meet me."

I put my fork down carefully and deliberately before taking a deep breath. "I was supposed to have you met. I did that."

"It would have been nice if you would have ..."

"Doctor Curtis, we have approximately eight months of comfortable working temperatures. I want to accomplish as much as possible in that time. I intend no disrespect when I say that my time was better spent at the site than it would have been driving to the airport." I picked up my fork and speared a piece of steak.

"Now, about Sandy, why did he not return to the site?"

"He couldn't. It took us all afternoon to--"

"Please! Don't give me any more details." *What am I doing? I'm asking her questions, but not allowing her to answer them.* This was so unlike me, allowing my anger to get the better of me. What was it about this young woman that so infuriated me? After all, how she lived her life was her business. I wasn't normally this judgmental. Sandy was an excellent student and very likable and perhaps I was being overly protective, but I didn't want PJ to cause him any grief.

PJ chuckled. "In spite of wearing me out, it was a lot of fun. And I was able to show Sandy a few of the things I learned."

I couldn't believe the audacity of this woman. I wanted to slap the smile off her face. "Of all the nerve." I threw down my napkin and started to rise, but thinking better of it, sat down again. "How could you take advantage of him that way?"

"What the hell are you talking about?"

"Don't play innocent with me." I was up again and leaning over the table. "You know damn well what I'm talking about."

"I haven't a clue."

"I told you before what you do off site and on your own time is your business. If, however, you choose to prey on my students," I wagged my finger in front of PJ's face, "then it becomes my business." I was making a scene and attracting the attention of other diners.

PJ's face flushed; her green eyes flashed in anger. "My gawd! You think that I bedded your protégé, is that what this is about?"

"You all but admitted ..."

"I admitted nothing of the kind." PJ tossed her wadded up napkin on the table and stood up. "I don't give a shit who you are. I don't have to sit here and listen to you accuse me of gawd knows what. You're as dried up and brittle as this damn desert and I'm outta here."

"But you said ..."

PJ was not listening to anything else I might have to say. "I'm guilty. Case closed. Is that it? I know all about my reputation ... I thought you'd at least give me a chance ..." Her voice cracked. "Damn it, this time I'm innocent. Sandy has a minivan with a faulty transmission. We worked on it all afternoon and got it rebuilt. If you can't trust him ... or me, then..." She stopped in mid sentence, turned on her heel and left.

I glanced at the other diners who immediately found that their meals or table partners demanded their attention. "Shit." I rubbed my eyes with my forefinger and thumb.

"Are you okay, Doctor Blair?" It was the hostess.

"Thank you, Betts, I'm fine." I sighed. "It was just a little misunderstanding between colleagues."

"Hey, I know how that goes. It's sorta like me and my daughter, we're always at loggerheads."

"Thank God," I inclined my head in the direction of the exit, "that she isn't my daughter."

"Who the HELL does she think she is?" I slammed the door, slipped off my sandals and threw them the length of the motel room. "Dried up old prune...Probably hasn't had a good lay in months."

My tank top and shorts sailed in the direction of the sandals. "Damn it!" I said to the mirror over the dresser. An irritated blonde in a white lace bra glared back at me. I paced the room in my underwear trying to control my outrage. "A shower ... I need a long, hot, shower."

Half an hour later, I toweled myself dry and wiped a circle through the steam-covered bathroom mirror. The skin on my face was already suffering the effects of the dry, Arizona heat. *Jesus! Living like this is going to take a ton of moisturizer.*

"Curtis, this is an all-time record for you." I poured cream onto my palms and administered first aid to my parched face. "You've probably been kicked off this project before you even set foot on the site. And the irony of it is you weren't guilty this time. You were screwed by your reputation for screwing." I laughed, mirthlessly and wiped the excess fluid off my hands.

"What the hell is the matter with you?" I pulled on my terry cloth robe and began to blow dry my hair, using a low setting and a styling brush. My initial gestures were full of unresolved anger. I frowned and grimaced at my reflection as I worked.

As my hair dried, the tension in my body dissipated. "Negative thoughts, beget negative energy...and negative energy is self-destructive." I snapped off the dryer and took a deep breath. "You've got so much going for you, woman. Why do you self-destruct when shit like this happens?"

I gazed at myself for several seconds. It had been months since I'd felt the need for a critical self-evaluation, but for some reason, it seemed necessary tonight.

You have a nice face, good cheekbones and clear, green eyes. You're short, but your body has good muscle tone with firm abs and a flat stomach, thanks to all those sit-ups and crunches. There's good definition in your arms and shoulders. Go ahead, flex your biceps, you know you want to. I pushed my sleeves back and grinned as the right bicep bulged.

Show off. You've got a decent brain and the ability to speak and write coherently...most of the time. Fortune Magazine considers you a hot prospect in the marriage arena. Conservatively speaking, you're worth twenty or thirty million. You're recognized in most of the best restaurants in Boston and several in New York. You could be anywhere in the world right now...with almost anybody. Why the hell do you need to be here, in this God-forsaken pile of detritus, with a crusty, old bitch who thinks you have the morals of an alley cat?

I left the bathroom and padded barefoot to the bed, the question echoing in my brain. Why is it so important? Why here? Why now?

A soft inner voice supplied the answer. *The timing is right. You saw the opportunity to work with Kim Blair. You know she can further your career credibility, so you went for it. Robert Frost spoke of a road less traveled, maybe you're at that point in your life when it's time to take the hard path ... prove you can do the work and jettison those harmful relationships from the past.*

I chuckled. *Geez! Is that all? I thought it might be something important.*

An unusual colored light filtered into the room through a crack in the drapes. I investigated, and though I couldn't see the setting sun from my east-facing window, I could see its light reflecting off several wispy clouds and painting the face of Superstition Mountain in rosy hues. It glowed as if on fire. How mystical and haunting those rocks looked. The vision was captivating.

Shit! The place is already casting a spell on me.

Are you out there somewhere, Amazons? I know Kim Blair thinks you are and she's determined to find you. I think I want to help her.

I sighed and turned back toward the bed. *Okay. What am I going to do about tomorrow? I have to show up on the project. Crusty's not going to have the satisfaction of running me off so easily. There are just a couple of problems. I don't know how to get to the site and I don't have any transportation.*

"Sandy!" I said, snapping my finger. That sweet fellow had given me his phone number. Maybe he'd be willing to help me find the site. I dug around in my purse for the scrap of paper with his number on it and gave him a call. His friendly voice calmed my anxiety and uncertainty.

"Hey, PJ. Whadda ya know? I was just wondering how your dinner went with Doc Blair."

"It was quite an experience, let me tell you."

He laughed. "I'm sure. Doc Blair is one amazing woman."

"You don't know the half of it."

"What's that?"

"Nothing…Listen, Sandy, I wonder if you could help me out."

I didn't have to go into the helpless female act. He was more than willing to pick me up along with two other workers in the newly repaired minivan. "Wait for us in the lobby," he said.

"What time should I be ready?"

"Five thirty should be about right."

"Gawd, won't it still be dark out then?"

"Well, yeah, but we gotta hike a few miles from the trailhead to the campsite. Now that we have the van, we can load it with supplies and carry them in with us. The Jeep couldn't hold all that much with the guys in it."

"Great. Well, I'll see ya bright and early then. Thanks again, Sandy."

"No problem PJ. Sleep tight."

I hung up the phone and groaned. *I don't do mornings very well. This just might kill me.*

I changed into my faded blue scrub suit. Stretching out on the bed, I contemplated my next move. Tomorrow was going to be a challenge. Would PJ show up at the site? What would I say to her or her father about this? And what would Sandy think? PJ would probably tell him what had happened. How could I have been so judgmental and insensitive? I put on my glasses and opened a half read mystery novel, but soon fell into a fitful sleep.

I was relieved, when I awakened in tears from another one of those strange dreams, to find myself safely inside my motor home. What is going on with me, I wondered? Pup fixed his yellow eyes on mine as if reading my thoughts. "I wish you could talk to me." I hugged him. "I'm sure in your wisdom, there is an answer for me."

The motor home did not allow for much pacing, but pace I did, a dozen steps forward to the cockpit, a dozen back to the foot of my bed. When my activity failed to quiet my mind, I went to the bathroom, drank a glass of water, and returned to bed, where I laid awake for the rest of the night.

Chapter Four

Rays of sunshine slanted through the canyon walls of the Superstitions, bathing patches of rock in yellow and gold. By the time we had trudged from the trailhead to the camp, carrying our load of supplies, Sandy, Mike, Donny and I were old friends.

We paused to catch our breath and observe the other graduate students working at the current grid site. I located Doctor Blair at the center of the activity and felt my stomach flip flop. Why was I so uptight? Kim and a young blonde-haired woman were engaged in animated conversation as they peered down at something in the dirt. The other students huddled around them, listening and gesturing.

"Something wrong, PJ?" Sandy had noticed my hesitation.

I smiled. "I'm getting used to the surroundings. I don't want to barge in on everybody while Doctor Blair is lecturing."

"Oh, Doc won't mind. She's very informal about things as long as we do our jobs."

I bit my lower lip. "To be honest with you, I'm not sure she wants me here. We parted on less than friendly terms last night."

Sandy's brow wrinkled, but he didn't ask for details. As we watched Kim and the students, Mike and Donny walked around us with their load of supplies. Sandy shifted his weight and coughed. "Do you want me to go first and smooth the way a bit?"

"No...really. I can do it. Just give me a minute."

He shrugged and moved forward with the guys.

Kim, in her natural habitat, was the consummate professor. The angry and irritated woman that I saw last night was gone. A contented, relaxed woman, dressed in cargo pants and long-sleeved work shirt, had taken her place. She chatted with her students and smiled often, making her face appear at least a decade younger. I noticed her lean, powerful build. Working long days in the outdoors had overcome a lack of good dietary habits and rewarded her with a fit body. She was taller than I remembered, but then, she'd been seated during most of our ill-fated meal.

One of the students said something funny and everyone laughed. Kim was still smiling when her head turned in my direction. Her expression of pleasure and contentment quickly faded. Was that surprise or dismay that replaced it? She wiped her hands on her cargo pants and closed the distance between us.

This is what you wanted, Curtis. You begged to be here working for this woman, learning what she can teach you. Take a deep breath and try not to blow it this time.

Feeling someone's eyes on me, I turned to see PJ standing at the end of the trail that led to the road. She had arrived with Sandy, Mike, and Donny. The fellows were loaded down with gear, but I noticed that PJ, too, carried her fair share.

I walked toward them, sure in my mind that PJ had discussed our misunderstanding with Sandy and wondering what kind of a reception I would receive from them. "Thanks guys," I said to the fellows, eyeing Sandy for any expression of displeasure. There was none. "You know where to stash the stuff."

When they left, I turned to PJ. The morning sun glinted in her hair and her green eyes bore into mine as if searching my soul for goodness knows what. "I'm sorry about last evening ... for assuming something that I shouldn't have." I drew a line in the dirt with the toe of my boot.

"Apology accepted. And by the way, I'm pleased to report that the minivan is running just fine." Her grin fell neatly into the category of one-upmanship. "It's just what we needed for hauling this stuff from town to the trailhead."

"I appreciate your helping Sandy with the van. It's going to save us a lot of trips back and forth." I took a deep breath. "You know, it isn't often I make such a complete ass of myself."

"Well, the jury's still out on that, but now, if you don't mind, I'd like to get to work."

"Of course, allow me to show you around." I relieved her of one of her bundles. "We'll begin over there, at the tent."

While strolling with PJ toward the tent, I was aware of the admiring glances of my male students. I knew what they were seeing in this young woman and hoped it wouldn't disrupt their focus. If she continued to dress conservatively as she had this morning, in cargo pants and a denim shirt, there was nothing to be said. She was, after all, to be my assistant so it would be up to her to keep things under control. I hoped I would not be forced to intervene.

"Looks like you're all set up," PJ said, looking around the interior of the tent and seeing the laptop, maps and charts on the table, and the haphazard pile of books on the floor in one corner.

PJ was about to sit on the edge of the cot when a low growl startled her. Pup emerged from beneath the cot, still growling.

"Is that what I think it is?" PJ asked, backing toward the open flap.

I couldn't help but smile. "Meet Pup. He's half wolf and half German Shepherd."

"He looks all wolf to me, and mean."

I knelt beside Pup. "It's okay, boy." I turned to PJ. "He's protective of me, but once he gets to know you...."

"I don't believe I want to get to know him."

"We'll take care of that right now. Stand very still because I'm going to have him check you out." I whispered a command and Pup slowly approached PJ who was standing so still she could have been mistaken for a granite statue. Pup sniffed her hands, which were hanging loosely at her sides. "Stay very still," I said quietly, not wanting PJ to make any sudden moves.

"I am," she responded between clenched teeth.

"Okay, Pup, what do you think? Is she okay … shall we let her stay?" He let out a low-throated growl and licked her hand. I thought PJ was going to faint so I went to her side. "He's comfortable with you now."

PJ's voice was shaking. "Well, that makes one of us. You know, I'm used to terriers and cocker spaniels." She tried to smile. "He's so big … and that growl is enough to stop one's heart in mid-beat."

"I'm sorry. I should have warned you."

"Yeah, well ..." She eyed the cot. "You stay here?"

"Occasionally. I have a motor home parked in Apache Junction that doubles as my home, at least for now, as well as my headquarters for this project."

"I see."

"Come, I'll show you around the project and introduce you to the rest of the crew." We walked over the rocky ground to the mouth of a small canyon where most of the activity was taking place. Pup followed close on my heels.

"It's pretty up here."

I stopped to look around. "It's not pretty, it's beautiful."

"Sorry."

"Beautiful, but deadly. There are creatures here that can give you all sorts of unpleasant problems, desert rattlers, scorpions, and spiders, especially the Desert Recluse. It's a close relative of the Brown Recluse and the only spider in the States that's really dangerous to humans. The venom can reactivate months after the initial bite causing the victim all kinds of distress, even amputation of the infected area. A bite from that little fellow is not a pleasant experience."

"How do I recognize this delightful creature?"

"Let's see, they're brownish, about a centimeter long, and have six eyes."

"You're dreaming if you think I'm going to hang around counting spider eyeballs."

I chuckled. "The easiest way to identify them is by the violin shaped patch on their heads and mid sections."

"Is that right? Well, I'm not checking for musical instruments with legs either. If I hear of one within a half mile, I'll be gone until it's gone."

"Most importantly though, watch out for dehydration." I tapped the water bottle hanging on my belt. "You need to drink lots of water, even if you aren't thirsty."

"Are you trying to scare me off?"

"Not at all. I'm just telling you what you need to know to be safe up here. Don't let the beauty of the place lull you into a false sense of security." I was feeling better about PJ's presence.

She might not be as difficult to get along with as I had thought, in fact, she was even exhibiting a sense of humor.

Now, if I could do the same...

We walked through a damp area left by an overnight shower and not yet dried by the sun. "I'm glad you didn't wear shorts." My remark was casual and without thought.

"Afraid it would distract the guys?"

I bit my tongue. "I suggest you do not wear shorts because of these," I pointed to a small Teddy Bear Cholla. When I put my leg close to the spiny cactus and drew it away, my pant leg was covered with tiny needle-like barbs. "They call these things Jumping Cholla. I seriously doubt you want them in your bare leg."

"Sorry. I was being a smart ass, as usual."

"I'll let it go this time." I pulled a narrow toothed comb from my pocket, the kind with a handle, and ran it downward and flat against my pant leg, ridding myself of the Cholla spines without getting them in my fingers.

"Hey, neat trick."

"It works."

PJ, peering at the Cholla, was careful to leave plenty of space between it and her. "How far do these things jump?"

"They don't really jump. It just seems like they do. As long as you wear long pants, hiking boots, and carry a comb in your pocket, you'll be okay."

"Thanks for the tip."

"You're welcome. I like to keep my people healthy."

"Hey, I'm sorry I misunderstood ... about the shorts."

"Apology accepted."

"One for one."

"I beg your pardon?"

"Nothing."

We arrived at the grid, a ten by twenty foot area where the crew was working. They were grouped together and talking excitedly over what appeared to be a small blackened, twisted piece of wood. "Take a look, PJ, and tell me what you think?"

PJ dropped to her knees to study the partially exposed artifact. "Who found it?" PJ asked, kneeling and leaning way over to view it from a low angle.

"I did." The young woman who had spoken moved to PJ's side.

"You didn't move it?"

"No ma'am. I know not to do that until it's been photographed and catalogued. All I did was clean a little of the dirt away with this." She picked up a small brush, the kind people use for cleaning the dust from automobile dash vents.

"What's your name?"

"Laine, ma'am."

PJ smiled. "Nice to meet you, Laine, but can you tell me what is it with you Arizonians that you call everyone ma'am? I'm Doctor Curtis, but you call me PJ, okay?"

"Yes ma ... PJ."

"And now, Doctor Blair, will you please introduce me to this merry band of dirt diggers?"

I laughed, delighted that the tension between us was evaporating. I made the introductions, "James, Lewis, Josie, Dewey. Laine, you just met, and you already know Sandy, Mike, and Donny."

PJ grinned. "I don't want to hear any of this doctor or ma'am crap from any of you, just PJ, if you please."

"So, Doctor Curtis ... um PJ, what do you think Laine has here?"

"We can't be sure yet, of course, but I'd say it's a piece of leather. It could be from an old sandal or from a carrying strap." She was silent as she examined the artifact again without touching it. "It appears to be very old, but I'd need to run some tests."

Lewis was already working on triangulation, pinpointing the find on the site with two thirty-meter measuring tapes and a plumb line. Josie was plotting it on a scale plan with the aid of a ruler and a drawing compass. Dewey was busy with the camera. "If we have no way of doing that, I'm sure we can approach the university," PJ said, thinking out loud," or Father can arrange for us to use some local government facilities."

38

"The people at the university have been most helpful. I'm sure they will continue to be so."

"That's it then." PJ rose to her feet.

"Let's go back to the tent," I said to PJ, "and I'll bring you up to date on what we're up against here."

"I'd like that."

"Would you care for a cup of Earl Grey?"

"I'd like that, too."

I was silent as I put the water on to boil. It was obvious that PJ's mind was still at the grid site and I didn't want to interrupt her train of thought. I took a couple of tea bags from a battered metal container.

"You know," PJ said, as I handed her a cup of tea, "that piece of leather, if that's what it is, could be Hohokam, anywhere from nine hundred to twelve hundred AD, or it could be relatively modern."

"Very likely." I motioned PJ to sit. This time she took the chair, searching first for Pup's whereabouts. He was curled up in the corner, his nose resting on the pile of books. He gave her a bored look. I sat cross-legged on the bunk. PJ, watching me from over the top of her cup, waited for me to speak.

"My work here is unusual in that we're not looking for a civilization or even a scattered set of ruins." I paused to sip. "What we are looking for is a needle in a haystack, a small band of women warriors who were on the move and as far as we know did not settle anywhere on a permanent or even semi permanent basis."

PJ crossed her leg, ankle over knee. "What makes you so sure they were here?"

"Word of mouth ... that's all I've had to go on. Greece, of course, is a land of legend and myth. Stories I heard there led me to South America where I interviewed literally hundreds of native people from areas deep within the rain forests and along the Amazon River." PJ sipped her tea absentmindedly as she hung on to my every word. "I interviewed old people from tribes barely infiltrated by outsiders and listened to stories that have survived generations of telling. Here too, local Indians have similar stories. What it all comes down to is that I'm working purely from legend and hearsay. Not exactly proof positive."

"But you really believe there is something to these myths?"

"Yes, I firmly believe they're based on actual events." Pup came over and placed his paw on the edge of the bunk, his way of asking that I rub him behind the ears. He responded to my attention with growls of pleasure from deep within his throat.

"Okay, so what do we expect to find?" PJ asked, her eyes on Pup. She was still uncomfortable in his presence. He sensed it, I think, and ignored her. "A small band of people on the move wouldn't have been carrying lots of stuff. They wouldn't have left much of a trail."

"That's true."

"And even if they had left any clue to their passing, evidence of it would have long since disappeared."

I nodded. "If we find anything at all, it'll be small stuff. Perhaps something like Laine unearthed this morning. We'll find out."

"Pottery?"

"We may find some, but it will more than likely be Hohokam."

"You know, Doctor Blair, you're crazy. You've staked your life and your reputation on next to nothing."

I responded sharply. "If you feel this is a waste of your valuable time, then you don't belong here."

PJ stared me down, her eyes steely. "I didn't say anything about it being a waste of time or that I wasn't interested. I was just stating the facts of your life. You've spent how many years now, chasing shadows?"

"I was just giving you the option of pulling out...should you feel it's a waste of your time."

"Shadows intrigue me, so why don't we just get on with it?"

I raised my cup. "To shadows, Doctor Curtis."

"To shadows, Doctor Blair."

I noticed that PJ had a lovely smile. I regretted that I had not given her much to smile about.

Chapter Five

Kim's project is going to be difficult. Excavating a site is not as exciting as television and movies make it out to be. When I tell people I'm an archaeologist, they often think of Indiana Jones and mummies in tombs. It isn't like that at all. As Kim said, we won't find features like temples or buildings, or cultures where a large group of people would be living. She likened it to searching for a needle in a haystack and that is probably true.

From aerial views and ground surveys she planned to try a series of test holes and trenches along one canyon wall. We would search for evidence of a few single occupation sites, a small band of women, following the likeliest sources of water through the mountains.

The survey work had already been completed and several test holes and a trench had been exposed by the time I joined the group. The leather piece that Laine found had been the star attraction so far. The only other excitement I faced was avoiding sunburn, blisters, bites from snakes and spiders, and painful contact with cactus needles.

The daily work is tedious and dirty and the routine gets monotonous. Usually, I'm on my knees with a diamond shaped trowel scraping through dirt, strata by strata, trying to determine and document what happened in that section of the grid and why. For every artifact we find, there are hours and hours of screening, scraping and processing a whole lot of extraneous matter. I like to think of it as working with three-dimensional puzzles that need to be re-assembled. It's the possibility of finding something worthwhile that gets everyone excited. Unfortunately, we weren't finding anything useful.

My interaction with Kim was limited to early morning meetings and short reports at lunch and end of day. Her

41

conversations were brief; her initial, light-hearted pleasantries fading as the search continued with nothing of consequence uncovered. Those infrequent smiles ceased altogether as her expression grew more somber. When students asked questions, they were likely to get one or two word responses. Morale was at an all-time low.

As the newcomer to the group, I knew it would take some time to fit in. To amuse myself during the days of boredom and tension, I visited with the crew, especially the guys. They were usually friendly and willing to chat about sports or cars, and joke about daily events. Carpooling with Sandy, Mike and Donny helped us develop camaraderie. When they learned that I came from Boston, they made me the brunt of every Red Sox joke they could think of starting with the Bosox's annual collapse during the pennant race.

Josie and Laine were friendly enough, but I noticed uneasiness whenever I worked with them. My instincts told me there was a bit of jealousy behind Josie's occasional hard looks. She had shown an interest in Sandy, but he ignored her. Instead, he found my company more pleasurable. I was flattered with his infatuation, considering the difference in our ages. Sandy had been in the army before seeking a degree and was in his mid to late twenties, which was still young by my standards.

Kim frowned whenever she'd observe us together talking. "I just don't want to see him get hurt," she'd say.

"Relax, Doc, he's a friend.... a sweet guy.... nothing more. I can handle it."

Kim just shook her head and remained silent. Something was bothering her beyond the worksite, but she wasn't about to tell me anything. There was a private side to Kim that I couldn't penetrate. I could tell that she was losing sleep over some problem. I hoped she would tell me eventually if it concerned our excavation.

One Friday, after another week of fruitlessly sifting rock and sand, Mike, Sandy, and I decided to socialize a bit in Mesa before going home. We ate a meal at the local fast food restaurant. I managed to find a salad that was palatable. Then,

Mike guided us to a place called The Oasis where we could kick back and relax with something stronger than soda.

"Grab a booth and I'll get us a round of Rick's Cactus Coolers," Mike said, already bouncing to the jukebox's pulsating country beat. Sandy and I shared one side and Mike slid into the seat across from us once he had placed our order. His dark hair fell over one eye in rakish fashion. When our drinks arrived, he pulled off his wire-rimmed glasses with a contented sigh. "Just what a tired dirt-digger needs to soothe his aching muscles."

I had to laugh at that remark. Mike was thin and wiry; if he had muscles they were lean and well hidden. Despite a wispy mustache, he still looked like a teenager. I carded him before we left the van to make sure he was old enough to drink with us. Still, it lifted my sagging spirits to be in the company of two good-looking fellas.

"PJ," Sandy cautioned, "you'd better go easy on those. They'll kick like an army mule."

I drained my second 'cooler,' marveling at the mellow, slightly fuzzy warmth that spread through my body. "Don't worry, Cowboy, I'm fine." I gave him my patented sexy, sweet smile and watched as his face reddened. *Well, well, Sandy, my man. It's not hard to see what you're thinking about.*

There was a guy with curly, red hair sitting at the bar. He kept smiling at me. After he sent a 'cooler' my way, and we saluted each other with our glasses, he sauntered over to our booth. He leaned over, flirted with me and managed to peer down the front of my shirt in the process. *What is it with guys? They think they're so subtle.*

"Hey, beautiful," he said, "I heard you talking about a dig site. You're with Doctor Blair's group?"

I exhaled and sat upright against the back of the booth, removing my cleavage from his inspection. "That's right, 'Red.' I'm her right hand gal."

"Well, how's it going? Did you find what you're looking for?"

"PJ, don't answer that." Mike scowled at the guy. "Move on, Mister. She's had a bit too much to drink."

43

"Mikey, I can talk for myself. There's nothing to tell. We're just chasin' shadows out there."

Sandy put his hand on my arm and addressed the man. "Mister Green, we know who you are and you'd better leave now."

The new guy winked at me and took a few steps backward toward the bar.

"Maybe some other time, Cutie," I said, blowing him a kiss.

"Jesus, PJ, He's not a 'Cutie.' He's Fritz Green from one of the TV stations in Phoenix and he's bad news." Mike looked so serious.

"Shit, I'm not gonna give away any secrets." I fanned my face. "Gawd, it sure got hot in here all of a sudden." I started to unbutton my shirt.

Sandy got a glimpse of my black lace bra and yanked me to my feet. "That does it. Definitely, time to go, PJ." He tried to pull my shirt together.

"Sure, Cowboy. My place or yours?" As he fiddled with my shirt I tugged a few of his buttons loose.

He pushed my hands away. "Jesus, PJ, will ya stop it!"

I just rubbed against him, grinning.

Mike's eyes widened. "Sandy, we're gonna have trouble with that Fritz guy. He's getting a real eyeful. He probably wants a juicy story for his viewers."

I leaned my head on Sandy's chest and listened to them try to figure out what to do with me. My tongue had grown fuzzy and my brain wasn't far behind.

Mike was right; 'Red' hadn't finished with us. "Hey boys, I have a few more questions for the lady. Why don't you two run along and let me take over. I'm afraid she's a bit more woman than you can handle."

I felt Sandy's body stiffen. *Shit! I may not be firing on all cylinders right now, but somewhere in that jerk's sentence I heard a compliment and an insult. I think the insult was directed at my adorable companions. Am I gonna stand here while these sweet young men get treated that way? Hell, no!* "You just...back off! This is a private party." I gave Sandy's waist a squeeze.

44

'Red' laughed. "Your fiancé thinks you're wasting your time up there on the mountain, Doctor Curtis. What do you think?"

"She has no comment." Sandy said, as he and Mike helped me out of the booth.

My mouth seemed to be working again, so I spoke up. "I told ya...down the tubes. Kim's not talkin'... There's nothin' out there."

Sandy covered my mouth, but I pushed his hand away. "Let me be!"

"PJ, you don't know what you're saying--"

"Please shut up," Mike added. "Doctor Blair will kill us if she--"

"Oh, c'mon. We all know what's happening. She's just wasted a shit load of my father's money..."

They managed to shove me out the door and into the minivan. Sandy drove Mike to his apartment and then headed toward Apache Junction. Somewhere along Highway 60, my stomach began to churn. Sandy glanced at me in concern when I moaned. He took the next exit and pulled off onto the side of the road.

I opened the door and swung my feet around so that I could lean my head down and breathe some fresh air. That helped, but I could tell that I was very drunk. When I get too drunk, I get rather amorous, or so I've been told. Quite often I can't remember shit when I've had too much. *What the hell was in those coolers anyway?*

I could feel those neglected hormones heating up, warming my insides and making my skin super-sensitive to touch. Standing outside the van made my knees weaken. "Sandy?"

"What is it, PJ?" He was at my side instantly. "Are you feeling sick?" His arms came around me. I tucked my head under his chin, hearing his rapid heart beat as we deepened the embrace. *Oh, Gawd. He's so strong...and protective. I really don't want to be alone tonight. Would it be so bad?*

"Do you think I'm pretty?"

He responded without hesitation. "I think you're beautiful."

I started to cry.

"PJ? Did I say something wrong?"

My hands moved across his back, feeling the warmth of his muscular body. "Do you want to make love to me?"

He inhaled. "God, yes." Then, he released his hold. "But...you're engaged."

My head was still pressed against his chest. "Not really," I mumbled. "That was Stephen's idea."

Sandy pulled back further. I could see conflicting emotions in his eyes. "PJ, we can't do this...not now. You're not in control of--"

"Hell, I've been out of control so many--"

"No. It's not right." He helped me sit back down, leaning in to fasten my seatbelt. I seized his face and kissed him, feeling his passionate response. With a soft moan, he broke away and climbed back behind the wheel. Before he could start the car, I slid my hand along his thigh and into his lap. "Jesus," he hissed, and placed his hand over mine. We both felt his undeniable arousal before he removed my hand and drove back onto the highway. He glanced over at me, and then focused on the road. "Dear God. I'm probably gonna hate myself for this, but I don't know what else to do."

I smiled and curled up against the doorframe. *Just go with the flow, Cowboy. It's nothing personal...just a bit of fun for both of us.*

"Thank God she's still up," I heard him murmur.

"What? Who?" Now, partially awake, I felt my nausea and pounding headache return. We had pulled along side a motor home. A thin, pale light shone behind drawn blinds. Strains of Mozart drifted through the screen door. *Where the hell are we?*

Sandy rapped on the metal frame. Inside, a dog growled. "Doctor Blair? It's Sandy. Are you awake?"

Oh shit. No! "Sandy how could you?" *Oh, Gawd.*

Chapter Six

As much as I tried not to feel discouraged, there were times when I felt like giving up. I'd been searching so long and seemed not to be any closer to finding the Lost Tribe. I imagined the walls of the motor home closing in on me and I felt the threatening panic of claustrophobia. I slipped a CD into the deck and stretched out on the sofa listening to Mozart's Magic Flute. Music was the companion that helped me cope with stress.

My mind drifted back to the project with less panic, less despondency. Testing had shown the strip of old leather to be six to seven hundred years old and Hohokam in origin. Something, a little voice, intuition, whatever it was kept nagging at me to start a grid closer to the canyon wall, some two hundred meters from our present position.

Pup, lying on the floor next to the sofa, raised his head and growled. "It's okay, boy," I whispered. "We aren't expecting anyone." Moments later, I heard the knock and Sandy calling out to me.

"Just a moment."

"Doc, PJ is with me. She needs help."

I opened the door in time to see PJ vomiting beside an old cactus. "What the hell is going on?"

Sandy avoided my eyes. "We went for a drink, Mike, PJ, and I, and ... um ... PJ had a little too much."

I sighed. "Looks to me as though she's had more than a little too much. Why did you bring her here? Why didn't you take her to the inn and let her sleep it off?"

"She wanted me to stay with her. I didn't want to do that." Even in the subdued lighting, I could see that Sandy was embarrassed. "May we come in?"

47

"I suppose so." Between us, we managed to help PJ into the motor home. "You look like something the cat dragged in," I said, when we had her seated on the sofa. She was disheveled; her hair was mussed, her blouse pulled out of her cargo pants and partly open. I looked at Sandy.

"Oh no, Doc, it's not what you're thinking. No one bothered her. It's just that she had too much to drink and wanted me to ... um ... I didn't think she should be left alone, but I didn't want to ... um ..."

"Sandy, I know this wasn't your fault. You can help me though by making a pot of strong coffee." I pointed to the cabinet above the sink. "The beans and grinder are in there. The coffee pot is above the stove."

"Yes Ma'am."

PJ was wearing that green look again, but I was able to get her into the bathroom in the nick of time. After a couple more sessions of john hugging, her stomach settled down. She returned to the sofa and flopped against the brightly colored cushions, her face still pale.

"Would you care to explain what this is all about?"

"No, it's none of your business." She glared at Sandy. "And thanks a lot pal, for bringing me here when you knew what I wanted. What kind of a sick joke was that?"

The music had stopped ... the tension in the motor home was palpable.

Sandy handed PJ a cup of very strong coffee. "PJ, I didn't think you should be alone, but I couldn't stay with you ... I'm sorry, I didn't know what else to do."

"You don't know what you missed."

"No way, ma'am, not in your condition."

"Well, you had plenty of interest in me on the way over here. You even had a condition of your own going there. Did you suddenly get a conscience or something?"

"Doctor Curtis! That is enough." I turned to Sandy whose face was pink with embarrassment. "Thank you for bringing her here. Go on home. I'll get her sobered up and back to the inn."

"Doc," Sandy shifted from one foot to the other, "I need to talk to you privately first, like outside."

It was a storybook desert evening, warm and star-studded. For a moment, I thought of the Lost Tribe and wondered how they might react to such a night. Would they have seen the beauty of the night or were they in dire straits after a long trek across the desert? How different was the desert then from now? No cities, of course, not even any settlements ... roving bands perhaps...

"There's something you should know," Sandy said, interrupting my reverie. We were a few steps from the motor home and out of PJ's hearing. "There was a reporter there, at the bar. PJ was flirting with him and he was buying her drinks, and ... well, she may have said more'n she should about our work here."

"Shit!" I turned and hit the back of the motor home with my fist. Pup, still inside, started barking and growling. When I opened the door to bring him outside, I saw PJ cowering in the corner. Pup's outburst had, I believed, sobered her up in a hurry.

"Who was this reporter?" I asked Sandy while Pup inspected the immediate surrounds.

"Fritz Green."

"Oh shit! I've had trouble with him in the past." I paced for several minutes, rubbing my arms while Sandy fidgeted. "What all did she tell him?"

"We warned her to go easy on the stuff, but ..."

"I can see how she is, Sandy. Just tell me what she said to Green."

"That she was your right hand and that you were looking for shadows. I don't think she mentioned the Amazons, but I can't be sure. Then he started talking to her about Stephen."

"Stephen? Stephen who?"

"Stephen, her fiancé."

I shook my head. "I didn't know there was a fiancé."

"Yeah. I don't know much about him except what PJ told me. Seems he travels a lot between the States and South America. Green seemed to know all about him."

I thanked Sandy as I touched his shoulder reassuringly, and sent him home. Before returning to the motor home, I was joined by Pup who had determined that all was well. Little did he know....

We had worked so hard to keep our project under wraps and PJ, of all people, had to blab to this Fritz Green fellow. I knew it would be useless talking to her tonight. Perhaps by morning, she'd be less belligerent.

When I stepped into the motor home, PJ was sitting on the couch, hugging her stomach. "You look like hell," I said, unable to conceal the disgust I was feeling.

"He had no business bringing me here, damn it. He knows how I feel about you."

I poured her another cup of coffee and one for myself. "And how is that?"

She lowered her head and mumbled. "It's not important."

"C'mon, tell me. You had no trouble whining about Sandy, blaming him for the state you're in. Don't you have courage enough to--"

She lifted her head. "You're a stubborn, sexually frustrated woman with absolutely no sense of humor." Her eyes were defiant, challenging. "You have no life beyond your work. Do you even have any friends besides your students and your dog? When was the last time ..." She fell silent.

"The last time what? If you're thinking it, you can say it."

"Nothing."

"Well, now that you've gotten all that off your chest, maybe we can get to the important issues. We're not here to talk about me, or Sandy. He did the only thing he could under the circumstances and now I have to cope with the mess you created." I took my coffee to the passenger seat, swiveled it around, and sat. "We do need to discuss your behavior though. What's the matter with you, woman? What in God's name were you thinking, talking to this reporter?"

"What I do on my own time is my business, you said so yourself." She avoided my eyes.

"What you do *is* your business except when it affects my project. Then it becomes my business. What you have done tonight may have seriously compromised our work here." I took a deep breath. "We've been trying to keep the lid on things because I didn't want a bunch of insensitive reporters bothering us. We didn't need you to go blabbing everything in a bar. Where's your sense, woman?"

PJ did not respond. Instead, she sat quietly, her head resting in her hands. I went into the bathroom and pulled out a fresh towel and washcloth, then found an old pair of pajamas. "You stink. Go shower. Clean your sorry self up."

While she was in the bathroom, I threw a blanket and a pillow on the couch. "Sleep it off," I said, when she came out looking more presentable, her face scrubbed clean and her hair freshly shampooed. "I'll deal with you in the morning," I added as I headed to my bedroom.

"Up yours with a wire gigi."

I stopped and turned around slowly. "I'm assuming that juvenile remark is the result of the alcohol so I'm going to let it go, but keep in mind that come morning, you're going to have to face up to your actions."

When I got up, PJ was not in the motor home. The blanket was folded neatly on the couch, the pillow on top of it. A quick glance through the window showed her to be nowhere in sight. I decided she had called a cab and left so I took my time showering and dressing.

When I stepped outside with a cup of tea in hand, I was surprised to see PJ behind the motor home, sitting beneath the sparse shade of a Palo Verde. I waited for her to speak. When she didn't, I did. "I don't want you on-site today. I'll drop you off at the inn. You can sit there and contemplate your actions while I spend my day doing damage control."

"I'm sorry ... I ..."

"I don't need excuses. You did what you did and I have to deal with it. I'll contact your father later today and explain why you're being relieved of your duties, then--"

"Please, Doctor Blair, I want to be part of your project. I made a mistake. You have my word that it won't happen again."

"Get in the Tracker."

She climbed into the white four by four. It was less than a ten-minute ride during which neither of us spoke. I really didn't know what to say to her. I believed from her silence and meekness of manner that she truly regretted her actions, but she had a lot of growing up to do and I didn't have the time or the inclination to mother her. "I'll speak with you later, after I've spoken to your father," I stated flatly when we arrived at the inn.

"Please, Doctor Blair, don't tell him. I asked for this assignment and if I flub it--"

"You already have. Your father agreed to fund my project provided I keep the media out of it. It was your choice to involve them. Now I have to ask his help to fend them off."

"It wasn't a choice, it was a mistake." Tears welled in her eyes.

"It may have been a mistake, but it shows lack of good sense." I could see she was distressed. For one fleeting moment, I wanted to hug her and tell her it would be okay, that we'd work it out. The thought didn't last.

"Out," I commanded. "I have work to do."

I called Sandy's cell phone. "I'm leaving you in charge today?"

"Sure, Doc. What's up?"

"I'm going to try for some damage control."

"Have you talked to PJ this morning?"

"I just dropped her off at the inn."

"Is she okay?"

"She realizes that she's created some serious problems and has to face the consequences. Frankly, I don't believe she's had to take responsibility for her actions before."

"Consequences? Are you going to fire her?"

"She wanted this assignment enough to ask for it … now … well, she's more liability than asset."

"I guess. You know, Doc, we all make mistakes."

"I'm considering all options."

"You know, Doc, I didn't provoke it … her coming on to me--"

"I know you didn't, so don't worry about it. If it hadn't been you, it would've been someone else. That seems to be PJ's way and it's going to get her in deep trouble one of these days."

"Yeah, I know, but she's so beautiful."

"Just remember, Sandy, that the most beautiful of Nature's creatures are sometimes the most deadly."

"I got it, Doc. And hey, I'll call you if anything comes up."

"Good enough."

As soon as I got back to the motor home, I tried to reach Fritz Green, but was told that he was out and could not be reached. I picked up the phone to call Frederick Curtis, but changed my mind. PJ could explain to him why she was no longer part of my team.

I spent the rest of the day catching up on paper work. So much had been shoved aside in order to take care of more urgent matters.

When I arrived at the site the following morning, PJ wasn't there. I called her later on the cell phone and told her to return to the site the next morning, that she wasn't off the job yet.

Chapter Seven

I was in the motor home that evening, having just finished a microwavable frozen dinner when the phone rang. It was Sandy. "Hey, Doc, we've got trouble."

"What now?"

"I'm sorry to be the one to tell you this, but Stephen what's-his-face was being interviewed on the six o'clock news. He talked about not wanting his fiancée involved with this project, that it was some off the wall operation led by some kooky Amazon wannabe."

I sat with the telephone to my ear. The anger started with a sickening ache in my stomach. It spread outward and upward until I felt its heat in my cheeks and I became momentarily dizzy, consumed by the fight or flight syndrome. Flight was out so I needed to fight, to strike out, but for the moment, all I could do was seethe.

"Doc, you okay?"

"Yes, Sandy, I'm here, but I'm not okay."

"Do you want me to come over?"

"No. I need to be alone to think."

When Sandy hung up, I threw the telephone into the corner. "Damn you, PJ."

Pup whined and backed away. "It's okay, fella. I'm not mad with you." I dropped to the floor beside him. "We're still together, but it looks as though our life's work just hit the manure pile."

I pushed the remote button to turn on the motel television with the telephone still to my ear, its cord stretched to the limit. *Damn it! Why can't motels have cordless phones? I guess people would only steal them.*

"Oh m'gawd, Sandy, it's Stephen. Why is he talking to Fritz Green?"

"You tell me."

I listened as my fiancé belittled the project and Kim, making her sound like a raving lunatic. "Oh Sandy, how can he say those things about her?"

"I figured you'd know what he's up to."

"Believe me, I have no idea. Poor Kim ... she doesn't deserve all this."

"Doc's not too happy."

"She has seen this interview?"

"Yeah, I called her before I called you."

"Oh, Gawd. Thank you for warning me, Sandy. And listen, about what happened between us--"

"PJ, we have more serious problems right now."

"I know we do, but I really need to talk to you."

"Okay, we'll find a time. Listen I gotta go, but I had Mike bring the minivan to the inn. The keys are at the front desk. You'll need wheels to come back to work."

"How do you know I'm still on the payroll? Oh right. You talked to Kim. Was she really angry?"

"More quiet than angry."

"That's it then. I'm history. She'll never want my sorry butt on site now."

"PJ, don't assume anything about Doctor Blair. I've learned from experience that she demands a lot, but she's fair. As long as you work up to your professional potential, she's very forgiving."

"Thanks, I think."

I paced the room. *What kind of a woman are you, Curtis? Crying on the shoulder of a student. You're supposed to be Kim's assistant for gawd's sake. Act like it.*

The telephone rang.

"Doctor Curtis." Her tone was cool, professional.

"Doctor Blair, I uh ..."

"I need to see you at my place at once. Can you find your way out here?"

"Well, it was dark and I wasn't exactly ... I think ..."

"But you're sober now."

"Yes, of course. I'll be there."

Pup growled when I tapped on Kim's door.

C'mon ya monstrous beast...tear through that screen and sink your teeth into my neck. Put me out of my misery.

Kim silenced him with a word and let me in.

My boss wore a black tee shirt and khaki cargo pants. Her damp hair released a faint scent of herbal shampoo. I remembered it from my recent shower ... mango something or other. Images of violent retching and painful headaches flashed through my mind, filling me with despair. I searched Kim's face for a clue to her inner thoughts, but her expression was unfathomable. Creases still etched the corners of her dark eyes, but her lips and jaw were rigid with a composure that seemed unnatural. It made a chill skip along my spine. I remembered wondering how it would feel to have those dark eyes boring into my soul. Now I was about to find out.

Oh, Gawd ... I do not want to be here.

"Tea?" She asked as I settled on the edge of the sofa.

"Uh...okay, thanks." *Well, at least she's acting civilized toward me.*

She drew two mugs from the cupboard, then turned her back to put fresh water into the kettle and heat it on the stove.

Take a deep breath. Stay calm. Get those nerves under control. Your voice will be strong ... you will not panic.

I found my mind wandering, disconnecting from the fact that I was here to be chewed out, and focused on Kim's movement within the confines of her kitchenette. In preparing the tea, she wasted no energy, took no unnecessary steps or turns. The whole task resembled a graceful, flowing dance, one that emphasized her long legs and powerful shoulders and arms. I watched her hands as she poured boiling water into a teapot, added tea bags, selected sugar, milk and spoons, and put everything on a tray with the mugs.

Why hadn't I ever noticed how expressive her hands were? So tanned, and strong, devoid of jewelry, with tapered fingers that ended in short, neatly trimmed, unpolished nails. I remembered our first handshake. She had a firm, calloused grip from working long hours at countless dig sites in pursuit of her life-long obsession.

Now, thanks to you, she'd been labeled a fraud, a pseudo-archaeologist in front of a vast audience of television viewers.

A lump formed in my throat. My eyes filled with tears.

Oh, Gawd. You will not cry in front of her.

Kim gave me a brief glance as she handed me a mug of Earl Grey. "Two sugars and a splash of milk. I believe I got that right."

"Yes, thank you," I whispered.

"Now then." Kim took a sip and I followed suit, almost choking.

For the love of God, will you yell at me. Rant. Rave. Scream. Curse me. I deserve all that and more.

She just sat and sipped her tea, thinking, her eyes revealing a quiet resignation.

"You've seen the interview." Her comment was more statement than question.

I cleared my throat. "Yes."

"And it was your fiancé?"

I stared at the floor. "Yes."

"When was the last time you spoke with him?"

"The day I arrived … No … I called him the day after that. So it would have been early September. I had no idea he felt so-"

"Did you and he talk about the project on that occasion?"

"Well." I searched my brain. "I think I might have told him … on the flight to Phoenix … about looking for Amazons." Kim made a noise in her throat, almost a groan. "But I told him it was Top Secret …" My voice wavered.

Curtis, that has got to be the lamest excuse you have ever used. You're an asshole! Tears trickled down my cheeks and I sniffed into my mug. *Shit, that's perfect. Now you're a blubbering asshole.*

"So he chose to discuss my project with the media?"

I kept my eyes focused on my tea. "Apparently."

She sighed. Seconds passed in slow, deliberate motion. "Do you love him, PJ?"

"What?" I stared at her, confused.

She shrugged and returned the tray to the kitchenette, keeping her back to me. "I was curious to know how someone who cares about you and, I assume, you care about, could do something like this."

"I honestly don't know how to answer that."

She looked back at me. "You don't know if you love him?"

"I thought I did, once. My father wanted me to ... that is, he and Stephen wanted me ..."

I shook my head and drank the last of my tea. "Doctor Blair ... Kim ... I am so terribly sorry. I would do anything to change my part in all of this. I know it's compromised the secrecy of the project. I know what was said in the interview hurt you deeply."

Kim returned to the seat facing me. She chewed on her lower lip for a moment and stared at me, deliberating. Then her eyes seemed to refocus at a point somewhere over my left shoulder. Her head nodded once. "You know, I think we need to dig a test trench closer to the canyon wall."

"The canyon wall? We? After all I've done, you still want me involved?"

"Your professional credentials are impeccable, PJ. It's your personal behavior that needs attention."

I gave a shaky laugh. "That's an understatement."

She picked up the cordless phone and handed it to me. I noticed a scratch on one edge and a chip missing from the end with the mouthpiece.

"You can start your behavior modification right now."

"I don't understand."

"You're going to call your father ... and tell him the whole story."

"No, Kim ... I can't ... Please don't make--"

"I believe you just said that you would do anything to change your part in all of this."

"But ..." I sniffed and swiped at my eyes. "I'd sooner run naked through a field of Jumping Cholla."

"Ouch!" A ghost of a smile flickered across her face. Brown eyes glinted, held my gaze, and made a connection. In that moment, I realized Kim had made a decision about my future

59

worthiness. Maybe she had been in my shoes at some point in her life. Maybe something in my demeanor had triggered a sympathetic response. I don't know … it didn't matter. She had found a reason to believe I was capable in spite of myself. Sandy had been right … Doc Blair was a fair person, treating me better than I ever deserved.

We would start fresh.

But first, I had to make a phone call.

When I finally reached Father, he was already in Arizona, somewhere on the road between Phoenix and Apache Junction. I should not have been surprised. Frederick Lane Curtis prided himself on searching out problems before they could escalate and destroying them. Once again, I appeared to be the problem. He told us he wanted to meet and plan strategy. Kim accepted this news better than I, but then, she was the brave one.

I handed the phone back to Kim and pointed to the damaged parts. "What happened here?"

She winked. "Oh, a little behavior modification of my own."

Chapter Eight

Pup growled when the black Mercedes pulled up next to my motor home. I put him in the bedroom. "Stay." I patted his muscular shoulders and closed the door.

I was back at the window in time to see the uniformed chauffeur jump out and open the car's rear door and stand at attention as Frederick Curtis stepped out. Where's the red carpet? I thought, wondering if Frederick Curtis ever drove himself anywhere.

PJ's father was a rather handsome, sixty something, with thick, white wavy hair. His complexion was that of a man who spent much of his time in the Board Room. Although thick of stature, he was not fat and his expensive, lightweight suit showed him to be in fine shape for his years.

I stood aside while he greeted his daughter. "I hope you are well," he said, in a manner that was rather formal, I thought. A mild level of tension resonated between them. It was my understanding, albeit through hearsay, that they had been estranged since the death of PJ's mother. I couldn't make any judgments without knowing both sides of the story.

"Yes, Father, thank you."

"Doctor Blair." He shook my hand with the same amount of familiarity he had shown his daughter.

I offered tea. PJ nodded, but he declined. For a moment, I thought I detected disappointment in her expression. She sighed and sat down on the far end of the sofa.

"Well, I'm going to make some for PJ and me, so if you change your mind--"

He pulled a PDA from his attaché case and tapped in some data. "We need to get down to business."

"Quite so." I put down the kettle, directed him to the other end of the sofa, and cleared the swiveled passenger seat of books and papers to make room for me to sit.

"We have a problem," Curtis said, looking first at me, then at PJ.

I nodded. "One we need to get a handle on right away."

"Father, it's my fault. If I hadn't--"

I silenced PJ with a stern look. "As near as I can tell," I said, crossing my leg, ankle over knee, "Stephen Cresswell has a problem with me and this project."

"But if I hadn't--"

Again, I interrupted PJ. "You had nothing whatsoever to do with what Cresswell told Fritz Green."

Curtis looked at me, frowning. "Stephen Cresswell is my daughter's fiancé. She has to be involved."

His way of speaking as if PJ wasn't present irritated me. In fact, I was annoyed by his whole attitude toward his daughter. Was it possible that her rebellious lifestyle was fed by his rejection, or did his rejection stem from her behavior over the years? Which came first, the chicken or the egg? Curtis had always been fair in business dealings with me, but right now, I tended to sympathize with PJ and make allowances for her rebellious nature, though I dare not show it.

"If you remember," I directed my remarks to Curtis, "Green was the reporter who caused us so much trouble when I first arrived. His methods are those of a tabloid predator and I can't imagine what he and Cresswell have in common."

Curtis turned to PJ. "Have you and Stephen had a falling out?"

"No, Father, I haven't spoken to him in a while. I thought he was still in South America." She glanced at me, perhaps wondering if I would interrupt again. I kept still. This was treacherous ground. I depended on Frederick Curtis for funding, but his daughter was my assistant … it was necessary that I tread a fine line.

"I told him when I was coming here," PJ said, "that I'd be working with Doctor Blair, and I may have mentioned Amazons, so if there is any blame to be placed it should be with--"

"Stephen Cresswell and Fritz Green," I was getting good at interrupting at just the right moment. "I can't imagine what Cresswell's gaining by talking to Green."

"I'll talk to Stephen." Curtis stood up. PJ and I followed suit, effectively ending our meeting. "I'm going to double your on-site security, Doctor Blair, then I'm going to talk to the powers-that-be at the TV station. They're going to have to understand that this project is off limits. In return for their cooperation, I'll guarantee them an exclusive when and if you find anything significant."

"Not if, but when." PJ's words were soft, but emphatic.

I smiled. Curtis acted as if he hadn't heard her.

"Fritz Green won't be bothering you again."

"Thank you, Frederick. I appreciate your help."

"Just protecting my interests." Curtis turned to PJ. "Priscilla, you'll have to settle things with Stephen."

"Father, I'm sorry but I can't continue my relationship with Stephen any longer. He has no regard for my career ... what I want to do with my life--"

Her father waved his hand, silencing her. "Do whatever you have to do. I just don't want to have to fix this problem again."

Curtis turned, shook my hand, then left.

I stood at the door, watching as the chauffeur opened the door and Curtis got in the car without so much as a backward glance. I could not tell because of the limo's darkened windows, whether or not he looked my way again. After waiting for the Mercedes to leave, I turned to find PJ sitting on the sofa in tears. "What's this about?"

"You didn't let me tell him my part in this fiasco."

"He didn't need to know."

I hated seeing so little outward affection between father and daughter and could not believe he was so callous with her. The person sitting on my sofa was no longer a self assured, scientific woman of the world. She was a little girl in tears because her daddy had dismissed her again. How many times had he done this to her? I swallowed hard as memories of my own past flooded to the foreground of my mind. I pushed them away,

63

refusing to allow them into my life again. I sat down beside PJ, put my arm around her, and held her while she buried her head in my shoulder and cried.

"Okay, that's enough." Somewhat embarrassed, I pulled away from the familiarity of the moment.

"Tomorrow will be a busy day. First thing we need to do is to protect the present grid with tarps and finish the field notes on it. Then, we're moving closer to the wall. We'll leave the site early and gather here to examine the survey maps and aerial photos and formulate a plan of action. I'll order pizza for everyone."

"Thank you for giving me another chance. You won't regret it, I promise." She looked at me through red-rimmed eyes.

"I expect you to treat this project as your own. Make it come first in your life. Do you understand?"

"Yes, I do." She wiped her eyes. "You can count on me."

"I hope so."

I watched PJ leave, knowing that despite her failings, she was a good person. Given half a chance she would go places. I'd see to it that she had that chance.

The motor home was crowded. Both the driver and passenger seats were swiveled, facing the interior of the coach. PJ sat on the passenger side, I on the driver's. The crew were scattered on the sofa and on the floor. Sandy was at the computer. We discussed the project and future plans to the aroma of pizza and beer, a combination that heightened the camaraderie we felt as a crew. I had a glass of wine; the rest had beer, except PJ who, I noticed, poured herself a glass of iced tea.

Laine attempted to extol the virtues of anchovies, but was shouted down by the others. "That's all right," she said, "all the more for me." She had brought her own can of the salty little fishes because she knew no one else would allow them near their pizza.

As the evening progressed and business was concluded, talk turned to other things, past experiences, and embarrassing moments. Despite PJ's earlier indiscretion, the crew had rallied around her. She was obviously feeling comfortable again. I was happy about that because she had the potential to be a good archaeologist ... I didn't want to see her lose faith in herself or her ability.

I'd closed Pup in the bedroom earlier because I didn't want the crew feeding him too much pizza, but now that it was all gone I brought him out and fed him good, big dog, fare, after which he socialized with everyone. It was amusing to watch him make the rounds, be noticed and petted before moving on and finally laying down in the hallway so that anyone going to the bathroom would have to step over him.

The crew left in ones and twos and with little fanfare, after all, we'd see each other on site in the morning. Soon there was just PJ and Sandy, who insisted on helping clean up the mess of empty pizza cartons, crushed beer cans, and the usual debris left after a gathering of mostly young people.

We had the motor home almost back to normal when Pup growled. The windows beside the door were open, inviting the breeze to enter, clear away the stale pizza and beer smells, and freshen the air. A red sports car pulled up in front. *Now who in the heck...* I opened the door and my world came crashing down around my ears.

"Hi, Babe, you're a hard one to track."

"Terry, what the hell are you doing here?"

"Hey, you never asked me that before. I was feeling horny, sweetheart. Who better to take care of me ... than you?"

My face flushed with embarrassment, I pushed Terry from the door and followed her outside. "What are you thinking ... coming here unannounced?" Out of the corner of my eye, I saw Sandy and PJ inside staring at each other as they hung on to Pup's collar. If it weren't such a disaster, it would have been funny.

"What are you so all fired mad about?"

"I have guests."

"I see that." Terry looked toward the window. "Hey, I like that little blonde. Bet she's hot, huh? You got a little action going with her?"

"My personal life is none of your business. And, by the way, whatever happened to my replacement? Sylvia, I think her name was ..."

"I was too much woman for her." I tried to steer Terry away from the open window. She wasn't moving. Too late anyway, I thought, they've heard more than enough to add two and two together.

"And since you're not woman enough for me, I suggest you take your sorry ass back to wherever you came from."

"Well, if that's the reception I get for stopping by to say hello, then I'll leave you with your little blonde." She craned her neck toward the doorway and snickered. "And, a boy toy, too. Kim, you're getting kinky in your old age."

"Those people are colleagues, nothing more."

"Oh, that's right." Terry slid her slim body into the driver's seat. "I forgot that you're still obsessed with that silly pursuit of yours. It eclipses all else in your life. I feel sorry for you, Doctor Blair."

"Don't …"

"You're a laughing stock, you know that, don't you?"

"Good bye, Terry." I turned my back as she burned rubber, trailing a cloud of dust.

I glanced toward the motor home and the open windows. Sandy and PJ must have heard every word. They were gathering their stuff. *Shit! What do I say to them?*

"It's okay," Sandy said, the moment I stepped into the motor home. Where was the awkward silence I had expected? "We'll see you in the morning," he said, "at the site."

PJ rested her hand on my arm. "Tomorrow's a new day."

I nodded.

"Kim? You okay?"

I smiled at the genuine concern reflected in PJ's expression. "I'm, okay. Exhausted and in need of rest, but otherwise … fine."

I sat, staring through the window, trying to read the shadowy bulk of the mountain and losing track of time. A book lay open in my lap but I was unable to concentrate on the words. Pup lay at my feet, opening an eye every now and then, checking up on me. *Why did she have to come back and open old wounds?* It wasn't that I was in love with her any more. It was just the memory of the hurt. She had played with my affection as she had with others.

After a while I changed into my old scrub suit and crawled into bed. It was a warm night and I was restless. I threw off the covers and after what seemed like hours I must have dropped off.

I awakened, soaked in perspiration as always when I had these dreams. They were so realistic. I was aware of having cried out, but there was no one close enough to hear me. It was a little after three and the motor home was dark and quiet, except that Pup must have picked up on my restlessness. He couldn't seem to settle. I needed a strong cup of tea. Tonight's dream had been the most vivid to date, and the most frightening. It had reached beyond the dream state and into the dark space of a nightmare. If only there was someone I could talk to about it, but I wasn't ready for that. I couldn't really explain it to myself yet.

Chapter Nine

After leaving Kim's, Sandy and I agreed to meet at my motel for that long overdue talk. I worried if it was wise to select a motel room for our discussion, but I hadn't had any time to find a more public place to chat that could still give us privacy. It was either my place or his and he shared an apartment with three other students. I had a fairly good idea of what I wanted to say and I trusted him to be the responsible gentleman he had always been with me.

We settled into the captain's chairs at a circular table near the window.

Sandy, I'm sorry...for everything. You're such a sweet guy, the least I can do is offer you a drink.

"There's beer, cola or water in the mini-fridge. Pick your poison."

"Water's fine, PJ. I had beer with my pizza."

I found two bottles of cold water and placed them on the table. We uncapped them in silence and took several long swallows.

"May I go first?" I wiped my wet hands on my pant legs.

"Absolutely."

Okay. If I want to cover both issues, I'd better get right to the point. "I want to apologize about the other night--"

"Really, you don't have to--"

"But first I want to ask if you're okay with what just happened over at Kim's? You seemed kinda quiet afterward."

"You mean this visitor of hers?"

"Yeah."

He shrugged and took another swallow. "Sure. I think so. I mean it was a surprise and all. Did you know she was gay?"

"No, not really. Doc is a very private person. We were kind of like oil and water when we first met. I managed to give her several other problems to worry about after that."

"She seems to have had a history with the woman, but they didn't act too friendly toward each other tonight."

I shifted in my seat. "It's Kim's personal business, really. She's still our boss, still the director of the project. Her private life doesn't change that."

He tapped the table lightly with his fingers. "Oh, you don't have to worry about me, PJ. Doc is the greatest. I think the world of her and I'm gonna show up tomorrow and do my job just like usual. It surprised me, that's all. I'll be fine. You sound pretty protective of her all of a sudden, though. Are you okay with it?"

"Me? Sure. I was...well ... you know, she looked so embarrassed when she came back in and a little sad. It bothered me to see her that way." *Why does it still bother me?*

He nodded and smiled. "Good, then. We both agree. Doc Blair is no different than she was before we found out about this Terry person. We're gonna work just as hard tomorrow..."

"And, if she wants to share any information about her personal life, then we'll be there for her as friends."

"Absolutely."

Well, that wasn't so bad.

We both exhaled and drank more water.

I studied Sandy's face, noting the bronze glow of his skin and the sparkle in his pale blue eyes. Such an open, honest face. Stephen's looks were darker, more guarded; even his eyes were a darker shade of blue. I couldn't imagine having a discussion with him about the personal life of my colleague. Stephen would have lost interest after two sentences.

"Now, about my behavior at The Oasis and afterward..."

Sandy leaned forward on his elbows, his folded hands supporting up his chin. He was trying to suppress a grin at my discomfort. "Yes?"

I gave him a shaky laugh. "I don't remember too much about what happened actually."

"Well, I can--"

70

I held up my hand and he grasped it gently. "Wait! I do remember a lot of what went on in the bar, it's just the afterward part that I'm a little hazy on."

He gave my hand a squeeze. *Oh, gawd. It's getting so warm in here!*

"I behaved badly, Sandy. When I get too drunk, I get rather...um..."

"Affectionate?"

My neck felt hot. Superstition Mountain was bathed in the rosy glow reflecting from the sun setting to the west. It rivaled the color I felt in my cheeks. "Yeah." I pulled my hand away.

Sandy grinned. "It's all right, PJ. These things happen. I tried to warn you about the potency of those coolers."

And as usual, I didn't listen.

"That's another thing. I showed very poor judgment ... made several bad decisions. It won't happen again. I remember coming on to you, practically undressing us both in front of Mikey."

"And he's still traumatized, let me tell you."

I brushed back my bangs. "Sandy, don't make jokes. If you hadn't been mature enough to resist, we'd have both done something regrettable."

He leaned forward again, his expression serious. "PJ, I stopped because it wouldn't have been right..."

"I agree."

"Then."

Oh Geesh. Here it comes...

He picked up my hand again, turned it over and placed a soft kiss on my palm. "You're not drunk now and I got the impression that you and Stephen were finished."

I swallowed and felt my eyes moisten. "Please Sandy, listen to me. This isn't going to work."

He hesitated, still holding my hand. "I know I couldn't really trust your actions toward me that night, but I had hoped ... that maybe... Look, I know I'm not rich or sophisticated like the guys you've been with, but I thought--"

"It isn't that, believe me. You're light years ahead of all of them."

His brow wrinkled. "Then, what is it? Do you doubt my sincerity? I think you're gorgeous and smart and sexy as hell."

I managed to reclaim my hand. "Thanks."

"You're saying there's no chance? I'm really attracted to you, PJ. I was hoping against hope that you felt something for me."

Oh, Damn...this is so hard. "Sandy, I'm so sorry. I don't feel that way about you. And I won't give you false hopes."

He sighed, and picked up his empty plastic bottle, squeezing it so hard its sides collapsed with a sharp crack. "I see. I should have realized."

I reached over and removed the smashed container. "I'm trying to explain, but there really isn't any easy way. I like you very much Sandy, just not in that way. Right now, I'm trying to concentrate on my career. I want to prove I've got what it takes to succeed. I don't want any romantic entanglements."

There was pain in his eyes. "So, the timing is wrong?"

Shit, I used to be able to dump guys without breaking a sweat. Can I be sensitive?

"The timing for us will always be wrong. You have been a good friend to me and I really want that friendship to continue."

The muscles in his jaw worked back and forth. I watched him struggle to compose himself and my heart ached.

"Sandy, I never wanted to hurt you. I really need you in my life as a friend. I've had so few true friends. We got off to a good start, didn't we, working on the transmission and all the kidding on the rides to work?"

He nodded and glanced away.

What else could I tell him? There's just no spark between us, not now that I've finally learned to look beyond the physical aspects of a relationship. Oh, crap!

We sat in silence for several seconds. Finally, he cleared his throat, took a deep breath and flashed a weak version of that familiar grin.

"Well ... uh ... I guess there's nothing more to be said. Can't blame a guy for trying, right?" His eyes locked with mine.

I was relieved to see his spirit return. "I realize that you took a risk by telling me how you felt, Sandy. I know it changes things between us right now, but I hope that, in the future, we can still work together as friends and colleagues."

"I guess," he murmured without much enthusiasm.

How do I make him understand?

"Sandy, you have a bright future ahead of you. You don't need my reputation tarnishing all that you've worked so hard for up to now."

"PJ--"

"It's a complication that would screw up your career big time. Trust me, I speak from experience."

"Okay." He held his hands up in defeat. "Okay, I believe you. It's just a little painful right now. Give me some time, okay? I'll work on it ... this friendship thing."

"Good. It's for the best, you'll see."

He stood up. "It's been a long day ... and night." His eyes lingered for a second on my bed. "I'd better go."

I walked him to the door, my hand rubbing lightly against the small of his back. "So, I'll see you at camp, tomorrow, bright and early?"

"Yeah ... sure. Tomorrow."

We faced each other with awkward looks. "Are friends allowed to give each other a hug goodnight?" he asked.

I grinned. "Absolutely. It's in the rule book." I moved into his embrace, letting my head tuck under his chin, inhaling the pleasant scent of his soap and cologne.

His arms tightened around my back and we stayed connected for several moments, and then we separated.

"You give very good hugs, friend," I told him.

"Thanks. I do my best."

"We both will. Friendships take a lot of effort."

He dipped his head. "Yeah." With a little wave, he was gone.

I closed the door and leaned my back against it, replaying the last few minutes of his departure. There was a point at which I could have leaned into him more ... let him touch my cheek ... and kiss me. The chance was there, for an instant, but we both resisted.

I did the right thing. Sandy is a good man, but he's not the one for me.

I sighed and folded my arms across my chest. *Is there one out there someplace who is just right for me?*

I took a shower and slipped an oversize white tee shirt over my head. My thoughts bounced back and forth between the talk with Sandy and Kim's unplanned visitor. Clearly relationships were not easy to maintain. Lovers came and went. I hoped Sandy would still regard me as a friend and that Kim would not be afraid to talk to me if she felt the need. A piece of her mysterious past had returned to haunt her in a sudden and alarming way. I had seen the pain in her eyes when she came back into the motor home. This Terry woman had caused her grief sometime in the past. Anger rose up inside me at the thought.

I stretched out under the covers and stared at the ceiling. "We humans are a complicated species, aren't we? We struggle through life, trying to do our jobs and find someone to comfort and love us. It doesn't matter if we're gay or straight. We all just want to belong, to have friends and share ourselves with someone special."

I sighed and shut my eyes. Kim had shown me friendship and trust. She stood up for me with my father and allowed me to keep working after I had sabotaged our efforts. My job now would be to help her professionally … and personally, if she'd let me. I could do that. I could be her friend.

When I arrived in camp the next morning, the silence in the main tent was deafening. Sandy and Kim gave me brief glances and continued to concentrate on their work.

Well, it seems that it's easy to say we'll carry on as usual, but to actually do it is another thing. Sandy is glued to the computer. His ego is still a bit bruised from my rejection. And he's afraid to talk to Kim. She isn't the most talkative woman on a normal morning. And, after last night, she must be expecting us to act like she has two heads.

Pup gave me his usual greeting, but even he seemed uncomfortable with the unnatural silences.

Okay. I can try to get them talking.

I plastered a hearty smile on my face and fixed us tea. Sandy reviewed Geographic Information Systems data on the laptop. I put his mug on the table to his right.

"There ya go, Cowboy."

He nodded. "Thanks, PJ."

"You doing okay?"

He took a swallow from his mug. "Yeah, okay."

I squeezed his shoulder. "Good. Uh, I see you've got new maps from the database. That system is something the way it can layer geographical data like that."

"Yeah."

Well, that went well. Sandy, you're a regular chatterbox.

"So, you can really tell different anomalies from those blips and graphs? I'm afraid I wasn't in on the initial plotting of the water trails. Is that the line for the ancient creek bed?"

"Mmm." Sandy kept his eyes on the monitor.

I touched his shoulder. "Maybe you could give me an update a bit later ... clarify some points for me?"

He looked up, took a long drink of his tea, and shrugged. "Okay. Only it will have to be later."

"Sure. No problem. Thanks."

He hunkered back over the keyboard as a new graph appeared.

Geesh! Now, on to the other quiet one.

Kim nodded her thanks when I gave her the steaming mug. I studied her eyes. The lines and shadows seemed less prominent today. That was encouraging.

Let's see...what to talk about. Something normal ... like work.

"Sleep well? Or are you too excited about the new plans?"

She took a sip while jotting down a few last minute notes on her clipboard. "Hmm? Sleep? What's that?"

We both chuckled.

Okay. She made a little joke. I'm all for that. Business as usual for her, then we'll pull Sandy into line. It'll work...

"PJ, today is going to be an important one. I can feel it in my bones. Big things are going to happen." She gave me a sly

75

grin and thrust the clipboard in my direction. "I need to go over the latest GIS data with Sandy. Will you do the honors?"

Huh? Well that came out of left field.

I took the pad and glanced at the chart. Kim used a thick pad on a clipboard to record our daily work assignments. With our new plans to close up one hole and relocate to another spot, there was more than usual outlined on the pages.

"You want me to tell the crew where they'll be working?"

"Yeah. We discussed it all last night. You had good suggestions and you're the assistant director. It's about time you got more involved in the administrative tasks."

I had been reading the lists of details in Kim's precise handwriting, but I looked up when she touched my arm.

"You'll be fine," she said.

I bounced once on my heels and grinned back at her. "Sure...I can do this. Thanks."

"Thank you," Kim said. I think she was referring to more than this assignment.

"All right, Dirt Diggers, listen up." I scanned their faces and realized one was missing. "Where's Donny?" The skinny redhead with the pale goatee was not among the group.

"He's coming, PJ," Josie answered. "I saw him talking to a really good-looking guy in a suit back at the trailhead."

"Well, if that guy turns out to be with the media, I'll pluck Donny's beard out one whisker at a time."

The others chuckled.

"That won't take very long," James said, and we all laughed.

"Let's get started and Donny can catch up. Kim and I worked out some new assignments for you as a result of the meeting last night. A couple of you lucky people will be helping us plot and dig a new site nearer to the canyon wall. This won't be a Wheeler Grid, more like a horizontal excavation with careful attention to stratification. Anyway it will involve lots of digging."

A loud groan greeted my words.

I smiled. "Ah, some things never change. Don't tell me you're afraid of a little spade work!"

"It's gonna be a hot one today, PJ."

"We've got plenty of water, Laine…and we'll take regular breaks." I looked down the list. "Hmm. Looks like you lucked out on this one, though. You and Dewey will close the old site."

She gave a happy cry and slapped Dewey's raised hand. "All Right!"

I handed her several printed forms. "Make sure all finds are classified, recorded and labeled. Ship the ones that still need lab work off to the appropriate places and stack the rest in boxes along the wall of the field lab. We'll bring in new samples as soon as the new site yields something."

"Okay, PJ. We're on top of it." Dewey gave me a confident nod.

"James, you and Donny will set up the new datum point and man the cameras when needed. The rest of you, grab your digging tools and plenty of water."

I noticed that their attention was drawn to something in back of me so I turned to see what it was. "Ah, the late Mister Benton and…" *Oh, shit!* The man brushing off his expensive Italian suit was none other than Stephen.

Oh, Gawd, I don't think this is the 'big thing' that Kim had in mind.

I turned back to the group. "That's it for the moment gang. Relax awhile." They moved off to find some shade.

"Look who I brought, PJ." Donny's gray eyes widened with delight. "I saw him talking with Security. When he said he was your fiancé, I thought I'd bring him along to surprise you."

"Thank you, Donny. You need to see James about your new work assignment."

"Sure thing, PJ."

Donny left and I faced Stephen feeling the eyes of the crew boring into my back.

"Hello, Stephen."

"Cilla." He gripped my shoulders and bent his head to give me a proprietary kiss.

"What brings you all the way out here?"

Stephen's scowl returned. When he spoke he made no effort to lower his voice. "What do you think, Cilla? I find out you're messing around with some college kid, digging up this mountain looking for ghosts and wasting your father's money with a dried up has-been of a relic hunter--"

"Stephen, please. Keep your voice down. Let's go over to the main tent. I don't know where you got this crazy information." As we walked, Stephen kept his arm around my shoulder. His possessiveness irritated me. Was I being too irrational? "In the first place, I am not messing around with anyone--"

Pup's menacing growl interrupted whatever else I might have said. We ventured inside the tent after Kim gained control of the animal. I made introductions. Though he no longer growled, Pup's fur stayed ruffled and he maintained a watchful surveillance on Stephen.

Kim and Sandy mumbled polite greetings and left with Pup so that we could continue our talk with a little more privacy. I couldn't read Kim's expression, but she gave my arm a brief squeeze on her way out.

I cleared my throat. "Tea?"

"No, we won't be staying. Get your things and let's get out of this God-forsaken--"

"What? Have you lost your mind? I can't leave, I have a job to do."

"Cilla, wake up and smell the cactus. You are embarrassing me by remaining here."

I folded my arms across my chest. "And you are embarrassing me by coming here, Stephen." I took a deep breath, trying to curb my temper. "Who the hell do you think you are coming--"

"Who? I'll tell you who. I'm your fiancé and I have every right to--"

"Well, let me tell you something Stephen. That title was not my decision. You and Father cooked it up between you and I just let it slide." I raked several fingers through my hair; brushing damp bangs off my forehead. "I should have talked with you long before this, but you were always too busy to hear

78

about my plans for the future. Every time I tried to have a serious conversation with you, we ended up in bed."

He looked at me. A smirk replaced his scowl. "What? What am I too busy to hear?"

"I'm sorry Stephen. I don't know how to make this easy for you. We just aren't compatible."

"Huh?"

"It's over … we're through … finished."

"I don't believe this!" He threw up his hands and started to pace. His hands clenched and his jaw tightened as anger welled inside him.

"You don't have any respect for my career, for my plans, what I want to do with my life."

He stopped and stared at me. "This is crazy. 'What you want to do with your life'? You don't need to do *anything* with your life!" He was shouting now. I knew the entire crew could hear every word we said. "You're *rich* Cilla! You don't need to do a thing … ever. You can stay home, look beautiful, entertain my associates and make me happy. Isn't that enough?"

I sighed. "In a word, Stephen … no. It isn't. Not by a long shot."

"God." He rubbed his eyes and shook his head.

"I'm sorry." My voice dropped. "Stephen, it's over between us. I can't marry you. I don't love you. Now, please leave and let me get back to my work."

I turned away to let him compose himself. In a minute or two he'd shuffle on down the trail, out of my life.

Instead, he grabbed my arm and spun me around. "You listen to me. Walk out of here on your own two feet, or by God, I'll carry you out. Your father will not be happy--"

"Father and I talked. He left it up to me." I pulled free of his grasp and rushed out of the tent.

Sandy and Kim were nearby holding Pup. When Sandy saw me, he moved to my side.

I touched his arm. "It's okay. He's just leaving."

Stephen burst from the tent. I had never seen him so enraged. When he saw my hand on Sandy's arm, he thrust his body between us. "That's right Sonny Boy, we're leaving. So, you can find another sweet thing to warm your bed. This one's mine." He tried to take hold of my arm, but I ducked away.

"Stephen, leave us alone. I'm not going with you. Not now, not--"

I never saw his fist. There was a sudden explosion of pain along my jaw. I fell to my knees, tasting blood, feeling tears on my cheeks. I watched Sandy and Stephen scuffle while Pup charged between them and launched himself at Stephen, driving him to the ground in a snarling, teeth-baring fury.

Gawd, open up a hole and let me fall in. I've never been so mortified in my whole life.

"Pup! Sit!" With fangs bared he crouched between Stephen and PJ. Sandy, too, rushed to PJ's side, but I warned him away. I approached Pup with caution, snatching him firmly by his collar as he focused his energy on protecting PJ. I had to defuse the escalation of what was rapidly becoming a dangerous situation.

Stephen's face was ashen. "That animal is a menace," he said, his eyes locked on Pup.

His voice shook, partly from anger, I thought, and partly from fear.

"He should be put down."

Although I was doing a good job of containing my emotions, I felt the heat of anger coloring my face. My heart was racing and threatening to strangle my breath. "It appears to me that it is you, not my dog that is the menace."

PJ was still on the ground, blood trickling from the corner of her mouth. A welt reddened her cheek and her left eye was puffy. I gripped her hand and slid my arm around her back, pulling her up and against me, supporting her weight. The firmness of her body surprised me and the spicy scent of her hair was a momentary distraction. "Easy does it," I said, reluctant to let her stand on her own.

"Ugh." She worked her jaw and grimaced.

"Can you walk?"

She nodded.

I let her go. She staggered. I reached for her again.

"No. I'm okay … really, I'm okay."

"Then go and wait for me in the tent. Take Pup with you and be sure to hold him."

Stephen moved in her direction, but Sandy put a hand out to stop him. Stephen brushed him away, directing his words toward PJ. "Cilla, if you don't come with me now, it's over. I won't be back."

Dazed, PJ looked at me, her eyes clouded with confusion. She gave no indication that she had heard Stephen.

He tried again. "You either come with me now and look forward to a good future, or you can spend the rest of your life with this rag-tag bunch of air heads."

"PJ, take Pup and go to the tent," I repeated. She glanced at Stephen, hesitating. Then, she looked in my direction and I saw recognition and comprehension in her eyes. I softened my tone. "Now, Doctor Curtis, please."

She sniffed and nodded, reaching for Pup's collar.

"Damn it, Cilla!" Stephen started toward her, but Sandy blocked his path.

I watched PJ stumble toward the tent with Pup, until I became aware of Stephen and Sandy shoving and threatening each other. PJ had reached the tent and was fumbling with the flap when I forced my attention away from her and back to Stephen and Sandy. "Enough, both of you! Mister Cresswell, I don't know what manner of man you are."

I do and I'd like to sic Pup on you, but that's not going to help PJ.

"You're not welcome here. I'm asking you to leave right now and I don't want to see you around here again … ever. Is that clear?"

"You bitch! You've filled her head with craziness."

"Mister Cresswell, you *will* leave, one way or another. I suggest you do so now."

"I'll leave when I'm damned well ready to and what's more, Cilla's going with me." He took a menacing step toward me, his fists clenched.

Sandy pushed him away. "Keep your filthy hands off of her. You've already hurt one of my friends. You're not going to hurt another one."

"Sandy, don't get into the middle of this. He's not worth it."

Stephen pulled back. He glared at both of us. "This is none of your damn business. It's between Cilla and me."

I heard Pup's growls and PJ's attempts to calm him. *For gawd's sake, PJ, hang on to him no matter what happens out here.*

"Give it up, Mister Cresswell. It's over." I took the two-way off my belt. "Unit one, come in, please."

The radio crackled, a man's voice responded. "Doctor Blair, this is Jackson. What's the problem?"

"We have a situation … a *gentleman* needs an escort back to the road."

"On my way, Doctor Blair."

I slipped the radio back onto my belt. "Your choice, Mister Cresswell. You can leave quietly before security gets here, or you can wait to be escorted." I wanted to get this over with. My jaw ached from tension. "And just so you know, I'll be reporting this incident to Frederick Curtis. I doubt he'll take kindly to your treatment of his daughter."

"What makes you think he'll believe you over me?" Stephen snarled.

"Look around you. We aren't alone here. There are plenty of witnesses, people who work with PJ, friends of hers." Several of my crew had witnessed the exchange. James, the freckled faced, youngest member of the group, the one who rarely showed any emotion, bristled with anger. And Josie, who for a while had exhibited some jealousy toward PJ because of her friendship with Sandy, was crying. The rest were a blur in my peripheral vision. And even though I could not see them clearly, I knew they were experiencing every emotion from anger to embarrassment to sympathy. "Mister Cresswell, you're no fool …"

"Your loss, Cilla, not mine," he shouted.

Our burly security guard prodded him toward the trailhead. *I hope that's the last we see of you, Mister Cresswell. PJ deserves better.*

82

My people gathered around me. "You shoulda let me take a punch at him," Sandy said, still clenching and unclenching his fists.

"Yeah, me, too," Dewey echoed.

Josie, her eyes still red, shuddered. "And I thought he was so handsome, the creep."

"I wanted to scratch his eyes out and feed 'em to him," Laine muttered.

"Why, Laine, such violence." My attempt at humor was forced but I needed to lighten the situation.

She gave me a sheepish grin.

"Anyway, people, the show's over so back to work all of you. I'm sure PJ appreciates your support. I'm going to check on her ... make sure she's okay."

"Anything I can do?"

"For now, Sandy, just keep things progressing out here. I may need you in a few minutes."

"Sure thing, Doc."

PJ sat on the floor of the tent, hugging Pup, crying against his shoulder. Pale blonde hair mingled with gray and black. It softened my heart.

"And I thought I was the number one human in his life."

She lifted her head and I stared into wide, watery eyes. *The most captivating eyes I've seen in a long, long time.*

Emotions long kept silent, threatened me. I wanted more than anything to comfort her, to be her friend.

I'm in so much trouble. If I don't stop now...damn it. I won't be able to help myself.

I reached out and trailed two fingers along her cheek and jaw. "You okay?" I whispered.

She nodded.

I reached into the cooler and wrapped some ice in a hand towel. I dropped to my knees in front of her. My hands shook. "Here, hold this against your cheek."

She reached for the compress and our fingers touched, her hand lingering on top of mine. "It's okay, Kim. I'm fine. Really."

"I'm supposed to say that to you," I muttered, disgusted with my lack of composure.

"Well, your hands were shaking. I thought maybe you were worried ..."

"Me? Not a bit." Then, I exhaled. "Well, maybe a little." We both smiled.

She took hold of the icepack and I leaned back on my heels.

"When you're ready, I'll have Sandy take you back to the inn where you can rest."

"No, I'd rather stay here, Kim. Just give me a little time, okay?"

I opened the first aid kit. "All right, but at least let me look at your mouth." I cleaned the blood away with an antiseptic soaked square of gauze.

"The only damage is a split lip."

"Helps to have a hard head, I guess." We chuckled and she winced.

I examined the inside of her mouth. "Your teeth are still in nice, even rows and your smile should be as dazzling as ever, once you get over that fat lip." I wiped my hands and closed the medical kit. "It'll be sore for a while, but it's not life threatening."

"Unless you count dying of embarrassment."

"C'mon, this wasn't your fault." I smiled. "You'll have a colorful face for a few days."

She shot me a stiff, lop-sided grin. "Will you still love me in black and blue?"

I laughed out loud for what felt like the first time in days. I got to my feet. "I'm delighted that your sense of humor is still intact."

Damn, I'm still feeling the after effects ... that idiot could have broken her teeth, smashed her jaw, or worse. Gawd, how I wanted to smack him! But, it's over. PJ is trying to get beyond it. I must, too.

I packed the first aid kit away and spread my sleeping bag on the cot. Now that I wasn't invading her personal space, my thoughts were more professional, more practical.

"All right, PJ, if you must stay on site today, I'm going to insist you lie down and rest awhile. No arguments. I'll leave Pup with you."

"You think he'll ... Stephen ... will be back?"

"I don't think so, but I'm not taking any chances." *If that bastard returns, he'll have Pup and me to deal with.* "I'm posting one of our security people outside."

"Thank you. I'm sure I'll be okay. And, Kim ... I'm sorry if I worried you."

I felt the tear on my cheek. Surprised by my depth of emotion ... I hadn't cried in years, I hastily swiped it away, hoping she hadn't seen. "I wasn't worried. Really. I uh ..."

"Just couldn't bear the thought of losing your assistant director after you had finally broken her in." She grinned. "Am I right?"

"Absolutely." I winked. "That's it exactly."

I can't believe she's teasing me when she's hurting, trying to comfort me when she was the one assaulted. What's more, I'm enjoying it. I don't like where this is headed. Or, maybe the problem is ... I like it too much.

PJ settled onto the cot, with Pup, ever watchful, at her side. "I'll check on you later," I said.

She responded with a crooked grin.

Two weeks had passed since the Stephen incident and the digging progressed smoothly. Despite the heat, the hard work, and the lack of anything tangible, everyone was in a good frame of mind. Laine and Dewey completed work on the old site, covered it, and turned in a detailed report. All the pottery shards were, as expected, Hohokam in origin. They represented several phases of development. It was not that the Hohokam culture was unimportant to us -- it was just not what we were about. We treated the shards with respect. We measured, photographed, and noted for the benefit of future study all aspects of the site. Even though we thought the material had been thoroughly documented by earlier expeditions, we believed that there was always more -- a site rarely revealed all its secrets. We, however, were looking for something much different, something that predated the Hohokam artifacts.

One evening, on the spur of the moment, I invited the crew to my place for a spaghetti dinner. I prided myself on my cooking ability, though I seldom took time these days to do much in the kitchen. Preparing fine meals was relaxing for me. Through the simple act of handling and preparing food, blending ingredients, and adding spices, I found companionship, not as in one person to another, but meditatively as in a Zen experience.

"I can't afford to let you spoil perfectly good food," Mother had told me time and time again so my first cooking attempts were as an adult and over campfires in distant places, where I would try anything to liven up the freeze dried meals that made up my diet.

Sandy, Josie, and Lewis were the first to arrive. I was struck again by how much Lewis reminded me more of a prizefighter rather than a scientist. He was heavyset and had, as a child, broken his nose, the shape of which remained unique.

PJ arrived right after Sandy and just before the rest of the group. She joined me in the kitchen.

"What can I do to help?"

"Not a thing. Thank you." I moved away from the arm that had encircled my waist. "Just go relax with the others. Food will be ready in a few minutes."

"I can at least serve the drinks." She tied a white, linen dish towel around her waist, grabbed a note pad and pencil, and left my little one butt kitchen to take orders in as professional a manner as she could muster and still keep a straight face. By then everyone had arrived and the interior of the motor home buzzed with conversation. And with that many people in such a small space, there wasn't much room for moving about.

We shared a relaxing evening during which we chatted about past work experiences and our dreams for the future. We were all dedicated scientists though we all brought differing philosophies to the table. The subject invariably got around to the Amazons and why the lost tribe had left their homeland so many centuries ago. It was suggested by Dewey, the most studious of the team, that the tribes had splintered and that, scattered as they were, they had not the strength to defeat their enemies.

"I don't agree," Mike said, cleaning his glasses on the tail of his tee shirt. "I believe they became infected with what ails civilization today ... they lost the ability to work together and disagreed so violently among themselves that it led to civil war."

PJ shook her head. "Get a group of powerful, independent women working in a community and you'll have disagreement, but surely not civil war."

Sandy grinned. "But you'd sure get a whole lot of bitching." His laugh was muffled by PJ's dishtowel apron landing squarely in his face.

Laine cheered. "Good pitch, PJ."

I began the evening totally involved in the conversation, but gradually found myself studying PJ and hanging on to her every lively word. We were colleagues, but more than that, she was a breath of fresh air in my life.

I was pleased to see that she had settled into the routine and appeared comfortable with the crew and more importantly, with herself, but it was time to get my mind off her and add my two cents to the discussion.

"We don't know why the lost tribe left their homeland. We hope to learn the reason, but the fact is we may never know. History is sketchy at best and what we hope to learn from a few artifacts ..."

"What if we find human remains?"

"Well, Dewey, that would be more than I dare hope for."

The conversation lagged and one by one and two by two, the crew left. Josie and Laine offered to stay and clean up, but I declined. It was getting late and tomorrow was another long workday. Then, there was just PJ and me.

"Like it or not," she said, pushing me out of the way, "I'm not leaving this mess for you to clean up by yourself." I threw myself into washing the pots and pans while PJ straightened the living room, picking up the used paper plates, cups, and napkins. Together, we had the place ship shape in no time.

"Would you care for a night cap before you leave?"

"I'd love one, but I'd better go." She laughed. "I'm so tired now that if I don't get going, you're going to have a bed partner."

A strange but sweet sensation crawled the length of my spine. "Then, you had better leave, pronto."

"Okay, be that way. Goodnight." She sashayed to the door and ignoring the two steps, leapt to the ground.

"Goodnight, PJ. Drive carefully, okay?"

I stood in the doorway and watched her go to the car. G'Night, Boss, and sweet dreams." She blew me a kiss.

I turned away and closed the door behind me. *Oh, PJ, what am I going to do about you?*

Several days after the dinner at my place, I decided to spend the night on site. It wasn't the first time and I didn't expect it to be the last. I was alone, except for the security team whom I glimpsed now and then as they made their rounds. When I was on site like this, at night, they were careful to maintain a discreet, but vigilant distance.

I needed to be alone. The strain of Terry's unexpected appearance and the incident with Stephen Cresswell had left me feeling stressed. PJ, on the surface anyway, had moved on. It was time for me to do the same. A night up here, alone with the nocturnal creatures and with the Amazons I knew had passed this way was the tonic I needed to recapture my inner peace. I sat in my low camp chair, closed my eyes and listened to the night. It was true that one's hearing was more acute when vision was compromised. There was life in the dark.

My thoughts turned inward. Seeing Terry again had nothing to do with the unexplained emptiness I felt. She had long ago destroyed anything I had felt for her. The deep-seated sense of loneliness began the day I comforted PJ after Stephen's visit. I realized then, how important it was to have a close, dependable friend for support ... someone who cared.

That's it. I have no one in my life that cares, really cares.

My thoughts drifted, but soon returned to PJ. We had gotten off on the wrong foot.

Do you remember, PJ, when we first met? You were a handful and our relationship was tempestuous to say the least. You were spirited though, and wild like a mustang.

I adjusted my chair into a semi-reclined position. The air was warm; the night sounds a symphony in the concert hall of the outdoors. Pup gave a low growl, sensing another presence. "Settle down, fella." I wasn't worried. Intruders were unlikely with the security we had in place. "Just a night creature going about his business."

Pup stood. He wagged his tail and whined as PJ emerged from the darkness.

When she saw me, she hesitated. "Oh! Um ... uh, I didn't expect to see you here."

"I might say the same thing to you."

She held up her hand. "Aw now, Kim, don't get all bent out of shape."

"Why would I do that?"

"Cuz I know how much you value your privacy."

I smiled, despite being a little miffed at the interruption. "What can I say?"

"I got tired of staring at the four walls of the motel. I wanted to see what it's like up here at night ... if it's as creepy as I thought it would be ... hearing the coyotes and all." PJ turned toward the chorus of howls. "They sound lonely."

"I doubt they're lonely ... they just make us feel that way."

"And I wanted to make sure that our security force is on the ball."

"And?"

"They are ... they stopped me on the trail."

"PJ, are you still worried about Stephen?"

"A little, and the media ... I wouldn't put anything past them."

"Security didn't tell you I was up here?"

"No. I guess they figured I knew ... that I was privy to what my boss was up to." She snickered.

I smiled to myself. "Well, now you know."

"Yeah. I guess I do."

89

"Right now, I'm concerned about how you'll get back down the trail in the dark."

PJ shifted from one foot to the other. I noted the hesitation. "I ... uh ... thought I'd stay up here tonight."

I sat up. "Why would you want to do that and compromise your comfort?"

"I'm not that fragile, Kim. I'll manage."

"It gets cold up here at night."

"I brought my sleeping bag this morning ... when I heard the temperature was to be above average. Mid fifties at night isn't so bad. Back in Boston, that would be considered a heat wave."

I chuckled. "I didn't expect company."

"Well, neither did I."

"I spend the night every once in a while. I guess to ground myself and refresh my thought processes."

PJ giggled. "And keep in touch with your Amazon friends wherever they are."

"Well, I know they're here, somewhere."

"You're sure?"

"I'm sure."

"Then, perhaps I should leave. My presence might make too much of a crowd." Her mouth twitched, suppressing a grin.

"Not necessary. You've every right to be here ... and you'll not bother me."

"Look, if you prefer, I'll go over there." PJ pointed to a hollowed out area about two hundred meters away. "You won't even know I'm here."

"Really, that won't be necessary. It's warmer here, near these rocks ... they hold the heat."

Pup had been whining around PJ's legs, seeking her attention. She dropped to one knee and scratched his ears. He rolled onto his back and whimpered with pleasure when she tickled his stomach.

"He really likes you," I said. "He doesn't usually take to people."

"They say animals assume the traits of their owners."

I frowned. *Was I that antisocial?*

90

Pup shook himself, and returned to lie down beside my chair. We watched him settle into a comfortable position. "I don't own him, you know. He has too much wildness to belong to anyone except himself." I ran my hand over his shoulders and back. "He honors me by staying with me."

"He'd kill for you."

I looked at my faithful companion. His coat gleamed in the moonlight. "He probably would. For you, too, I think."

"Where did you get him?"

"I found him beside the road. He'd been shot."

"My Gawd!" PJ rocked back on her heels. "How could someone do such a thing?"

"Unfortunately, there are people out there who have no respect for life … in any form."

PJ moved to a nearby rock and sat down. "Mmm, it is warm." She shrugged her shoulders and stretched her legs.

I continued stroking Pup's head, whispering soft endearments. I didn't realize that PJ had been observing us until she spoke. "He looks all wolf to me. How do you know he's part German Shepherd?"

"The vet who attended him thought so." I buried my hand in his ruff. "I think he's more than half wolf."

"Me, too."

"I'm glad he's taken to you."

"He should after scaring the pee outta me that first day."

I chuckled. "Would you like a cup of Earl Grey?"

"Yeah, but let me fix it." She stood up and stretched. "It's the least I can do for invading your privacy."

"You're not in …" She had already turned toward the tent. Her hips rolled in a sexy, seductive way. *I wonder if she's aware she does that?* PJ was petite, blonde, and attractive. I could see why men were drawn to her. *Am I attracted to her? Is she the reason for my unexpected loneliness?* My chest filled with exhilarating warmth at the possibility. *Stop that! She's straight for gawd's sake. Besides, the last thing I need is another relationship to complicate my life.*

I thought about Terry and the night she had just dropped in. *What was she thinking? Did she honestly believe that I'd welcome her with open arms and invite her into my bed?*

Thinking about Terry reminded me that I should say something to PJ. She and Sandy had heard so much more that night than I would have shared willingly. If either of them was homophobic, they hadn't shown it and I was grateful for that. As key players on my team, any resentment on their part would likely create problems.

Does it make you nervous to be up here alone with me on this mountain, PJ? I hope you know that you have nothing to fear.

She returned with two cups of tea and the cookie tin under her arm. After handing me my cup, she set hers down on a rock and struggled to remove the dented lid from the tin. I took a fat chocolate chip cookie and waited for her to settle on her rock.

I hadn't realized my concern was showing until PJ gave me a curious look. "Something wrong with the cookie, Kim?"

"No. It's fine." I sipped some tea. "I um ... I know it's behind us, but I still need to talk to you, Sandy too, about Terry's visit that night. I'm sure it was awkward for you both and ..."

"You don't owe us any explanation."

"Oh, but I do. You witnessed an embarrassing encounter and I need to address it, even though I'm a little late in doing so."

"Kim, our only concern was for you. It was obvious that you two had a history ... that she had hurt you. Other than that, we thought nothing of it." PJ shifted and hugged her knees.

"If you're cold, there's a blanket--"

"No, I'm fine. My butt's going to sleep. I guess the rest of me should too, pretty soon."

She knew how to inject humor into a situation.

"Well, I feel better for having spoken ..."

"Look, Kim, what you do with your life is no one's business but your own. Besides, I should judge ... look at the mess I've made of mine." She giggled. "Talk about fodder for a novel..."

I smiled. "It would make for some interesting reading."

"I'll be sure you get the first copy of the first edition. I'll even autograph it for you."

I laughed and felt more relaxed, but I wasn't about to let the discussion of that fateful night go unfinished. "You're right about Terry's leaving. It did hurt. It was a difficult time for me, but it's all in the past. I'm over it."

We sipped our tea in silent respect for the night. I could see PJ's green eyes glinting, studying me in the low lantern light reflecting outward from the open tent flap.

I was sure that PJ was sincere and that she had accepted my right to choose so I continued. "Terry and I were together for a number of years," I said, surprised at my willingness to share some long buried pain.

"What happened?"

"Someone else, another woman, came along. Terry was always ready to trade the old for the new. Guess I always knew she'd move on, that I wasn't exciting enough to hold her." I sighed. "But, as time went on, I began to think and hope that she'd found a life partner in me. It didn't turn out that way though."

"I gather from what little I heard that she's not with that other person now?"

I shook my head. "I guess she's just another of Terry's discarded trophies."

PJ reached for the cookie tin. "Want another?"

"Not right now, thanks."

She replaced the tin and brushed crumbs from her lap. "So, how'd you two meet?"

"At the home of some friends in South America. Terry is a forensic anthropologist, a very good one. She was conducting a study of a remote band of headhunters, the last of their kind who lived along the banks of the upper Amazon River. I liked her intelligence, her ability to converse on my level. I guess I was vulnerable in that I wanted love in my life. I was attracted physically, too." The words slipped out. I felt myself blushing and hoping she didn't notice.

"She can't be very good if she doesn't recognize your worth, Kim. You're better off without her."

"I guess."

PJ jumped lightly to her feet. "Tea makes pee. I'll be right back."

I watched as she headed for the little tent that housed the porta-potty. Dewey, the quiet member of our crew, had painted a half moon on the outside and placed an old battery radio on the floor inside the flap. When the music was playing, the 'think tank' as it was sometimes referred to, was occupied. PJ turned on the radio. I wondered why since there was just the two of us and we would know when the teepee was occupied. Sounds carry at night, though. Perhaps PJ had a shy streak. I grinned to myself. Maybe I didn't know my assistant as well as I thought I did.

"You can stay in the tent if you want to and sleep on the cot," I said to PJ, when she returned with her sleeping bag rolled up under her arm. "I'm staying outside."

"What, and let you do all the stargazing? No way. I intend to count all the stars in the Milky Way." She looked around. "How about I go over there?" She pointed to a flat area several feet from where I was sitting and between two large rocks.

"Wherever you're comfortable."

I got up then, and headed for the tent to fetch my sleeping bag, but with a short detour to the teepee. I sat down on the chemical toilet. As an afterthought and with a smile, I turned on the radio.

When I returned, PJ was already tucked into her sleeping bag. I spread mine alongside a long flat rock where I was sheltered from any wind that might come up in the night. "Looks like you're ready for sleep," I said, not knowing if she was still awake. "I know I am."

"Yeah." She yawned. "It's been a long day. That woman I work for is a real slave driver."

I chuckled. "Yeah, and I'll bet she gets you up at the crack of dawn to make her some tea."

PJ snorted. "She wouldn't dare … would she?"

I turned onto my side to face her. "Oh, she can be ruthless with her assistants. Or so I hear."

PJ gave an exaggerated sigh. Then, she rose on one elbow. "Wait a minute. Just how many assistants have worked for her?"

94

I laughed out loud. "Okay, I'm busted. You're the first one."

"That's what I thought and I want to thank you."

"For what?"

"For taking a chance with me … for teaching me what real archaeology is all about … most of all, for being my friend."

"Hey, it hasn't been nearly as bad as I expected. Perhaps I should be the one thanking you."

"Well, fine then. You're welcome. Good night, Kim."

"Good night," I replied, then added, "sweet dreams, friend." I don't think she heard me.

I lay on my back, savoring the moments between wakefulness and sleep. For a minute all my cares and worries vanished. The stars were as bright and as big as I had ever seen them. There's something about the night sky that makes a person stop and take stock … think about the journey to this moment and what the path ahead might have in store for a solitary traveler.

That thought brought a resurgence of the hollow, lonely feeling. It didn't last, though. I drifted off to sleep with the realization that I wasn't really alone anymore. At this point in my life, I had a friend.

Pup was howling and running back and forth between us. PJ scrambled from her sleeping bag. "What the hell was that?"

"A trembler, I think, a mild one." I held onto Pup, who was shaking. "It's okay, fella. We're all right and you are, too."

"You mean an earthquake?"

"Somewhere, maybe in California. We barely felt it."

"The hell we did. It woke us up."

"Probably because we were lying on the ground. Being in contact with the Earth like that, we can feel Her breathe." I glanced at my watch … it was just after four.

PJ was standing in the middle of the clearing, looking around as if expecting to see something. She shivered. "I didn't know there were earthquakes in Arizona."

"There are a couple of faults just north of here, Sugarloaf and Horseshoe."

"You said it was coming from California."

"I said maybe it was California ... the epicenter could have been in any number of places ... California, Nevada, Mexico. Anyway, it was too far away to affect us."

"You'd better be right." She took a deep breath and finger-combed her hair. "I remember all those things you warned me about the first day of camp ... cactus needles, snakes, spiders and dehydration. Earthquakes were not on the list."

She pulled on a hooded sweatshirt. I wasn't sure if she wanted protection from the early morning chill or the shaky ground.

Pup was calm now, so I let go of his collar. He stayed close.

"Now that you're up and about, would you like some bacon and eggs?"

PJ grinned. "You have the fixings?"

"In the ice chest."

"Then I'd love some." She laughed. "Ya know, this could all have been an elaborate trick to get me to make tea for you."

I grinned back at her. "Not even I could be that diabolical. But, you can get the frying pan ... it's in the box under the table. I'll get the camp stove going."

Pup trotted between us. He was still unsettled but he seemed content enough as long as he was close to one or other of us.

Chapter Ten

"What?" Kim looked up from her breakfast plate, her fork still poised in the air. She stared at me.

"I said, I think you're trying to kill me. This breakfast, delicious as it is, is full of fat and cholesterol." I chuckled and her smile delighted me. *You need to smile more, Kim. It does wonders for your disposition.*

The smile widened. "And that would be a bad thing?"

Hmm, smiling and making jokes, too. Incredible.

"Oh yeah ... bad stuff. Before I came here I was focused on all that nutritional stuff ... fats, cholesterol, HDLs and LDLs. I would have fruit or bagel and juice or herbal tea for breakfast. Now look at me." I sighed and stretched, rubbing my stomach. "All fat and sassy... Do you know that the guys stop for French fries and cheeseburgers after work several times a week? I'm ashamed to admit that I've joined in a few times. When you add that to the pizza and--"

"You have nothing to worry about. There's not a stray ounce of fat on you."

I bowed my head. "Why, thank you."

"Besides, hiking to and from the site every day--often carrying loads of supplies will keep anyone trim."

"I hope you're right about that." I drank the last of my tea. "Can I get you another cup?"

"No, I'm fine. We'd better wash up and get ready for the crew's arrival. You use the tent and what's left of the hot water. I'll go check out our elegant bathroom."

I shrugged. "Why don't you use the tent, I don't mind making do with--"

"No, this is fine." She was already moving toward the potty tent. "We'll change places in a bit."

97

I rinsed our plates and utensils, being careful to save as much hot water as possible for both our needs. I stripped off the sweatshirt, sweatpants, and tee shirt I had worn to bed. I had a fresh shirt and underwear stuffed into my daypack. Yesterday's cargo pants would have to do another day. Ugh ... also yesterday's socks. Dressed in cargo pants and fresh panties, I washed and applied deodorant. I was just pulling my sports bra over my head, when the tent flap rustled.

"PJ, are you decent?"

"Depends on who you ask," I answered, my back to the entrance.

"What's that? Oh Geez, I'm sorry."

I turned to see her backing up. "Hey, no big deal. Just making a joke. I'm almost finished." I pulled the bra into place and picked up my shirt. Kim had her back to me, but remained standing inside the tent.

"All yours." I tapped her on the shoulder. "And don't worry about--"

She winced.

"Kim, what's wrong?"

"Oh, it's nothing ... just my shoulder." She turned toward me, rubbing the left side of her neck. "I fell and dislocated it several years ago while working in Greece. Sleeping on the ground makes it ache sometimes."

"Why didn't you use the cot?"

"Because I wanted to sleep outside under the stars ..."

"You could have moved the cot outside."

"I know, but sometimes I like to sleep on the--"

I cut her off. "Never mind that." I nudged her toward the cot. "Go lie down. I'm going to make it all better."

"But, really--"

"Don't argue." She tried to walk around me, but I blocked her path. We grinned like a couple of children in a schoolyard game of tag. "Kim, don't fight with me. I want to help you."

"The pain will go away on its own, really." She rubbed the offending shoulder.

I grabbed her by the hips and waltzed her to the cot. "Bend yer knees, Dearie," I said in my best imitation of my childhood nanny. Constance Hazleton was a prim and proper Englishwoman. She expected and received total obedience. I doubt she'd ever heard of Mary Poppins. "Now, sit," I commanded.

"Okay. Okay ... I give up." Kim flopped face down on the cot. "You sure you weren't an army drill sergeant in a former life?"

I placed my hand against my chest, feigning astonishment. "How can you say such a thing when I have only the best intentions? You are our leader, Kim. It is imperative that you be in tiptop shape for the coming day." I cracked my knuckles and wrinkled my nose. "I intend to see that you are."

Kim groaned. "That's what I'm afraid of."

"Hush. Take your shirt off and stretch out on your stomach."

She protested again, but I was persistent. "Now, now. Doctor Curtis will make it feel all better."

I rummaged through my daypack. "Damn, if only I had some massage oil." I found a tube of moisturizing lotion. "This will have to do." I looked toward my patient. "I hope that cot will hold both of us."

"Really, PJ ..." She started to rise, but thought better of it.

I chuckled. *Modesty, Doctor Blair, is going to force you to obey.*

"Now try to keep your arms and shoulders relaxed. This won't hurt a bit." I straddled her hips. "I'm a doctor and I know what I'm doing."

"I'd like to remind you that your degree is in archaeology, same as mine."

"Details ... details." I coated my hands with lotion and began to knead the tendons on either side of her neck. "I learned from the best ... Carlos Montega, my father's personal trainer."

"Who? I'm not sure this is going to ... ahhhhhh, yeah, right there ... ohhhh. Whatever you're doing, it feels wonderful."

"Uh huh. And you doubted these magic fingers. Carlos taught me how to give the best massages. Course, he taught me a few other things, too, before Father fired him for corrupting my seventeen-year old morals. But, that's another story."

My fingers were tingling as they made contact with Kim's flesh. *What's that all about? Must be some alcohol in the lotion or something.* I kept my eyes focused on the wide expanse of her muscular back and swallowed.

Gawd, what am I doing? This is Doctor Blair, naked from the waist up...and I'm acting like a comedian here. We started out so playfully, but this was a definite step forward in our friendship. I hadn't expected to feel anything by it. *Oh, come on. I'm a friend helping another friend who happens to have a sore shoulder. That's all it... isn't it?*

"Whoa, I bet your parents had something to say about that." The padding on the cot muffled Kim's voice, but it was loud enough to bring me out of my reverie.

"What? Oh, well … it was just my father who got after Carlos. Mom died when I was fourteen. Killed in a plane crash near Cairo."

"Oh, that's right. I remember reading about it. I'm sorry, PJ."

"It's okay. I … um … took her death pretty hard. I'm afraid I was a bit of a handful after that."

Kim coughed. I ignored her and continued.

"My mom was a super lady. She was a photojournalist for the Boston Herald. A real independent, stubborn woman."

Kim coughed again.

"Hey, are you trying to tell me something?"

"No … not me." She shifted her hips and we both rolled to one side.

"Hey, you're rocking the boat, here. Take it easy, you'll undo all my hard work." I moved us closer to the center.

"Sorry, PJ. I'm not used to getting the spa treatment." She sighed and turned her head to the right, before lowering it to the mattress.

I patted her shoulder. "The next time you get to Boston, let me know and I'll take you to my favorite health club. It has the most wonderful day spa."

"I don't know about that. This may be my one and only experience. I'm not into this luxury stuff."

I continued to work out the knots and smooth out her tense muscles. "Kim, it really isn't extravagant to keep your body healthy and flexible. Bodies need a little help every now and then."

She snorted. "Especially mine. Is that what you're saying?"

"Certainly not ... not at all. You have a great body." I felt my face flush after I said it. "That is ... uh ... what I see here ... is very toned. Your back is strong, your arms and shoulders ... uh ..." *Oh Gawd.*

She started to laugh. "It's okay. I was only teasing."

"... And your butt is so firm..." *Shit! Did I say that out loud?* "Uh, sorry. Forget I mentioned..."

Her laughter continued. "Goodness, such flattery. I think I'll come to this spa more often. You are very good for my ego, PJ, and your massage seems to have my neck moving again."

PJ was straddling my hips. *Does she realize what a compromising position that is?* I tried not to squirm, to keep my thoughts under control. *Gawd, PJ, if you only knew what you're doing to me.* I fought the desire to turn beneath her, to face her and pull her into my embrace, to pull her hips to mine -- to feel her bra-constrained breasts pressing against my naked ones. My face was burning. *Gawd, if she should notice! What will she think? Hot flashes, that's it, I can tell her I'm having hot flashes.* I gripped the wooden sides of the cot.

"Relax," PJ ordered in a most demanding tone. "Let go of the cot ... you're hanging on for dear life, like I'm planning to tip you off onto the floor."

"Okay, okay."

Her therapeutic fingers were working wonders for my shoulder, but they were doing much more than that. *It's been so long and she's so desirable. But she's straight and would probably be insulted if I were to ...* I remembered Terry and the hurt she brought into my life when she left ... and she was gay. *A dalliance with PJ, even if she were a willing participant would be so much worse...so much more complicated. Besides, she's my assistant ... I need to keep this on a professional basis.*

PJ continued to chatter. My thoughts were out of control. I hoped my responses to her made sense.

"Glad I could help, then. And, I meant it about Boston. I go to Sunny's every time I'm home."

I had lost the thread of the conversation. "Oh, you mean, the spa thing. I really don't have time for that kind of thing, but I'll keep it in mind."

PJ's fingers continued to work their magic. My body was feeling the heat of passion and the pain of subduing it. I tried to focus on conversation. "I guess you'll drop in there next month, then, during your Thanksgiving break."

PJ stopped. "Probably not. Father goes to Newport for the holidays and takes his staff with him. He has long, work sessions that are anything but restful. Boring as hell, actually. Last year I was with Stephen." She made a face. "Ugh. I doubt I'll be doing anything with him. So, I guess I'll stay around here. How about you, Kim? Will you go home for Turkey Day?"

"When I'm close enough to Santa Fe, I like to spend time there. I have a ranch there, you know."

"No, I didn't know."

"The house is a fixer upper, but I consider it my official residence. It'll hardly be worth the trip though, not for just a couple of days. So, I'll probably stay in the motor home in Apache Junction. If you'd like to come for dinner, I could cook a--"

"Kim, you cook for us, the crew, all the time!"

"Thank you, PJ, for the thought, but ordering in Chinese or pizza is hardly cooking."

"Why don't I take you out for dinner? My treat. What do you say? We could go into Phoenix, to a really nice restaurant. Have turkey and all the trimmings. How about it?"

"I guess we could do that. But, nothing too fancy, okay?"

"I'll call around and let you have the final choice ... and I promise ... nothing fancy."

Pup stood up and gave a happy bark. Kim turned her head. "What is it, fella?"

"Hey Doc!" Sandy burst through the tent flap and stopped abruptly. "Ooops! I'm sorry. Jesus, forgive me." The sight of us on the cot, Kim's bare back, and me with my shirt unbuttoned left him slack-jawed.

I started to giggle at the thoughts that must be going through his mind. Kim sputtered a little, but stayed down. Sandy turned and started out of the tent, his face turning a most adorable shade of pink.

"Hold it right there, Sandy m'boy. Just stand still and keep your back to us." I couldn't control the giggles.

"You're a big help," Kim said, lifting her head. "Sandy."

"Yes Ma'am."

"This is not what it looks like. I had an ache in my shoulder and Doctor Curtis was rubbing it out for me."

I got up and tossed Kim's shirt over her back. "Let me handle this."

She grabbed my wrist. "You've done quite enough already." Her tone was stern, but I could see she was smiling. "And it really does feel much better. Thanks."

I gave her a gentle pat on the shoulder. "My pleasure."

"Okay, Sandy, what is it?"

"Did you hear about the earthquake?" He was still facing away from us so I walked around to talk to him, remembering to button my shirt before moving into his line of sight.

"Yes, we felt it."

"Wow! That's amazing. The epicenter was in Sonora, Mexico. Seven point four on the Richter Scale, the radio said. There's property damage and several fatalities, mostly in Mexico, close to the border."

Kim climbed back into her tee shirt. "That's not good news, Sandy. I was hoping it wasn't too serious. Did you notice any ground disturbances on your way up here?"

"Nothing that I could--"

"C'mon, Sandy," I interrupted, giving him a gentle push toward the entrance. "Doc needs to finish dressing and washing up."

"Oh, sorry. Sure thing."

As I followed Sandy out of the tent, I called over my shoulder to Kim. "Hope what little hot water I left you didn't cool off too much."

Ten minutes later, I sat with the crew while the sun made its grand entrance. Kim joined us to hear more stories from the arriving students. Laine reported that the seismologists feared more quakes and damage in the days ahead. "Probably aftershocks," Sandy said, "not as strong and not as damaging as the main quake."

Kim shook her head. "It depends on how much slippage occurred along the fault line. The stress builds up over the years, often hundreds of years, and is released by an earthquake. If the initial shock released all the tension, then we can expect only some minor shakes as the fault settles. Let's hope that's what happened and that it wasn't a strong foreshock. But since we can't do anything about it, I suggest we get to work."

Chapter Eleven

After many days of digging, we had found little other than some shards of traditional Hohokam, red on buff pottery and a small animalistic figurine; a legacy, we believed, from their Mexican neighbors.

Watching PJ work and the way her fingers caressed each piece as she examined it reminded me of the healing touch of her hands that day, when she had rubbed the ache out of my shoulder. What an awkward, yet pleasurable experience it had been for me. Just thinking about it now made my spine tingle and my stomach flutter. I had come as close as I dared to revealing my feelings for her. Not only was she straight, but she was an employee ... coming on to her would be unprofessional.

Oh, PJ, if you only knew....

I was impressed with how much PJ had matured since we first met just three months ago. There were no more indiscretions with alcohol, no more flirting with all the guys, and no more screw-ups. She had changed, too, after her altercation with Stephen. Her dedication to our project was complete. I watched her interact with the crew. She was friendly, but with an air of maturity. She seemed comfortable as my right hand, an assistant with the capability of holding a team together. I had learned years ago, after some disastrous situations, that when in a position of authority, you can be a friend, but never a pal.

I was pleased when, on her own initiative, PJ established weekly dinner meetings at Missus O'Brien's Home Style Dining. She had suggested to the owner, none other than the portly Missus O'Brien herself, that we have a standing reservation for the private dining room. I smiled to myself when I thought about it. When PJ suggested, people listened. She had a knack, that one, except when it came to her father. He and she remained politely aloof. And on more than one occasion I had seen her in tears after talking to him on the telephone.

I found our off-site gatherings at Missus O'Brien's both stimulating and relaxing. Pictures and posters of the Faire Isle decorated the walls of the private dining room. It was there, usually over dessert and coffee, that we reviewed suggestions from every team member and discussed any current problems.

"Don't you wish," PJ said, with a sigh, "that our Lost Tribe had migrated to a lush green spot like that?" She pointed to one of the pictures. A stone wall in the foreground led the viewer's eye into a pastoral scene of rolling, green fields dotted with wild flowers. "Why in gawd's name did they pick this place?"

"Maybe they were lost," Josie said.

"The lost Lost Tribe," James quipped.

"Could be," Mike said, "after all they didn't have a man along to show them the way."

"Smart ass!" Laine was close enough to Mike to grab his arm and twist it behind his back.

"Hey, that hurts."

"So apologize."

"Okay, okay. I'm sorry."

"Gawd, what a grouch," Mike said, when Laine released his arm. He rubbed his shoulder.

"Okay, peace in the ranks," I said, trying to sound severe. I don't think it worked because I couldn't stifle a chuckle. I liked the way my team could banter together and tease each other. It helped carry them through those long, dusty days of hard work.

With dinner over and business talk out of the way, we retired to the bar, a replica of a Dublin pub, to play darts. The play was deadly serious and stress relieving. The winner was excused for one week from all the unsavory on-site jobs like packing out trash and emptying the Porta Potti tank into the blue, wheeled honey bucket and hauling it out to the dump station down on the highway.

I had lost count of the days we scraped and turned the dirt. The daily high temperatures had slowly dropped from the high nineties and low one hundreds into the seventies. This brought blessed relief when working, as we were, in the open with no shade and with the sun bouncing off the rocky surface.

I was feeling particularly lethargic when we broke for lunch, as was everyone. It was that kind of day. The air was warm, sweet smelling, and still -- so very, very still, though charged with the buzz of unseen insects.

I was sitting on the ground taking advantage of the scattered shade of a scrawny juniper. When I leaned my head back against its rough bark, it crackled like dried grass. I closed my eyes.

When I opened them again, I saw that PJ had shifted positions. She was now lying on her back, her body shaded by a large rock. Her eyes were closed. I put on my sunglasses and with my head tilted, observed her out of the corner of my eye and from behind my shades.

PJ, you're something. But you know that, don't you? If you only knew how much I admire your healthy body, your shiny blonde hair, and those devilish green eyes. I adore your sense of humor and your ready smile. You add so much to my day ... I leaned my head against the tree again and closed my eyes. And, I have to admit, my nights as well, because I think of you often when I'm lying there in the dark ... when I'm lonely and can't sleep. Sometimes I have difficulty remembering that you're a trusted colleague and friend, nothing more.

An insect buzzing around my head brought me out of my reverie. The juniper bark was beginning to itch though my shirt. I scanned the clearing and the crew's lunch-break activities. Off to my right, Sandy and Laine were discussing the destruction of ancient sites in the Middle East and the implications of its loss to historians as well as the worldwide archaeological community. Josie was lying on her side on a piece of faded blue tarp. She was engrossed in a Patricia Cornwell mystery. As far as I knew Josie was straight. I think though that a little piece of her was in love with Cornwell's Kay Scarpetta character. Better to fall in love with a fictional character than a live being, I thought. Less heartache.

I was proud of the way we worked together, and how well we relaxed together as a group. *Was that my doing or PJ's?*

107

We've come closer, I think, since her arrival. She has a way, that one. I chuckled to myself.

The rest of the crew were clearing away their lunch trash and preparing to return to work.

Pup's limbs were twitching. I imagined he was dreaming about roaming free with the wolf pack. "Enjoy it, fella," I whispered. "Enjoy the moment."

I rolled onto my back and with my hands behind my head and knees bent, watched the scattered, fluffy white clouds drifting across the otherwise brilliant blue sky. Cactus wrens twittered. The occasional tapping I heard was a Gila woodpecker hard at work. From where I lay, I was able to identify Juniper and Net Leaf Hackberry. I prided myself on my knowledge of the desert environment. Knowing it and coming to terms with it helped me understand what my Amazons were up against when they entered this unforgiving land.

It's such a perfect day. I should give everyone the afternoon off.

Too late, PJ was on her feet and moving toward me. She stopped in front of me, saying nothing, but looking at me with a raised eyebrow.

"What?"

"C'mon, Doc, or are you planning on lying about all afternoon?"

"Slave driver," I muttered, dragging myself to my feet.

"What's with the birds?" PJ asked. They were flying in erratic circles and screeching loudly enough to awaken the dead. I scrambled to my feet. "What the hell ..."

Without warning, Pup howled and ran toward me, almost knocking me over. By now, everyone was on their feet. I was disoriented. My vision was blurred. I couldn't focus on anything. My balance was off. The rumbling sounded like an approaching locomotive. I saw Laine scramble to her feet only to fall down. The ground heaved beneath me. Why did I take that moment to remember a white water raft trip I'd taken down the Colorado? The difference; I had some control in the raft, here I had none.

"Oh, my gawd, Kim!" PJ grabbed me. We both fell. The earthquake lasted a long time though in real time it was less than a minute.

I pried myself from PJ's tenacious grip. "It's over."

"Are you sure?"

"Well, I can't be sure, but ..." PJ's eyes reflected her fear. "Yes, I'm sure."

"You'd better be right, lady."

I squeezed her arm. "I know one thing," I said, choking on the cloud of dust that enveloped us, "that was no aftershock."

"That's an understatement."

The alarm in PJ's eyes was close to panic. I put my arm around her shoulders. "It's okay ... we're okay."

The dust covered us like fine rain until we were all looking like human dirt devils. I could taste the grit, which had gotten into my mouth and lungs. I needed to rinse my mouth but couldn't see my water bottle anywhere.

I tried to spit but my saliva had dried up. PJ was coughing, trying unsuccessfully to clear her throat and lungs.

"There it is." My water bottle was lying in a hollow six feet away. I let go of PJ and dashed for the bottle, grabbing it, and returning to her side.

I offered it first to PJ. "Here, wash out your mouth."

She did, spitting a brown stream onto the ground. "Thank you, Kim, now you."

I took the bottle from her and did the same. It helped -- a little.

Everyone was coughing, spluttering.

I looked around. Every grubby face was wide eyed. "Sandy, are you okay?"

"Yeah, Doc, I'm good."

"Laine?"

"I'm okay."

"Josie?"

"I broke a nail."

"No self respecting archaeologist keeps her nails any longer than nubs."

"Mikey Boy, unlike you, I have a life down there." She pointed toward Phoenix.

Their banter relieved some of the fear we all felt.

"The rest of you are okay?"

They answered in unison. We had sustained a few scratches but nothing more serious.

"Okay, I guess we were lucky. Let's go get those scratches cleansed and band aids on them if necessary."

The slightest sound caused everyone to jump. Although it was hard to see beneath the grime, I was sure everyone's complexion was several shades whiter than before the quake. I walked over to the partially fallen tent and grabbed the first aid kit and several bottles of water. Sandy relieved me of my load and handed them around.

I returned to PJ and stood next to her, my back to the group. "We're okay," I said, my voice calm and under control. "You look like hell though."

"Yeah. Who'd know I even showered this morning."

"Only you, darling, only you." I blushed under the grime when the endearment slipped out. I cleared my throat, as much in embarrassment as to clear the grit.

Sandy went for the radio and twiddled the dial until he found a Phoenix station that was broadcasting. There was fear in the announcer's voice, an excited trembling as he rattled off the latest news. "Early reports indicate some structural damage both in the city and in outlying communities." He went on to warn of broken glass everywhere, but fell silent when a small aftershock rumbled through the area.

"Kim!" PJ dropped to the ground, I suppose because she felt safer sitting rather than standing.

I went to PJ and dropped to my knees beside her. "Relax, it was just an aftershock," I said, addressing the group. Josie, following PJ's example, sat down. I put my arm around PJ's shoulder and pulled her close to me. "We'll feel a lot of those for the next few days, but the worst is behind us."

"I feel so silly, but the thought of an earthquake scares me to death," PJ said. "I'd rather deal with tornadoes. At least you can see them coming."

"Hey, it's not silly at all. We're all scared when the earth trembles. We feel vulnerable because there's nothing stable to hold onto."

"Except each other. Thanks." She gave me one of her adorable lop-sided grins.

"Anytime." I wanted to hug her, but I didn't. That would scare me more than the earthquake.

The announcer came back on the air, his voice devoid of the smooth patter so recognizable on the morning news. His nervousness was evident in his frequent pauses and the slight tremble that weakened his trained speaking voice. "Many areas of the city are without power but utility companies are dispatching crews to assess the extent of damage. Early reports place the epicenter of the seven point nine quake ten miles north of Santa Ana in Sonora, Mexico. Fragmentary information indicates severe damage there with loss of life in Hermosillo and smaller communities."

Sandy shook his head. "Geez, those poor people...."

The birds had settled down but Pup was nowhere to be seen.

"Hey!" It was Laine. She had wandered away from the group clustered in front of me. "There's been a rock slide ... over here."

I turned toward the sound of her voice. She was standing near the pit where we had been working earlier, before the quake. Rocks and large boulders had rolled into and had obliterated our work site.

"Shit!"

What if we had been there ... working? I felt the color drain from my face. *How fortunate for us all that it happened while we were at lunch.*

PJ, her fear of earthquakes forgotten, was off and scrambling up and over the rocks.

"PJ, get back here, we don't know how stable--"

"I'll take care, but I gotta see ... looks like we have a cave up here."

111

Even from here I could see a small opening in the canyon wall, about five meters above the rubble. "C'mon, people, let's go assess the damage."

"Look at this," Sandy said, voicing my earlier thoughts. "What if we'd been working ... if we hadn't been on a lunch break ... if we'd done what we usually do, eaten individually as the mood struck?"

I shivered. *What if, indeed? We'd probably be digging out the badly injured or, worse yet, the dead.*

Josie crossed herself and looked upward. Her lips were moving.

I continued to stare in disbelief at the pile of rocks and boulders that had buried our pit. I didn't want to think about what might have happened if the quake had occurred earlier. Sweat oozed through my pores. Although I wasn't a religious person, I was spiritual, and mouthed gratitude to my Higher Power.

PJ slid on some loose rocks and tore her pants.

"Be careful."

"Yes, Mother Hen."

I chuckled nervously.

She had made it to the opening in the cliff face. It wasn't terribly large, more like a horizontal slit, wider in the middle. I imagined that it was likely home to some critter.

"PJ, do be careful ... you don't know what's in there. It could be a rattlesnake lair."

"Don't worry, I will." She peered into the hole, then turned toward us and scanned the area. "My flashlight's in the pack over by that old juniper. Could somebody throw it up to me, please?"

I happened to be closest so I went for it. The pack, like everything else, was coated in gritty, brown dust. I returned with the Mag Lite and tossed it to her.

The crew waited, chatting among themselves. I wasn't listening to them. I was way too concerned about PJ whose head, right arm, and shoulder had disappeared into the opening.

"PJ, please be careful." I wasn't sure she could hear me.

My concern for her was overwhelming.

Gawd, don't let it show.

"PJ, please, there are likely to be more aftershocks."

112

She withdrew, but not because of my warning.

"Kim, you'd better get up here."

Her excited tone hushed the conversation. I scrambled up the jumble of rocks to join her. My hands and feet grasped for the bigger boulders, testing each one, making sure it was stable before putting my weight on it.

"Watch out, Doc!" I heard Sandy's warning just as a large rock loosened under my hand. I grasped for another handhold as the loose boulder rolled to the bottom of the slide. Sandy, who was closest, leapt out of the way, scattering the already jumpy crew.

"Take a look inside," PJ said somberly, when I reached her. She had stepped to the side and was partially kneeling on a relatively secure boulder and holding on to another one. I couldn't read her expression, but I knew from her tone that she had seen something in that dark and forbidding hole.

I squeezed my head and arm into the opening and, for a moment, was aware of nothing except the overpowering smell of stale air and dust. I sneezed. I forgot everything else though when my beam of light picked up an incredible sight. "Oh, my gawd!"

I backed out of the opening to face PJ. Her expression was serious … one hundred percent archaeologist. I scanned the faces of the crew. They stood in silence, in a semi circle at the base of the slide, waiting for us to say something.

"It's a cave and … well, you best get yourselves up here, one at a time. But please be careful. This stuff is unstable and I don't want anyone breaking a leg."

"Stay put," I said to PJ as I moved away from the opening and positioned myself between two precariously balanced boulders. PJ gripped my arm then let it go quickly, as if she felt she had taken liberties. "Kim, do you suppose…?"

I shook my head. "It's way too soon to even hazard a guess. As to what happened here … well, we just don't know yet."

Hushed whispering from below accompanied each crewmember as they climbed up one by one and peered into the gloom of the cave.

"Geez, Doc," Sandy said, as he withdrew from the hole. "Could be, you know, it very well could be." He made his way back to the base of the slide.

"Let's not get ahead of ourselves."

James was the last to climb into position at the opening. His exclamation, "Jesus!" sounded like a distant echo. He withdrew and searched my eyes for an answer.

I shook my head. "We can all think what we want, but whatever our thoughts, they're no more than guesses."

"Educated guesses," Josie said. She had been the first, after PJ and me, to see into the cave.

Minutes later, I was back at the opening, staring at the skeletons of two individuals. One was lying on its back, straight out as if laid carefully in place. The other was lying face down across the first one. Clutched in one bony hand was an ornate dagger, dulled by time, but a beautiful weapon nevertheless. The blade was imbedded deeply between the ribs of the one who held it. Bits of hair, cloth, and leather clung to the remains.

I backed out. Strange fluttering sensations gripped my stomach. I needed fresh air. For some reason, perhaps the after effects of the earthquake, I wanted to run, to get as far away from the cave and its occupants as I could. I wondered if Howard Carter had an urge to run when he first discovered Tutankhamen's tomb. I didn't think so. As I made my way down the slide with PJ right behind me, I tried to explain to myself the reason for my unease.

The crew bunched up around us.

"Could they be ...?" Sandy asked, letting the sentence hang. We all knew what he meant.

"They appear to be old," Mike said, "maybe old enough ..."

"Now, people, let's not get carried away. It'll be some time before we learn enough about these people and what they were doing here. And for that matter ... if this is an ancient crime scene ..." My stomach was churning.

"The remains are small," Sandy said, "very likely female--"

Laine interrupted. "Which means they could be Amazon."

"Yeah, and then there's the dagger," James said. "It's ancient like ..."

PJ could barely contain her excitement. "We've done it, Kim ... we've found them."

"PJ, all of you, let's not jump to conclusions. We won't know *anything* until we've investigated further." I was shouting now, afraid that PJ's enthusiasm was getting the better of her, and the crew.

"Hey, gang, listen to what Doc is saying," Sandy said, trying to help me by putting a lid on the runaway conjecture.

"I know all that," PJ said, "but, from what I can see of the markings on the dagger..." She shook her head. "It isn't anything even remotely native to this area."

The group started again, shaking hands and hugging each other.

"And that's all we know for sure," I said, glancing uneasily back toward the cave. I half expected to see a fully muscled and fleshed Amazon warrior walk out of there.

I had to stop the runaway conjecture. Stepping onto a large boulder, the one I had loosened earlier and which had come to rest at the bottom of the slide, I addressed the crew. "Listen up, people. Don't jump to conclusions. This may or may not be what we're looking for. However, it is a significant discovery. I need time to think about how we're going to proceed ..." I looked at my watch. "... and since it's already mid-afternoon ..." A wave of nausea passed over me. I glanced around, still with an inexplicable dread gnawing at my stomach, and took some deep breaths.

PJ sensed my discomfort and picked up where I left off. "Everyone, it's too late in the day to start moving rock. I think Doc wants you all to take the rest of the day off." She looked to me for confirmation.

I nodded.

The buzz of enthusiasm turned to good- natured grumbling. The chatter stopped when a low frequency trembling rumbled beneath our feet. Strangely, it relaxed me.

"Let's not forget," PJ said, "that we've experienced a severe earthquake. You need to go home to check your apartments, rooms, whatever. Call your loved ones and let them know you're okay. We'll meet here in the morning."

I touched PJ's arm. "You too, you have to call your dad."

"Like he cares, but yes, I will."

I turned to face the crew. "I don't have to remind you that mum's the word. And because of that we cannot risk bringing strangers in to help access the cave. We'll have to do the heavy work ourselves. That means stabilizing the slide, building easier access, and expanding the entrance. We have a lot to do before we meet these people face to face." I paused; scanning the eager faces looking up at me. The prospect of several days of hard labor had not fazed anyone. I was blessed with a dedicated group of young scientists who were about to become laborers.

Mike stepped forward. "You referred to them, the remains as people … are you pretty sure we've found our Amazons and you feel bonded to them?"

"I'd like to think that they're our Amazons, but I referred to them," I inclined my head toward the cave, "as people rather than remains because that's what they are … human beings who have moved on, transitioned to the beyond."

"We'll get started in the morning then," Sandy said.

"Righto." I turned to PJ. "Do you have anything to add?"

"Well, the real archaeology won't begin until we get in there. Then we'll need samples of everything including the soil."

"What are you expecting from the dirt?" Josie asked.

"Good question." PJ looked at me. "Would you care to …?"

"Go ahead." I folded my arms across my chest and listened to my assistant who was in her element. I was proud of her and damn glad she was involved in my expedition.

"We don't know for sure what the matrix will yield … traces of blood, bits of pollen, microscopic bone fragments, perhaps. That area could give us a wealth of information. We won't know until we have it analyzed."

I stepped forward, resting a hand on PJ's shoulder. "What happened in there is a mystery waiting to be solved. It could be a murder or a murder-suicide. We have some detective work to do. Just remember that the only difference between this and a modern day mystery is that we do not have witnesses. We have only the dead to speak to us."

"Well, for sure, they won't be apt to lie."

"No Laine, they'll tell us the truth, but don't expect them to share their secrets easily."

I turned to PJ. "Anything else?"

"Just protect the context of the site. Don't disturb it any more than necessary." She shrugged, looking at all of us. "But, you already know that."

Heads nodded agreement.

"Sandy," I threw him my keys, "will you stop by the motor home?"

"Sure thing, Doc."

"Just check things out, mainly the computer. I don't know what you can do if it's been damaged, but check it out anyway."

"Gawd, I hope it's okay."

"Motor homes are relatively safe in earthquakes, but they rock like hell."

"Don't worry, Doc, I'll take care of it."

I surveyed the wide-eyed faces hanging on to my every word. "Okay, off you go. Remember, not a word … this is a sensitive location and we don't need reporters or anyone else snooping around and disturbing the purity of the site."

"What are you going to do?" Mike asked, wiping his glasses on the tail of his grubby tee shirt.

"Stick around. Pup took off. I don't know where he went. I want to be here when he returns."

Everyone was reluctant to leave, but did so with a little urging on my part. Mike and Josie left first, then Laine hurried to catch up to them. The rest straggled along behind them. Sandy waited until everyone had left. "You're sure I can't do anything here?"

"We'll be fine, Sandy. Thanks. Your checking the motor home is enough."

"If you need me, you can call, at least I think you can." We checked our cell phones, which appeared to be working okay.

When Sandy left, PJ and I checked out our tent headquarters. We righted the corner that had collapsed and secured it. We were amazed that it had fared so well in the quake. Papers were scattered about on the floor and some books that had been stacked on the table had toppled. The laptops had survived, though everything was coated with dust.

PJ took the cell phone from her belt and blew the dust off the dial panel. "Guess I'll call Father ... get it over with."

I moved outside to allow her some privacy. It took her several minutes to get through, but when she did I could tell by her tone of voice that he wasn't around. I squatted on the ground and without really thinking about it, picked up a handful of dirt and strained it through my fingers. I could still hear PJ.

"Okay, thanks anyway, Barbara, I just wanted him to know I was alright. I'll try again tomorrow."

"Not likely," she added quietly, exiting the tent.

"As usual, he's not available," she muttered in my direction. She dropped the phone in its case on her belt. "Why am I surprised that he's in one of his high- powered meetings?" Then, she squared her shoulders and set about making tea.

I sighed and righted a low camp chair, which was lying on its side. I shook off most of the dust and sat down.

"You know," I said, when PJ handed me a cup of tea, "I should be elated, but I feel strangely subdued ... like I've seen a ghost."

"In a way you have, ghosts from the past."

"Yeah, but that's not it." I gazed toward the burial site and beyond. Dust still hung in the western sky. *That'll make for a lovely sunset.* "It's as though I've seen my own ghost."

Oh, brilliant! Why did I say that to her? She'll think I'm batty for sure.

PJ shot me one of her lop-sided grins. "Hey, Kim, don't get all weird on me."

We sipped our tea in silence though PJ kept shooting looks my way.

"What?"

"You haven't called anyone."

"There's no one to call."

She wrinkled her brow and continued to stare at me.

"That's it. I have no one to call. End of conversation."

"Okay." She looked toward the cave then back at me. "What now?"

"Nothing."

"I can't explain it ... my odd behavior."

"I didn't ask."

"I know, but ..." *You're disappointed, aren't you ... over my reaction to the discovery?*

PJ got to her feet. "C'mon, Doc, let's go eyeball the situation again ... secure the entrance for the night and figure out a way of attacking it tomorrow."

"Secure it?"

"I'm going to hang a tarp over the entrance. We don't want critters going in there and disturbing those bones."

I shuddered. "Of course. I should have thought of it."

"Kim, you're just so elated about finding the Amazons that you're not yourself."

"We don't know for sure ..."

"I do, and you do, too, I think."

PJ picked up the faded blue tarp that was lying beside the tent.

A few minutes later, she was scrambling up the rocks with the tarp dragging behind.

"Want some help?"

"No, I've got it."

"Thanks." *I don't want to go near the cave again today... tomorrow, but not today.* PJ covered the entrance and neatly anchored the tarp with rocks.

Then, when she was finished, she joined me, sitting on the ground our backs against a rock. A spectacular sunset painted the sky, wrapping itself around us like a colorful Navajo blanket. I glanced up at the blue tarp and wished I could share the beauty of the evening with them, the two women, and I was sure they were women, sleeping with their secrets inside the cave.

PJ, sensing my emotional state, put her arm around my waist. "Kim, I'm here for you, you know that, don't you? If there's ever anything I can do ..." She rested her head on my shoulder. I drew a modicum of comfort from her action and fought back the tears that threatened to spill onto my cheeks.

She cleared her throat. "May I ask you something?"

"You may ask, but I won't guarantee an answer."

"Does this business of seeing a ghost have anything to do with your dreams?"

"I'm going to stay here tonight."

PJ sighed. "Okay, so you don't want to talk about it. That's all right. And I think you should stay. I will, too, if you don't mind." She grinned. "I promise I won't ask any more questions."

I raised my hand and brushed her bangs back from her forehead, resisting the urge to bury my face in her hair ... lose myself in the soft beauty of it, dust and all.

"Don't you want to check your room at the inn?"

"Nah, that won't be necessary. I just have a few clothes there, nothing of importance. My laptop is here. And we have a shower, such as it is. No change of clothes though so I'll just have to shake 'em good."

"Then, I'll be happy to have you stay. I have a strange feeling about all this and I really don't care to be alone."

She gave my waist a tight squeeze. "You're not alone, Kim."

Chapter Twelve

I awoke in darkness, sitting up to untangle my legs from the sleeping bag. *What the hell was that noise? It sounded like a wounded animal.* My eardrums throbbed as I strained to listen. *Had Kim heard it, too?*

Jesus, it's so dark.

I rubbed my arms, shivering. *And cold.*

Was it a coyote? I remembered how they scared the hell out of me when I first arrived in the Superstitions.

"Leeja ... NO! NOOOOOO!"

Gawd! It's Kim and she sounds like she's in pain.

I squinted in the direction of where Kim had been sleeping, detecting the outline of her body, thrashing about in her bedroll.

Must be a nightmare. I should wake her, but she'll freak out even worse if I startle her.

I crawled free of my covers and approached her with great care.

"Kim? ... Kim, can you hear me?" She shuddered when I put my arm around her shoulders. The back of her shirt was damp with sweat. "Kim, you're having a dream... a bad dream."

Her eyes opened. She clutched at me. "What? Who?"

"It's me ... PJ. Take it easy, okay. We're at the site ... sleeping peacefully by the light of the moon and the stars. At least we were."

"Oh, PJ, I'm so sorry." Kim released her grip. "That dream again. It was so real..."

I sat back on my heels. "Let me get you a heavier shirt; you're chilled to the bone. I can light the lantern. Do you want some tea?"

"No, really. Thank you, it's not necessary." She shuddered again. "I guess I could use my sweatshirt, though."

121

I found my pocket flashlight and collected the shirt. I also dragged my sleeping bag closer to hers.

"Um ... it's still early. Can you go back to sleep?"

Instead of answering, she stared in the direction of the narrow cave. Moonlight reflected off the blue tarp and sketched a faint outline of the rocks along the canyon wall.

"Pup? Did he return?" Her voice was strained, confused.

I sighed, rubbing her shoulder. "Not yet. I'm sure we'll find him once it's daylight."

She looked at me and nodded. "Daylight," she repeated.

C'mon Kim, snap out of it. I don't know how to talk to you when you're like this.

I turned my head and stared at the shadows on the canyon wall, taking a slow, deep breath, collecting my thoughts, examining my options.

Maybe the light-hearted approach will work.

"Sure. You know how Pup loves your bacon. He'll be hungry." She nodded again, brushing her hand across her eyes, perhaps clearing some mental cobwebs.

I pulled our bedding up around us and rubbed gentle circles against her lower back with my fingertips.

This is scaring the shit out of me. I feel so inadequate. What has happened to the Kim Blair I met two months ago? That woman was confident, feisty, and authoritative. Damn it, I want her back.

I can respect that she's a private person and reluctant to share things, but I'm her friend. We've shared weeks of hard work together. Friends are allowed to ask questions and try to help. Jesus, I've been through enough therapy. I should be able to remember some of the touchy-feely stuff.

We hunkered down in our sleeping bags, facing the cave opening, waiting for the dawn. I cleared my throat. "Ya know, Kim, sometimes it helps to talk about things. These dreams ... or whatever...."

Her silence lasted so long, I figured she hadn't heard or was ignoring me.

"There's two women ... Amazons ..."

Her voice faltered and her head dropped to my shoulder. My arm circled her waist in a gesture that seemed as natural to me as breathing.

Okay, that's a start. She's telling me something. Poor thing must feel like she's trapped between two worlds. These dreams ... these women ... are as real to her as all of us working this site.

The dark sky paled to a grubby, grayish-white. Morning colors replaced our monochromatic shades. The shadows vanished and a familiar reality came with the clarity of a new day. Canyon walls, so sinister moments ago, materialized as the common buff and sandy borders that we recognized as the focus of our narrow work site ... leaving behind mystery, but no further mayhem. A fresh, new workday was about to start. I knew Kim would welcome our early routine, but I might never get the chance to draw the demons from her mind again ... so I prompted her for more information.

"Kim? You said there were two Amazon women ..."

"Yes ... part of a small group." Her voice tightened. "Those two loved each other ... so much."

"Well hey ... that's good ... isn't it?"

Kim's lip trembled. "One of the women was gravely wounded."

"I see. And ...was that Leeja?"

She lifted her head. "How did you know?"

"You ... uh, cried that name in your sleep."

Kim's anguished sigh barely suppressed tears. Her fingers plucked at a thread on the hem of my sweatshirt. "Sometimes, when I dream that part, PJ, I feel like I'm seeing it happen ... watching her die. I'm right there with her ... as her companion ... and lover. In the dream, my name is Marna."

She sniffed and swiped at her eyes.

I pulled the sleeping bag up around our shoulders, tightening my grip. I couldn't stand to watch her cry; it hurt too much. "It's going to be okay," I whispered, trying to convince us both. "It was a dream--vivid and terrifying, to be sure--but, just a dream."

I was reluctant to leave Kim's side, but daylight was upon us and the chilly shadows disappeared. She sat straighter, looked more confident, and made eye contact with me.

"Kim, we need to get ready for the gang. How about I fix us both some tea?"

A tight smile creased the corners of her mouth and her eyes glinted with familiar warmth. "Thank you, PJ, I think we both could use some."

Once the rest of the crew arrived, I had little time to think about Kim's troubling dream and my efforts to comfort her. Mike had sprained his ankle playing touch football and Josie wanted to leave early for a dental appointment. The schedule would have to be changed. As Acting Director, I was in charge of assigning specific jobs for the new excavation and for the immediate task of rock removal. The shallow cave opening had to be enlarged before anyone could work in there, even in pairs. That meant hours of heavy lifting. We would have to create a rough set of steps to traverse the rubble left by the quake.

It was November. Our mornings were cool and our afternoon temperatures reached the mid-eighties ... delightful weather for strolling or watching wildlife, but add a little exertion, and we'd soon be sweaty and irritable.

I found Kim's clipboard and made a new schedule.

"Okay, gang," I said with a hearty smile, "I'm posting the work orders inside the main tent right next to the lunch cooler. "Check your assignment, grab a bottle of water, and let's get the show on the road."

There was a minimum of complaint, which surprised me. We trudged to the side of the canyon. Sandy and Lewis climbed up to the hole, removed the tarp, and we formed an assembly line to gather rocks and place them into rough layers of steps reaching from the cave opening to the ground. Kim and I worked side by side on the lower part of the hill.

It was slow, dirty work, but necessary.

"Wouldn't it be cool if we found the Lost Dutchman's treasure hidden in the back of this cave?" Laine looked at her fellow workers after we'd been moving rocks for an hour. Sandy

124

shook his head, but she refused to give up on the concept. "It could happen. The legend says it's buried up here someplace."

Sandy removed his ever-present cowboy hat and wiped his forehead. "That would be like finding a needle in a haystack. We should be so lucky." He replaced the hat and picked up another piece of rock.

"Don't listen to him, Laine. He's just a wet blanket." Josie grinned at her friend. "What would you do with the gold if we did find it?"

Laine laughed. "That's easy. I'd pay off my student loans. There's a mountain of debt there, let me tell you."

"I hear ya," Dewey said. "And I can match ya mountain for mountain. Let's keep working. The sooner we get our staircase constructed, the sooner we can explore the cave."

"Well, I feel like a convict on a chain gang," Lewis said, standing up to straighten his back. He was working on the upward slope and had moved most of the heavy boulders with help from Donny and James.

Laine scowled at him. "Quit complaining. You're stronger than all of us." She held up her hands with a melodramatic sigh. "See these poor fingers? My manicure is ruined, I've got blisters and I'll probably have a permanent stoop--"

"Yeah, right." Sandy laughed as he slid a flat rock into place above us. "You haven't lifted anything heavier that a textbook all morning, Miss Treasure hunter."

Laine glared at him before grinning. "That's Mizz Treasure hunter to you."

Kim and I glanced at each other. "Gives you a keener appreciation of those Egyptian pyramid builders, doesn't it?" she said in an undertone. "My back is going to feel this tonight."

I dusted my gritty hands on my cargo pants. "Maybe that's our problem. We need a huge army of slave labor with ramps, pulleys and sleds to get this job done. And lots of overseers and waving palm branches to fan us. And plenty of back rubs for everyone."

"Slave labor? What do you think we've been the last hour?" Mike wiped sweat from his glasses.

Kim eyed him intently. "Oh, I'm sure we could find something even more tedious for you to do, if you're not happy with this."

"I hear ya, Doc. I'm not complaining, really."

"And, you realize that these stones would have to fit much tighter, if we were actually building a pyramid," I couldn't resist adding. "None of this 'close enough for government' stuff."

Josie snickered. She handed me the next rock to put into place on the lower rise. "Don't forget, the pyramid would be a tomb for some dear departed ruler. We don't have a dearly departed person..." She gave Mike a penetrating look. ".... yet."

"Sheesh!" Mike threw up his hands and shook his head. "You women have no sense of humor. You're forced to do a little physical labor... and right away you turn on us poor guys."

"All right," I said, putting my stone into position. "Time for another rest before we fight a battle of the sexes."

Relieved groans and sighs greeted my words. Everyone relaxed in whatever shade was available. James fashioned a makeshift canopy with the blue tarp against a side of the rock mound, so we could take turns getting out of the direct sunlight.

Kim worked with us for several hours more before her attention flagged. I gave her a smile of encouragement, but she squeezed her eyes shut and sighed with fatigue. "I'm afraid my lack of sleep is catching up with me, PJ."

"Take a longer break, we'll be fine here." I nodded in the direction of the hole. "It's not going anywhere."

Her smile was fleeting. "I do have some data to load into the laptop." With a little wave, she turned and trudged toward the main tent.

When we broke for lunch, Kim had not returned. Laine and I found her inside the tent, asleep on the cot, the laptop beside her on the table.

"Ah," Laine whispered behind me, "she looks so peaceful."

"She didn't sleep well last night. Let's get the cooler and take it out under the tarp ... give her a bit longer to sleep."

"Sure thing, PJ."

The crew sprawled in various shady spots, munching sandwiches, gulping down water and sports drinks from the cooler, comparing blistered hands and sore muscles. I joined them for a few minutes, but my mind kept returning to the tent and Kim. I rewrapped the remaining half of a ham sandwich, snatched up my water bottle and started back to the main tent.

"What, are we too lowly to merit your company at lunch?" Sandy teased.

I shook my head. "Rank has its privileges."

James and Josie chuckled.

"I ...uh, want to check on our fearless leader."

"Doc's not sick or anything, is she PJ?" Sandy asked.

"No, no, just a bit tired. Keeping up with all of you guys can be a full time job, ya know."

They laughed and I continued on to the tent.

Kim was still asleep. I sank into a folding canvas chair, uncapped my water bottle, and watched her sleep. A fragile smile played across her lips. No lines of tension marred her face; the skin was smooth and tanned. In slumber, Kim had recaptured her youth.

I took a long gulp of water and my stomach fluttered, spreading a warm glow to parts of my chest. *Gawd, I'm so unsettled when I look at you lately. My insides are churning and my head hurts so much I can't think straight.*

I took another long drink and sighed.

I used to think you were a dried up old bitch with no personality. Now, I realize that you are a remarkable, inspiring, and intelligent woman. We've become good friends and ... now I'm worried because in just a day I've seen you change. You were so strong and confident, standing up to my father for me, and protecting me from Stephen. You believed in me ... you still do, or you wouldn't have put me in charge of this operation. Nobody has ever given me a chance to prove myself before, Kim. Even though I've never led a whole project before, I'm going to try my best to live up to your faith in me. I really will. I value our friendship so much. I hope you know what a major force you've become in my life ... in all of our lives. We're all lost without you.

I blinked back several tears.

Kim stirred and opened her eyes. "Hey."

I sniffed. "Hey, yourself."

"Something wrong?"

"Nah. I got some sweat in my eyes." I wiped the moisture away with my sleeve. "Uh ... you look rested."

She smiled and her eyes crinkled. "You finally look like a real archaeologist, PJ."

"What's that supposed to mean?" I poured the last half of my water bottle over my head, gasping as the cool liquid trickled down my neck and onto my chest.

Her laugh was unforced, natural. "When you first joined us, every hair was in place, your makeup was flawless ...your clothing straight out of a catalog."

I grinned and stuck the tip of my tongue out. "So, your idea of an archaeologist is a smelly, sweaty slob with dirt in places it has no business being in." I swiped my forearm across my forehead, no doubt leaving a smear of grime, and pointed my empty bottle at her. "You, on the other hand, are the epitome of archaeological splendor ... reclining on your posterior while your team of slaves--"

"Doctor Curtis?" Laine poked her head through the tent flap. "Ah, sorry to interrupt, but we think it's wide enough now."

"I guess I lost track of time. I'll be right there."

She left and I turned to Kim. "What's with this 'Doctor Curtis' all of a sudden?"

"You're in charge of this phase of the operation. I imagine Laine is trying to show you her respect."

"Hmm. More like kissing butt." We chuckled. I stood and held my hand out. "C'mon Doc, let's go give the troops their battle orders and get a clearer view of those remains."

She let me pull her upright, but held onto my hand.

"PJ?"

"Yeah?"

"I don't know if I can work inside the cave just yet." She took a steadying breath. "There's still something holding me back. Will you stay in charge for now?"

"Sure, Kim." I gave her hand a squeeze. "As long as it's just for now."

I reviewed my notes, feeling a trickle of sweat slide down my neck. We would work this site 'by the book,' from start to finish. I scanned Kim's precise, tidy, handwriting, knowing her to be a stickler for details.

What we find here could be the most important data she's ever uncovered in her search for the lost Amazons. I am not going to allow any screw-ups. She has placed great trust in me and I refuse to let her down no matter how little experience I have in directing digs.

I double-checked the team's areas of expertise before making my final assignments. Dewey and Lewis would take color, black and white, and videotape pictures from every angle and at every step of the work. Sandy and Mike would measure and establish a new datum point and lay out a grid for inside the cave, paying particular attention to the matrix around the remains. If Mike's ankle gave out, he'd have to switch with Lewis or James.

"Let's try a combination grid pattern to develop a horizontal area trench around the remains," I told them, as we assembled at the base of the slope, "and random vertical test trenches in other parts of the cave. We'll probably not need to go deeper than the second level of stratification."

"How many centimeters down should we dig?" Josie asked.

"I think we should follow the stratification lines carefully and not worry so much about the exact depth for now. We don't want to miss anything. Even though it looks to be a primary context here, with just some sand blown in over time, it was an earthquake that revealed it to us and we can't assume anything. Every bit of information we can discover will be important to Kim ... and to the excavation."

Josie located her diamond shaped trowel and gave me a mock salute. "I'm good to go, Doctor Curtis."

"Excellent." My smile was brief. *Another kiss up attempt? C'mon, I'm getting too cynical in my old age. They mean well.* "While we're on the subject of how deep to dig, the caliche is closer to the surface inside the cave. Chances are there won't be anything useful to our purposes below that bedrock."

They all nodded their agreement. No doubt they were more experienced than I was working with the caliche, the hard subsoil that underlies so much of the Arizona desert.

"What should Mike and I do after we get the grid set, PJ?" Sandy took off his cowboy hat to wipe some sweat from his brow.

"I think Josie and James should be the small finds directors. They can use a portion of the field lab tent. Why don't you and Mike help them classify whatever artifacts we locate."

I looked directly at Mike. "If your ankle gives you trouble, sit, pack some ice on it and keep it elevated. Okay?" He nodded.

I turned to look at the rest of them. "We'll all take turns working inside the cave, but because of space, we can only enter a couple at a time. Any problems or questions?"

"You forgot me," Laine said smiling. "And Doc."

I glanced over at Kim. She had been watching me from the vantage point of a shady rock. "Doc, what do--"

"I can help log in the finds as they come out. Or I can label and code whatever you bring me." She stood up and addressed the crew. "Doctor Curtis has a good plan going. Let's help her out." She gave me a tiny wink and the gesture made a butterfly pirouette in my stomach.

I managed to pull myself together long enough to tap Laine on the shoulder. "You, my friend, have knowledge of forensic anthropology. So, we are going into the cave and meet the remains 'up close and personal' right after our photographers finish."

Laine's smile was expansive. "Awesome. I'll get my gloves and small tools."

I cleared my throat and raised my voice. "Folks, before we start, I just want to remind you that we are facing an important task." I risked a quick glance at Kim, noting her serious expression. "I'm sure each of you has heard this before from every professor or site director that you've ever worked with, but I'm still going to say it, because it's true. Excavation is--"

"Destruction," they said in unison. Then, we laughed.

"Exactly. Let's make this destruction mean something."

My team settled down to work.

I paused before the remains. Laine and I had brushed away the sand and soil clinging to the fingers, toes and various small bones. It was time to collect samples of hair, bone, fabric, and leather from the skeletons and soil specimens from the surrounding area.

Aware of Laine's curious glances, I continued muttering a few words as we kneeled beside the skeletons. I offered an apology for disturbing the solitude these two women had enjoyed prior to our discovery. I had worked on nearly a dozen burial sites in my career. My professors and directors always reminded us to revere the lives that had left the remains we worked on and remember they were once human beings much like us. So, I gave Laine a brief look and raised my voice so she could hear.

"Ladies -- and we are fairly certain that you are that, after making our observations and calculations of your pelvic regions -- we ask your cooperation during these procedures. Whatever you suffered in life that led you to this place, we ask you to help us uncover your secrets. It is our intention to do our jobs with as much respect as possible." Laine's head was bowed as if in prayer, so I decided to finish on a less somber note. "So relax, gals, it shouldn't hurt a bit."

Laine snickered. "Professor Hubbard always quotes Shakespeare when he examines remains."

"Whatever works," I said, sitting back on my heels. I let my eyes roam over the provenience that contained our two subjects. I remembered something a beloved professor had once told me. 'Don't get so focused on the trees that you forget the forest,' meaning that we should always consider the whole environment in which our artifacts and remains are presented, their provenience. We may find important clues just by observing the way everything relates to everything else and once we disturb one item, we lose the original picture.

I turned to Laine. "I wonder if we should try to separate these two, maybe consider them as individual sites in our record-keeping. What are your thoughts on the arrangement of the burial?"

Her forehead wrinkled in concentration. "Well, I've seen several Native American burial sites here in the southwest. We had to stop while the tribal councils went through the legal stuff about reburying."

I nodded. The Native American Graves and Repatriation Act, commonly called NAGPRA, was a powerful law. It was used throughout the North American continent whenever suspected remains of Native Americans were found so that descendants could claim their kinfolk and return their bones to an honored final resting place.

"But, honestly, PJ, this is different. There's nothing much in the way of grave goods, for example, and the fact that the dagger is still sticking in one of the bodies..."

"Yeah, that's hard to ignore. And, it is difficult to tell if the woman on the bottom was already dead when the one on top died, or if the knife killed them both. At some point, we'll have to separate them enough to do more detection. The knife will be the key, I think. It's not native to this area and if the time frame fits, neither are the two women." I sighed. "You ready to pull out the dental tools and small brushes and get started on the bones themselves?"

"Absolutely," Laine said. "I'm hoping that we can solve the mystery of who killed whom and determine if knife wounds exist on both. That, along with the origins of these two, should give us plenty to talk about in the weeks ahead." She sat back on her heels and looked about the narrow cave. "I can't help feeling sorry for them both, though."

"I know what you mean. If they prove to be the Amazons we seek, whether from Greece or Anatolia, they were a long, long way from home. To have died in a strange and hostile land far away from friends and loved ones is tragic."

We finished our work with a minimum of words.

When I consulted with Kim the next morning, she indicated that the dagger should remain in place for the time being. I wondered if she might be thinking of bringing in an expert on weaponry to advise us. Her participation in the excavation had been brief, but supportive, so I didn't ask any unnecessary questions.

One day merged with another. We worked and slept, slept and worked, a routine that seemed to go on forever. Though Kim worked along side us, she seemed to slip in and out of a mental fog. She was distant at times, as if in another place altogether. When she was lucid and aware of our efforts, she favored me with nods and smiles. I was pleased with her confidence in me, but bothered by the fact that she was not leading us, not experiencing the same excitement of discovery. It was her triumph; I wanted her to relish it.

When all our material was collected, boxed, zip locked in baggies and tagged in black marker with identifying codes, I supervised the loading of it into the minivan, for transport to the labs at the University of Arizona in Tucson. Kim gave us minimal hands-on assistance, but it was the crew that pulled together to get it all packed. Sandy, Mike, and Donny would take our precious cargo to the labs and conduct the tests. I hovered about them in the parking lot at the trailhead, offering last minute admonitions, which they listened to for as long as their patience allowed.

"Listen Sandy, you're in charge, but if it takes more than a few Accelerated Mass Spectrometer tests for some of those specimens, then go for it. I'll pay for them myself. They require fewer grams of sample material--"

"I know, PJ." Sandy put his hand on my arm. "It will be fine. Don't worry, okay. We can handle this."

I exhaled and nodded, feeling sheepish. "I'm sorry. You're right. You know what to do."

"We won't let any of it out of our sight," Mike said.

"Right," I added. "You can sleep in the dorms next to the labs."

Donny grinned. "Well, at least we get to sleep. I was afraid you'd make us stay awake the whole time."

That broke the tension and even I joined in their laughter.

"Sorry, guys. I guess I'm a little stressed out about this."

"Just a little," Sandy admitted. "You've done a great job, PJ." He gave me a quick hug before climbing into the driver's seat. "Just take good care of Doc for us, okay?"

"I'll do my best, Cowboy." I smiled confidently. "Now you take care of yourselves and call when you have some results."

"You can count on us." Mike took his spot up front in the navigator's seat.

"That better be true or I'll skin all of you alive with my dental picks and a very rusty pocketknife."

"Ooo! So cruel!" Mike clutched at his heart.

Donny gave a quick wave. "All that power has gone to her head, guys. Let's get out of here while we still have our hides."

I watched them pull out, leaving a cloud of pale dust in their wake.

Well, that's that. Now we wait ... for results. God, I hope it will be good news. Kim deserves it. We all do.

Chapter Thirteen

It bothered me that I was relying so heavily on PJ. Not that she wasn't doing a great job ... she was. She had far exceeded my expectation, having taken the helm while I was brooding in the background. Brooding is a harsh word. The fact that I haven't been feeling too well can hardly be described that way.

What do you think, PJ? Am I brooding, and if so, about what? I wish I could describe to you the way I feel. But how can I when I can't describe it to myself? It's like I'm standing on a precipice, knowing that soon the ground is going to give way beneath my feet, but I can't move ... my shoes are lead weights. I can't go anywhere. Not that I really want to go. There's something, a premonition perhaps --

I was sure the remains we had discovered were those of the Lost Tribe of Amazons, but I'd have to await the test results to prove beyond a shadow of doubt that these were the warrior women I had sought for so long.

I wish I knew why I feel strange whenever I approach the cave. It has some connection to those damn dreams. But what could they have to do with the facts before us? Dreams are nothing more than tricks of the mind. The tenants of the cave are the reality.

We had heard nothing yet from Sandy, Donny, and Mike. The tests would take time and I had to exercise a little patience, something I had very little of these days.

The next evening, after an especially hard day, Laine and Josie appeared back at the site with steaks. "We thought you guys would like a real meal," Josie said, grinning.

Their thoughtfulness overwhelmed me. "Thank you." A lump formed in my throat. It concerned me that I was getting way too sentimental about things. "It was kind of you to think of us."

"'Twas nothing," Laine said, "it's known as kissing up to the boss." PJ and I exchanged glances, she with a silly grin on her face.

It wasn't long before the four of us were sitting around our blackened, well-used, portable grill watching the meat sizzle and splatter. The sparks created, in their few seconds of brilliance, a vision of fireflies. Corncobs wrapped in foil cooked on one side of the grill, potatoes baked on the other. The aroma was delicious. Our kisser uppers had thought of everything.

PJ speared a thick, juicy steak and plopped it on a plate, removed the corn from its foil wrapping, and the potato, arranged them beside the steak, and handed me the plate.

"Hey, I can wait on myself."

"Of course you can, but right now I'm doing the honors. Call it kissing butt."

My response was something between a snort, choke, and a giggle.

With a lop-sided grin, she passed the tub of soft butter. "You can slather."

After serving Laine and Josie, PJ loaded her own plate and sat close enough to me that the warmth I felt was not totally from the grill.

"I can't get over how much you've changed," I said to PJ. "Whatever happened to the salad-eating, cholesterol watching?"

She nudged me with her shoulder. "Someone I know corrupted me. Now, hush up and eat."

PJ, you're a good friend, one whose strength is buoying me through difficult times. But that's not all, there's something about your smile that makes me desire the unattainable. I cannot turn fantasy into reality so I'm not going to dwell on it. Just having you on the team, being here at my side is enough. It has to be.

"You okay, Doc?" Laine asked. "You seem far away and we've noticed that you haven't been yourself lately."

"I'm fine, Laine. But thank you for asking. I haven't been up to par, but it's nothing to worry about." I was aware of PJ's sidelong glances. "Besides, things are progressing nicely with PJ at the helm."

"PJ's doing just fine, but this is your project and we want you in there with us."

PJ reached over and squeezed my arm. "You know, don't you, that you're the one in charge … I'm just helping out here."

"You tell her, PJ." Josie said, reaching for another cob of corn.

"Let's not forget that I'm the one who put you in charge," I said, smiling at PJ.

"Right you are, Doc."

I couldn't resist chuckling because she rarely called me Doc any more.

Later, after we had eaten, cleaned up, and stowed everything neatly away, Laine and Josie picked up their sleeping bags. "We've found the neatest side canyon, just down the hill, that way," Josie said, pointing east. "We thought we'd camp there for the night."

"Sounds great," PJ said, "but watch out for biting critters."

"Well, you'll be close enough that if you get lonely, you can always pick up your stuff and join us back here." I smiled and added, "Bacon and eggs will be served at five o'clock in the morning."

Josie rolled her eyes. "You wouldn't consider making that noon, would you?"

I lay back in my sleeping bag and studied the night sky. "PJ, look at the Milky Way. It's so bright tonight."

"The Ancients believed that every point of light is a soul departed."

I watched PJ open and spread her sleeping bag, close to mine, but far enough away that we couldn't touch. She crawled in and lay on her back, staring skyward with her hands behind her head. She appeared delicate, as she lay so close and yet so far, protected by the dim light of the waning moon. She reminded me of a doll I had once seen, an heirloom, made from the finest Dresden china. The vision was false, for in reality, she was as strong as they come. I felt the urge to reach out, invite her into my space, hold her in my arms and kiss her, but I knew I could not.

If I don't stop now and focus on another subject, I'll never get to sleep.

"PJ, I'm thinking of bringing in a forensic anthropologist, a trusted friend and colleague, to work with us on the remains."

She sat up and turned to face me. 'Tell me more."

"Have you heard of Doctor Samuel Westermeyer?"

"Yeah, who hasn't? He's kind of an outsider though." PJ assumed the lotus position. I wondered if I could do that any more. "As I recall, he made some enemies in the scientific community. Several years ago, he sided with the Native Americans who were demanding the return of ancestral remains, locked away in museum vaults."

"That's Samuel." I chuckled, remembering the controversy. "You know him well?"

"Yes. I've worked with him on occasion. And furthermore I trust him." I sat up, supporting my head and resting my elbow. "We don't have all the answers and we don't have access to the scientific equipment we'll need to solve the riddle of these women. Samuel is an independent, not subject to the rules and regulation of the University labs. There'll come a time when I'm ready to share my Amazons with the scientific community at large, but that's down the road apiece."

"I understand and I'm with you … whatever you decide."

"The remains themselves have to be scrutinized scientifically and I'm afraid if word leaks out before we're ready, we'll be overrun with people wanting bits of this bone or that. The integrity of the site will be destroyed and I'm not going to allow that to happen to our Amazons."

PJ's eyes glinted in the moonlight. "You love those women, don't you?"

I laughed. "When you've lived with them as long as I have, you have to feel something. They're close, like family."

"Kim, that's the way I feel about y--" PJ stopped in mid sentence. "What was that?"

I turned toward the sound to see a pair of yellow eyes as Pup bounded across the clearing toward me. "Pup! My dear,

dear Pup, where the devil have you been?" He knocked me flat on my back into the sleeping bag and washed my face with his tongue. After a minute or two, he left me to greet PJ in much the same manner.

I watched them roughhousing. It delighted me to see the two of them playing together ... the wolf and the heiress. I laughed to myself. *That would be a great title for a movie.*

"This calls for a celebration," PJ said, disentangling herself from Pup's puppy-like greeting. "Earl Grey for two coming up and some doggie biscuits for the prodigal Pup."

When the phone rang the next morning, it was Sandy.

"Well," I teased, "I thought you guys had taken off on vacation."

"Yeah, sorry about that. It took longer than we thought. We called."

"I know, PJ told me. So what do you have for us?"

"Good news. We'll be back tonight. It'll be real late though before we're done here, so if it's okay with you we'll wait until tomorrow to come out to the site. We're all kinda tired ... we had to keep on those guys to get the tests done quickly. I think they thought that if they procrastinated we'd share more with them, like the location and the who and the what of this operation."

"You didn't ..."

"Gawd, no!"

"You're a good man." I took a deep breath. "The results, Sandy, are they promising?"

"Better than that, Doc. We're right on time-wise. It looks good ... real good."

I exhaled and nodded at PJ. "All right, Sandy. You drive safely and we'll see you up here in the morning." PJ and I seldom went home at night any more, preferring instead to stay close to the Amazons.

PJ's grin turned to shouts of joy when I repeated what Sandy had said. She hugged me with such exuberance that I had to caution her against wild speculation on the topic until we had gathered all the data. In truth, however, I had trouble containing the happy bubble of excitement that swelled in my chest.

139

We spent most of the next morning in the tent studying and discussing the reports, which, as Sandy had indicated, appeared promising. The remains themselves would tell the tale.

I told the crew about Doctor Westermeyer and they all agreed that his expertise would prove beyond a shadow of doubt that these were our Amazons.

Samuel Westermeyer's thinning gray hair and sun damaged skin made him appear older than his years. Since I had last seen him, he had grown a beard, which he kept neatly trimmed. I watched him work with gentle precision around the remains. PJ was at his side. It was still difficult for me to be in the cave, but I forced myself, despite the gnawing sensation of unrest in my nether regions. I put it down to the atmosphere in the cave, that I might be allergic to something there. Surely the fresh air coming in from outside would clear whatever it was that was bothering me. I hoped that would happen soon.

"You know, I would really like to take the skulls back to the lab in Los Angeles." Samuel paused, knowing the reaction I would have to his words.

Before I could open my mouth, he held up his hand. "I know you're reluctant, Kim, but you know me. I'd prefer to let these two rest in peace. But, knowing you as I do, you're going to demand answers, and to provide those answers I must have them at the lab. You have my word that I'll be the only one working with them and that they'll be returned to you in the same condition they're in now."

I reluctantly nodded agreement. "I trust you, Samuel. And I'll let PJ help you prepare them for their journey. I trust her completely. She knows what I want and you can tell her what you need." PJ flushed at my unexpected compliment. I turned my back and headed up the slope away from the site with Pup close at my heels.

"Where were you for so long?" I asked my four-legged friend as I sat on the hillside overlooking all the activity. I held him close to me, needing to hold a living, breathing entity. I knew Pup would provide the comfort I sought and ask nothing in return.

140

I watched Westermeyer leave with Sandy and Mike carrying their precious bundles. Shortly afterwards, PJ joined me on the hillside. "Kim? You okay?"

"Yeah, I'm fine. I worry about them though." I smiled, more to myself than at PJ. "Here I am worrying about a bunch of bones like they're my kids or something."

"In a way they are ... like your kids. You've been chasing them for a good part of your life."

PJ sat down beside me on the dusty ground and reached for my hand. "Westermeyer took the knife, too. I hope that's okay. He'll bring it back so don't worry, okay?"

I nodded. "He'll take care of them ... I know that."

Pup wriggled out of my arms. He sniffed around, checking out new and different smells. Soon, he was out of sight. Twenty minutes later he returned, agitated and wanting us to follow him. PJ leapt to her feet. "I'll go." I watched her jog after Pup.

I dozed in the warm sunshine, but awoke concerned. PJ and Pup had been gone for over an hour. I was getting ready to go look for them when PJ returned with a strange expression on her face. Her arms were scratched and bleeding. "What the hell?" It looked as though she had fallen into some Cholla.

"There's more."

"More what?"

"Bodies, remains, like the others."

I stood up. My stomach cramped. "Damn! Where?"

"Over there." She pointed toward the ridge. "You'd better come and see for yourself what Pup was so excited about."

"Show me."

I followed PJ to where she had commanded Pup to stay. He was lying beside a dense thicket of prickly desert plants but got up and whined when we arrived. I could see parts of what appeared to be a cave entrance that had been overgrown and concealed until Pup discovered it. PJ, in order to see what Pup was excited about had scrambled up toward the opening, pulling just enough of the thorny brush to one side to get through ... not an easy task. It was no wonder her hands and arms were in such a mess.

"You'd better go tend to those."

"I will, but first, you've gotta see."

The cave was much larger than the first one, but higher up, possibly chosen for visibility and protection. I climbed and scratched my way to the opening, thankful that I had on a long sleeved shirt. Though not total protection from the thorny bushes, it saved a little of my flesh. The sleeves though were being shredded.

The three skeletons were in sitting positions, their backs to the rear wall of the cave, their bony hands laced together as if trying to provide comfort to each other.

"Three," I said. "Two and three make five."

PJ stared at me. "What does that have to do with anything?"

"There were five, don't you see, five in all."

"How do you know there were five?"

"I just know."

I felt better after Westermeyer's visit and PJ and I fell easily into the routine of being co-directors of the operation.

"Kim," PJ said, taking my arm and moving us out of earshot, "you feel better about Site Two, so while we're waiting for Westermeyer's reports, I'll take Laine and Josie and we'll manage Site One. There's still a lot of delicate work to be done in there and that'll free up the rest of the crew to work with you at Site Two."

"Sounds like a plan."

I worked alongside Sandy, Donny, James and Lewis, clearing brush and vegetation from the entrance, all the while cursing the prickly nature of the vegetation. We found, on the opposite side from where we were scrambling and slipping our way to the entrance, a rough track of sorts leading into the cave. "Let's try not to disturb the dirt more than we have to."

"Gotcha, Doc," Donny muttered as he chopped away at a particularly stubborn bush.

"I wonder if the Amazons entered the cave by way of this track?" I asked, as much of myself as whoever happened to be listening.

"Possible, I suppose," Sandy said, taking his hat off and wiping his sweaty brow.

"Is it feasible that their footsteps," I inclined my head toward the cave entrance, "are still here, under a layer of dirt and dust?"

"I doubt it," James said, studying the layout. "This looks like a game trail. Their footsteps, if they had left any, would have been obliterated."

"Maybe not," Sandy said. "The remains don't appear to have been disturbed so it's unlikely there have been any animals in there ... snakes, maybe, or insects, but that's all."

"Depends, too," Donny said, talking to himself more than anyone else, "on how long they were here and how much tracking in and out they did."

I tried to visualize their activities, their comings and goings. "That's right, the bones would have been scattered if they'd been visited by carnivores."

I turned at the sound of PJ's voice. She had come up from Site One to check on our progress and to take a break and stretch her limbs. "How come we're so lucky?"

I smiled. She was a good-looking woman even when coated in sweat and dust. "We must be living right."

With most of the brush removed, it was much easier now to see into the cave. Besides the human remains, there were two swords, and a dagger, less ornate than the one found in Site One, but a functional weapon nevertheless. Remnants of what appeared to be a litter were half buried beneath a layer of dirt and dust. There were scraps of cloth and leather; two of which looked like leather water flasks.

"Kim, it's good to see you feeling better, and involved again."

Together, we peered into the gloom of the cave.

"I just wish I could shake this feeling of impending doom. It's like a premonition. I don't know what that's about. Whatever it is though has to do with Site One."

PJ wrinkled her forehead. "Must be that there's something in there that you're allergic to. Whatever it is doesn't bother me so I'll keep working it. You can 'snoopervize' from a distance."

I laughed. "PJ, you're one in a million." I wasn't sure if she blushed or if it was the heat. Who could tell anyway, through all the grime?

I watched PJ as she made her way back down to Site One. It was time for me to pull myself together.

Chapter Fourteen

I crouched in the shallow cave next to Laine, scooping minute soil samples into plastic bags. We'd compare the samples to our Munsell soil chart for proper coding. Laine or Josie would take the bags and place them under the windows in the pages and make further notations in our record book regarding color, density and the associated materials contained in the dirt. Now that we had two sites to compare, we might determine their respective ages through this type of testing. My hands acted automatically, but my mind was on more personal issues.

I have to get my act together. Now that Kim is working with the crew in a nearly normal capacity, I've got to take some time and examine my situation. It's a mess...and I can't figure out how...

"PJ!" Mike's shout snapped me back to reality.

"Be right out!" I handed the bag to Laine. "Wonder what the problem is now?"

"I'm sure he'll let you know." She grinned and took over my task as well as her own.

My knees creaked when I stood up. *Gawd, I'm not as young as I used to be. Thirty-four isn't that old except when compared with these fresh-faced college kids.*

Mike was standing on the rock ledge waiting for me when I exited the cave. "Your cell phone was ringing, so I took the liberty of answering it."

I blinked at the late afternoon sunlight. *Where had the day gone?* "Who was it?"

"Your motel in Apache Junction. They have to close down for several days because of damage to the electrical system and stuff. You know, the earthquake? Anyway, they got you a room in the Casa Grande across the highway, but you need to go move your things."

145

The Casa Grande. I chuckled at an image of Kim fuming at me across our table in their restaurant. She had been so angry at my tardiness. She even accused me of seducing Sandy. *It seems like ages ago.* "Casa Grande, huh? Now, that's ironic."

Mike gave me a blank look.

"It's where Doc and I first met. We had a momentous dinner in the restaurant there ... nearly started World War Three."

"Oh."

"I guess you had to be there to appreciate it."

I looked back toward the cave interior and then at my watch. "One more hour before quitting time," I muttered. "Can you hike over to Site Two and tell Doc I have to be away overnight?"

"Sure thing, PJ. You might as well enjoy the new room once you get moved in."

I smiled, rubbing my lower back. "Yeah, I'm thinking nice, hot shower, good meal, and a bed with no threat of scorpions."

"Sounds like paradise." He started down the rocky steps. "I'll get right over to the other site."

"Thanks Mike. I'm glad your ankle's improved."

He waved his hand in a gesture of dismissal. "It's fine. No problemo." Just to prove it, he demonstrated a tricky hop and jump to the bottom.

"Ah youth," I muttered. *I seem to be doing a lot of muttering lately. Is that a sign of senility or is it required of site directors?*

Laine and Josie agreed to stay overnight at camp and keep an eye on Kim for me, so I hiked to the trailhead and took the minivan to the Holiday Inn. It was a short drive but one that spanned centuries of culture. Like Kim, I had become obsessed with the Amazon women and that small plot of ground in the Superstitions. It was hard to let go of the time and the place.

I'm also letting thoughts of Kim mess up my life. What am I going to do about that? Being around her so much of each day has me consumed with her; what she looks like...how she acts ... what she has to say to me.

The trailhead dirt road merged quickly with a winding two-lane road called Old Apache Trail. There wasn't a single old Apache in sight and very few vehicles either. In short order, I was through the scrub brush and saguaro cactus and at the intersection of Idaho and Apache Trail. The Casa Grande was off to the west and the Holiday Inn was on the other side of the road a quarter mile or so in the opposite direction. I paused to look at the mountains surrounding and controlling this area of the Valley of the Sun. The most prominent peaks were the Superstitions, old Moody Mountain as the natives called it.

I wonder what Kim's doing up there now?

She had become such a big part of my life. I missed her presence already. Talking with Kim during the down time in the evening was the best part of my day. She knew so much about everything. We compared notes on projects, other archaeologists, and places we'd visited. I remember one evening we had heard some coyotes calling to each other, making loud, doleful sounds. Kim told me they had a wide range of vocal calls for communication. I was astonished to learn that coyotes were present in every one of the continental United States and even in New York City.

The afternoon sun was still warm so I rolled down the window and breathed in the dry desert air.

Kim knew all about coyotes. She said the Alpha female usually had the young, though the Beta females helped raise them and it took a year to train the pups to be independent. When they found mates, coyotes bonded for life. I was quite touched by that concept.

"That's so sweet," I told her.

She nodded. "Yet, they're the most despised animals in our country. Even the government wants to kill them."

I said something sympathetic and Kim got a sly grin on her face. Her brown eyes sparkled in that intense way. "Even after decades of slaughter, there are more coyotes alive now than ever before. They've found a way to survive despite the odds against them." I could tell that Kim admired their tenacity and fighting spirit. The warrior within … animals or humans.

I pulled into the motel parking lot, noting the plywood covering one side of the spacious glass front door. Several trucks and work crews clogged the front driveway. Workers wearing overalls, hard hats and heavy boots traipsed in and out, tools clanking from their leather belts.

Dennis, the assistant manager, was on duty. He looked like a deckhand on the Titanic. There were no guests checking in, only individuals and a family or two wheeling luggage down the hallway toward the parking lot.

Dennis made commiserating small talk with all of them. When he noticed me, he put on a brave face. "Doctor Curtis, I'm so sorry for this inconvenience."

I shrugged. "Who can predict the whims of Mother Nature?"

"That's the truth." He ducked behind the counter and pulled up a small pile of envelopes and journals, handing them to me. "Here's your mail. You haven't been around for quite a while."

"Thanks." I tucked the bundle under my arm. "I've been up on the mountain, working."

The ringing telephone distracted him, so I waved and walked along the deserted corridor to my old room. A fine coating of dust covered the doorknob and some of the furniture inside. I surveyed my accumulated possessions with a sigh. None of it was irreplaceable, but it all had to be packed and taken to a new location. I heard a noise in the hallway and discovered an employee with a luggage cart. *Dennis, you thoughtful man.* Together, we managed to load my books, clothing, duffel, cosmetics and assorted paraphernalia.

When the minivan was packed, I tipped my helper and returned to the lobby to settle my bill.

"Thank you, Dennis." I pumped his hand gratefully. "I added a bit extra to the total for you and the staff. You've gone way beyond the call of duty."

"Thank you, Doctor Curtis. That really wasn't necessary. It was a pleasure to serve you." Dennis smiled despite his weariness.

"I appreciate your finding me a new place and I hope you get things restored in short order."

He nodded. "Me too. Please come back and stay with us when we aren't having earthquakes."

The lobby of the Casa Grande was busy, but not crowded. I paused to take note of the decor and experienced a feeling of deja vu. It was predictably southwestern in motif, a mixture of Native American and Mexican cultures. Colorful woven blankets hung on one wall and covered the backs of two over-stuffed sofas. Sturdy oak tables held replicas of Hohokam pottery as well as travel brochures and maps. A cactus garden held center stage, displaying examples of Arizona's abundant prickly plants. I'd managed to avoid most of them during my hikes to and from our camp and I gave them a wide berth now.

As I approached the front desk I could hear faint Spanish-sounding guitar music and the scent of tamales and refried beans wafted from the corridor leading to the onsite restaurant. Several of the employees, dressed in bright red vests, white shirts and black slacks, smiled and greeted guests with practiced efficiency.

One of the energetic, college-aged fellows gave me a stunning smile. He had wavy black hair and bright brown eyes, not quite as dark as Kim's. "How may I help you today?" he asked. His nametag said: Joel Weaver, Assistant Manager.

Joel must have started working here when he was still in middle school.

Now that I was closer, I could see that all of their vests had adorable saguaro cactus logos embroidered on them.

"Hello, Joel. My name is PJ Curtis. I'm a refugee from the Holiday Inn and I hope I have a reservation."

His fingers raced over the computer keyboard. "Uh...yes...Oh, yes! We most definitely have a reservation for you, Doctor Curtis." He swallowed. "We have a two bedroom suite with a view of Superstition Mountain. Would that be acceptable?"

"Wow. That sounds like more than acceptable. Thank you very much." *And I must remember to thank Dennis next time I see him.* I signed in and Joel provided me with assistance moving my heavier luggage.

As I walked through the lobby on my final trip to the car, I noticed a commotion at the front desk. A man and woman with two young children clustered around Joel.

"I'm sorry, Reverend Parker, but the only room we have left is a single."

From my position in front of the elevators, I glanced sideways at the family. They had an air of wrinkled weariness about them, the curse of long distance travelers. The man remained composed, but I could see that the kids were getting on the woman's last nerve.

"We've been on the road since sun up," she said, fatigue showing in her voice. "Now, this earthquake and the motel closing..." She made a snuffling sound.

Her husband put his hand on her arm. "C'mon Rose, honey..."

"Neil, if you're about to say: 'God will provide,' I'm not in the mood to hear it right now."

His hand gently rubbed her back. "It will be okay, really. We'll just have to make do."

"Sir, you don't understand. We can't let you have the room. It's against regulations to put four people in one that small." Joel was polite, but firm.

The little boy gave the woman's arm an urgent tug. "Mommy, I gotta pee."

She sighed. "Timmy, hold on a second."

The husband continued to negotiate. "It's just for one night. We're driving to California...leaving early tomorrow. And, really, it's just two adults—the kids can sleep on the floor in--"

"I'm sorry sir. Rules are--"

Before I had time to consider my actions, I wandered into their discussion. "Excuse me, Joel. I couldn't help overhearing and I have a suggestion."

He gave me an apologetic look. "Oh, Doctor Curtis, it's really--"

I turned to the minister and stuck out my hand. "Hi, I'm PJ Curtis. You seem to have a problem."

His palm was moist, but there was firmness in his grip.

"Hello. Neil Parker. My wife, Rose."

I nodded and smiled in her direction.

"And our children, Jessica and Timmy."

The girl gave me a shy smile, complete with dimple and twinkling blue eyes, but the boy was beyond social graces. A pained expression creased his flushed face and his legs were now crossed. One chubby hand struggled to keep the dam from bursting. "Mommy, I *really* gotta pee!"

"Um, okay, Timmy. Uh..." She looked toward the desk. A woman working beside Joel noticed her distress signal and led them to a restroom.

"Now, I think I may have a solution to your problem, Reverend Parker."

"At this point I'm willing to hear anything. Thanks."

I motioned him over to the end of the counter where we could confer privately with the assistant manager. "Here's the deal, Joel. Reverend Parker and his family need a bigger room."

"Yes, but--"

"I know, I heard. You have only a single left."

"Right. It has a double bed, but there's just no room for two more--"

"Yes, of course." I nodded. "And regulations are regulations. But you've just assigned me a two bedroom suite and I'll be the only one in it."

Joel squared his shoulders and pulled at the hem of his scarlet Casa Grande vest with the saguaro cactus logo. "Well, under the circumstances, Doctor Curtis, it was the least--"

"'Under the circumstances,' I think the obvious solution is to have the Parker family switch with me. Then we'll all have room enough."

The minister's expression brightened. "That is so generous of you, Doctor Curtis."

"Think nothing of it," I said. "Now, we'll just rearrange the--"

"But, we can't afford anything that lavish."

"Oh." I thought for a moment. "You're only staying for one night, right?"

"Yes, we'll be away as early as we can get 'our ducks in a row' so to speak."

I turned to Joel with my most persuasive smile. "We'll just keep the rooms in our own names but switch places for the evening. I'll pay for the suite and the Parkers can cover the price of the single. That should work, shouldn't it?"

His forehead wrinkled into a frown. "Well, these are unusual times. I suppose it will be acceptable."

Reverend Parker breathed a relieved sigh and took my hand. "Thank you. That is so kind of you. I'm afraid our travel budget is already stretched to the limit. This will really help us out."

Mrs. Parker returned with the children to find her husband in a much happier mood.

"Honey, Doctor Curtis has offered us the use of her two bedroom suite for the night. She'll take the single."

His wife's jaw dropped, but she recovered quickly. "How wonderful. Thank you." She stared at me. "You look so familiar. Where have I seen you before? A magazine perhaps?"

Oh Gawd, I hope not. "No, I don't think so," I muttered, and turned back to the men.

Joel completed the transfer of electronic room keys and gave me an embarrassed look. "I'm so sorry, Doctor Curtis. That single is on the same floor as the suite but in the corner by the elevators. It has no view of the Superstitions and no Jacuzzi. No real amenities at all."

"The suite has a view of the mountains?" Rose Parker gave a wistful sigh.

"And a Jacuzzi?" There was a gleam in her husband's tired eyes.

I chuckled. "Don't worry about it. All I need tonight is a hot shower, some food, and a mattress thicker than a bedroll. I'm too tired to care about extras."

The Parker family gathered their luggage. "Doctor Curtis," Reverend Parker said, shaking my hand again. "You are truly our Guardian Angel."

"Glad I could help, but believe me, I'm no angel." I bent to pick up my gear, and an employee rushed over to assist me. We rode the elevator to the third floor and I joined the Parkers long enough to remove my earlier baggage from the suite.

The management had provided a basket of fruit and a canister of whole cashews as a welcoming gift for me. While the Parkers exclaimed over their plush new surroundings, I appropriated an orange and the nuts, nodded to the hotel employee who grabbed my bags, and we made our way to the single.

Ten minutes later, I was under the shower, letting the hot, steaming spray flow over my body. *This is divine! I may never leave. The sun showers at camp can't compare to the real thing.* I squeezed a stream of raspberry scented body wash into my palm and worked it into a lather. I imagined Reverend and Mrs. Parker enjoying the Jacuzzi after their long drive and smiled.

Feeling clean and drowsy in cut-offs and a fresh tee shirt, I turned on the television to catch the latest news and explored dinner options from the hotel's extensive room service menu. I settled on pork medallions with mango chutney, candied yams, and mixed green salad with balsamic vinegar. A pot of hot tea and chocolate mousse completed my order. *So much for watching my waistline. But, hell, digging in dirt all week and doing good deeds for ministers and their families can work up an appetite.*

The phone rang just as the meal arrived. Cradling the receiver between my chin and shoulder, I indicated the table by the window -- with a view of the highway -- to the young woman with the tray and pressed a ten-dollar bill into her hand with my thanks. She smiled her appreciation and left.

"PJ Curtis, thanks for holding," I said into the phone, my taste buds already stimulated by the entree's aroma. My stomach was so empty I feared the caller could hear its rumblings.

"Priscilla, finally I found you. I couldn't get you on your cell phone and when I called the Holiday Inn, they gave me this other number."

"Who is--Vivian? Is that you?" What did my father's personal assistant want with me? "Cell phone? Oh, yeah, probably needs charging. Wait, is Father--"

"He's fine, dear. And we are relieved to know that you and your group weren't injured by the earthquake."

I could smell the tangy fruit sauce on the pork and swallowed some excess saliva. "So, uh …what is the problem, Vivian?" *Can we get to the point before I die of starvation?*

"Your father wants to send flowers to Kim and he needs to know where to have them delivered."

"Flowers? For Kim? Because of the earthquake?"

She laughed. "No silly. Surely, you know that it's Kim's birthday on Thanksgiving Day."

Jesus! And she was going to spend the day alone. "Well … no. She uh… Listen, why don't you send them to the site the day before? If you offer a big enough tip, I'll bet they'll take them as far as the trailhead and our security team can handle the delivery." I gave her identifying landmarks and assured her it would work out.

"Would you suggest roses?"

Shit! I don't know. Kim likes the wildflowers that grow wild in the rocky crags along the desert trails. She told me they bloom so sporadically in the spring, after a rain. I know she admired their toughness. But, as for a favorite kind... I'm clueless…

"I guess that's always a good choice." *How's that for a lame answer? Sorry, I don't think well when I'm drooling.*

We finished our conversation and I settled on the bed with my feast. In between tangy bites of meat, I thought some more about Vivian's call. Kim had agreed to a Thanksgiving dinner for the two of us. The big day was just a week away. I had originally thought to make reservations in Phoenix, but now I wasn't so sure. I sat and made notes as I chewed. If I could keep the suite for the duration of my stay in Arizona, and if the restaurant would provide us with turkey and all the trimmings, then we could stay right here at the Casa Grande. *Well, not here, here. In the suite.*

I licked the last of the mousse off of my spoon and sighed. *There is something so decadent about the taste of chocolate.*

Reluctantly, I placed the spoon beside the empty dish, rolled off the bed and grabbed the phone. The hotel was more than happy to accommodate my needs. I pumped my fist into the air at the conclusion of that call. Next, I called Boston to arrange for Kim's birthday gift. That took a little doing, but I knew it would be perfect for her as soon as I thought of it. Mitch agreed to pack it and ship it by air charter to Phoenix. Then a messenger service would deliver it to the site on Wednesday in time for the celebration that I was sure we'd be springing on our unsuspecting boss. I caught myself grinning. It was all coming together so well.

You said nothing fancy, Kim. Well, Thanksgiving Dinner will be a quiet meal for two. You don't have to travel far and you don't have to dress up.

I finished my meal and leaned back on the bed. Closing my eyes, I imagined the whole event. *There would be soft music, good food, and a view of our workplace—but we wouldn't talk shop, unless Kim wanted it that way. I'd much rather spend the time getting to know her better. Finding out her favorite flower, for instance. We could talk long into the evening. There was the Jacuzzi ... and room to sleepover if she wanted.*

Whoa! Wait a minute.

I sat up, feeling overly warm.

It's time I faced this. It's time I gave this situation with Kim some serious thought. Every time I think of her in a non-work related way, my thoughts turn romantic.

The most amazing lightness filled my chest. It was as if a bottle of champagne had been opened and all the tiny bubbles spilled into my blood stream. It felt wonderful and scary at the same time.

C'mon, it's not really romantic, is it? I'm just feeling the need to give something back to the wonderful woman who guided me and supported me for the past few months. I like being with her even when we're not working. We're friends ... just good friends.

I sighed and leaned back against the headboard, my fingers laced together behind my head.

My feelings for Kim have changed so much during the time we've worked together. I've grown to respect and care for her as a mentor, colleague and friend. She's shown she cares about me, too. I'm not imagining it. Several times I've caught her smiling at me and giving me certain looks. Her touches have been special, too. But, she's never said anything further.

What am I going to do about her and this feeling I get when I'm with her? We've become good friends, but it's more than that for me now. I feel more for her than any other female friend I've had in the past. What is it? Where is it coming from?

I mean, sometimes when she touches my arm, I feel like electrodes are attached to my skin. And my stomach gets all crazy. Kim makes me feel so much more alive than I've ever felt. And it's more than my body reacting. I want to work harder, be smarter ... make her proud of me. My heart races, my palms sweat and sometimes my toes even tingle when I think about her ... not to mention what she does to my more erogenous zones. I've never experienced that sensation with anyone else before ... and I must admit, it doesn't feel bad at all. In fact, it feels damn good.

So why am I so worried? I've never sacrificed my own pleasure for any reason before. Why am I walking on eggshells over this? I can't deny it any longer. I'm in love with her.

It does surprise me that it happened here and now, when I least expected it. I've spent years drifting in and out of casual relationships, dropping lovers like petals from a dead flower. All that time, I was looking for the right guy ... and it was a gal that I needed! Now, it makes sense. I spent so much time trying to please men, hoping I'd find a deep connection, a feeling of comfort and belonging with one of them. When it didn't happen, I just moved on to the next, thinking surely if I found the right one...

I bit my lip and swallowed.

Okay. I know I'm not sick, just in love with my boss. That could still be a sticky situation. What if she doesn't want anything more than friendship from me? She's had that bad affair with Terry. What if she's sworn off love?

My heartbeat quickened. Sweat dampened my skin.

Images of Kim flooded my mind. I recalled the smooth, muscular feel of her back as I massaged it that morning in the tent ... the way she hugged me when the quake hit, an experience so intense I could feel our hearts drumming against our chests ... those long, lean, powerful legs ... the supple skin at the base of her neck where her shirt's unbuttoned ... her firm, well-rounded butt, so visible through the thin fabric of her cargo pants as she climbed over rocks.

Can I stay just a friend when images like those pop into my head all the time?

So many images.

The long, expressive fingers as they tighten around her trowel or fix our hot tea... the mornings, when we wake up in our sleeping bags and her hair is all tousled from sleep.

Her face ... I've memorized every line and wrinkle ... and her smile, the one that reaches all the way to those warm, brown eyes, making them crinkle in such an adorable way. I like to think she smiles like that just for me. And those sensual lips. I've imagined kissing those lips so often.

I took a deep shuddering breath.

I'm confused and exhausted, much too emotional. My mind is stuck in sexual overdrive.

Damn it! It's never going to work. Kim thinks I'm straight. Even if she knew I was interested, she'd think I was experimenting with the idea ... with her. And, I'm probably not her type, any way. She'd want someone more experienced ... more interesting. I remembered Terry's impromptu visit to Kim's motor home. *More voluptuous.*

Gawd, this is making me insane. What do I do? Confront her? Stay away from her? Keep the status quo or boldly go where I've never gone before? I wish I had someone to talk to about this. I wish I had some sort of confirmation.

I stared at the ceiling, seeking answers. "If I'm supposed to pursue this passion, I need a sign that I'm on the right path. Ya hear me? Show me a sign!"

I took another deep breath and waited for a full minute.

Nothing happened.

This is stupid. How can I think talking to a ceiling--

The phone rang and I nearly levitated off the bed.

"I hope I didn't wake you," Reverend Parker said.

157

Calm down and say something. "No, no ... I was ... uh ... just thinking." *That was brilliant.*

"I wanted to ask you a favor, even though you've done so much for us already that I don't have any right to even ask."

"What is it?"

He coughed and lowered his voice. "Uh, I can't exactly explain it over the phone. Would it be okay if I brought it over to show you?"

Right now? Hell, maybe I need a distraction. It can't hurt to see what he wants. I can always go back to thinking about Kim when he leaves. Ha! As if I could stop myself. "I'm in room three twelve, just to the left of the elevator. You can't miss it."

"Thanks, I'll be right there."

I ran a comb through my hair and waited by the door. *So, is this the sign I asked for? Fat chance.*

A faded polo shirt, khaki shorts and bright red tennis shoes had replaced his wrinkled traveling attire. He'd never be mistaken for a GQ model in that outfit, but there was something about Reverend Parker that put me at ease.

"You sure don't look like any minister I've ever known, Reverend." He laughed. "Not that I've known very many," I amended and waved him in. "Welcome to my humble abode."

"Thanks. I guess I am a little casual. Rose doesn't like me to run around in this old shirt, but it's so comfortable. Like an old friend, ya know?" He looked around. "Nice place you have here. I'd offer to switch rooms, but we've gotten very attached to the suite. It's amazing what a nap and a soak in the Jacuzzi can do for a person's well being. We even ordered dinner from room service. This 'lap of luxury' stuff is quite exciting."

"It can be very addictive."

"I hear you. Listen, Doctor Curtis..."

"Hey, it's PJ, okay? The doctor part isn't necessary."

"Oh sorry. Well, please call me Neil."

"Okay ... Neil."

"You're not a medical doctor, then?" His voice was deep and very soothing. I found myself responding to his lack of pretension and his seemingly genuine interest in me.

"I'm an archaeologist."

He nodded. "Ah, I see. Well, that's good, I guess." His laugh was nervous. "I don't really know any archaeologists."

"We're harmless most of the time." I gave him a brief smile.

"Right." The nervous laugh again. "Listen … PJ, I think I've maybe intruded on you at a bad time." His gentle, gray eyes examined me with intensity. "You look preoccupied…"

"No, really. It's … a personal problem. I'm working on it. What can I do for you?"

He held out a white square card with printing on both sides. "The management wanted to offer you a complimentary half hour massage. Rose got all excited when she saw it, before she realized that it was meant for you. I thought perhaps … if you didn't--"

"You want her to have the massage in my place?"

He shifted his feet and a shock of light brown hair fell across his forehead. His lips turned slightly upward. "This trip has taken a lot out of her. We've been on the road for several days … and, well, she's never had one before. We don't have the money for many extras."

I tapped the card against my palm. "Sure. Why not? Does she want it right now?"

"Uh … she doesn't know I'm asking about it, but …yeah, I guess now would be good. The kids are asleep. I can go down to the lobby and wander around for a while to keep out of the way."

I picked up the phone and made the arrangements. "All settled. They'll be up in twenty minutes. You'd better go and warn her."

He exhaled and the grin appeared. "Thank you again. I really had no right to ask."

I shook my head. "It's no problem, really."

There was an awkward pause. He shook my hand, lingering a moment, holding it in both of his. My hand was rough and very tanned compared to his. I stared at the simple gold band on his ring finger.

"She's going to be so tickled. You are very kind to do this."

The simple gesture of his holding my hand and the words of appreciation brought sudden moisture to my eyes. I used my free hand to wipe the tears away.

"What is it PJ? Can I help you in any way?"

"I don't know." I sniffed. "I'm very mixed up right now." I swallowed. "Probably not... Thanks for offering, though."

He shrugged. "It's my job ... helping people when I can. And I'm used to tears. I have three sisters. Course, I was usually the one crying."

I forced myself to laugh and kept staring into his gentle eyes before making a decision. "Maybe, if you wanted, you could come back here for the half hour ...uh ... we could have a soda or something. It would save you wandering around the lobby."

"I'd be honored to join you." He gave both my hands a squeeze. "Be right back."

I leaned against the door once I had closed it. *Why did I do that? I barely know the man. Does he look like he can solve my problem?*

I managed to find ice, glasses and two cans of soda. Neil arrived with a bag of corn chips, so I broke open the canister of cashews. I was still angry with myself for inviting him back to the room. My social skills were definitely lacking, but he didn't seem to mind.

"I hope root beer will be okay." I held out both cans.

He sighed and accepted one. "My all time favorite."

We settled at the small table by the window. He peered down at the busy highway. "Quite a picturesque view you have here."

I managed to smile at his little joke. "Hey, after my last few days on the mountain, this room is palatial, believe me."

Reverend Parker sipped his drink and watched me with a thoughtful expression. He made some idle conversation about the weather and started talking about his family's drive from Indiana to Arizona and their plans to see a lot of California along the way. "I've been called to be an associate minister in a church south of San Francisco. Rose's brother lives out there and we're anxious to see him again."

"That's nice," I replied, not really concentrating on the conversation.

"He's had a rough time of it since his partner died."

Whoa. What was that? "His ... his partner? As in same sex partner?"

The minister nodded, acting like he imparted this sort of information to strangers everyday. Maybe he did. Maybe it was no big deal or at least he thought it wasn't to me. *Well, cool. Neil is not going to be uptight about my relationship with another woman.*

"John lost Brian three months ago. He was killed in a car accident. Rose and I were very fond of him and she took his death almost as hard as John did. They were members of the church I'm going to serve. The congregation is a congenial mixture of gay and straight, old and young, rich and not so rich. John isn't the only one who has lost a partner recently, what with the AIDS situation. I'm looking forward to the challenge of getting out there and helping wherever I can."

He tapped his fingertips on the edge of the table. "I've been doing all the talking. Why don't you tell me something about yourself? Sometimes it helps to get a fresh perspective on things."

"Okay," I said, not very convincingly.

"We'll start with an easy question, at least I hope it is. How did you get interested in archaeology?"

"Oh, it's a long story. I got interested while I was a college undergraduate. A favorite teacher of mine went on digs during the summer and talked me into joining her."

He crunched on a few corn chips, still watching me with those gentle gray eyes. "Rose said you were from Boston."

Uh huh. What else does she know? "I live there now. I went to school in the Boston area and my doctorate is from Boston University. How did your wife happen to know that?"

He gave me a sheepish grin. "I'm afraid I don't keep up with the society pages, but she was so sure she had seen you before. She went through some copies of *People* that we had in our luggage.... there must have been five back issues...and there was your picture at some function for the Boston Symphony."

"Oh." I felt my face flush. "Well, at least it wasn't the clambake with the Kennedy clan. *I think I was wearing a string bikini in that picture.* Sometimes it's hard to avoid the press, especially when your father expects you to show up for events like that." I took a long swallow of soda.

"So you're the daughter of Frederick Curtis, the multi-billionaire?"

I shifted in my seat. "Uh ...yeah, something like that. When he wants to admit it."

"You two don't get along?"

"Let's just say there are issues between us. I don't think he wants to acknowledge our kinship."

"Is that why you're troubled tonight?"

"No." I sighed and took another swallow of root beer.

"I see." He waited a moment, before asking more questions. "How come you don't have a Boston accent?"

"Well, we didn't move to Boston until I was about ten. I was born in New Jersey and lived near Philadelphia after that. My father's main business is in shipping so we spent a lot of years living in port cities. I guess my accent is from the whole east coast."

"Any brothers or sisters?"

"Nope. I'm an only child. In fact, it's just Father and me now. My mother died when I was fourteen." My voice caught on the last sentence. *Even after all these years, it still hurts.*

He heard the quaver. "I'm sorry."

"Me too. I sure could use her advice right now."

He glanced at his watch. "Well, I could never replace your mother, but I've been told I'm a pretty good listener." His eyebrow arched. "And, I left my clerical collar in my luggage so I won't get 'all preachy' on you."

I felt my throat tighten and the room seemed to grow warmer. "It's kind of you, Neil, but I don't know if my problem can be solved in ten or twenty minutes. It's been building for several weeks."

He drained his beverage and placed the glass on the table, giving me a reassuring smile. "I understand. And I don't mean to pry, but you're clearly bothered by something. You've been so kind to Rose and the kids and me, I just want to help if I can."

I didn't intend to say another thing, but all at once, the words tumbled out in a jumble of pain and confusion.

"I've gotten myself into a situation … with … a romantic situation ... an affair of the heart, I guess you'd call it … with someone at work."

"I see." He leaned back and folded his hands.

"I don't know how it happened..." I felt a lump form at the back of my throat. "I don't know if I should pursue it … and I'm confused."

He reached across the table and took my hand.

"Affairs of the heart can be like that. And you say it involves your workplace?"

I nodded, keeping my eyes focused on the table. "I think I've fallen in love with one of my colleagues ... a woman."

"Ah... I see. And you're worried about what people might say? What they might think of you?"

I shook my head. "No, not at all. I don't give a damn …oops, sorry, about what people think."

"Oh, well, perhaps you should start at the beginning. I've jumped to the wrong conclusion already. I could use a few more facts."

I took a long breath. "Okay, in a nutshell... I came to Arizona because I was interested in working on a certain project with a certain group of people. I've had a lot of experience working in a supporting capacity, but nobody has helped me learn to lead a project. Nobody ever cared whether I progressed in my profession. I hoped I could get some of that guidance here."

"Has that happened?"

"Yes. I got off to a rocky start, but I learned a lot and for the first time in my life, I've proven myself to be a capable worker. I've taken charge of a group and made a contribution. I've been encouraged for my brain and not my money or my looks."

Neil squeezed my hand. "That's great, PJ."

"My father lost interest in me when my mother died. We were a very close, loving family when she was alive. We even went to church regularly."

"That's good to hear."

"But, when she was killed, things just fell apart. My father went to the office or away on trips and I was sent to private schools and summer camps. At home, I had a housekeeper, cook and chauffeur to supervise me. I tried all sorts of things to get Father to notice me, and when he did it was for all the wrong reasons. He considers me a screw-up and I guess I am ... or at least I was until I came here. I made friends with my colleagues, one in particular. Now, I've got to decide..."

"Decide what?"

I took a final drink of soda. "We became friends first, good friends. This friendship ... I value it so much, but at the same time, I really think I'm in love with her." I swallowed against the lump in my throat. "I can't lose her friendship, Neil. I don't know if she feels as strongly as I do about this. What do I do? How do I know it's love that I'm feeling? And if it is, how can I tell if she loves me back?"

Neil chuckled softly. "And I was afraid you had a hard problem to share with me. That's about the hardest, most universal problem that humans can face. Maybe we can take one part at a time, okay?"

I sniffed and wiped my eyes. "I seem to be getting a little emotional. I'm sorry."

"For what? Falling in love?" He paused and searched his pockets, producing a crumpled tissue. "Don't ever be sorry for falling in love, PJ." He handed me the tissue and then moved to take it back. "Oh, wait ... I used that on Jessica this morning. She had chocolate ice cream. Be careful of any brown spots."

I found some safe corners to blow my nose. "I'm okay. Thanks."

He leaned back in his chair and folded his hands in thought. His eyes closed for a few seconds and I felt a calm settle over me. Then, his eyes were open and on me. "You want to know how you can tell if it is real love?"

"Yes."

"I take it you've never been in love before?"

"I was engaged to a guy for a few months, but it was all his idea. There's no comparison."

"Okay. Close your eyes, picture this woman in your mind and tell me what you feel."

I did as he requested and my tears dried, my throat cleared. A broad smile replaced my tense expression. I relaxed into the experiment with a sigh. "When I think of her, I feel warm, comfortable, and safe. I can't help smiling a lot. She makes me feel capable, smart and funny. It doesn't matter where we are or what we're doing, I'm just happy being there with her. I can tell her things that I've never told anyone and she listens. Before she came into my life, I was practically invisible. I had no concerns beyond my own pleasures. I was a rich, empty-headed bitch or at least, that's what people thought and I tried to live up to my label. She taught me so much about acting responsibly toward people, animals and the environment. She's my best friend and I think about her all the time."

"Okay, good. Keep your eyes closed and pretend she's sitting beside you right now. What sort of emotions do you feel? How does your body react to her?"

"Oh, gawd…. Uh … my heart races and my neck gets hot. My palms sweat. Sometimes I try to talk but my words get all tangled up because she's smiling at me. I'm struck dumb. And, when she touches me." I sighed again. "I wish she'd do more of that. When we sleep at the site, I think about how it would be to zip our bags together and just snuggle for days on end. That image gets me aroused, I must admit."

Neil cleared his throat. "Then, I take it you haven't expressed your feelings toward her in a physical way yet?"

"No. I react to her touches, but I haven't … we haven't made any moves in that direction."

"I think we've explored that avenue enough. You can open your eyes now."

I blinked and blushed, realizing how much I had confessed.

"Hey, relax. You had me remembering my first date with Rose and how I daydreamed all the way back to my dorm room."

I leaned toward him. "It went well for you? Was it love at first sight?"

"Ha! No, as a matter of fact, she thought I was the most boring, obnoxious guy on campus. It took us several dates and I had to be very persistent before she realized that it was easier to give up and love me back. I sent her poems, flowers, and candy. Nothing seemed to soften her up ... until one day.... "

"What? What did you do?"

"I serenaded her in a rowboat on Lake Discovery. That was a small body of water near our college campus."

"Hmm. That sounds very romantic."

He grinned and I sensed there was more to this story. "Yeah, it does sound romantic. It was meant to be romantic. But, I couldn't row a boat, so I lost an oar right off the bat. We got sun-burned and a speed boat came by and soaked us right when I was doing my best Barry Manilow impression."

I started to laugh. "No. You're making that up."

He made a cross over his heart with an index finger. "Swear to God! Ooops!"

We both laughed.

"Oh, Neil. Thank you for making me laugh."

"Well, listen. I want to relieve some of the tension. You just remember old Neil trying to woo sweet Rose and I hope you'll realize that there is only one way to truly know if you are in love."

"And that would be?"

He paused for dramatic effect. "That would be ... if you are willing to persist in spite of all the embarrassing things that can happen when you're trying to make a good impression and if the object of your affection can keep on going out with you, in spite of the fool you make of yourself, then it must be true love. And both of you were meant for each other."

"Okay. I'll remember all that. Now, about the second part."

"Ah, yes. Part two. Why wouldn't she return your love? You're a very attractive woman."

"Thank you." I bit down on my lower lip. "Well, for one thing, she thinks I'm straight."

"Oh."

"And she's had a very nasty experience with an old love affair and I don't think she wants to think about loving anyone again for quite some time."

"Hmm. You *do* have your work cut out for you."

"I was afraid you'd say that."

"But, it's not hopeless. It's *never* hopeless. Remember Neil in the rowboat. Have faith in yourself and in your love for her. If she's got a brain in her head she'd be a fool to turn you down."

"Yeah. I keep telling myself that."

Neil tapped his fingers on the tabletop, beating out a brief tattoo. "Let me ask you a serious question. You don't have to answer, but I wish you'd think about it, okay?"

"Okay." My body tensed.

"Do you love yourself, PJ? Have you looked deep down inside and forgiven yourself for your teenage years?"

Well, have I? I looked down at the table and then up at him. "Yes, Neil. I believe I finally can say that I do love myself and, except for the problems with my father, I am at peace with my past."

"Good. It's hard to love another if you don't first love yourself."

"Should I risk destroying the friendship we have, though? If I tell her I love her and she isn't willing to love me back, I will jeopardize all of that."

He heaved a mighty sigh. "The sixty-four thousand dollar question. I can't say for sure one way or the other. I haven't met your intended so I can't give you my impressions. Maybe I can suggest that you take it very slowly in that direction, watching for the right opportunity to bring it up. If you are patient and if she continues to want to be around you, then I'd say you could probably risk it. Be patient. Don't ever be sorry for falling in love."

"I'm not. I just never expected it to happen this way. It sort of came at me from out of the blue."

His laughter was soft, full of warmth. "Love is just like that, PJ. Sneaky, so very sneaky. It takes hold of us and won't let go. It seeps into every pore, sealing up the cracks, suffocating us with the most wonderful feelings. It picks its own time and place. It's overwhelming and amazing and the world needs a whole lot more of it, in my opinion."

He popped a few cashews into his mouth and rose. "I'm afraid I'd better get back to Rose. She'll be so relaxed she might fall asleep on the massage table."

I stood up. "Thanks so much for talking with me, Neil. It's been a real help to discuss this with you. I'm afraid I haven't been very religious for many years, at least not in an organized way. I believe in a higher power ...God ... or whatever name he or she goes by, but I've read so much about other cultures both ancient and modern that I'm afraid no organized church fills my needs."

"You'd be surprised how rewarding a personal relationship can be. God is like the boss of a big company. Some of the employees work together and some maintain individual ties." He took both of my hands. "Anyway, it's never too late to get reconnected."

"I'm not so sure your boss would approve of my life up until now."

Neil grinned. "My boss loves every employee."

"I'm afraid I gave up on your boss when Mom died. I asked all sorts of questions and never got answers."

"Give him another try, won't you? The 'boss' I know wants all of his 'employees' to be happy. He loves us, no matter who we are or who we choose to love."

He went back to the table for a final handful of cashews, tossing them into his mouth. "Love these things."

"Me too."

His hand brushed my shoulder. "You call me if I can be of further help."

I followed him to the door. "Thank you, Neil, I will."

"'I'll put in a good word for you, but try him yourself, okay?" He winked. "I bet your name is still in his Rolodex."

That made me smile. "Yeah, right."

He paused in the doorway. "There's no big mystery about it, you know. It's all about love. Feel it. Share it. Pass it along."

We gave each other a hug. He pulled out his wallet and gave me a card. "This is the number of the church in California. Let me know how things turn out, okay?"

"I will. Thanks so much for listening."

"Any time. Thanks for the cashews ... and the root beer." He walked on down the hall to his family.

I changed into a nightshirt and prepared for bed. The room was illuminated by the faint glow of moonlight from behind closed drapes. Tucked under a light blanket, a thick mattress supporting my back, I stared at the ceiling, composing my thoughts.

Finally, I took a deep breath.

"Okay, I know I haven't made much of an effort for a long time, but if you're listening...Thanks. I think I'm finally getting some answers."

I fell asleep, then... dreaming of Kim.

Chapter Fifteen

I lay in my sleeping bag trying to concentrate on the night sky. My mind though had other ideas. It kept returning to my Amazons. They weren't really mine, of course, even though I'd like to keep them that way. All too soon they'd belong to the world of academia. Their lives would be dissected. Disagreements would arise between archaeologists, anthropologists, and historians, some of whom would refuse to believe that Amazons existed at all. I sighed and shifted to ease an aching hip. The women had rested in silence for centuries, until I had come along and disturbed their repose. What had happened to the cold, hard scientist in me, the archaeologist who believed all things are better revealed?

Westermeyer had taken longer than I had expected to get back to me, to return the skulls to their resting place. But I managed, thanks to PJ, to refrain from calling him, bugging him.

"I know you're worried about your Amazons," she had said, "but no one knows better than you that it takes time."

"I know … it's just that…"

"And it's not like we don't have plenty to do here."

I smiled. *You've come a long way, baby.*

Finally, Doctor Westermeyer called to say that he would return to the site on the Monday before Thanksgiving.

Sandy and Mike assisted Westermeyer in carrying the precious bundles back from the trailhead to the site and replacing them in the cave where I felt they belonged. As soon as they arrived on site, I gathered the rest of the crew together in the tent so that they could hear his report first hand.

I made room on the table for Westermeyer to spread out his reports. I gave him the one good folding chair. PJ and I sat on our battered, aluminum framed, camp chairs; the others either sat on the floor or stood. Sandy and Mike followed the scientist into the tent and placed two boxes on the table.

"Samuel, I thought you returned the skulls to the cave," I said, nodding toward the sealed boxes.

Westermeyer raised his hand. "I did." He stared hard at me a moment before scanning the assembled crew, waiting, I thought, for the right moment to begin his command performance. I smiled to myself. *Oh, Samuel, I always knew you had a flair for the dramatic.*

The group was silent, a rarity. The mood was solemn. The clearing of collective throats reminded me of my childhood, when I was forced every Sunday to wear a frilly little dress and go to church. It had amused my child's mind that the clearing of congregational throats was a necessary prelude to the singing of praises. *Gawd, where did that come from?*

First, Westermeyer took the dagger from a padded envelope and handed it to me. I held it for a few moments, feeling the heft of it before handing it to PJ.

"It's of Greek manufacture," Westermeyer said, after what he had deemed an appropriate pause. "The engravings are what are believed, at least in myth, to be Amazon. And we all know, don't we, that myth is the historical record of a preliterate world?"

I sucked in my breath. "Proof positive."

"I'm not through yet." The undertone of excited whispering that followed his initial statement ceased.

"With the scrapings I took from the skeletons and from the examination I had performed here, I determined that both women appear to have been in relatively good health, better, I might add, than many young women of their age today. Their battle scars, however, would have caused discomfort and physical pain."

"As warriors, they would probably have put up with the pain without complaint," I said, feeling pride in these women who had traveled so far. "It's not fair."

PJ looked at me. "What isn't fair?"

"That they would have come so far just to die in this gawd forsaken desert."

Murmured agreement filled the tent.

"But think, Kim. You found them." PJ's eyes were brimming. "Look at it this way, you brought them out into the light. Their story is yours to tell."

I was about to respond when Doctor Westermeyer interrupted.

"I took the liberty of going further with the skulls." He peered at me from beneath bushy eyebrows. "Would you like to know, Kim, what your Amazons looked like?"

My eyes riveted on Westermeyer. The silence in the crowded tent was so profound that I was sure I could hear the collective hearts beating.

"You all know, of course, that archaeology is not an exact science. There are so many unanswered questions, most of which will have to wait for future generations with far more sophisticated equipment than we have at the moment. But, with modern testing procedures such as isotopic analysis we can determine so much more than we could just a few years ago."

Westermeyer was in his element. The man was a gifted teacher. He held himself in high esteem, a flaw that he had admitted to me on several occasions. He was playing now to my students and they were wide eyed with admiration. I listened attentively, but as a colleague, I was coming from my own knowledge and experience. My credentials matched his in every way. I knew as well as he all the modern methods of ancient identification, but I gave him the stage. I owed him that and sat beside PJ absorbing all he had to say.

He looked around at the assembled crew. Even though he had their complete attention, he punctuated his presentation with dramatic pauses. I loved the man, had the utmost respect for him, perhaps because he reminded me in some ways of myself ... a trifle arrogant at times.

"The secrets of the past are being revealed as never before. You're undoubtedly familiar with computed axial tomographic CAT data and how it is being used in archaeology."

"It's used to reconstruct facial features," PJ said. "Basically, pegs placed at key points on a model of the skull reproduce the normal thickness of tissue, then material representing muscle and skin is molded on to the model. There's a lot more to it than that, of course, but it's been used successfully in criminal cases to identify remains."

"Right you are, Doctor Curtis." Westermeyer scanned the group. "And now, ladies and gentlemen, are you ready to meet face to face the female who was on the bottom?"

James snickered and found himself on the wrong end of a withering look from PJ. For one fleeting moment I felt sorry for him.

Westermeyer was too busy opening the first of the two boxes to express either amusement or annoyance over the exchange.

I was eager to see the features of the women I'd sought for so long. One can learn much from bones, but looking at a face can reveal what the bones cannot, the mirror of personality. I felt it would help me put aside once and for all, the unrest I had felt since the discovery of Site One.

As I stared at the face on the table, I was vaguely aware of the excited buzz of conversation behind me. The reconstruction was as life-like as I had ever seen. She was a beauty with classic Mediterranean features and dark, almond shaped eyes. Westermeyer had dressed her in a wig of long, blue-black hair, matching as closely as he could the hair that still clung to the remains. The eyes seemed alive as they stared back at me.

"Oh, Samuel, you have performed a miracle." A lump formed in my throat as it became clear that I was in love with the face in front of me. I was feeling all the confusion and delight of young love. I couldn't tear my eyes away. And although I knew better, I would have sworn she felt the same about me.

I was aware of PJ's hand on my arm and her asking, "How does it feel, Kim, to see one of your Amazons face to face?"

I was beyond response.

The crew's excited conversation faded into the background. I was riveted to my chair, just staring at the lovely warrior's face.

PJ squeezed my arm. "Kim, are you okay?"

I nodded.

"So what do you think?" Westermeyer asked.

PJ looked at me. "Kim, Doctor Westermeyer asked you a question."

I thought I had answered him but obviously I hadn't.

"You have only to look at her, Doctor," PJ said, squeezing my hand. "This has been a life-long journey for her, and to see a likeness of one of the Amazons is for her like the second coming."

"I can't even begin to describe my feelings," I said, pulling myself together.

"May I congratulate you, Doctor Westermeyer," Sandy said. "I've seen this done before, at the University, but this is the first time for a project I've been working with ... kinda spooky if you ask me."

There was a murmuring of uneasy mirth and of agreement from the others.

"Thank you, young man. But, you know that as archaeologists, we often disturb ghosts."

Westermeyer returned his attention to the assembled scholars. "I determined this young woman to have been in her mid to late twenties when she died. She was in her prime, as was her companion-in-death."

Just like a man, I thought, to say that a woman in her twenties is in her prime. That puts the rest of us on the slippery slope to invisibility.

I returned my momentary lapse to Westermeyer as he broke the seal on the second box.

"The woman I am about to reveal was older, in her early thirties, but I would say that she was a pillar of strength and good health."

I could have heard a pin drop as everyone's attention was focused on what Westermeyer was saying. Except mine ... I couldn't get past the way in which the first face had affected me.

"The dead can reveal a lot about themselves," Doctor Westermeyer said, his eyes scanning his attentive audience. "It's quite obvious to me that this little lady," he pointed to the already revealed face, "the one on the bottom..." He smiled at James and winked.

Laughter broke the serious nature of the moment and snapped me back to reality. All eyes turned to James, who I'm sure wished he was someplace else.

"As I was saying, the dead speak to us in many ways. And now ..." Westermeyer turned his attention to me, "Doctor Blair ... Kim, I need your full attention. What I am about to reveal will, I'm afraid, be disturbing. It was for me and it will be to you, ten fold."

"Not any more so than that young woman." I glanced again at the face and the eyes that seemed to draw me in.

"I suggest you take a deep breath."

PJ covered my hand with hers as Samuel slowly opened the box.

A loud gasp escaped the assembled crew. In a split second of time my heart stopped momentarily, before beating again, erratically.

"No ... no ... NO!" PJ's denial was frantic.

I was aware of her nails digging into my hand but I was beyond feeling the pain. I was angry.

One look from me was enough to squelch the excited muttering. I stood up, kicking my chair out of the way.

"As you can see, Doctor Blair, this one is a fair likeness of yourself."

"Doctor Westermeyer, if this is your idea of a joke ... it's a sick one. I don't find it the least bit funny." I could feel all eyes focused on me.

"Kim, you know me better than that." Westermeyer's tone was kindly but firm. "I don't play tricks on people. I certainly wouldn't do that to you. The second skull was reconstructed by the exact same method used with the first one. This is what she looked like."

My stomach churned as I stared in fearful amazement at the second Amazon.

"I can't explain it," Westermeyer continued, "but what you see is the result of cold, hard science. I know there's a resemblance--"

"A resemblance! My gawd, man, I could be looking in a mirror."

Without waiting for further discussion, I turned and left the tent, shoving Dewey who was standing in front of the tent flap, aside. I walked, ran, and scrambled up hill, straight up, and fast

176

until my breath was ragged. When I could go no farther, I dropped to the ground, bowing my head and hugging my knees.

Moments later, PJ found me. She was breathless and sweating after chasing me up hill. She sat down beside me, took me in her arms and rocked me.

"It's okay, Kim. Everything's going to be all right ... it was a shock, it was to all of us."

"It was me ... he made an image of me."

Pup was licking my hand. PJ was holding me, rocking me. Despite their comforting presence, I could not immediately respond.

I've been involved with these women for too long. I'm ready to believe anything ... now this. Am I crazy or what?

"It was the dreams, PJ. I knew it all along."

PJ placed a tender kiss on my forehead. "Why don't you tell me about those dreams?"

"I suppose I should, though you're going to think I've lost it."

"Never! Not after what we've seen today."

I took a deep breath and wiped a grubby hand across my face.

PJ chuckled. "Oh, now you look lovely."

I didn't feel like smiling but I couldn't help it. *Oh, PJ, what would I do without you?*

"The dreams began with five Amazon warriors, Marna, Leeja, Peli, Shanna, and Solana. They were heading across the desert, that desert." I pointed toward the vast, empty land that surrounded the City of Phoenix. "It was mid summer and the heat was unbearable. They were making their way, against overwhelming odds, toward a distant mountain range, our mountains, the Superstitions."

I paused to take a deep breath. Sharing my dreams was like sharing a long forgotten memory ... it frightened me.

"Go on." PJ's soft voice and the feel of her arms around me were reassuring.

"The band was in bad shape after an encounter with an unknown tribe of dark skinned warriors. Leeja had been severely wounded and was being transported on a litter. They were all concerned for her, but Marna was especially so. They were in love, you see, and Leeja, with bloody puss seeping from her festering wounds, was weakening."

"Marna was their leader?"

"No, Leeja was, until she was wounded and could no longer carry out her duties. It was then she appointed Solana as her interim lieutenant."

"Not Marna?"

"Leeja knew she was going to die and that Marna in her grief would not immediately be of sound mind. That would come later. Besides, she knew that Solana would listen to and benefit from Marna's experience, once Marna moved on beyond her initial grief."

"Leeja was a wise woman."

"She was indeed."

I paused. PJ continuing to hold me, waited.

You'd probably want to kill me, PJ, if I told you this, but you have a strong mothering instinct.

"I could see it all clearly, PJ. Marna and the others survived this far by gathering the few berries that could be found, and killing a rabbit or a snake now and then. It was enough to keep hunger at bay, but not for long. They found water by tapping into the Saguaro."

PJ drew my head onto her shoulder. "When did the dreams start?"

"When I was in South America."

"And you said they were repetitive?"

"They were for a while. Then they changed." I paused. In my mind's eye I was trudging with my small band across the limitless desert. There were times when I wanted to give up, to just lay down and go to sleep. I had others to consider though. And there was Leeja, my beloved Leeja ... I could not, would not leave her.

"There's more to tell?"

"When they reached the mountains, they found a small canyon, our canyon ... it has changed little. They set up camp. It was a good camp. Occasional showers during the night left small pools of water in depressions in the rocks, enough for them to fill their skin flasks. Marna lay beside Leeja and cradled her in her arms. It was like it was happening to..."

"To you."

"Yes. Soon Leeja's breathing became even more labored and she slipped quietly away."

"Oh, Kim, that is so sad."

"Normally, we would have had a funeral pyre, but wood was scarce. Besides, even if it had been available, we wouldn't have had the strength to build one. We began without further ado and by the light of the moon and our campfire to place Leeja's body in a small cave."

"Kim, are you aware that you're speaking in first person?"

"PJ, I was there ... in my dreams. You think I'm crazy, don't you?"

"Kim, I ... no ... I don't know what to think, but I want to hear the rest of the story, so please go on."

"Then I'll try to keep it in perspective and relate it as a viewer and not a participant. They used almost all of their reserves of strength to block the entrance with rocks and stones. When they were about to roll the last boulder in place, I ... there I go again. Why do I keep referring to myself?"

"Because you were there, at least in your dreams you were. What are dreams but another reality?"

I shifted, releasing myself from PJ's comforting embrace.

"Marna crawled through the small opening, 'one last time,' she said. She leaned over and kissed Leeja, then without another word, plunged the dagger into her own heart." I gripped my chest against the searing pain.

"Kim, for gawd's sake! Are you okay?"

I nodded. "I'm okay. It's just that whenever I think or dream about that I have severe chest pain. It's as though the knife has entered my own body, my own heart."

I leaned back, far enough away from PJ's face so that I could focus clearly on her expression. "Am I losing it, PJ? Am I going insane?"

"Of course not. What do you expect when you've been involved with these women for what ... twenty years or more?"

I nodded.

"Sometimes we confuse dreams with reality, especially when one is involved to such a degree. A writer friend of mine once told me that she becomes one with her characters. Is your situation so very different from hers?"

"You sound like you almost believe the story."

"Given what we know, it makes sense, though I can't explain where your dreams are coming from."

"It's like it happened yesterday, the pain and my ... Marna's blood running off Leeja's body and pooling in the dirt, her falling across Leeja."

"Sacred ground in those caves, Kim, we have and will continue to treat them with great reverence."

"I ... she was dead before the others could do anything so they rolled the remaining boulder across the entrance. I was dead, in my dream, and holding Leeja in an eternal embrace, just as the remains were when we found them. Even though I was dead, I could hear the others keening. Shanna's funeral chant was haunting and in some ways like a beautiful lullaby. It was as if my ... as if Marna's spirit was watching the events after her death. And I saw it all, you see. I knew before Westermeyer's testing, before the reconstruction of the skulls. I knew as soon as we entered the cave. I knew what had happened and how it had happened, and why it had happened."

"Oh, Kim." PJ got to her feet and extended her hands to me. "Come on, let's go back to camp. Everyone's concerned about you. I'll fix us all some tea."

I got up and brushed myself off. "PJ."

"Yes."

"Thank you for sticking with me."

"Hey, don't mention it." She grinned. "But, you owe me ... big time."

I laughed. "I need to go set things right with Samuel."

"Now you're sounding more like my boss. I like that."

Chapter Sixteen

A sharp stone dug into my shoulder and my hips and back complained of stiffness from contact with the hard ground. My sleeping bag kept me warm, but not as comfortable as that luxurious bed at the Casa Grande.

It's the day before Thanksgiving and I'm up here on the mountain, sleeping a scant few yards from the woman of my dreams. Tomorrow, I'll be alone with her, sharing a sumptuous turkey dinner in the suite and relaxing afterward with some romantic music, stimulating conversation ... and maybe, if I can get up the courage ... some serious lip locking.

Oh Gawd.

Excitement and fear wrestled with my nervous system.

Today is the day of Kim's party, and I haven't made any progress in advancing our relationship to the next level. I can't help it. The timing is wrong and it has been since I got back on the mountain. When we're alone, we're working or discussing work and when we don't have work to do, we're not alone or too exhausted to talk about it. Kim is still obsessed with her Amazon Women and the amazing likeness she shares with one of them. I can't intrude with my concerns when I know she won't be able to concentrate.

I pinched the bridge of my nose and held my thumb and forefinger against my closed eyelids, rubbing gently.

Let's face it; I've been too chicken-shit scared to bring up the subject. What could I say to her? 'Oh, by the way, Kim, I'm not as straight as you think I am? Want to have hot, monkey sex with me sometime, huh?' Shit. Now, beside my case of nerves, I could add sexual frustration to the mix.

I rolled over in my sleeping bag and propped my head up. The cause of my frustration slept on, one hand curled under her chin, her hair adorably tousled.

Today will be a big one for you, my friend...and for me, if I can ever get you alone long enough. I'll start to tell you how I feel...I swear I will.

Pup stirred from his spot at Kim's side. He lifted his head and gave an expansive yawn that ended in a squeak. The effect was comical coming from such a large, ferocious-looking animal. He rose and shook his entire length. When he noticed me watching him, he padded over to greet me. Before I could resist, he was all over me, whining and nuzzling my neck, giving me slobbery kisses.

"Yeesh, Pup. Stop it," I whispered, wiping my face, but I threw my arms around his shoulders and hugged him. "You're such an old softy. A few months ago, I was scared to death of you." I scratched behind his ears and he flopped onto my stomach, emitting moans of pleasure. "Shh! Honey, you'll wake the boss." I tried to roll his hefty bulk off of me with little success.

"Too late," came a sleepy reply. "The boss is awake. Now, you both will suffer." Kim stretched in much the same manner as her pet, even down to the moans.

I gave Pup a final hug and stood up. He joined his mistress, greeting her with a barrage of wet kisses.

Pup has the right idea. If I were an animal I'd just sniff her a few times and if she didn't bite me, I'd plant wet, wild kisses all over her body. Hell, I'd probably do it even if she did bite.

I smiled, watching them. "Two of a kind, that's what you are. You both pretend to be so tough and all the time you're a couple of cream puffs. It's so cute."

"Enough, Pup. Get down." He obeyed instantly. Kim gave me a stern look, except her eyes were bright with amusement. "I heard that, PJ. If you expect to get scrambled eggs for breakfast, you'd better stop comparing me to a wolf. Some people would not be flattered." She rolled her bedding with swift, practiced strokes.

"Is that so?" I imitated her moves until my sleeping bag was rolled and secured. "All I can say in my defense is that *you* are not *some people* and Pup is no ordinary wolf."

She tucked her bedding under her arm and waited for me to fall into step beside her. "Touché," she said with a pat on my shoulder. We ambled along the path to the main tent. "But, I do have a reputation for toughness to maintain."

"Don't worry, your secret's safe with me."

She grinned. "Why don't you have first dibs on the half-moon facility and I'll put water on for our tea."

I nodded and continued along the path.

Just an ordinary day...up here on the mountain. Little do you know, my dear, that our entire crew has planned a big old party for you at lunchtime. They all know about your birthday tomorrow and they can't wait to surprise you. They love you, Kim. We all do. No matter what state you've worked yourself into lately. Don't ever forget what an extraordinary teacher you are and how much we value your opinion of us.

As Kim mixed the egg batter and stirred it into the heated skillet, I poured the tea and set out two plates with utensils. We'd set our chairs outside the tent for our meal so we could enjoy the first few rays of morning sunshine.

I reentered the tent, chewing my lower lip.

Let's see. Sandy's mom baked a cake.

She lived nearby with three of his five brothers and sisters.

James is in charge of the gift from the crew.

I told them I had a present for Kim, so they left me out of their plan.

I can't imagine what they picked out for her.

Donny, Mike and Lewis are in charge of getting party supplies, beverages and snacks.

I did contribute to that fund.

Josie will coordinate the delivery of everything and help me divert Kim's attention while the tent is decorated.

As far as I can tell it's still a surprise for our guest of honor.

"PJ?"

I jumped. "Sorry, what?"

She held up the pan with a mountain of fluffy cooked eggs. "I asked you to hold out your plate and tell me how much you wanted."

"Oh, um… Two scoops should be fine." I picked up one of the plates and thrust it toward her. "Here ya go."

She plopped two large spoonfuls and a piece of fried bread onto my plate and fixed a matching plate for herself. We eased into folding chairs with our breakfast on our laps. I pulled over a box so we could rest our mugs on it. My hands shook and I dropped my spoon before I could stir my tea.

She watched me for several seconds. "Is there something wrong, PJ?"

I gave her an innocent look and started shoveling eggs into my mouth. "Huh-uh, this is delicious."

She shook her head. "Not with the food, with you. You seem nervous and a bit preoccupied this morning."

I shrugged and kept chewing. The chair made a creaking sound as I squirmed. "I'm fine, Kim. I'm just thinking of all the work we have to do today. The gang will be heading home or wherever … for Thanksgiving, and we've got so much to finish before then."

"Well, good." She seemed to relax. "I was afraid you were still concerned about my actions when Samuel was here…when we saw those women's faces and I got a little… crazy."

I put my fork down and swallowed. "Kim, you had every right to go crazy. In your place, I'd have done the same thing, especially after you described those dreams."

She gave me a faint smile and swallowed her mouthful of egg. "Thank you for understanding. I know you don't know what to think about my relationship with that one woman."

"Marna?"

She wiped her lips with a napkin. "Yes, Marna. I've lived with her in my dreams for so long and now we've located them and the site of their final struggles." Her eyes glistened and for a moment I was afraid she'd start crying.

I took a sip of tea and swallowed the last of my fried bread. "It really doesn't matter what I think about it, Kim. I'm not the one in the middle of it all. I believe what you tell me you

184

experienced. So far, what you've said fits with what we've found. By the way, Father wants to know how soon we can have a press conference. I've been putting him off until we had definite results, but it looks--"

"Yes, you're right, PJ." Kim stood and collected our plates and cups. "We owe your father a complete report and we should set up a time when the media can come to take photos. Maybe we can do that this morning. Let's go over to the shallow cave and put everything in order. It would make a pretty impressive photo opportunity to have those women waiting for the reporters, 'in situ'...don't you think?"

I pondered her idea as we cleaned up our breakfast items. "Finding them just as they were when we first saw them would be very impressive. Are you sure you are up to that? You won't be bothered by working so close to them?"

Kim pulled out the washbasin and poured leftover hot water into it from the teakettle. "Do you want to wash or dry?"

"I'll wash." I found the liquid detergent and squeezed in a few drops as she poured.

"To be honest with you, PJ, I don't know how I'll feel in there, but I've got to do it. We're coming down the homestretch of our project. This is the time for announcing our discovery. Your father has invested a great deal of money in this venture and I'm certain he'll want to bask in the glory of our findings." She poured rinse water into a spare bucket and then dipped our plates and utensils into it, drying everything carefully and putting it all away for our next meal.

My stomach churned with excitement. *Your next meal is going to be on paper birthday plates. We'll probably have plastic forks and spoons too. Gawd, I hope we can pull this off.*

My reverie was interrupted by a shout from outside the tent. Crew members were arriving.

"Good thing we dressed before breakfast," Kim murmured. "We don't get much privacy when the gang gets here."

No, damn it. That's part of the problem.

I dried my hands on a clean towel. "I noticed that. It's like living with a great big family."

"A big, happy family, I trust."

185

"Oh, definitely," I assured her.

"Hey, Docs," Donny said, poking his head into the tent. "Uh...Sandy is gonna be a bit late today. He has some personal business."

That's secret code for Sandy's stopping by his mother's to pick up the cake on his way to work.

"That's fine," I said. I looked sideways at Kim to see if she had her thick padded clipboard in hand. We'd gone over the list of chores together last night, but I had neglected to ask her who was giving the orders today.

She smiled at me once we were outside facing our assembled co-workers and handed over the paperwork. "You can handle this. You've been doing a superb job so far."

The warmth in her eyes made my mouth go dry. "Thank you, Kim. I've learned from the best."

She put her hand on my shoulder and gave it a squeeze. "I'll get our packs so we can get going."

I turned my attention to the students. "Okay, people. Are we all here, except for Sandy?"

"Looks like it, PJ," Josie answered for everyone. She had a sparkle in her eyes that clearly hinted at mischief. Fortunately, Kim was back inside the tent.

"Good, then let's get to our assignments." I cleared my throat. "Before you all scatter to the four corners of the earth for Thanksgiving and a long weekend, we have a few little loose ends that need tying up."

There was a series of groans. "Hey, it's not bad, really.... just some paperwork for the most part. 'Course we know you have no real lives beyond these canyon walls and if we left you to your own devices, you'd probably forget Thanksgiving altogether."

There were a few chuckles now. "Yeah, right. Like that's gonna happen." Mike shook his head, smiling.

I noticed that Kim had returned and was laughing, too. She called Pup to her side and gave his head a loving caress. A happy flutter stirred somewhere near my heart and I forgot what I was about to say.

Get a grip, here.

I took a deep breath. "Seriously, Doc and I are extremely pleased and proud of the work you have conducted during our weeks here. We've all come together like a well-coached team."

"Three cheers for the coach!" Laine called out, and a chorus of yells erupted.

"Goodness, aren't we chipper this morning," Kim said, with a grin.

"Don't forget the assistant coach!" Mike shouted. The group responded with more cheers.

My cheeks burning, I tried to continue. "Thank you all. I guess the fact that we've made some momentous discoveries lately hasn't hurt us either."

"Yeah!" Several cried at once and a few hands slapped together in triumph.

"PJ, could you wrap this up, please," Mike grinned. "Some of us have long trips ahead of us."

I grinned back at his impertinence. "Sorry. I'll stop all these compliments, then. Mike and Laine can finish the reports and data entry on the first excavation. Josie, you and Donny can do some more field specimen cards on Site Two." I noticed that Kim had picked up our daypacks and was walking toward the shallow cave with Pup at her side. "Doc and I are going to work at Site One in preparation for a press conference and possibly a taped documentary on the discovery." I said that loud enough for her to hear.

"I'll meet you at the cave," she called back to me, urging Pup to keep up.

"Okay. I'm almost finished here." I gave the rest of the orders and lowered my voice.

"Is everything on schedule, Josie?"

She looked around at her peers. They nodded with big smiles. "I think we'll be fine, PJ. Just make sure you and Doc stay in the shallow cave while we decorate. We'll send someone to get you when we're ready, okay?"

"I'll do my best." I tucked the clipboard under my arm. "Any questions?" I asked the rest of them.

"We're cool," Donny said. "Don't worry, we'll get our work done and be ready to boogie in short order."

I grinned at them. "I've no doubt about the latter part of that comment. Okay, dismissed. Let's get to work."

Kim was sitting on the ledge outside the cave waiting for me.

"Hey." I looked for signs of worry or concern on her face. "You okay?"

She took a deep breath. "As ready as I'll ever be, I guess. It helps to have you with me, though."

We walked in and approached the final resting place of our Amazons.

I knelt and compared their positions with the Polaroid photos we had taken on our first trip inside. "Looks like this skull should be turned slightly." I pointed to the photo for Kim's comments.

She looked at the ground and the picture and took out her notebook. "I took measurements. Give me a second to find the sketch with the data attached."

I rubbed my hands on my cargo shorts. "Take your time. We want to get it just right."

"Yes," Kim murmured. "We want everything in perfect order."

We continued to maneuver the remains and associated artifacts into position. Kim put the dagger into its proper place and we stood back to survey the entire area. She had kept up a steady conversation with me while we worked. I was relieved to know that she was present with me in body...and spirit.

We had not been in total agreement about the media events that would occur as word of the discovery spread to the outside world. Kim promised one Phoenix television station an exclusive interview and taping session. Father had his own ideas about the grand announcement. As long as we had nothing concrete to report, we had stalled everyone. Now, we had proof. We could no longer keep this amazing find to ourselves. My father, the local area, and the whole world must see what Kim and her crew had found...and soon.

After several hours of work, I noticed Kim had grown quiet. She took a few swallows of water and sat back on her heels, staring off into the dark corners of the cave.

"You okay?" I asked, crouching beside her. "Want to go outside for a bit of air?"

She shook her head. "I'm fine."

Why don't I believe you?

"Kim, I can certainly understand if this is getting to you. I can visualize them now, too, after the facial reconstruction and what you told me of your dreams. Are you seeing them again? Feeling their pain?"

She shook her head slowly. "No, not that exactly. I just..."

"Talk to me, Kim.... Please." I didn't know whether to touch her...whether it would make things better or worse. "Are you having second thoughts about any of this?"

She stared at me for several seconds. "I don't have any doubts about these women, if that's what you mean. I know who they were and what they represent to me...and to all of us in the field of archaeology. My search is over. My prayers and questions have been answered by what is here in this cave. I should be jumping for joy...and I guess, in some ways I am. But..."

"But, it troubles you, too. I can see that when I look at you. Please tell me what it is. Let me share it with you."

She took my hand. "It's such a personal thing, PJ. I don't really expect you to understand all of it. This quest I've been on has taken me so many years. It's consumed me for so long that it's hard to realize that it is over."

Her expression was so bereft, I wanted to wrap her in my arms and make everything all better. I did put my hand on her shoulder. "You're wondering what will happen next?" My voice was husky.

A tear slid down her cheek. "Yeah. Where do I go from here? My life's ambition was to find evidence of The Lost Tribe of Amazons. Now, we have. What's next?"

I brushed the tear away with my thumb. *How about a new love, huh? And it could last a lifetime...if you're willing to give me the chance.*

189

"It is going to be okay. You'll see. There's plenty more to do for you."

She sniffed and nodded. "I guess."

"Sure. You'll have a book to write, talk shows to appear on...maybe a trip to Disney World."

"What?" She stared at me as if I had two heads. "Disney World?"

I laughed. "Take it easy. I just threw that in to see if you were still listening."

Kim grabbed me by the shoulders and shook me. "You're crazy, do you know that?" Then, she smiled. "Thank you, PJ. I don't know how I'd keep my sanity without you and your humor."

I took a deep breath. "Well, I do have a few ideas of my own to discuss with you."

She let her hand slide down to my waist where it rested gently against my hip. "Do your ideas concern the project?"

"Uh...no. Actually, my ideas concern--"

"Yoo Hoo! Docs! It's time for lunch!" There was a scraping of boots against the rocks and Laine poked her head inside.

Damn...Damn...Damn. Timing. We've got to work on timing.

Kim stood up and I joined her. "I'd like to hear your ideas, PJ," she said. "Perhaps another time."

I picked up my pack. "Sure, Kim. Another time."

Sandy lingered outside the main tent. He held a long box behind his back, so I dropped a step or two behind Kim as we walked along the path.

"Doc, I think these are for you," Sandy said, whipping the box in front of him with a flourish.

"You're kidding," she said. When she read the card and opened the box to find a dozen red roses, she was dumbfounded.

Laine read the card aloud. " 'With all best wishes for a Happy Birthday, Frederick Curtis and the Curtis Foundation.' "

"How did he know?" Kim looked at me, suspicion glinting in her dark eyes.

I held up my hands in surrender. "It wasn't me, honest. I didn't even know it was your birthday. He has spies everywhere."

Sandy grinned at both of us. "Oh, PJ, something came for you. I put it inside on the computer table."

Oh, my gift for Kim. I'll just tuck it away for a quiet time later when we're alone.

"Thanks, Sandy. Let's get our lunches, shall we."

We let Kim go inside first. When she heard the chorus of 'Surprise!' followed rapidly by an off key rendition of "Happy Birthday," her expression was priceless. Josie took pictures so we'd have them for posterity.

The tent was crammed with bodies, balloons, streamers, cake, sodas and sandwiches. All of it created a warm, festive atmosphere.

Kim sat on the cot and pulled me down beside her. The students clustered around us. "Did you have anything to do with this?" Her tone was gruff, but her eyes sparkled in delight.

"Hardly a thing, I swear."

James thrust a package into Kim's hands. "We...uh...didn't have much money, Doc. I wish we could afford to show you how much you really mean to us. Anyway, happy birthday."

Kim looked around at her students. "Really, you didn't have to do this. The party was plenty."

"Open it!" Mike called.

Kim chuckled. "Still in a hurry to get out of here, are you, Mike?"

We all laughed and watched her tear the wrapping off the gift. It was a hand-tooled leather belt with a silver and turquoise buckle. I gave James a nod and a 'thumbs up.' "Nice choice, big guy." He blushed.

"It's beautiful. Thank you all so much." Kim admired the craftsmanship in the belt and turned the buckle over. "Goodness, you had it engraved." She held it up to the light. "Amazons Rule...November 1999." She stood and gave them each a hug.

"Okay, PJ," Laine said when Kim sat back down. "It's your turn."

191

Dewey found the package on the computer table and passed it to me. "Well, I thought maybe I'd give it to her in a little--"

"Aww. C'mon," Josie urged. "We're really curious."

I shrugged and handed the box to Kim.

"Oh my goodness, PJ. You shouldn't have." The group 'oohed' and 'ahhhed' when she held up the gift. "It's a Krater, isn't it? A Greek mixing bowl for wine and water."

"A replica, yeah."

"And it looks like there are Amazons on the side." She held up the red and black bowl so the group could see the figures depicted on the exterior.

"It's an exact copy of a Greek Krater that the Boston Fine Arts Museum has on display. The original was created about 450 BC in Athens. The black figures are thought to show Amazon women fighting a monster of some sort."

Kim studied it intently. "A griffin, perhaps."

I shrugged. "Maybe so."

She put it down carefully and gave me a hug and a kiss on the cheek. "Thank you. It's perfect."

"You're welcome," I mumbled against her shoulder.

Just perfect. I couldn't help my frustration. My perfect moment was lost…again.

Chapter Seventeen

I lay in the moonlit silence of the motor home, unable to sleep. Pup was on the floor beside the bed. He was snuffling and twitching, dreaming, I suppose, of being the Alpha Male, running free with the pack. "I wish, Pup, that I could return you to the wild where you belong."

He opened one eye and looked at me as if questioning my comment. He was content, I think, to be with me. And where it had once been just he and I ... now there was PJ. He was the Alpha Male and we were his pack.

The dial on my wristwatch glowed ... a dim beacon in the otherwise dark room. It was well past midnight and even though I was tired, I could not go to sleep. My mind, a confusing jumble of thoughts, kept me awake and restless.

Yesterday had been quite a day. The crew, bless them, had surprised me with an on-site birthday party. I don't recall ever having had a birthday party, surprise or otherwise.

Usually my birthday passed without a second thought on my part. Yesterday's party in a tent on the side of a mountain made up for all the lost years. It had affected me more than I wanted to admit.

And, PJ, that beautiful Krater. That's a gift that would normally be reserved for that special someone ... not your boss.

Despite the fact that we were closer after having survived a stormy beginning, I was still her boss, nothing more, nothing less.

Well, yes, it's more than that, isn't it, PJ? We're friends.

You've seen me through some dark days. You've stood by me when I was at my most vulnerable, when I was overwhelmed by the scope of our discovery. You were there, still are, if I need you, to handle the day-to-day operations of the project.

I scrambled out of bed and pulled on my Acorns, the slipper socks I found so comfortable for padding about indoors.

193

It was warm enough that I didn't need to pull on a sweatshirt. I was comfortable as is, in my faded green, sleep scrubs.

Pup yawned and stretched. "Sorry, fella," I said, running my hand through his ruff. "Just cause I can't sleep doesn't mean you shouldn't."

When I opened the privacy drapes that covered the windshield of the motor home, the light of the full moon streamed through the glass and spilled over into the interior of my mobile headquarters. My monitor caught the moon's reflection and glowed ... a ghostly eye inviting exploration. But, I was not in an exploratory mood. I just wanted to be here now and in the moment.

Ever since we discovered the remains, I've been in a state of confusion, not knowing who I really was. I need to know myself again and be who I am now ... in this world and in this time.

I moved mechanically to the stove and put on the teakettle then I turned to the cabinet and pulled out a mug and a box of Carnation Instant Chocolate. By the time I had split open a package of powder and found a bag of mini marshmallows, the kettle was whistling for my attention. There was something inexplicably comforting about making hot chocolate, even when it's done the easy way, with instant ingredients.

I was aware of the fragrance of roses. Frederick's bouquet of red roses stood on the table, a surprise gift from the man who had, by way of a grant, turned my desire to continue my search in the Superstitions into reality.

How thoughtful of you, Frederick, to remember my birthday, yet how thoughtless you are with your daughter. She needs you in her corner ... you are her father after all.

I nursed the steaming mug of chocolate in a small square hot-pad and took it up front where I settled in the passenger seat, swiveling it so I could face the enormous, bulk of Superstition Mountain. It was a beautiful sight with the moonlight playing hide and seek among the mounds and gullies that dotted the mountain's surface.

Sitting there alone in the motor home, my safe place, a home away from home, and sipping hot chocolate in the light of

194

the moon, I was myself and in the moment. Where else would I be? Except it wasn't enough. My mind struggled to stray while I fought to keep it confined.

I gazed at the mountain ... my mind wandering. I thought about Laine and Josie camping out up there, in their favorite side canyon. They had invited PJ to join them and she had accepted. I wondered how they were doing, the three of them? Were they asleep, all snuggly rolled up in their sleeping bags or were they sitting up, talking girl talk, and sharing the light of the same moon that illuminated my space? Why was I feeling hurt because PJ hadn't invited me to go with them?

"Come off it, Kim Blair. You know you had work to do. PJ knew it, too, and even if she hadn't ... so what?"

So I've finally come to this; talking to myself and feeling put out because my Assistant Director didn't see fit to invite me for a sleep over. We had shared many nights on the mountain, so why the big deal?

Pup crawled into the small space at my feet. "You old softie, you'd be a lapdog if I'd let you," I said, uncrossing my leg, allowing him more room.

When Pup had settled down, my thoughts turned again to PJ. I hadn't wanted her in my life, yet she had landed there with all the delicacy of an asteroid crashing into downtown Phoenix. I chuckled to myself. Despite earlier disagreements, she had become a close friend and to some degree, a confidant.

I loved the way she stretched in the sunshine after working in the cave and how she'd run her fingers through her hair ... hair the color of the sunrise on a spring morning. If I were an artist, I could capture her image in a painting that would hang on my bedroom wall where the sunlight would illuminate it by day and the moonlight at night.

Perhaps, PJ, sometime when you're not looking, I'll take a picture and have it enlarged and framed and put it on my bedside stand. I smiled to myself. I wonder what you'd say about that?

"Oh Pup," I said, trying to move my foot, which was going to sleep beneath the bulk of his muscular shoulder, "what do I do about her?"

PJ had been on my mind a lot lately and I was not happy finding myself attracted to a colleague. I had never before mixed business with pleasure. This was new for me, having a colleague for a friend, and she was that. It bothered me though, that she had witnessed my vulnerabilities. On the other hand, her friendship had gotten me through some tough days.

Although Terry had been, in some respects, a colleague in that she was a scientist, I had never worked with her, nor was I likely to … her field of expertise was different from mine.

PJ was straight and that put us on different sides of a fence that I was not about to step across.

Whatever my feelings for you, PJ, they must remain just that, very personal and private, shared with no one, except myself. You must never know that I think of you in that way.

I was aware that my feelings would not make my working with her easy. If she had any idea that I thought of her in that way… This was a woman who liked men, one who would feel threatened by another woman's attraction to her.

What the hell am I thinking about anyway? Is it that I'm frustrated?

I thought about the last time I had made love. I was still with Terry … just before our breakup, and that was what … four years ago, or five?

That's a long time, and I'm not dead from the head down…I have my needs, but it doesn't give me the right to be thinking of forbidden fruit. Besides, that which follows love is spelled h-u-r-t.

Pup opened one eye as if to tell me I should be in bed and asleep. "I know, my friend, she has us both by the heartstrings." He was right, of course, about bed. I got up, rinsed my mug, and crawled back under the covers.

Despite having had a restless night, I was up early. I had not dreamed of the Amazons. In fact I had not dreamed of them at all since we discovered the first cave. I understood that the dreams were no longer necessary. Marna and Leeja and the others had shown themselves to me. They were so much more than remains. Instead of bones I saw two dark haired warrior women with olive complexions and strong bodies. And now, since the facial reconstructions, they were as familiar to me as anyone could be. Their story was, in some ways, my story.

I could not explain the fact that Marna looked so much like me or why I identified so strongly with her. Were she and I one and the same? Had we, through some quirk of time and space, come together with ourselves after centuries apart? It didn't make any sense, but perhaps it wasn't supposed to ... yet....

One thing I was sure of was that Marna, Leeja, and the others were real. They had at one time walked upon this earth together, fought together, and more importantly, Marna and Leeja had loved each other. Their love had been so strong, so much a part of them, that they could not continue on alone. Leeja could not journey into the afterworld without Marna any more than Marna could have continued in this life without Leeja. As death overtook one, so the other followed, anointing her lover's body with blood and holding her forever in her arms.

What must it be like, I wonder, to have a love such as that?

The glow of a new dawn was touching the shoulder of the mountain when I stepped into the shower. The warm spray felt good after a night of tossing and turning, and no real rest. I was sure though that it wouldn't do anything for the dark circles under my eyes.

Thoughts of PJ crowded into my mind. Our momentous discovery had changed her, too, in ways I was sure she hadn't yet shared with me.

PJ, could you have been Leeja in my past life? Do you even feel a connection to her?

I didn't think she did, not in that way.

When I looked in the cave that first time and saw the two of them in an eternal embrace, I knew but wouldn't admit that Marna and I were connected, and that a window had opened, bringing us together. They had caught up with me and had forced me to confront a past that I had not been aware existed.

Is that what my life-long search had been all about?

I shrugged my shoulders and moved my head in a circular and side-to-side motion, ending up with my eyes closed and my face to the spray. I could feel my knotted muscles loosening up and the stiffness evaporating. I thought about the time that PJ had massaged my back. The woman had fingers of magic. When I opened my eyes, she was there, an apparition in the steam filled cubicle.

I quickly stepped out of the now cooled shower and grabbed the towel from the rail. My image, another year older, stared back at me from the full length, closet mirror. I was in good shape for my age. Working outside agreed with me and was apparently all the exercise I needed to keep me fit. I didn't have an ounce of fat on my body despite a not always perfect diet. I was brown as a berry from exposure to the sunshine.

I towel dried my graying hair, applied a little styling gel to tame it, and brushed it into place.

I saw PJ in the mirror …stepping out of the shower behind me and taking a soft, rose-colored towel off the rail. Her hair looked darker now that is was wet. Drops of water clung to her pert breasts … catching the morning light. Her still wet abdomen was taut. She didn't dry herself off as I did, with a good rubdown. Instead, she caressed her body with the towel… "NO! STOP!"

I was to meet PJ, later; at her hotel … we were going to spend Thanksgiving together. How could I look her in the eye after having lost control of my thoughts like that? It wasn't going to be easy.

I threw my towel into a corner and dressed hurriedly.

Chapter Eighteen

"I wish I'd insisted that Kim join us last night. That side canyon you two found is beautiful."

Laine poured more hot water into my mug. I reused my teabag and added two heaping teaspoons of sugar, taking a moment to stir my tea and collect my thoughts. It was Thanksgiving morning and soon we'd scatter to our various holiday activities.

Laine, Josie and I were sprawled on the cot and camp chairs in the main tent, enjoying our breakfast. The stove in there was dependable and familiar.

Everything about this tent is familiar. The only thing missing is Kim.

Josie shook her head. "One thing we've learned about Kim is that you can't make her do anything she doesn't want to and if she thinks work is more important, then that's that."

"Besides, PJ, you were telling us about life at Boston University." Laine's eyes glinted with amusement. She and Josie had regaled me with stories of college life at the University of Arizona and the dating scene on campus. Now, it was my turn.

"Okay, where was I? Oh, yeah…B.U. Beach. They called it that because you could lie down on the knoll near the road and the cars passing by would sound like the crash of the waves at the ocean. Or so Ted told me."

"And did it?" Josie asked before biting into a crisp slice of bacon.

"I never found out. When I stretched out, he climbed on top of me and I had to wrestle my way out of his clutches. What a pig!"

The girls laughed and I joined in.

Laine finished her meal and stood to gather our dirty dishes. "Boston University doesn't sound much different from the University of Arizona."

"It was years ago," I said, handing her my plate, "maybe things have changed."

Josie looked at Laine and they giggled. "I doubt it, PJ."

Laine nodded her agreement.

We had enjoyed our night on the mountain. I kept thinking of our leader, though, and how much I missed her company.

I should have invited her. I might have convinced her to join us, even though she said she had computer data to crunch. She works too hard. And today's her birthday. She shouldn't have to work on her birthday.

The girls and I had chatted about everything from Arizona's early inhabitants to where the Lost Dutchman, Jacob Waltz, might have stashed his gold. Beside the courses they were taking at the University of Arizona, books, movies and boyfriends, I'd even managed to wrestle a few facts about Kim out of them that I hadn't known before.

Both Laine and Josie had taken Kim's classes as undergraduates. They were impressed with her ability as a lecturer and her vast knowledge. Laine was especially intrigued with Kim's expertise in the field of dendrochronology. From what they told me, Kim had been instrumental in establishing a nationally recognized facility at the university for the study of tree ring dating. My research into Kim's background told me her dissertation had been in that field, but I had no idea she was so well known and so respected. I guess I should have realized that UA would have some good resources since A. E. Douglass was at the university when he developed the technology during the 1920's.

Why am I surprised she never mentioned this to me? She's full of mystery and so closed mouthed about her accomplishments.

"Sandy isn't like that, though," Josie said after a few moments of silent thought.

"Like what?" I'd lost the train of our discussion.

"Like Ted." Her cheeks flushed with the intensity of her comment. "He's not a pig."

Ah ... she's got a crush on the cowboy. "No, he isn't," I assured her.

She cast a glance at Laine who was busy washing our dishes. We found dishtowels and helped with the cleanup. Josie took a few deep breaths and forged ahead with the topic as we worked. "You know, PJ, I used to be so jealous of you when you first got here. Sandy followed you everywhere." She held my gaze, the dishtowel bunched in a tight fist. "It is over between you, isn't it?"

"There was never really anything there to begin with, Josie. He's a wonderful guy and I love him dearly, but not that way."

"Really?" Laine looked over at me. "I'm surprised to hear that's all it was. He used to watch you all the time in camp when he thought you weren't looking. Josie tried everything to get his attention, but he had eyes for you alone."

Josie's cheeks still burned. She slapped Laine with the towel. "Hey, that's enough, pal. Quit telling all my secrets."

They gave each other playful shoves.

"Sandy and I had a talk and decided to be friends and colleagues, nothing more. It was best for both of us. So, if you want him, Josie, you have my blessings…just treat him right, hear?"

She heaved a sigh of relief and returned my grin. "Absolutely."

We packed our food items, dishes and utensils away and went back outside to find some flat rocks to sit on and relax in the fresh, morning air. The sun's rays had gained a measure of warmth just in the hour or two that we'd been awake. The rest of the day held the promise of sunshine and glorious opportunity.

"Ya know, I wonder about Doc sometimes." Laine lowered her voice as if the object of her comment was lurking about the campsite. A tendril of curly, blond hair tickled her cheek and she tucked it back behind her ear.

"Wonder *what*?" I asked, my muscles tensing, ready to come to Kim's defense.

She gestured, making a wide sweep of our tent and campsite. "Her life away from this project. She's so private, PJ. It's not natural. Since you two have become friends, she's opened up a lot more, let herself relax and have fun. We can all see how good it's been for her to have you to talk with, but ... I wonder if she has a real life ... a boyfriend, ya know ... a secret lover, or something?"

I coughed. "Whew! That's kinda personal, don't you think?"

Josie shook her head. "We're not trying to be nosy, PJ. We love Doc. We just want her to be happy."

"Oh, I'm sure--"

"Ya know, several years ago, there was a rumor going around that she was romantically involved with a woman anthropologist."

Josie nodded. "I heard about that, too, Laine. I wonder if it was true?"

I cleared my throat. "Well, I'm sure it's none of our--"

"Wait, PJ." Laine's hand touched my arm. "Don't misunderstand. Josie and I don't care one way or the other about her sexual preferences. We're only worried that she's so alone all the time with just that big wolf for company."

"Yeah," Josie added. "Pup is a wonderful animal, but Kim is too terrific a person to miss out on love and friendship in her life. That's all we're saying."

"Okay. I understand." I brushed an imaginary bit of dirt off the cuff of my cargo pants. "But, don't expect any juicy tidbits from me. I don't think she's involved with anyone right now, but she doesn't exactly tell me everything."

Josie smacked her thighs. "We appreciate your position, PJ. And, we won't go any further with this discussion."

"Right," Laine added. "Besides, we've got to get going." She stood and pulled Josie up beside her.

I got to my feet hastily. "Um... I was wondering what you two were doing for Thanksgiving. Didn't Sandy invite you to his mom's for dinner? I think he's taking several of the guys over there."

Josie sighed. "Yeah, he asked us, but ... I uh ... felt a bit nervous going there with so many people ... and his parents and all."

Laine laughed. "She'd rather have Sandy all to herself."

"Oh, stop it!" Josie punched her friend's shoulder. "Laine Watkins, you just wait until Jimmy gets home on leave and then we'll see who's making jokes."

From our overnight chat session I had learned that Laine's high school sweetheart was an Army Communications Specialist, stationed in Germany. Laine flushed and held up her hands in surrender. "Okay, okay. Truce. I'm sure PJ doesn't want to hear any more about our romances."

I grinned. "Oh, I don't know. It might be very entertaining."

"Or not," both of them said in unison and we laughed.

"So, if you aren't going to Sandy's, where are you going?"

"Oh, we have a big day planned, don't we, JoJo." Laine grinned at her friend.

"Ah, sure ... we do." Josie shrugged. "I guess it's no big secret. Most of us are staying here in the area for the simple reason that we can't afford to go home for Thanksgiving. Laine's from Virginia and I'm from Delaware. It's too expensive for us to fly home for such a short time."

I paused in mid-stride. "Oh...I see. I'm sorry. I never considered that possibility."

"Don't feel sorry for us, we've got plans," Laine assured me. "Just not real big ones."

We went inside the tent, picked up our gear, and sauntered along the path to the trailhead parking lot.

"So, what *are* the plans?" I asked.

"We bought a couple of frozen dinners ... turkey and stuffing, of course, which we'll 'nuke' in the apartment microwave for our feast." Laine gave Josie's shoulder a hug, which her friend returned.

"And, then, if we're not too full and over stimulated from that," Josie added, "we'll probably go to a matinee in Mesa. *The Sixth Sense* is playing ..."

"Or we could see the new James Bond adventure," Laine said. "We haven't quite decided yet."

We continued our trek while I wrestled with an idea.

Why hadn't I considered the crew's financial status before this?

I remembered Mike teasing me about travel plans the day before. He had taken a bus to Denver for his holiday. Sandy very thoughtfully provided a dinner invitation for the rest of the guys.

These students have to watch their expenses. Perhaps there's a way to make things a little easier for them in the future. I need to do some research on the subject. For now, though ...what do I do? How do I help these two?

I pictured them shoving trays of cardboard into a microwave, chewing tasteless clumps of food, and shuddered.

I can't let them spend Thanksgiving like that. It's a time for friends and family to share with each other. Kim would agree with me. I know I was hoping for some quality time alone with her, but hell, it's a big suite and maybe...just maybe, I can figure out a way to make Laine and Josie happy and get Kim to myself as well.

"Say, you two ... I have another idea. How would you like to spend your day in a suite at the Casa Grande? There's a big TV, VCR, CD player, two bedrooms, two baths, one with Jacuzzi ...oh, and an Olympic size swimming pool ..."

Laine looked at me in astonishment. "Are you kidding?"

"We'd kill for an invitation like that." Josie grinned.

"Oh, you don't have to do anything that rash, just pack your swimsuits if you want to use the pool and come to the Sonora Suite at the hotel around three. Kim and I are having a turkey dinner with all the trimmings and you are welcome to join us."

"Wow!" Josie looked at Laine who was grinning. "I think you can count on us, PJ. If you're sure?"

"I am."

"But, what about Kim?" Laine asked. "Is it okay with her?"

I laughed. "I'm certain she'll be fine with it."

We finished the walk to our cars with firm plans to meet in the lobby at three o'clock. I called Kim while they were still in the parking lot and she assured them it would be a great treat to have them join us. In fact, she sounded quite relieved by the idea.

The staff at the Casa Grande went all out to create a dining experience that was a treat for our eyes as well as our stomachs. They set a festive table with dried flowers, candles and ceramic figurines of a pilgrim couple. Real china plates, crystal wine goblets and linen tablecloth and napkins added an elegant touch to the overall ambiance.

The best part was the aroma that filled the room when the wait staff uncovered the stainless steel trays. With great gusto, we tucked into the turkey, stuffing, sweet potatoes, beans, cranberry relish, rolls and pumpkin pie topped with thick whipped cream.

Conversation was sparse while we devoted our attention to the meal, but once we had stuffed ourselves, we gathered in the living area to relax on the sectional sofa, with more wine or tea and coffee.

I put some CD's in the player, lighted the candles and we stretched out.

"I brought a selection of music with me from Boston, so feel free to play whatever you like," I told them. "There's some Beatles, Bruce Springsteen, Beach Boys, Eileen Ivers, Anne Murray and I think I even threw in some classical selections."

Kim grinned at me. "You didn't actually throw them did you?"

"Figure of speech, I assure you." I sorted through my stack. "Here's Dvorak and Mozart--"

"What do you have of Anne Murray?" Kim asked.

"I've got some early stuff and a Greatest Hits I'm sure." I shuffled the stack.

"I've always liked her singing," Kim said.

"Who's Eileen Ivers?" Laine asked. "I don't think I've ever heard of her."

I picked out my copy of *Crossing the Bridge* and handed it to her. "She plays a mean fiddle. You'd probably know her from Riverdance."

Both girls nodded. "Oh sure," Josie said. "All that Celtic music and dancing. Now I remember. That might be a little too lively for after our dinner, though."

"What do you want to hear, Doc?" Laine asked. "It's your birthday, after all."

Kim groaned. "Don't remind me."

I looked at her. "It hasn't been that bad, has it?"

"No, it's been wonderful. The best one I've had in a long, long time. I love my gifts and that party yesterday... How did you all keep it a secret?"

The girls chuckled.

"Our secret," said Josie.

"Right," added Laine. "And we'll never tell." She winked at me.

"I must say, I can't remember ever getting such nice presents," Kim said. "The belt is very well-crafted and I'll treasure the buckle for years." She tilted her head in my direction. "That Krater is a beauty, PJ. You really shouldn't have done that."

"Sure I should. It was the perfect gift for an Amazon hunter, don't ya think?"

"Perfect," she said.

"I remember one birthday, I got this cute little kitten." Josie smiled at the memory. "It was white with a brown spot on its back, like a mound of mashed potatoes with gravy in the center."

Laine groaned. "Did you have to mention food?"

We laughed.

"I got a pair of inline skates one year for my birthday, but my brother tried them on a week later and got them all scuffed up."

Josie looked at her friend. "Which brother was that?"

"Peter," Laine replied. "He was three years younger than me. I used to call him Peter the Pest. Now he's six foot, two hundred and ten pounds."

"And really cute," Josie added. "I've seen his picture."

"I got a tattoo for my twenty-first birthday," I said, and immediately regretted it.

"Whoa!" Laine and Josie sat up and Kim gave me a curious look.

"Oh, Geez." My face felt warm. "Let's just forget I said that, okay?"

"Oh no." Laine shook her head. "We're not letting that go so easily. Right, JoJo?"

Her friend leaned closer to me. "What is it and where is it?"

I looked at Kim with a silent plea for help. She just smiled at my discomfort. "I'm afraid you got yourself into this, PJ. You'd better confess all."

Oh, Hell. What would it hurt? If I tell them where it is, they'll probably believe all those tabloid stories, though. Gawd, sometimes my mouth gets me into so much trouble.

"Well, it's a small one...a shamrock."

"And the location?" Laine persisted.

I bit my lower lip and tugged at some loose strands of hair at the back of my neck. "Um...it's uh...covered up most of the time." I could feel the heat on my cheeks.

"Aw, c'mon, PJ, tell us." Josie grinned and looked at Kim. "Make her tell, Doc."

Kim shrugged. "If she doesn't want to reveal her secrets--"

I leaned toward her and whispered in her ear. "It's on my butt."

She swallowed. "Oh, really?"

"Well?" Laine asked.

"What did she say?" Josie added.

Kim smirked. "Sorry, that's classified information."

"Thanks, boss." I smiled at her.

"No problem," Kim assured me. "Now, I suggest you play some more music and we'll change the subject."

"Shoot." Josie glanced at her friend. "Somebody pulled rank on us."

I stood up. "Well, if there's no objection, I'll put on some Anne Murray. My mother got me hooked on her music. She used to sing along with her records and tapes and attend her concerts whenever possible."

Kim smiled at me. "Your mother had good taste."

I returned her smile, losing myself in the moment, forgetting anyone else was in the room until Josie yawned.

"Um, PJ, would you mind if I stretched out on one of those spare beds? I'm getting so sleepy after that meal."

"Me too," Laine added. "I noticed there were twin beds in the guest room and I'm about to doze off here."

"Help yourselves, ladies. 'Mi casa es su casa' as they say in these parts."

They stumbled off to the guest bedroom. "And maybe later, you'd like to try the pool," I called after them.

"Later," Josie mumbled.

"Much later," Laine added.

Kim and I stretched out side-by-side on the sofa. We smiled at each other.

"A tattoo on your butt, huh?" Her grin was almost seductive, but I'm sure I was mistaken.

She's just teasing me…and I'm enjoying it.

"Yeah, it was kind of a dare. And I did it when I got to be twenty-one so Father couldn't stop me."

"I see."

I made a face. "And I had a few beers for courage."

"Naturally."

I cleared my throat. "Not one of my more adult decisions, I assure you."

Kim laughed. "Could be worse, I guess. Could be some guy's name or something."

I shook my head. "No, that's never gonna happen. Now, if you don't mind, I'd like to drop this subject. Put it behind me…so to speak."

We chuckled at my inadvertent pun. Anne Murray finished her last song and the next selection was Dvorak's *New World Symphony*.

"Oh, I love this," Kim murmured.

"Me too."

We listened for several minutes and then I remembered something I wanted to ask her.

"Kim, how come you never told me you were so involved with the Dendrochronology Center at Arizona? I had to learn about it from Laine and Josie."

She shrugged. "Oh, I helped out a bit a few years ago. I haven't kept in touch with them lately, though."

"Well, it sounded to me like you were one of the founders of the facility."

"No, not really. I worked with a group and did some contacting, wrote some grant proposals, you know ... that sort of thing."

I sighed. "Kim, you're way too modest."

"Are you interested in the tree ring dating methods, PJ?"

I shook my head. "Not that per se, but I'm fascinated by the bristlecone pines used for much of the testing. You worked with them a great deal, didn't you?"

Her eyes sparkled with fond memories. "In California, yes. You wouldn't believe the majesty of those trees. I spent some of the best times of my life doing fieldwork with those grand specimens."

"I'll bet it was a humbling experience to be in the presence of something so old."

"Exactly. They look so gnarled and lifeless and yet, there's growth on them. They're like living monuments to our history, silent sentinels of our past."

I felt sudden goose bumps on my arms. "That's so poetic, Kim. I can tell you were, and still are, affected by your work with them."

She thought a moment and then looked at me intently. "Would you like me to show you a few of them? We could take a short trip, probably a weekend would do...to California where I worked, or even Colorado. There are several great old trees on Windy Ridge. The trees even have names."

"I'd love to go. Thank you so much for asking me."

She smiled. "The oldest one is called Methuselah. It's over four thousand years old, but the ones in the Windy Ridge area are only eight hundred to a thousand years old."

"Only," I murmured with a grin, catching her enthusiasm.

She rubbed her chin in thought. "Seems to me, the oldest one in Colorado is near Griffey and it's about twenty-five hundred years old."

"Kim, it really doesn't matter which ones we see. I'll leave it to your judgment."

Really, any place at all sounds like a great adventure if you're going to be there.

"Okay, then, we'll set something up. You'll need me to guide you. Most of the trees are not marked in any way."

I leaned closer. "Why aren't they identified?"

"Security. The park service and government want to protect them from vandals and relic hunters."

"Oh, I see. You're right. Somebody someplace would want to chop them down and sell pieces for profit. They'd never let a little thing like being a national treasure stand in their way."

Kim beamed at me. "You understand perfectly. Some of those trees were seedlings when the Pyramids were created and some stupid jerk with a chainsaw would think nothing of removing them for all time. That doesn't even count what we'd lose in the ability to date wood out here in the west. Speaking as an archaeologist and as a conservationist, it infuriates me to think anybody could be so ruthless." Kim's eyes darkened in anger.

I got up and changed the CD's in the player. "I'm with you, Kim. Pot hunters, bone diggers, relic thieves and now those who would threaten the Bristlecone Pine … they're all scum and should be locked up."

Kim settled back on the sofa, her posture lost its angry tension. "Sorry, I got a little carried away with my devotion to the cause."

I relaxed, too. "No problem, I understand." *And I love it when you get passionate about a cause.*

"I think a change in the conversation is in order." Kim chuckled. "This has been the best Thanksgiving meal that I can remember. Thank you for making all this possible, PJ."

"My pleasure." I gazed into her deep brown eyes and glowed with happiness. "Don't forget, it's a birthday celebration, too."

"Ah, yes. That part I'd like to forget."

I shook my head. "Well, I won't let you. Happy Birthday, Kim. Are you having a good day, so far?"

"The best. It's been wonderful."

I sighed. "Good."

"You, know, it was very kind of you to ask Josie and Laine to join us."

"Oh, Jesus!" I slapped my forehead. "I forgot my call to Jonathan!" I stood and walked to the desk where the phone rested. "I'll just be a few minutes. Some business I need to finish up. Relax and enjoy the music. There are earphones in the cabinet under the TV."

She gave me a bemused look, but plugged in the earphones and slipped them on, while I dialed the number of my accountant. He was an employee of my father's and I knew he'd be spending the holidays in Newport. I watched a dreamy smile appear on Kim's face as she listened. Her eyes closed in contentment.

You look so peaceful… and so beautiful by candlelight.

I sighed, punched in the number, and waited for Jonathan to answer his cell phone.

"Fletcher here," came the terse voice.

"PJ Curtis here," I mimicked his speech. "How's it going, Jonathan?"

"Hey there, sweet pea? Why aren't you with us?"

"Long story, I'm afraid. Listen; if you aren't too busy right now, can I go over that fax I sent you earlier?"

"I'm free as the wind, for you, sweetheart. Tell me what you need." His voice warmed with the usual paternal tone he used on me. I had known him forever it seemed and he had known me since I was in diapers … a fact he delighted in recounting to anyone who would listen.

"Can you get the money transferred like I requested?"

"Sure. No problem there. You want checks made out to those names you sent, and I should post them to the Foundation account."

"Yes, that's right."

"But, the money will actually come from your discretionary fund?"

"Yes, nobody needs to know the actual source. I think it will look better coming from the Curtis Foundation."

I heard him wheeze a bit as he made notes. No electronic notepads for Jonathan; he used a yellow legal tablet and scrawled his notes with a wide-tipped fountain pen. "No problemo. I can make some electronic transfers and Express Mail everything to you tomorrow if you like. You father has some documents going out then."

"Great. We still have lots to do here. Our next step is arranging for press coverage and publicity for the project, but I'm sure it won't be a problem if the checks come early."

"Do I tell your father ... or keep it confidential?"

"Hmm. I don't think he'll object. It isn't illegal, the money is mine from my trust fund, right?"

"Yes."

"Okay, then I don't care if you tell him or not. He can't change my mind, it's already made up."

He chuckled. "If you only knew how much you sounded like your mother just then, Priscilla."

I felt a rush of heat to my chest. "Thank you, Jonathan. That's a lovely compliment."

We talked for a few more minutes and then I replaced the receiver with a satisfied smile.

Kim was still stretched out on the sofa tethered by the earphone cord to whatever music soothed her soul. I watched for several minutes, admiring the view.

That's a very becoming blouse you're wearing. It fits you so well and the rich, burnished gold color gives your skin a healthy glow. I especially like the way your chest expands under the silky fabric. Gawd. I'm going to have to talk to you. I'm turning into such a pervert, admiring your chest.

I checked on the girls. They were asleep in the twin beds, so I closed the door and walked back to the sofa. As quietly as possible, I sank into the plush leather cushions and stretched out beside Kim. She stirred, but didn't open her eyes.

Okay. You're obviously still enjoying the music. I'll just wait until you finish and then we'll talk. Laine and Josie are safely tucked away. There's nothing to disturb us.

212

I yawned. My eyes seemed full of sand. Everything grew soft and hazy; my mind focused on the warm body only inches away from my own.

Something firm pressed against my hip and I came awake as if surfacing from the depths of a deep, sensual dream. When I shifted and stretched, my thigh nudged Kim's.

My God, I fell asleep next to her. I'm practically on top of her. How embarrassing...how mortifying...how pleasant and comfortable. Why didn't she wake me up or push me over to the side of the sofa?

I let my hand graze her hip. Kim gave a quiet moan and turned toward me, her face close to mine, her lips parted slightly in sweet temptation.

Jesus, she's asleep. I guess she's been asleep for some time. What do I do now?

I reached around her head and gently slipped the earphones off. Kim moaned again, louder this time. My brain entertained a warm and wicked thought.

What if I ... um ... just tried a tiny kiss? Right now, while she's sleeping. She'll never know and I've been dying to find out what it feels like.

What would I risk if I tried it?

The answer came back with jolting clarity.

Everything.

Is it worth it?

My body heat elevated. My back and chest grew damp with tense anticipation.

She won't stay asleep forever. Do I ... or don't I?

I leaned in as close as I dared, breathing in the scent of her hair. It was a spicy, fragrant herbal concoction. Her skin had a clean, warm essence that enticed me further. I took a huge breath and held it. My head tilted to just the right angle and then I touched my lips to hers. Tiny wisps of air escaped as I exhaled.

Incredible. They're so soft ... like velvet. Better than I imagined. And there's no stubble on her chin, no five-o'clock shadow, only smooth, tender skin. Look at those long eyelashes. Oh, God. I want to do it again.

213

Her mouth opened a fraction and I inhaled the aroma of pumpkin and cream.

Delicious.

I nibbled her bottom lip. She sighed and her lips responded, pushing with intensity against mine. I felt dizzy. The next sigh I heard ... was my own.

Passion flamed in my abdomen, spreading upward through my chest, making my breasts tingle.

I've got to stop... now. I've got to break this off, sit back, and act as if nothing happened.

Yeah, right.

I squeezed my eyes shut, concentrating on my heart rate, the alternating chills and fever coursing through my body and my overactive libido. Those stolen kisses, as brief as they were, nourished my soul like gentle rain over a desert arroyo.

I would never have believed I'd feel such intense pleasure from this. She's not even awake. Imagine what it would be like if--

There was a blast of moist of air against my cheek. When I opened my eyes, two startled brown ones stared back at me.

Oh, Shit! Shit ... Shit ... Shit.

She sat up quickly and I slid off the edge of the sofa onto the floor.

"Hey!" we both cried.

Kim stood up, fingers probing her lips, her expression dazed.

"What?" Her voice was husky. "Was I dreaming ... or did you just kiss me?"

My butt was bolted to the floor, my legs too weak to support me. I couldn't escape anyway. There was no place to hide ... nowhere to run.

"I ... uh ... I wanted to see ... that is, I had this overpowering urge ...You were sitting there ... and I didn't know you were asleep until ... but even if you--"

Exasperation knotted Kim's brow. "PJ, a simple answer will do, okay. Did you or did you not kiss me while I was sleeping?"

Oh God. You're in shock now, but when you get over that ... I'm toast.

I struggled to my feet. "Yeah ... I did ... um ... kiss you."

"I see." She took a deep breath. "I think I'd better go." She slipped her feet back into her shoes and picked up her bag and jacket.

"No ... Kim, please." I held up my hands. "Don't go, not like this. Let me explain. I've wanted to kiss you for a long time. I know I shouldn't have done it when you were asleep, but I just couldn't help myself."

I could have sworn you liked it as much as I did. Oh, shit, I've blown it. The realization of that fact produced a pain in my chest.

We moved in slow motion, two trains on a collision course, despite all attempts to avoid disaster, glancing at each other and then quickly away, evading even the slightest possibility of touching by accident. I murmured apologies; she gave vague, one syllable replies, all the time gathering her gear, moving toward the door.

She paused with her back against it, her hand on the knob. "PJ, you're a very attractive woman. Our friendship means a great deal to me, but I'm not going to let myself be used to satisfy your curiosity--"

"But, that's not--"

"And I won't become another name on your long list of conquests, just another notch on your bedpost. I'm going home now. I'll see you onsite Monday or whenever you return to work. I'm sure by that time, we will have forgotten this unfortunate situation."

She turned and opened the door.

"Kim, please don't go. Let me explain--"

"Thank you for a wonderful dinner. It ... uh ... it was a lovely birthday." She dipped her head and was gone.

I stood with my forehead pressed against the closed door, wishing like hell I could replay the last half hour. I slapped my palms against the wood, welcoming the stinging pain of despair.

Damn it! Why did I have to kiss her? Why didn't I stop sooner?

215

She did seem to enjoy it, though. I'm sure that was a good moan I heard.

It doesn't matter; she doesn't want to remember any of it. She wants to forget everything that happened.

How can I do that?

My body was numb; I acted purely by rote. I scribbled a note for the girls in case they woke before I did, assuming I could ever get to sleep now. I put an extra keycard with the note that told them to come and go as they pleased, use the pool, charge any meals to my account.

I wasn't sure what my plans were for the next day. In truth, I wasn't certain about any plans for any days. I turned out all the lights in the living area, blew out the candles, and made a weary trek to the master bedroom, snatching up a clean tee shirt and cotton, drawstring shorts for sleeping. I stripped off what I had been wearing, my clothing landing in a pile at the bathroom door. Sadness enveloped my body like a heavy robe.

I stared at myself in the mirror over the sink.

I gambled and I lost. Kim doesn't trust me now. I saw it in her eyes...the confusion, the uncertainty. When she first woke up, though, and realized what I had done, there was something else in her eyes ... need. There's a need in her ... and there's a need in me ...

My vision blurred. I bit down on my lower lip and turned to fumble with the shower faucet. Feeling thick, choking tears at the back of my throat, I stepped into the stall and let them mingle with the icy spray.

What do I do now ... about that need? Do I give up on us ... on our friendship ... on any love there might be between us? Or do I find Kim and force her to listen?

It was all too painful right now. I finished my punishing shower and rubbed my body dry. I dressed for bed, knowing full well that a long, tear-filled, sleepless night awaited me.

Chapter Nineteen

I stepped into the motor home and was greeted enthusiastically by Pup. He was such a good companion, always pleased to see me. I could always rely on his unconditional love. He didn't play the head games that we humans are apt to.

I dropped my shoulder bag onto the sofa and removed my jacket, hanging it in the closet. Stuff left lying around in the close confines of a motor home led to chaos. There was a place for everything and as long as everything was in place, living in such a small space was tolerable.

Why did I act like such an idiot, PJ, when you kissed me? I was aware of it. I liked it and even responded to it. You kissed me. So what! Why am I so afraid to admit any of that?

Because I'm afraid of being hurt again, that's why.

I undressed and caught sight of my naked body in the mirror.

Is there any chance that you, a young, extremely attractive and desirable woman could love me? I covered my breasts with my hands. *I wonder what it would be like if you ...?*

"No!"

My cry startled Pup. He growled ... his way of scolding me for my outburst.

"Sorry, friend," I whispered, pulling on my faded green, sleep scrubs.

I tossed and turned until the bed was a shambles, the covers in a heap. I couldn't turn off the replay of the kiss. It repeated over and over like a tape with no ending.

"Don't be an old fool," I told myself.

We had been in a romantic setting ... in a comfortable, nicely appointed suite. Soft music had been playing in the background; candles reflected flickering shadows on the walls. The stage had been set.

I should have been prepared, but I didn't think....

You were carried away in the moment, that's all ... a big meal and wine will do that ... cause a person to do strange and foolish things. I know it doesn't mean a thing.

Pup, who had been sleeping on the floor beside my bed, turned over and looked at me with just one eye open.

"She hasn't dated in a while, Pup, and she has needs." He ignored my profound statement and settled back to sleep. I tried to clear my mind, but the thoughts kept crowding in making sleep impossible.

It was easy to fantasize while lying there in the dark, but as fast as my mind wandered, I reined it in.

Perhaps, PJ, you think I can satisfy your physical needs since you don't have a man around at the moment. You think I don't know it's just curiosity on your part? Or is it that you think I'll jump at the chance to hop into bed with you. Having it on with the boss would be quite a notch on your bedpost. But you should have known better. You do now, don't you, after my hurried departure? You know I'm not about to satisfy your idle curiosity or any physical frustrations you might have, that I'm not one of your pick up and drop 'em suitors.

I don't go for one-night stands and a relationship is the last thing I need in my life, however tempting the prospect.

I went to sleep thinking about her impetuous act and how it would complicate our working relationship.

If only we could erase yesterday or pretend it never happened. I don't want to lose you, PJ, as an assistant, but how do we get around it? It would make life so much easier if you just didn't show up for work on Monday, or ever again.

On Friday morning, with the events of Thanksgiving Day still on my mind I prepared to head for the site. Since I had given my people time off to visit with family and friends, I was looking forward to being alone on the mountain.

It was a lovely, sunny morning, a little on the cool side, but it would soon warm up. I filled my backpack with enough food for the weekend, and while it was heavy, the framed pack fit snuggly on my back. Pup carried his own supplies in a doggie pack slung across his back like a saddlebag. The hike from the trailhead into the site felt good after an over indulgence of food and wine.

I was more comfortable with the Amazons now that the immediate shock of my likeness to Marna had settled into my consciousness. I gave up questioning the why or the how of it and just accepted the fact that she and I were somehow connected. I looked forward to spending time alone with them, perhaps even asking their advice about my situation with PJ.

I concentrated on my feet as they moved up the trail, one booted foot in front of the other. Tiny eruptions of trail dust accompanied each step. It was mesmerizing. This was travel at its most basic level … one step at a time.

Life should be lived that way, one step at a time.

Proof positive, I thought to myself, that the passage of even a single being changes the face of the landscape. I felt the tingle created by the combination of exercise, fresh air, and the touch of the warming sun.

This tingle I feel … it's almost like making love, but not exactly. Could you make me tingle, PJ?

"Stop!"

I was in trouble enough already without fantasizing and dismissed the thought.

I still hoped against hope that she would leave.

Once inside our tent headquarters, I stowed away the food supplies, lit the camp stove and put on the teakettle. Soon I was nursing a cup of steaming Earl Grey. I noticed the Krater that PJ had given me. I put down my cup and picked up the Krater. It was a special gift, one that would forever hold her in my heart, but one that I should not, under the circumstances, keep. I touched it to my lips and set it down on the table where it reflected an aura of its own.

Oh PJ, why did you have to go and spoil it all when we had been getting along so well?

I made my way over to Site One and climbed into the cave. I sat cross-legged beside the two Amazons and pulled on a lightweight, cotton glove before laying my hand on Marna's bony shoulder. I chose always to wear gloves when handling human remains to protect them from me rather than me from them. But sitting there alone in the silence of the cave, I didn't like the barrier the thin material created between us. I removed the glove. This time, when I put my hand on Marna's shoulder, it felt warm ... as if there was life there yet ... as if she knew I was there and was reacting to my presence. I felt strangely comfortable.

I thought about PJ. My question was directed at Marna. "If she doesn't take the initiative and resign on her own, do I have the right to insist? She's all I could ask for in an assistant, a damn fine archaeologist. You know that. You know how careful and respectful she was of you and Leeja, and the others. Do you know they are near by, that you're all together on this mountain?

"Oh, Marna, do I have the right to fire PJ for an indiscretion that has nothing to do with the job, and doesn't affect the project in any way? It's not as though I hadn't thought of kissing her myself ... on several occasions. She just acted on something I had fantasized about many times. The only difference is that she acted and I didn't. If I had taken the initiative, would the outcome have been any different?

"She'll probably come to the site to pick up her stuff, or maybe not. She might have one of the crew gather her things together and deliver them to the hotel. I'm sure she's as eager as I am to avoid a face-to-face confrontation."

Let's face it, that would be the least embarrassing way out for both of us.

"I wonder what you would do, Marna, in these same circumstances?"

I got up and waited until I was outside the cave before brushing the dust off my pants.

I returned to the tent and gathered some scribbled notes together, picked up my laptop, and a bottle of water to take outside where I could sit in the sunshine and start working on a report I needed to prepare for Frederick.

"Oh Geez!"

I stepped outside and found myself face to face with PJ. She had dark circles under her eyes and looked as though she had been crying. I could see she hadn't slept.

"Kim, uh … I have to apologize …"

"I didn't expect to see you this morning."

PJ teetered from one foot to the other. "I didn't know if you'd be here, but I had to come … to try to explain."

She was struggling with herself, and I wouldn't or couldn't help her.

I wanted more than anything to reach for her and hold her and tell her that I wanted her more than she could ever imagine. But I was terrified of what would happen if I gave in to my feelings. I closed my eyes and pushed away the desire that threatened to get the better of me.

"Kim, are you listening to me?"

"Sorry, I was distracted."

"You sure as hell were." PJ was angry and embarrassed. "I'm trying to explain my actions. This is important to me."

I took a step backwards, widening the distance between us.

"There's no need to explain …"

"I don't know what got into me. I guess it was the dinner, the wine, the comfortable surroundings, our being together in an intimate setting. It was all those things plus--"

"Stop!"

"What's the matter?"

"You're babbling." I resorted to my 'take charge' mode. "We have to sit and talk this out like adults."

PJ took a deep breath and gave me a faint smile. "Earl Grey?"

I chuckled. "PJ, what the hell am I going to do with you? Sure, I could use a second cup."

I followed PJ into the tent where she immediately busied herself with the tea kettle. My mind whirled like a tornado destroying all rational thought. Soon she handed me my cup and wrestled with the bent cookie tin lid.

"Here," I said, putting my tea down and taking the tin from her. "You have to handle it gently, like this." The lid came off easily.

"You'll have to show me how."

"Grip this corner and pull it sideways like this and it'll--"

"Kim."

"Mmm."

"I'm not talking about the *damn* cookie tin lid."

I found it difficult to ignore what I thought to be a direct invitation.

My lack of response brought her again close to tears. I didn't want her to cry.

"PJ, let me explain something. It's not that I wouldn't like to be with you, but this curiosity of yours ... this experimenting is not--"

"Curiosity! That's the second time you've intimated that, and damn it, it's not true."

"But why else would you ...?"

PJ put her teacup down on the table beside her chair. She turned her back to me. "You really do think I'm just curious ... that I would use you like some guinea pig?"

"Yes, I do. Why else ...?"

I was angry again though I had no reason to be. We were both being confrontational, which, I thought, stemmed from our mutual embarrassment and the fact that this was a live performance with no rehearsal time.

PJ whirled around to face me. "You think," she pointed an accusatory finger at me, "that because I know you're gay that I want to play the game, too? Maybe add another, a different kind of trophy to my experience. Is that it?"

"That's about it."

"Did it ever occur to you that it might be something else? That I might be attracted to you, that I might have fallen in love with you?"

I sat, unable to move or speak, just staring at PJ and trying to absorb what she had said.

"Say something, damn it!" PJ ran her fingers through her hair. "I'm standing here, declaring my heart to you, and you just sit there with your mouth hanging open."

"But, you're straight ... for gawd's sake."

"How do you know what I am?" PJ stood with her hands on her hips and a look of defiance on her face. "You're so damn busy thinking about yourself, your reputation, the project, and God knows what else. You've never taken the time to see who I am."

She picked up her teacup and took a sip. "Damn tea's cold." She slammed her cup down shattering it. "Oh, shit!"

"Don't worry, it's not our best china."

PJ attempted to smile but despite her struggle to keep control, tears washed it away.

Breaking the awkward silence that followed, I asked, "So who are you?"

"I'm a woman who finally knows what she wants. Amazing, I know. All this time, I've chased after men, looking for comfort, fulfillment, and the answer to my purpose in life. I never imagined that it could be any different."

She sniffed and took a deep breath. "And then, I learned that you were starting up a project here in Arizona. The great Kim Blair was going to work for my father's foundation. I knew you were one of the finest archaeologists in the world and that you'd make a superb mentor, if you'd give me half a chance."

She wiped tears from her cheeks and paced back and forth in front of me. "So, I asked, no I begged my father to let me come here to work with you. Little did I know that you would befriend me and give me the power to act as a professional ... to even lead a project for a time. You made me visible, Kim. You forgave my stupid mistakes and you believed in me. I was so grateful."

Her voice cracked, but she continued. "We became good friends. We talked, we laughed, and we worked together. When bad things happened, we consoled each other. Believe me, I wish I could have kept my feelings at that level ... kept us friends. But, it grew into more than that. I can't imagine my life now without you in it, Kim. I want us to be more than friends. I think of you all the time..."

She glanced at me and bit down on her lower lip. Tears made her eyes luminous. "I want you ... physically ... I didn't ask for it to happen and I know it isn't the best time to be telling you all this, but I can't help myself. I'm so sorry, but I've fallen in love with you."

PJ's lips trembled and she lost her battle with the tears. She turned on her heels and left the tent.

"Wait!" I followed her outside. She was striding toward the cave.

I caught up to her, grabbed her upper arms and whirled her around.

"You're hurting me," she cried.

I let her go, but prepared to grab her again if she turned her back on me. "I'm not through talking to you."

PJ rubbed her upper arms. "How am I going to explain the bruises?"

I couldn't resist a smile. "I'm sure you'll find a way."

"I guess I can't claim sexual harassment since I was the one who came on to you."

I sighed. Her flippancy was getting in the way of rational thought. "This is a serious discussion, PJ."

She bent her head and kept her eyes focused on the ground. "I'm sorry, Kim. I tend to make jokes when I'm nervous." Her head came up. "You have my full attention."

"I'm sorry, too, PJ. I didn't intend to make light of your feelings."

I paused, not wanting my emotions controlling my words.

If you only knew how often …

Voices broke the tension of the moment, the stillness that was pulling us together.

"Shit!" I looked at PJ.

She covered her face with both hands. "Oh, gawd, I wasn't expecting them … not today."

"Neither was I."

"Good Morning, Doc, PJ," Sandy said. The others were straggling into camp behind him.

Of all the inopportune times …

I stepped in front of PJ so she could wipe her eyes and pull herself together.

"What are you all doing here?" I asked, as my people were removing their packs and jackets and dropping them beside their favorite tree, shrub, or boulder. "I thought I gave you the weekend off?"

"We got together and decided," Sandy said, "that we'd prefer to be on-site doing something constructive than messing around in town."

"Yeah," Josie said, "we'd just get to drinking and stuff with the boys if we hung around with nothing better to do."

"Besides," Laine pointed to the cooler still strapped on her back. "We talked the people at the hotel into fixing us turkey sandwiches and pumpkin pie. We have enough to feed a small army."

"And Sandy brought some of his mother's home baked cookies," James said. "We can have a picnic."

PJ moved around me and started toward the group.

"PJ, our discussion is not over with."

She looked back at me for a moment. "Later then."

It was Sandy who asked, and who it seemed was always looking out for PJ's welfare, "PJ, are you okay, you look like you've been crying?"

"It's nothing," she said off-handedly. "I had a go around with Father on the telephone. I was just talking to Kim about it."

She put her hand behind her back, appearing to fiddle with her belt, but I noticed the crossed fingers ... she was taking no chances with a white lie to get out of this jam.

I noticed Josie looking a little too intently at PJ.

What, if anything, does she know?

Everyone else seemed to accept PJ's explanation on face value.

PJ seemed not to notice. She went to help Laine take the cooler off her back.

"You guys are too much," PJ said, as she placed the red and white cooler on the ground beside a large boulder.

Laine shrugged her shoulders and stretched her upper body after being relieved of the weight. "Well, when we looked into your bedroom and saw that you were gone already, we figured you'd be up here."

"We called Kim's motor home first to see if by chance you were there," Josie said, still scrutinizing PJ's facial expression.

"And when you weren't," Laine said, "we were sure you'd be here. That's when we came up with the idea for an after Thanksgiving picnic and called the guys to join us."

"And that," Josie said, as she neatly rolled up the straps that had held the cooler in place on Laine's back, "after what you did ... the dinner and sharing your suite and all ... well, we wanted to do something for you. The picnic lunch seemed like a good idea."

"You're the greatest," PJ said.

"And you're okay?" The inflection in Josie's voice indicated that the compliment was in fact a question.

"I'm fine," PJ said. "You know how it is when I talk to Father ... we're not always on the same wavelength."

While PJ had been talking with Laine and Josie, the fellows had lunch spread out on a blue and white checkered tablecloth that Sandy had borrowed from his mother. They had packed in some beer. There were still plenty of soft drinks in the tent.

We sat on the ground, in a roughly formed circle around the brightly colored picnic tablecloth.

Stephen had referred to my people as a rag-tag bunch of airheads. To me, they made up the best crew I had ever had the pleasure of working with ... they were the greatest.

"Sandy," I said, "your mother isn't going to be happy about her tablecloth being spread on this dusty ground. Couldn't you find something in plastic?"

He grinned. "I can wash it and even iron it if necessary."

"Mmm," Josie said, her eyes sparkling, "you're going to make someone a good husband."

Sandy grinned sheepishly.

Even though food was the last thing on my mind, the sandwiches were delicious.

PJ sat, as she usually did, beside me, but she avoided my eyes.

What would have happened, I wonder, if the crew had not arrived when they did?

We had finished eating and were in various stages of gathering up the empty soft drink cans, bottles, paper plates and utensils when we heard the first faint rumble before all hell broke loose.

The ground rolled like an angry sea. The noise was fearsome as an avalanche of rock rolled down the hillside. I had been standing, but I couldn't keep my balance and fell to the ground. I tried to get up and fell again.

PJ, who had been on her knees gathering up the tablecloth, dropped it and reached for me. Pup, who had been restless all morning, perhaps for reasons of animal intuition, tried to crawl between us. When the violent motion subsided, we were battered and bruised. I covered my mouth against the choking dust and indicated to PJ that she should do the same. She seemed to be in shock until I took her hand and pushed it to her face.

"This was no aftershock," I whispered into PJ's ear, "it was the main event."

Her look was not kind. "I should have left during the overture."

"You okay?" I asked, seeing the panic in her eyes.

"Apart from being scared shitless, you mean?"

I noticed a red stain on her shirtsleeve. "You're bleeding."

"A rock glanced off my forearm."

"Let me see," She rolled up her sleeve. I checked for a break. "It doesn't appear serious, but the skin is broken. I'll get some antiseptic from the first aid kit."

"You will? Have you looked at the tent lately?"

I turned in that direction. "Oh, my gawd!" The tent and the Peepee Tepee were buried under the rockslide.

"I have water here in my bottle, let me wash it ..."

"Save it. What about you? You're bloody, too."

"Nothing serious ... just some cuts and bruises. Some of your blood got on me so it looks worse than it is. We'd better check on the others."

Sandy's pants were torn and his leg was bleeding.

"Let me check that," Laine said. She appeared to be unscathed.

"Nah, it's okay, just a superficial cut."

I walked over to where Dewey was applying a crude splint of sticks to Lewis's lower leg.

"Let me see," I said, dropping to one knee.

"I don't feel a break," I said, after feeling along the bone.

"It hurts like hell."

"I suppose it could be a hairline fracture, so I'd go with the splint until you can get it checked by a doctor."

"Good work," I said, turning to Dewey. "Are you okay?"

"Yeah, Doc, just bruised is all."

Sandy was attending to a cut on Josie's forehead. Like all head wounds, it was bleeding profusely, but when I examined it, the wound appeared superficial. Josie was relishing Sandy's attention so I left them to it.

A rock had bounced off Donny's shoulder creating a sizable bruise. Nothing appeared broken and Laine was applying ice from the cooler, which was lying on its side in the dirt. It seemed to me that it was only moments ago it had being filled with delicious sandwiches and pumpkin pie.

After checking on the humans, I took time to examine Pup. I was happy to see that he had weathered the quake and the slide without injury. He remained unsettled though and kept rubbing his shoulders against my thigh. I can't explain why I took that moment to think about his size, but I did. He was big and he was powerful, but his need of me right now was that of a small, frightened child. No matter where I moved he was right there.

PJ had gathered herself together and was making the rounds … checking on everyone.

"It's okay, fella," I said, kneeling beside Pup and hugging him to me. "You're okay … we're all okay."

"Doc," Sandy called from behind me.

"Yeah."

"It's gone, Doc." His voice was hushed. I turned. He was pointing toward the small canyon and the cave, Site One. "The cave is gone, buried under hundreds of tons of rock."

No one said a word. We all stood there, just staring at what used to be a small canyon. The landscape was unrecognizable.

I looked at PJ.

Her eyes were round and wide. "I don't believe it, Kim. I'm so sorry … so incredibly sorry."

A huge sense of loss enveloped me and yet, at the same time, a fleeting sense of closure.

"Let's just be thankful we weren't working there," I said, scanning the distraught faces of my crew.

"I know," Laine said, "but the Amazons…"

"They're where they belong … better that than being separated and ending up in glass cases somewhere."

PJ stifled a sob. I went to her and put my arm around her shoulder. "It's all right, really."

I don't know how long we stood, all of us, trying to comprehend the enormity of the disaster and the changes it would mean for all of us.

I looked up toward Site Two. It, too, had been obliterated.

So this is how it ends … the years of searching for the Lost Tribe.

They were here for an instant in their time and returned in our time, just long enough to reveal their secrets. But, this is not all there is. We're connected with our past more than we know … a past that spans the centuries.

Chapter Twenty

"Doctor Blair! Is anyone hurt?" Sean Jackson arrived slightly ahead of his partner, Diego Rodriguez. The two security guards carried first aid kits, picks, shovels and machetes when they rushed into camp.

"Are we ever glad to see you," Kim told them. "Take a look at Lewis's leg. It may be broken. Otherwise, I think we just have a lot of cuts and bruises."

While they worked, the men related what they had heard on their portable radio. The ground-rolling, rock-shattering event that had brought us to our knees was an earthquake measuring an unofficial 8.4 on the Richter scale. Jackson and Rodriguez had left their post immediately to assist us, but were forced to blaze a new trail from their hut to our working site. It had taken them over an hour to reach us.

Rodriguez touched Kim's arm as she walked past him. "Wait a minute, Doctor Blair. I'd like to check that shoulder of yours. You aren't moving your left arm very well."

She waved him off. "It's nothing much...just a little sore. Why don't you bandage PJ's arm? She's got a nasty cut."

He focused his attention on my injury and Kim moved on to talk with Sandy and Donny. I tried to follow Kim's progress, but dust and debris made visibility difficult. Grit burned my eyes and my throat clogged when I tried to talk. Jackson put some drops in my eyes and that helped ease the burning. It took a few minutes before I could see clearly again.

Sandy materialized beside me. "PJ, are you sure you don't need me to help you and Doc clean up?"

I grabbed his arm, holding on to it for balance. "No, we won't be much longer. They want us out of here until they can assess the damage and security risks."

He gave me a hug, resting his chin on the top of my head. "We'll be okay. We're all in one piece, that's what counts."

"Yes," I said, "we were very lucky. Kim wants us to clear out and check with our families."

"I'm going to call Mike when I get to a phone. I want to tell him we're okay before he hears about this on some news bulletin."

We broke apart. "My gosh, I forgot all about Mike. He's still in Denver?"

Sandy nodded. "As far as I know, he's staying with his old roommate. I have the number. Don't worry, I'll take care of it."

I gave his waist a parting squeeze. "Thank you, Sandy. Help Josie and the others, okay? And keep us posted on Mike and his travel plans."

"Sure thing, PJ." He stopped to speak with Jackson. I couldn't hear the conversation, but they used their hands and pointed back down the trail so I assumed Sandy was getting new directions to the trailhead.

Gawd. I hope the vehicles are still in one piece. This is so unbelievable.

Pup nudged my hip. "Easy, boy." I gave him a pat. "You're okay now, yes you are." I looked around. "Where's Kim?"

He whined and bumped me again. "Can you find her for me?"

He snorted.

"Lead on, then."

He gave a sharp bark and bounded toward our collapsed main tent. I was right behind him.

Kim was on her knees, pawing through piles of scattered debris.

"Kim!" I called and skidded to a halt beside her.

"Oh, gawd. It's gone too." She wiped her hands on her jeans. "Only pieces...so many pieces."

I dropped to my knees. "Pieces of what, Kim?"

She looked at me, her eyes filled with tears. "Oh, PJ, that beautiful gift...is smashed to bits." She held up a few tiny shards of the Krater. "This was all I could find."

232

"Hey, it's okay. Really, it is. We can order another one."

Kim sniffed and wiped her face leaving a smear of dirt across her cheek. "It's just...oh, hell...the final straw, you know?"

She bowed her head. Her body shivered, giving way to shock now that the initial danger had passed. I sensed it too, a contagious fear. We all had come so close to being killed. I put my arms around her and touched my forehead to hers. Our bodies trembled against each other.

It's okay, now. We can be frightened together. The whole damn mountain can come down on us, but we'll manage.

"You need to get off this mountain and rest," I told her, giving her shoulder a gentle squeeze. I heard her breath catch.

"There's too much to--"

"Did that hurt you, Kim?"

"What? No, it's just--"

I gave her a penetrating look. "Don't give me that crap. It's your shoulder again, isn't--"

"PJ, please, not now."

She pulled away from me and we glared at each other for several seconds. I shook my head, trying not to smile. "Could there be anyone more stubborn on this whole damn mountain?"

Her lips twitched. "Uh huh... and I'm looking at her."

"Oh, please. There's no contest."

"Well, anyway, we have things to do. We have to leave the area."

I put my arm around her waist and she leaned into me.

This is much better. A gal could get used to this kind of support.

Dewey and James began a systematic search for our gear. Kim and I split up and wandered among the group offering our support and thanking the security guards for their monumental effort to get to us.

I saw Laine and Josie sitting together on the ground talking, their voices so calm it was surreal. Clean, white bandages made a sharp contrast to the dirt and grime on their arms and faces.

"Well, you two could be the cover girls for *Disaster Magazine*, if such a thing existed." My teasing earned me weary smiles, as I crouched beside them. "But, I guess you don't look too bad, considering you've been through an earthquake."

Laine laughed. "Haven't you heard? Grunge is in."

"How about you, PJ?" Josie eyed my arm. "That looks pretty nasty."

Laine gripped my elbow. "You look awfully pale under all that grit. Why don't you sit down here next to me and put your head down."

"I'm fine. I don't plan on fainting any time soon." I glanced in Kim's direction. "Doc may have re-injured her shoulder, though. I'd like her to go back to the motor home and rest."

Sandy joined us in time to overhear my comment. "Good luck getting her to leave if she thinks there's more to be done here."

I stood up and he pulled me into another hug. "Thanks, I needed that. We've already had a few words on the subject." He relaxed his embrace, but kept his hand on my back.

I noticed his cheek was cut and his arms were scraped, but otherwise his grin was as comforting as ever.

"How are you holding up?" I asked him.

"I'm fine for now."

"And the guys?"

"See for yourself." He motioned them over. "PJ wants to take a good look at you." He turned back to me. "They're a filthy bunch of hardheaded bone diggers. But I think you'll agree that it takes more than a little old earthquake to rattle us." He made eye contact with all of them, Laine and Josie included. "Am I right?"

"Oh, yeah!" Lewis and Donny nodded.

Dewey put his hands on his hips. "Good to go," he said.

"We're cool," James assured me and the girls gave me a couple of thumbs up.

You guys are amazing. You really are like family to me.

I felt a lump in my throat, but tried to keep smiling. My knees shook and I felt the trembling start again.

"Easy," Sandy said. The arm at my back stiffened and he and Donny helped me sit back down.

Josie rubbed my back. "Please put your head down, okay, PJ? It's bad for the troops to watch their leader keel over."

I nodded and lowered my head. "I'll try to remember that."

"We're all gonna be fine, physically, PJ." I looked up at Donny. His bloodshot eyes held tears. "It's just hitting us so hard that we've lost the Amazon remains and all."

I found a tissue in my pocket and blew my nose. Emotion and dust kept my throat tight. "I know, but it could have been so much worse." I looked at them standing around me, reflecting various stages of grief and shock. We had suffered physical and emotional trauma, yet we were alive and we would survive.

"Please, sit down here a minute." I indicated a space that we'd just cleared to assemble our gear. Someone handed me a bottle of water and I drank half of it before speaking again.

"Gawd, I am so proud of you." My eyes filled with tears. "We've uh...had a little setback here. But, after we have a chance to regroup, we're going to search the area and reclaim whatever we can of our notes and our data."

Kim joined our huddle.

"Hi, Doc," I said, as she crouched beside me. "I'm telling them all how proud we are of the way they've handled themselves."

She nodded and cleared her throat. Her hand slipped into mine and stayed there for the duration of her speech to the crew.

I doubt you realize what you're doing right now, but I'm not going to object. It's a great comfort to me.

"Yes, I agree," Kim said, her voice strong and steady. "I've called you the best team I've ever had and you've demonstrated that today. PJ and I will need to go over our options, and make some plans. Right now, though, I think it would be best if you all took off. The security people told me that you'd find debris on the roads, some power lines down, and buildings damaged. Be prepared for detours. Police will be out there to help you get home. See what needs to be done and contact your loved ones. Give them a phone number or a contact person so they can reach you. You can always use the guard post number or the local police number."

She took a crumpled up piece of paper out of her pocket. "I wrote that down here. I'll pass it around and I'd appreciate it if you'd list your most recent phone number and address on that. If you find you have to move, then let me know as soon as possible. My cell phone and home number are on that list."

I held out my half-filled water bottle. "Drink this. That frog in your throat will soon be dried and petrified."

"Thanks, PJ." She drained it and turned back to the group. "So, I guess that's it for now. Keep me informed of your whereabouts. I'll be at the motor home, assuming it is still there."

A few sardonic chuckles greeted her remark.

"What about Mike?" Lewis asked. "He's missing all the excitement."

"I'll contact him," Sandy said. "Doc can let us know what will happen next." He looked at her and she nodded. "So, for now, we do what Doc says and take care of business."

Kim and I collected what we could of our gear and left the camp, pausing at the guard station to talk with Jackson and Rodriguez.

"Thanks again for all your help," Kim said. "We're going to return tomorrow, if we can, to make a longer search of the area."

"Don't you worry, Doctor Blair," Jackson assured her, "we'll keep the place secure."

"Have you both checked with your families?" she asked them.

Rodriguez nodded. "Just a few minutes ago. Everyone's fine, so we'll stay here."

"Let me know if your relief doesn't show up and I'll see what I can do."

"Okay, Doctor Blair. Thanks." We said our goodbyes and headed for the parking lot.

"Looks like we lucked out on something." I pointed to the strip of flat gravel where our vehicles were parked, side-by-side. "I sure didn't relish the idea of walking all the way to the hotel."

"Don't forget to call your father," Kim admonished me, once we reached our cars. "After you get cleaned up, of course."

236

"Will do." I climbed into the minivan with a wave. "You go home and rest your shoulder. I'll call you later to see how you're doing."

Kim leaned against the Tracker. Her smile was a tired one. "We need to talk, PJ... about a lot of things."

I returned her smile. "We do...and we will. Right after we deal with all this."

Kim pulled out of the lot and I followed her as far as the turn off to the Rest-A-While Motor Home Park. I took the right fork, heading west. Apache Trail continued to the highway junction where the Holiday Inn and the Casa Grande were located.

Only, I never got that far. A police cruiser blocked my path a few hundred feet along the road.

What now? Another detour?

A young, well-built deputy approached my window. The nameplate on his neatly pressed, navy blue uniform said: J. T. Collison. He favored me with a tight smile and removed his mirrored sunglasses. "Sorry, miss, you can't go beyond this point."

"I have a room at the Casa Grande and I really need to get cleaned up. Is there some sort of detour?"

He acknowledged my disheveled appearance, then his eyes glanced upward behind me. "You're one of the archaeologists, aren't you? Did you just come off the mountain?"

I nodded. "Smack dab in the middle of the quake and the landslide...or so it seemed."

His spotless uniform, clear blue eyes and carefully combed, reddish brown hair only intensified my discomfort.

You haven't been anywhere near this disaster, Deputy. And right now, you're all that stands between me and my shower and clean, cool sheets.

"Look, officer--"

"I'd like to see some identification, please."

"What?"

"You said that you're staying at the Casa Grande?"

"That's right."

"I need to see some identification."

I exhaled. *Stay cool; he's only doing his job.* "Yes, sir." I fumbled through my daypack, located my wallet, removed my license and handed it to him.

He peered at it. "Massachusetts, huh? You're a long way from home, Miss Curtis. I'll just be a minute." He took it to the patrol car.

"I haven't broken any laws, you know!" I called after him. "Unless being filthy on an Arizona highway is a crime!"

"No, ma'am. Not that I know of."

Jesus Christ! He's unflappable. I can't even have the satisfaction of insulting him.

He consulted a list and made a call on his radio. I heard plenty of static, but nothing in the way of intelligible human speech. Sweat was trickling down the back of my neck and I could feel the gash on my arm throbbing. Deputy Collison muttered a bunch of gibberish and returned to my car with my license.

"If you'd be kind enough to come with me, Miss Curtis. Someone at the Casa Grande wants to speak with you."

"Someone at Casa Grande?"

"Yes, a Joel--"

"Joel Weaver?"

The patrolman rubbed his cheek. "I believe so."

Thank God. Now, we can get this cleared up. "Good," I told the deputy, "Joel is the assistant manager."

We walked to his patrol car and he handed the microphone to me.

"This is against regulations, Miss, but under the circumstances--"

"I won't tell if you won't."

"Hold it up to your mouth and push on that tab. That's right. Now release the tab and listen. Push the tab and hold it to talk. Release it to listen. Got it?"

Why do I feel like a six-year-old child?

"Yes, Deputy Collison, I believe I can do that."

He caught the sarcasm in my voice and his jaw tightened. I didn't wait for him to change his mind. "Joel? Come in. This is PJ." I released the tab and waited.

"Doctor Curtis? Oh, goodness. Is it really you?" Joel's voice sounded a million miles away.

"Yes, it's me. What's the problem there?"

There was a burst of static and then his voice came through clearly. ".... the fire after the quake. And we had to evacuate..." A squeal drowned his next few words. "...and about six more are missing. You were one of the six. I'm really glad to hear from you."

I clicked the tab. "Wait, Joel. Say again. There was a fire? Anybody hurt?"

"A short in the wiring... on the third floor.... near the roof. ...everybody out and try to account for... There were about ten injured, but not seriously."

"Thank goodness," I added.

"Yes, thank goodness. But, we still can't find five people."

"Oh, I see. That's terrible. Is the fire out?"

Another squawk...and then static. "...When the roof caved in, we feared the worst."

"Where? The roof caved in where? On the hotel?"

"... third floor section ... where your suite was. .... smoke and water. Oh, it's a real mess."

My mind stalled on the part about the roof over my suite.

Gawd. If I had been in there...or Laine and Josie.

I closed my eyes and sagged against the doorframe of the patrol car.

Deputy Collison grabbed my elbow. "Sit down. Put your head between your knees."

I handed him the microphone and complied, feeling better once the dizziness stopped. He pressed a water bottle into my hand. "Take small sips. It will help."

I looked up and took the bottle from him. "Thanks, I...it just hit me that I could have been killed...twice today." I uncapped the water and drank. The cold liquid hit my parched throat and I coughed.

"Easy," the deputy said, patting my shoulder. "You're fine now. It's going to be okay."

I tried to smile. "I think I must have a bull's-eye painted on my back or something."

For the first time since we'd met, Deputy Collison relaxed his professional demeanor. A hint of a smile creased his face. "I've had a few days like that myself."

Jesus, you're right, you must have had terrible days. I'm sorry to have thought otherwise. I'm so damn tired and achy and this day has gone on forever. But, I shouldn't have taken any of it out on you.

The radio squealed and the deputy took back the microphone.

"Did you have any more information for Miss Curtis?" he asked.

"Call your father," we heard Joel reply.

"My father? Why--"

Joel continued without hearing my question. "He called us because of an express mail package, but when he heard about the quake and the fire.... well he got a bit frantic."

Oh Gawd, he probably thinks I started it. Okay. I'll add it to all the rest of the stuff to do.

I realized that I was homeless for the time being and gave Joel Kim's phone number for contact purposes. There was little hope of retrieving my things anytime soon, if at all. I promised to call my father as soon as I reached a working phone.

"Are you strong enough to drive now, Miss Curtis?" the deputy asked, when I returned his water bottle.

"Yes, I'll be fine...and thank you for all your help." I climbed into the minivan. "I guess I'm going to have to drive clear to Mesa to find another room and get cleaned up."

"Well, take it easy. To get through, you'll have to go back that way on Apache Trail, take a right on Tomahawk, then go west on the Superstition Highway."

"Okay. You be careful, too." I retraced my route according to his instructions.

I'm going right by Kim's park; I might as well stop and tell her I'm relocating.

I smiled. *I'll use any excuse to see her again.*

I parked the minivan and approached Kim's motor home. As I raised my hand to knock on the metal door, Pup started a joyous greeting on the inside.

Kim held him back long enough to let me climb up the steps.

"Hey, you two," I said, "long time, no see." I bent to ruffle Pup's fur and he gave me a sloppy kiss on the chin.

"PJ, for goodness sake. Did you get lost driving to the Casa Grande?"

I chuckled. "Well, Kim, the Casa isn't so Grande right now." I told her about the fire. "I'm on my way to Mesa in search of a room."

She motioned me toward the sofa and dining nook. I perched on the end of one of the bench seats and she sank back on the sofa. There was an unmistakable scent of liniment in the air and Kim's posture was overly rigid.

"That shoulder is really bothering you, isn't it?"

Her left hand moved to her right deltoid area. "Maybe just a bit."

Gawd, you've got to be in serious pain if you'd admit that much to me.

"Do you have any pain killers for it? Or a heating pad?"

Kim's lips pursed and she made a dismissive gesture. "PJ, relax. It's a twinge or two. Yes, I have some pills for the pain…big ugly things the size of jawbreakers."

"How about I give you a massage with that smelly stuff you've been using?"

She made another face. "Let's stop worrying about me for a minute and decide what to do about you."

"Well, I'll drive into Mesa and find a room. I gave the Casa Grande people your phone number as a contact. My cell phone is still somewhere on the third floor there, so I doubt it'll be of any use to anyone."

She thought for a moment. "Okay, that's fine, but you don't have to go to Mesa. You can stay here. The power is touch and go, but I have a generator and the water tanks are full. I can be self-contained for a whole week if necessary."

Kim…self-contained. Why does that not surprise me?

I took a deep breath. "Are you sure about this, Kim? It would be helpful, certainly, but a lot has happened to us today. And I know you have work to do and you'll want to have some time to yourself."

Kim stood up. "What I want is to see that you get a hot shower and some clean clothes. I can put those filthy things to soak. Do you have anything else to wear or is that the extent of your wardrobe?"

I stood up and opened my soiled daypack. "Not quite destitute. Here's a change of underwear, a pair of cotton shorts and a tee shirt for sleeping...I think all my toilet articles survived, too."

Kim smiled. "Traveling light, aren't you?"

"Reduced to the bare necessities." I grinned. "So to speak."

Kim took a deep breath. "Okay, then it's settled. You'll stay here. The sofa makes into a bed and I have a sleeping bag and some old sweatpants if you need them, probably a shirt--"

"Wait!" I tugged at a lose strand of hair. It felt gritty and in desperate need of shampoo. "Um, I think there's a sleeping bag and a denim work shirt in the minivan. And a pair of running shoes." I looked down at my feet. "Thank God, I still have my favorite hiking boots."

I gathered the added supplies from the van and Kim escorted me to the bathroom where she supplied a washcloth and two towels. "You can dump your dirty things outside the door and I'll soak them. Do you remember how the shower works?"

I looked around her compact bathroom. "I'm sorry, Kim. I don't really remember. And I sure don't remember all these mirrors." There must have been six of them on the walls and over the sink. I stared at myself and shuddered. "Quite intimidating."

She laughed. "You don't ever have to worry about looking in a mirror, PJ. And, it's not surprising you didn't remember. The one time you used this shower, you were drunk as a skunk."

"True." *You had me blushing with that compliment, but your last remark brought me right back down to earth.*

242

She touched my forearm. "Does that cut need a new bandage or should we cover it?"

"I guess I'd better try to keep it dry if you can find something." She left and I stripped off my clothes, using one of the towels to wrap around myself.

Kim returned and taped plastic wrap over the bandage. "There's shampoo and soap on the sink. Use as much as you need."

"Thanks, Kim. I know this must be awkward for you."

She smiled and patted my shoulder. "We'll deal with things as they come up. Have you called your father yet?"

I shook my head. "After the shower, if your phone is working."

"It's been off and on, but we can check." She slid the door back open. "I'll put the kettle on for some tea. Are you hungry?"

Our pre-quake picnic seemed a lifetime ago, but I had little appetite. "Just tea, I think, Kim. And thanks... for everything."

She held up her hand. "It's no problem, honest. We need to work together anyway to get this project settled, and then we can have some long talks about more personal things. We're both adults. I know we can work things out."

She moved through the door and slid it closed, leaving me with a pounding heart.

Two adults ... discussing more personal things. What if one of them suffers from a lack of patience?

I emerged from the bathroom squeaky clean and dressed in shorts and tee shirt. My hair was still damp, so I rubbed it with a towel as I walked to the table where a hot cup of tea waited for me. One of Kim's flannel shirts was draped across my seat. I slipped it on for warmth. Kim was on the phone with someone, but smiled broadly when she saw me.

"Ah, Frederick, she's out of the shower now. You can talk to her yourself. Hang on." She covered the mouthpiece. "He was so worried he could hardly talk. Please PJ, tell him you're alive and well. I don't think he believes me." She thrust the phone at me before I could make any comment at all, so I just nodded.

"Father?"

"Priscilla, is that you, honey?"

"Yes...it's me." My voice echoed as if in a long tunnel. "The reception is pretty bad. I guess Kim told you the phone has been going in and out on her."

"Yes, but I had to try to get through to you when the hotel gave me this number."

"I'm sorry, Father. I would have called you sooner, but--"

"It's okay, Princess, I'm just so relieved to hear your voice."

Princess? Did I hear that right? He hasn't called me Princess since I was a child...since before Mom died.

"I'm fine. Really. Just a cut on my arm and some scrapes and bruises."

"You don't know how awful it was not knowing if you were hurt...or worse."

"Father, I told you and I'm sure Kim told you...we are fine. We were all very lucky. But, we lost the Amazon women in the landslides. We won't be able to get them back."

"Oh, honey, I'm not concerned with that right now. I know you and Kim are upset after all your hard work, but I'm just so glad that no one was seriously injured."

I sat back against the bench. "I guess that is..." The line went dead for a few seconds. We called to each other and then I could hear him clearly again.

"Okay," he said, "I guess the connection is breaking up, so I'll make this short and sweet."

His tone produced a tingle along my spine. *Oh God, what have I done now?*

I looked at Kim and shrugged. She had been sitting on the sofa opposite me, but stood and squeezed my shoulder. "Sit over here and be comfortable, PJ. I'll go get some food for us."

"Kim, there's no need--"

Father interrupted me. "Priscilla? Are you still there?"

Kim moved into the kitchen area and I concentrated on Father's urgent tone. "Yes, I'm here. I'm listening."

"We've been at odds for so many years, honey, and that's mostly my fault. I'm ashamed that it took almost losing you to make me brave enough to tell you this, but--"

"I understand." My voice cracked and I swallowed hard. "It's okay, really. I'm sure you had your reasons."

"Oh, God, Priscilla, it was…there was so much pain, you know…. when your mother died. I couldn't deal with it."

I squeezed my eyes shut, nodding. "Yeah, I know what you mean."

I'm not really up to talking about this now. It's been a hell of a day. How much more raw emotion can I stand?

"I threw myself into my work and I just didn't have the energy to cope with you. I know it wasn't the best thing for you, but it was so painful. You reminded me so much of Rachael…"

Shit. He's choking up. I'm choking up. We're going to be blubbering all over the place in a minute.

"I'm so sorry, honey. I want to make it up to you if I can. I've been so damn proud of you these past few months. Kim's reports have been so positive. Just glowing."

Really? Glowing reports about me?

"Thank you, Father. That means a lot to me. Kim's been a wonderful teacher and we've become good friends."

"Yes, she told me she cares for you a great deal."

"There's more to it than that for me, Father. I'd like to talk with you about that when I can."

I heard him exhale. "I'd love to hear all about your adventures in Arizona, Princess. Can you come home for Christmas? Or maybe sooner?"

"Well…"

"I know you and Kim have lots of work to finish and reports to complete, but I'd love to have you come home for a long visit. Maybe you could persuade Kim to come along with you."

I turned in Kim's direction. She had her back to me, stirring some soup on the stove. I saw a plate beside her with sandwiches cut into triangles. "Uh, well…I'd like that very much. The three of us might need to sit down and talk about some things."

There was relief in his voice now. "Anything. Anything at all, honey. I'm so glad we made a start at patching things up."

"Me too."

"I've neglected you for so long and you've grown into a beautiful, intelligent, capable woman. Jonathan told me about the checks you are going to give your students. I'm very proud of you for thinking of that."

"Thank you." I could feel tears threatening.

"I'd better hang up now. I imagine the connection won't hold much longer. Just let me say…. I love you…I've always loved you. And I can't wait to see you."

A sob caught in my throat. "I love you, too…Dad."

I sat with my head in my hands, the phone in my lap. Kim took the phone away and sat down beside me, putting her arm around my shoulder. "Everything okay?"

I nodded, sniffing. Tears trailed down my cheeks. "Everything is great."

We sat across from each other eating ham sandwiches and sipping vegetable soup. My tea was hot and steamy. It tasted wonderful.

I was surprised to discover that I was ravenous.

"Dad wants me to visit him at Christmas," I said. "And he'd like you to come, too. Would you like to tour historic Boston in all its winter splendor with me?"

Kim swallowed a spoonful of soup. "We do need to present our reports to the foundation." Her eyebrow arched. "I suppose I could force myself to stay in a stately Back Bay mansion with a beautiful, native guide."

I giggled. "Okay. I'm not exactly a native, but I know where to find some great seafood."

"Don't forget baked beans."

"Of course."

She stretched and winced. "Right now, I'd like to take you up on your offer of a shoulder massage. As soon as we're finished with our meal."

I wiped my mouth with my napkin. "You're on."

We decided that the sofa had a firmer mattress than Kim's bed, so she stretched out on it while I rubbed my hands to warm the liniment.

"Whew! This stuff sure reeks, doesn't it?" I felt my eyes water and my nose itch once my hands were covered with the lotion. "I'll try not to sneeze on your lovely back."

Kim chuckled. "Thanks so much."

My hands worked on her deltoids and across the upper part of her back. From her groans and moans, I could tell my effort was working. "You did take the pills before we started, right?"

"Yes," she replied. "They can cause drowsiness, though, so forgive me if I drop off."

I noticed that Pup had snuggled up on the floor close to his mistress. His alert ears twitched with every sentence we spoke. "Don't worry. Pup and I will have ourselves a nice chat if you fall asleep. Won't we, fella?"

He lifted his head and yawned.

"Gawd, that feels wonderful, PJ." Kim's sigh was long and heartfelt. "Do you remember the first time you gave me a rubdown?"

I thought for a few seconds. "Ah, yes, in the tent up on the mountain. And Sandy came running in to tell us about the Mexican quake."

She laughed. "Caught us half dressed. Goodness only knows what he thought about that."

I continued to knead her muscles and tendons, moving further away from the source of her discomfort so that I was giving every area of her back my attention.

"Speaking of Sandy, have you heard from him or any of the crew?"

Kim turned her head so she could watch me with one eye as we talked. "He called just before your father. His apartment had no power, so he and Donny and James went to stay with his mother. Laine and Josie had no problems with their apartment."

"Did Sandy reach Mike in Denver?"

"Yes. Mike can't get a flight to Phoenix for a few days. They've closed Sky Harbor because of some cracks on several of the runways. He might try to take a bus back here, but it probably won't be until Wednesday or Thursday."

"Hmm. Well, maybe I'll have my clothes back by then, if there's any that weren't burned up."

Kim grinned. "You may have to go shopping."

My hands paused while I contemplated the possibilities. "I don't suppose there's a Neiman Marcus nearby?"

"Your best bet for something open in our neighborhood is Walgreen's. They're everywhere."

I sighed. "Oh, gawd. I can imagine what choices I'll have in underwear. Fruit of the Loom or Hanes, right?"

"Hey, my back's getting cold. Could you work while you talk?"

"Oops, sorry." I renewed my assault on her tight muscles. "You have a beautiful back, Kim. Has anyone ever told you that?"

"Ah, no. Not that I can remember." Kim's face flushed.

"Sorry, I didn't mean to embarrass you. I'm trying to be patient and wait for our personal talks."

Her body stiffened. "I appreciate that, PJ. It's a very serious subject, you know. With all we've had going on, I don't want to treat it lightly."

I bit down on my lower lip. "I don't treat it lightly, either, Kim. I thought about the situation for weeks before I talked to you. Believe me, I meant every word of what I said on the mountain."

She turned her head to the other side. "I'm having trouble believing that you could change your ah...preferences so suddenly. And for someone who's much older and--"

"Kim, we should probably talk about this after a good night's sleep, but I can't let that comment go unchallenged. I know you decided your preferences very early in life. You were painfully aware that you weren't like other girls in your town, but you had the courage of your convictions."

"It's not an easy life, PJ. You've got to know what you stand to lose by making that choice."

"I'd prefer to think of what I'd be gaining."

"Oh, PJ--"

"No, wait! Let me speak. You brought it up and it sounds like you're putting yourself down. You need to hear things from my side this time, okay?"

248

Kim chuckled. "Since you're straddling my back and your hands are making me feel the most relaxed I've felt all day, I guess I have no choice."

I put more lotion on my hands and rubbed them together. "We're almost finished here, but I need to tell you what I've learned by working with you...some interesting observations I've made about Kim Blair...how we differ and how we're alike."

"Sounds fascinating," Kim muttered with sarcasm.

"See, you like to take your time before making decisions and you give a great deal of thought to problems. Remember how you decided to move the excavation to that canyon wall? And when we went out for those weekly dinner meetings, you always took a long time to decide what to order. Those are traits of an introverted person. It's why you need time to ponder the future of our relationship and why I'm going to be so patient with you."

She snorted. "Is that a fact?"

"Yes, it's true. It's not a good thing or a bad thing. It's just how you are, how you were made. I, on the other hand, tend to talk and think at the same time, which often gets me into trouble."

Kim snickered, but didn't comment.

"I seem to be an extrovert. Most of the people in the world are. I crave energy from other people and love to be with a crowd. Being around people helps me recharge my batteries, but you do better with a couple of friends or keeping to yourself to relax and get your energy level back to normal."

"Huh! You know, PJ, I think you're right about that. Very astute of you."

"Thanks, Kim. I must confess that I noticed the difference soon after we met and did some reading on the subject."

She smiled. "I'm flattered that you devoted so much time and effort to understanding me. But, if we're so different, maybe we aren't compatible."

"Oh, I never said that. We have lots of differences, but that only makes us more perfectly matched. Your strengths are my weaknesses and vice versa."

"You've got it all figured out, huh?"

"Not all of it." I gave her back a light tap. "Here's something else I realized. I've always said 'yes' too often."

She coughed. "Oh?"

I realized she had taken that wrong. "Jesus, you've got a dirty mind. I'm not talking about sexual encounters, Kim."

"Me? I... uh... no comment."

I laughed. "I'm talking about life in general. I've tried to please everyone by saying 'yes' too often, trying to be all things to all people."

"Oh, I see."

"You've learned to protect yourself by saying 'no.' "

She smirked. "Probably too often."

"Well--"

"But, you and the crew have helped me loosen up quite a lot, PJ."

"It's still okay to say 'no'... and should we find ourselves getting together on a more permanent basis, I'm not going to try to change your basic nature." I traced a heart across the widest part of her back and felt her shiver.

"And 'should we find ourselves getting together on a more permanent basis,' I would never try to dampen your spirit, PJ."

"So, I'm extroverted and you're introverted ... and it's okay."

Kim's smile was expansive. "We can say 'maybe'...a lot."

We laughed and I worked the muscles of her triceps and biceps, first on one arm and then the other. "You know, Kim, I'm glad you listen to all of my ramblings. I've admired the way you give folks a chance to talk no matter how crazy their ideas seem. It's one of the many things I love about you." I finished her massage and climbed off her back.

"I'm sorry, I know I shouldn't have said the L word just then, but it's how I feel, you know. I'll give you all the time you need, but it won't change how I feel about you. I love you, Kim."

She didn't respond.

"Kim?" I crouched beside her cheek. Her eyes were closed, her breathing steady.

I talked her right to sleep.

I'm better than a sleeping pill.

Do I wake her or let her sleep here?

I pulled the blanket from her bed and covered her up. "Sweet dreams, my love," I whispered, ruffling her hair.

"C'mon Pup, let's get you settled for the night." He stood up and stretched, finishing up with a good shake. I took him outside for his nightly constitutional and then he resumed his sleeping position on the floor beside Kim. I filled his water dish, and put out all the lights but the one in the bathroom.

Well, I was supposed to sleep on the sofa. Where do I go now?

I looked at the dining area.

I'm sure that makes into some kind of sleeping platform, but I haven't the faintest idea how.

After a few minutes of deliberation, I used the bathroom, unrolled my bedding on one side of Kim's bed and pulled the zipper halfway down.

Notice that I am sleeping 'on' your bed and not 'in' it because I've not been invited...yet.

There were two pillows on her bed, so I borrowed one, taking time to breathe in its distinctive mango and pear scent, before I placed it at the top of my sleeping bag and crawled in. Sleep came quickly, but once during the night I thought I heard a throaty voice speak to me.

"Look who's been sleeping in my bed," it said. "Hello there, Goldilocks."

But, I knew it was only a dream.

Chapter Twenty-One

"What the..." I awakened on the sofa, not in my bed ... but the blanket was from my bed. *What's going on here? It must be the medication.* The interior of the motor home was dark, except for the fading light of the waning moon. Other than Pup's deep breathing, all was quiet. Everything was normal.

Slowly the awful events of the day before came into focus. It was hard to believe they really happened. *It was a dream ... that's all, a bad dream.* I wanted to believe it was a dream, but it wasn't. I knew that.

I rolled onto my side but was stopped in mid movement by a searing pain shooting through my shoulder and neck. *I remember now ... re-injuring this darn shoulder ... just what I didn't need to have happen.*

Then I remembered PJ massaging my shoulder and back.

That wasn't a bad dream ... it was a most pleasurable experience.

But I must have fallen asleep, PJ, while you ... then you left ... without saying goodnight ... why?

I told you you could stay here ... I thought you understood. But, I guess, under the circumstances you would have felt uncomfortable. Or would you? You seemed confident enough in expressing your love for me. I'm the one treading on eggshells.

I kicked the blanket to one side and swung my legs over the side. The floor was cold. I hadn't turned on the heat last night ... hadn't needed to.

I sat on the side of the sofa bed, rubbing my shoulder. I was stripped from the waist up, but still in my sweat pants.

Of course, PJ, you had me strip off my top so you could massage me. Darn you anyway, you're such a little devil, teasing me like that because I was reluctant to strip in front of you. Things have changed, don't you understand that? Things are

253

different now that you've told me you love me. And then, when you giggled and said you wouldn't look … but that massage … oh, how that made up for the embarrassment.

I stood up, stiff from lying in one position. My shoulder ached like hell. *I suppose I'll have to swallow another one of those horse pills.*

Where did you go, PJ? If you left and went to Mesa I'm going to scold you but good. I smiled to myself. *Scolding you would be like tickling a killer whale with a hummingbird feather.*

I snickered at my own silly thought and pulled on my sweat top, still laying draped over the back of the driver seat. I winced when my shoulder complained.

Well, now that I'm up I might as well stay up. Off to the bathroom … prepare to face the day.

The door from the bathroom to the bedroom was open and that's when I saw PJ in her sleeping bag and stretched out on one side of my bed.

"Look who's been sleeping in my bed," I said, leaning against the doorframe. When she didn't respond, I walked around the bed and stood over her. "Hello there, Goldilocks." No response.

Poor dear, you're exhausted. You were so busy yesterday trying to take care of everyone else, including me, and not paying one bit of attention to your own shocked system.

I sat down on the edge of the bed next to her. She looked so peaceful. Her mouth was open just enough to allow small sounds to escape unhindered. Her sleep-tousled hair framed her face, a golden halo in the fading moonlight.

I had to pee so I left PJ's side and went into the bathroom, sliding the door between the bedroom and bathroom closed as quietly as I could, and opening it again when I was through. I hoped the flushing of the toilet or my running water to wash my hands had not disturbed her.

Gawd, this shoulder … where the hell are my pills? I went into the kitchen and found them where I had left them, on the counter. *Damn these childproof caps anyway.* I finally pried it open and choked one down with a half glass of water.

254

I grabbed my blanket off the sofa bed and returned to the bedroom where I stretched out alongside PJ. She moaned but did not awaken.

I doubt, PJ, that this is your image of our first night of sharing a bed.

I lay on my back with my head turned toward PJ. I watched her as she slept and was so tempted to cuddle up to her and take her in my arms, but I knew if I did there would be no turning back. If I kissed her, I would make love to her. It was that simple. I shivered, not so much from being cold, but from the desire that spread through my body.

I turned my back to PJ and lay in the dark, listening to her even breathing. Thoughts jumbled together in my mind ... thoughts of wanting PJ and grieving for the loss of my Amazons.

After all that hard work and all those years--

But, I accomplished what I had started out to do. I had found the Lost Tribe. My efforts had been rewarded.

And, PJ, I met you. How that will pan out though is yet unknown.

I must have fallen into a stuporous sleep because when I awakened it was full daylight. PJ's sleeping bag was folded neatly on the foot of the bed. I touched her pillow. It was cool so she had been up awhile. The door between the bedroom and bathroom was closed.

I sat up on the edge of the bed and peered through the window. A dirty, yellow haze hung in the air, dust disturbed by yesterday's earthquake had not yet settled. It would be several days before we would see clear skies again.

I looked around my bedroom, my inner sanctum. It was small, claustrophobic to some, I supposed, not that I had ever had guests. *Not until PJ, that is.* I chuckled when I thought of her sleeping on the top of my roomy, queen size bed. The room was all bed with its two small nightstands, and two equally small closets. I shivered. It was cool even though the sun was up.

I toyed with the idea of using a heating pad on my shoulder. *Better not ... it might increase the inflammation.* I couldn't stand ice so that wasn't an option.

255

I tried to see the bedroom through PJ's eyes. The sidewalls were mostly window leaving little space for pictures. The overhead cabinets had mirrored, lift-up doors, which gave the illusion of space to the ceiling only. There was a small TV in a specially built alcove close to the ceiling. I hadn't used it in years and wondered if it even worked any more. I thought about my ranch in New Mexico and longed for its rambling interior. I had bought it with the thought of eventually being semi-retired and spending my time writing and guest teaching. I wondered if PJ would be happy living in a sprawling ranch house at the foot of the Sangre de Cristo Mountains. *What am I thinking?*

I got up and knocked on the bathroom door but got no answer. I slid it open a couple of inches, just enough to make sure PJ wasn't inside. I did not want to walk in on her taking care of personal matters.

I walked through and slid open the door into the kitchen. PJ was seated at the dinette hunched over a stack of papers. I glanced at the counter and sink. There was no evidence that she had eaten, but there was a used teabag lying in the miniature teapot shaped teabag holder.

PJ didn't hear me approach and was startled when I walked up behind her and touched her shoulder.

I stepped back. "Good Morning."

"Gawd, you scared me."

"I'm sorry." I sat down on the hide-a-bed, which had been folded back into its sofa position.

"No need to apologize," PJ said, turning so that she faced me. "I'm jumpy that's all, you know, the quake and everything. I think it's just now catching up to me … the enormity of what has happened to us, all of us … you and me and the students…."

"Yes, it's changed the course of all our lives, that's for sure."

PJ looked fresh and rested, yet older somehow, as if the events of the day before had filled several pages in her Life Journal.

"Kim, I can't begin to know how painful it must be for you. I'm so sorry. You've lost something that has been so much a part of you for so long. Those Amazon women were here one minute and gone the next."

"It hurts all right, but in a way it ended the way it should have. Marna and Leeja are together forever and their friends are close by ... it's a fitting ending to their saga and our expedition." A lump formed in my throat.

"*Your* expedition Kim. You always believed you'd find them and you didn't give up until you did. I was just a late comer to the project." She smiled. "I'm proud though that I had some part in it, however small."

"You were there when it counted, PJ."

I glanced again toward the kitchen counter. "You haven't eaten?"

"I wasn't hungry, but I had a cup of tea." She picked up her now empty mug and saluted me with it.

"How long have you been up?"

She glanced at her watch. "An hour or so."

"Then I'll fix us some breakfast," I said, getting up from the sofa.

"Wait!" PJ stood got up and pushed me down, taking care not to touch my shoulder. "You stay put. By the way how's the shoulder this morning?"

"Truth?"

"Of course the truth. Why else would I ask?" There was a note of impatience in her voice.

"It hurts like hell."

"Did you take a pill?"

"Yes I did, but they don't do much except to make me groggy."

"I'll fix breakfast." She gave me a lopsided grin. "And try not to poison the both of us."

I looked at her. *Aren't you going to mention, PJ, that we shared a bed...?*

"It's the least I can do after sleeping in ... on your bed."

I squirmed. "Are you reading my mind or what?"

"Were you thinking about that, too?"

Here it comes, the smart-ass remarks, the making light of a serious situation.

257

"Yes and no."

PJ tapped my forehead with two fingers. "Can't be both ... it's either yes or no."

"Well, yes. We can't ignore the fact now, can we?"

PJ shrugged. She turned and began rummaging through my kitchen cabinets.

"What are you looking for?"

"Pancake mix. Do you have any?"

"Top left."

"Got it."

"Measuring cup and mixing bowl?"

"Lower shelf on the right."

After putting the teakettle on to heat, PJ measured some of the powdered batter into the bowl.

She stopped momentarily and turned to face me. "You'd prefer, wouldn't you, to ignore the fact?"

"That we slept together ... well, we have to talk about it, PJ. We're beyond ignoring it."

"I wouldn't call it sleeping together," PJ said, handing me a cup of steaming tea. "I found some English Breakfast blend."

"Thank you." I reached for and caught her hand. "I'm struggling with my feelings, too, but there's no sense dancing around the issue."

"Don't tell me that the great Doctor Blair has feelings...."

I let go of her hand. "That's not fair."

She shook her head and pinched the bridge of her nose. "No it's not, Kim, and I'm sorry."

"Go fix the pancakes," I said, dismissing her.

She stared at me for a moment, sighed, and turned her attention back to the mix. She measured the right amount of water and beat the mixture into a smooth batter. "I'm not a great cook so I can't promise that my pancakes will be anything more than acceptable, maybe not even that, but since I'm doing it out of ...um ...deep friendship, I don't want to hear any complaints, okay?"

I sighed. "PJ."

"Yes, Kim." Her attention was focused on ladling the mix onto the griddle.

"We need to talk seriously about our future, but first, we have a job here to finish."

She nodded. "I know. We're not through yet. We have reports to complete and we have to go back to the site and salvage whatever we can."

"Are you up to doing that today?"

"Going to the site …" PJ put a plate of pancakes in front of me. "…sure, it's okay with me, but how about you … your shoulder?"

"I'd just as soon do it." I poured on enough maple syrup to drown any self- respecting pancake.

PJ smiled. "Are you trying to disguise the look and taste of my lovely pancakes before you've even tasted them?" she asked, sliding onto the seat across from me, loaded plate in hand.

"No. I always slather my pancakes."

"Oh. Well, that's good." She picked up her napkin with a smirk.

We were both hungry and didn't waste any time clearing our plates.

Before leaving the motor home we packed a couple of apples and some cheese in foil baggies and loaded them into our day packs. We loaded Pup's pack with his food and water, filled two water bottles apiece for us and headed out the door and into the Tracker. Pup bounded into the back and took his place with his head between the front seats. I reached back to pat his head before starting the motor. Pup was a good traveler. It would be distracting to me, the driver, to have an animal pacing in the vehicle. I snickered. Of course with Pup being so large and the Tracker so small, pacing would be out of the question.

At the trailhead, we clipped the water bottles to our belts, fastened Pup's pack in place, and slung our day packs onto our backs. Well, PJ slung her pack … I wasn't able to sling anything so I put mine on gingerly. The pack, though light bothered my shoulder. I didn't let on about it though because PJ would have insisted she carry my stuff along with her own and I wasn't about to let her to do that. As it was she was already carrying extra stuff, like the small folding fire shovel she had found in the

Tracker and brought along. It was old and battered and had come in handy on many an occasion. I remembered that time when I was in New Mexico and driving along an old logging road ... someone had carelessly tossed an empty bottle into the dry brush at the side of the road. The sun shining on the glass was enough to start the small fire that was just starting to flame when I came by. I was able to put it out with the help of my trusty shovel.

PJ walked half a dozen paces ahead of me. Pup loped along ahead of her, tongue hanging out and turning often to make sure we were following.

"I wish this dust would clear," PJ said, stopping to drink some water.

I followed suit. The liquid, though no longer cold, was still cool from the refrigerator.

PJ dug into Pup's pack, got his bowl and put some water from his jug into it. His slurping drowned out the excited twittering of the nearby Cactus Wrens.

She shook the bowl when he was done and stowed it back in his pack. I remembered how scared she had been of Pup when she first met him.

"PJ."

"Yes, Kim."

"I'm not procrastinating. We'll talk, I promise you ... it's just that I have to wrap up this Amazon situation before I can focus fully on other things ... personal things ... you and I."

"I didn't say anything."

"I know you didn't, not now anyway, but I know you're thinking--"

"I understand, Kim, and I'll try to be more patient." She coughed. "Damn, this dust is making my sinuses ache and my head feels tight."

"I have some antihistamine in the motor home. Not much use here, I'm afraid, but if you still need one when we get back--"

"Okay. Thanks." She grinned. "I'm sorry if I'm a little cranky, Kim. I've waited this long and I can wait a little longer. Besides I agree with you that we have enough to concentrate on just bringing the Amazon affair to a satisfactory conclusion."

We resumed our up-trail hike toward the now unrecognizable site. Thoughts floated about in my head like the well-disturbed dirt that floated about us with every step we took.

Oh dear, P.J, am I capable of giving you what you want, of being all things that you expect of me? Can I be the lover who will satisfy your physical needs? What am I going to say to you when we finish up here and I run out of excuses to put it off any longer? We're going to come to a point where we will have to part ways or continue on together. Are you fully prepared, I wonder, to devote your life to me? Am I prepared to risk being hurt again?

We were met at the site by Sean Jackson and Diego Rodriquez. "Good Morning, Doctor Blair, Doctor Curtis. All's quiet up here."

"Yes, I'm sure it is," Kim said. "We're just going to look around and see if there is anything salvageable."

"I doubt it," Diego said sadly. "There's nothing much left of the way it was. I'm sorry your work here ended like this."

I wondered why I hadn't noticed Diego's eyes before now. They were beautiful, black pools, windows into his Navajo/Mexican soul. The open neck of his light blue shirt revealed a silver crucifix resting in the curly, black hair of his chest.

Sean, on the other hand was typical Irish, even to his red, unruly hair. They were good men.

"There's really no reason for your staying here any longer, so if you'll stop by my motor home later today, I'll pay you off. You're entitled to a decent severance and I'm going to see to it that you get one."

"Thank you," the two men uttered in unison.

"It's been a pleasure working for you," Sean added, "a real pleasure, and I'm sorry it's over."

"We won't leave until after you do," Diego said, "just in case you need anything. Then, we'll pack up our stuff."

"Not much to do there either." Sean said. "The quake dismantled our hut for us."

"I'll see you later then, at the motor home," I said, dismissing the men.

It was dirty work, sorting through the dirt at the tent site. All that was left of the tent were two bent poles and a shred or two of tenting material. We wore masks and worked in silence. There wasn't much to salvage. We found a few scattered papers and the battered remains of my folding chair. The strapping was torn and the metal frame twisted. The tent itself, the laptop, books, and everything else was buried. It would take heavy earth moving equipment to dig them out.

I gathered what few shards of the Krater I could find and dropped them into a plastic bag.

PJ came and knelt beside me and took my hand. "Don't worry about those. I'll get you another one."

I looked into her eyes and remembered the feel of the Krater in my hands. "It won't be the same, PJ, as this one ... so special ... it was so special."

"Keep it in your heart, Kim. And maybe, someday, you'll find room for me there, too. If you don't ... well, it wasn't meant to be."

Her expression revealed the pain in her heart and the courage it took to utter that last sentence.

I had to respond ... with something, but to extend hope ... would that be fair to her?

"You're already in my heart, PJ, and you're likely to be there for a long time. That isn't the point and I think you know that."

"I do and I'm not pushing, it's just that... Aw hell, let's get back to work, shall we?"

She grabbed the shovel she had carried from the Tracker and started scraping away at the dirt, turning over rocks and pushing aside loosened brush in her search for anything of ours that might have survived the quake and rock slide.

We were stopped dead in our tracks on numerous occasions as small aftershocks rumbled through the ground beneath our feet. They were mild, but strong enough to set small stones rattling downhill. Even though the disturbances lasted only a few seconds they were enough to freeze us in place, as if any movement on our part would bring the rest of the mountain down on top of us. Nothing was as it should be any more. The Amazons were gone and I was struggling with issues concerning PJ. Besides that, the very instability of the ground was driving me to the edge. *How much longer can I hold myself together?*

"This is futile," I said, after we had been scratching through the dirt for what seemed like hours.

PJ agreed. "We need bulldozers to dig through this mess."

"Well, we're not going to those lengths." I stood up and brushed off my jeans. "Luckily, I have most of our stuff backed up on computer disks at the motor home. That's what I was doing the night you stayed up here with Laine and Josie, bringing my master files up to date."

"That seems so long ago now ... as if it happened in another life."

"It did, PJ. Everything pre-quake happened in another life. Things changed the moment the earth shook and the mountain came tumbling down."

" 'The Damndest Finest Ruins,' that's what they said of San Francisco after the earthquake of 1906. In fact I believe someone wrote a book with that title. Is this, Kim, our damndest finest ruin?"

"It qualifies."

"Don't worry, I'm sure that between us," PJ said, looking around and shaking her head as if contradicting what she was saying, "we can reconstruct whatever is missing."

"You're right. So let's go pay our respects to Marna and Leeja, then get the hell out of here."

PJ reached for my hand. "Kim, would you prefer to do that alone? I'll wait for you here."

"Nonsense, we're in this together. You're as close to them as I am."

She smiled. "Not quite."

We climbed over rocks and boulders, dirt, fallen trees, and uprooted, low growing, desert shrubbery.

After twenty minutes of scrambling we had arrived at the spot that, though unrecognizable, we thought was right above the cave.

I looked at PJ. "I have to say a few words."

"I'll wait over there."

"No, I want you here with me." I took her hand in mine and bowed my head. "Marna, Leeja, it's been a pleasure. I'll never forget you. And, Marna, well, I guess, like it or not, you're part of me and I'm part of you. May your Gods and Goddesses keep you safe wherever you are, and if you're inside of me, may they show me the way to honor your memory."

I started to leave but PJ pulled me back. "Wait!"

"Ladies," she said, her head bowed. "I'm not as close to you as Kim, nor can I understand your connection, but you've helped me come to terms with my life ... you've given me a reason for being and I thank you for that."

As we turned to leave, PJ stumbled over some loose rock. I steadied her.

"Kim, what's that?"

We dropped to our knees and scraped some dirt aside to get a better look at a shiny object that was caught between two boulders. It appeared to be a metal disk on a leather strip, like a thong. PJ pulled on it but it was well and truly stuck. A second thong was entwined with the first one.

"Damn, I left my pack at the tent site," PJ said. "If I had a tool I could pry.... I'll go get it."

"Wait," I reached into my pocket for my Swiss Army Knife. "I have something here that might work."

I pushed the stubby screwdriver down into the crack and wiggled it, taking care not to damage the object or push it farther into the crevice. I pushed and pried while PJ held the thong taut. Then I used the butt of the knife as a lever. After a while it started to rub a blister in the palm of my hand and my shoulder was screaming its displeasure, but I felt the object move ever so slightly. We changed places. I pulled on the thong while PJ worked the knife blade down into the rock. Suddenly, the medallion was free of its rock prison. The second thong was attached to a dried up, leather pouch. Inside was another medallion, identical to the first one.

"What do you make of them?" PJ asked.

"I don't know. We'll have to take them back with us and do some research."

"Whatever they are, they're not indigenous to this area."

"You know, PJ, looking at the lettering, they could be ancient Greek, which means they more than likely belonged to our Amazons."

"But why didn't we find them before, in the cave, or outside?"

"I can't answer that. Perhaps we weren't supposed to find them until now."

"Now, Kim, don't get all funny on me again."

When I looked up, she winked. "Just teasing."

"I'll get you for that, you know."

"Is that a promise?"

I raised an eyebrow, swallowed, and turned my attention back to the medallions. The two appeared, on the surface anyway, to be exactly alike. "You know, PJ, don't you think it strange that they're so shiny? If they'd been here all along, they'd have been dulled with age."

"What are you suggesting?" PJ asked.

Geez, I'd like to kiss that frown from your forehead. "I dunno ... perhaps it was no accident that we found them."

She looked at me intently. "There you go again, getting all spooky..."

I stiffened and grabbed PJ's arm. "Don't move ... Stay very ... very ... still."

"What ...what is it? Kim, you're scaring me."

A snake with various brown, geometric markings slithered across the rocks in front of us. It had a flat, triangular head.

"Kim, is that what I think it is?"

"If you're thinking rattler, the answer is yes, but if you stay perfectly still chances are it'll glide on by."

"That works for me," PJ said, her voice weak and shaky. Her nails dug into my forearm.

"Shit," I muttered, as we knelt rigidly across from one another.

"What now?"

"There's a couple more."

"Sweet Jesus! What do we do?"

"Try to relax."

"Relax! You've got to be kidding. I'm about to pass out. But, I don't want you to get bitten when I fall and they strike, so-"

"PJ. Please shut up. You must remain calm."

She gave me a lopsided grin. "Maybe we're going to stay here with the Amazons after all."

"Don't be so melodramatic. They'll meander along and we'll be on our way."

We heard the low throated growl from somewhere behind and off to my left.

"That was your stomach, right?" PJ said, "And not a hungry grizzly or something equally horrific."

"Pup, quiet," I ordered softly. I had to repeat myself, but he got the message, though a low whine now and then indicated that he was not happy about not being allowed to protect us. He stayed put while the longest minutes of our lives ticked by.

"Kim. I've gotta pee."

"Well, either squeeze your legs together or pee your pants, but don't you dare move."

"Some help you are when my eyeballs are floating."

I stifled a giggle. "I can't think of anyone I'd rather be with at a time like this."

"Thanks a lot." PJ was pale under her suntan. "You want to be with me in the last moments of our lives. Where the hell were you when I had years ahead of me?"

I was scared, too, but I didn't want to let on to PJ that I was. Our first aid kit was in the buried tent.

If they strike there's little we could do to treat the bites. I wonder if Jackson and Rodriguez have left. Maybe not ... they said they'd wait until we left.

Now that I have a chance at happiness, a love in my life, has it come too late? And if we get out of here alive, will I have

266

the courage to give myself to her, or will the dread of future pain keep my heart in a deep freeze?

The standoff ended finally when the snakes slithered into a crack between the rocks.

PJ was trembling. I pulled her into a hug, unable to ignore how comfortable she felt against me with her head tucked under my chin. "It's okay," I said, rubbing her back and kissing the top of her head. "We can leave now."

"This feels so good," PJ said, "that I'm not sure I want to leave right now."

I chuckled. "There could be more rattlers."

"That's it! I'm out of here." She broke apart from me, stood off the jumbled rocks. "Gawd, my legs feel like Jell-O."

I followed her, but stopped for a moment when we reached the trailhead. I turned to take one last look back. *There's nothing left for us here. The Amazons, of course, but they live in my heart.* I glanced at PJ. *In our hearts.* I stretched my eyes toward the cave's location. "Sleep peacefully, Warriors."

"We'll never forget you," PJ added quietly, reaching for my hand. "C'mon. Kim, let's go. You've done what you set out to do."

We were dust covered and grimy so the first thing we did on arriving back at the motor home was to clean up. I sent PJ into the shower first. When she emerged, she looked a great deal better.

I had a cup of Earl Grey ready for her. "You know, you really do justice to my old sweats."

Sexy, too, with your hair still wet. What are we going to do, PJ, about us?

"Yeah. Well, they're a little baggy. Thanks to those rattlers, I lost ten pounds in sweat." PJ said, as I handed her a cup of tea and a cookie.

I swallowed a couple of mouthfuls of tea and headed into the shower.

After showering I put on my oldest and most faded sweats. I was still toweling my hair when I joined PJ in the living area.

She smiled. "And you look mighty ... uh ...well, never mind."

"I hope your thought was complimentary."

She shot me a saucy grin. "I tried to get into the computer," she said, "but the power went off again and I didn't know how to fire up the generator."

"You just need to flip this switch, the red one here under this cabinet." She had turned around to see where in the kitchen it was. I flipped the switch and a moment later I heard the generator hum and saw the surge protector glowing brightly, indicating that we had power.

I turned back to the living area and stood beside the table. "I'm curious about those medallions ... I have a feeling that I've seen them before."

"Kim, don't start.... I'm so firmly rooted in the here and now that it spooks me when you get into this former life thing."

"Relax. I meant only that I've seen something like them before ... in a museum in Athens. I was there for a conference and was waiting in line to check in and pick up my packet ... there were glass cases along the wall displaying small artifacts, one of them held some medallions and coins... Damn, I could kick myself for not having paid more attention, but my mind was on the conference schedule."

I reached into the passenger compartment for a pile of archaeological and mythological journals and papers. "But I do remember seeing some drawings in one of these ... here, you take half and I'll take half."

I handed her one of the medallions for comparison purposes. I kept the other one on the sofa with me. But before delving into the books, I studied the medallion closely under a simple magnifying glass.

I handed the glass to PJ and cracked open one of the journals.

"We've nothing on hand to decipher the script," PJ said, after studying the medallion, "but I'm positive it's of Greek origin." She paused and looked at me. "You know what bothers me?"

"No. What?"

"These are metal medallions ... why aren't they corroded or weathered or dirtier, or something?"

"Now who is hinting at the unexplained?"

"Not really ... I just ...well, it's a little strange, that's all."

"PJ, are you suggesting that they're fake ... that someone planted them?"

"No, Kim, nothing like that."

I put my journal aside, got up, and slid onto the seat beside PJ. I rested my arm across the back of the seat. "There are powers at play here that I can't explain. You'll just have to go along with me on this, however strange--"

"No, Kim, not that again--"

"*You* brought up the condition of the medallions. And how do you explain all that has happened?"

"I can't, Kim, that's the problem. But I'm not able to accept that there are forces beyond our control playing with us."

"Darling, they're not playing with us, they're speaking to us."

"Did you mean that?"

"I have to ... how else can I explain--"

"Kim, you called me darling. Did you mean it?"

"*I did?*"

"You did."

I covered PJ's hand with mine, squeezed it, and moved back to the sofa. "We have work to do."

"Kim, what are you going to do when you run out of excuses?"

I grinned. "Wing it."

"Yeah, and I bet you will."

For the next half hour or so the only sounds in the motor home were those of pages turning and Pup's heavy breathing as he napped beneath the table.

"Kim, I think I've found the drawings you were talking about."

"Here," she slid the journal in front of me and while I looked at the drawings, she typed something into the computer.

I studied the drawings. "Yeah, I'm sure these are the same ones I remember seeing."

"And here they are again," PJ said, pointing at the monitor. "Photographs from The Archaeological Institute based in Athens."

"Good work, PJ. They're so similar to ours, if not exactly alike." I put my arm around her shoulder and hugged her to me.

"Mmm, I like the reward for a good job done so if there's anything else you need, I'm your woman."

I side glanced her with a raised eyebrow before turning my attention back to the journal.

"It says here that, according to legend, they were Amazon insignias of bravery much like our Medal of Honor or Purple Heart. They were awarded by the reigning Amazon Queen for bravery and wounds received in battle."

I picked up the medallion and noticed something strange. I reached for the other one, which was still lying on the sofa along with my stack of journals. When I held both of them, one in each hand, one felt warmer than the other, as if possessed by some powerful magic.

That's crazy. I'm suffering from some post earthquake trauma or something.

"PJ, I want you to do something for me?"

"Do I get a reward afterwards?"

"Be serious."

"Okay." She covered her face with both hands, then opened them to reveal a serious expression.

"Hold out your hands." I dropped one medallion in each of her hands. "Do you notice anything?"

"Oh, my goodness. It's…" She looked startled. "Kim, this one," she opened her right hand, "is so warm … it's almost hot. How did you do that?"

I shrugged. "I didn't do anything. I noticed it, too. Only the other one was hotter for me, the one you have in your left hand." I took it back and confirmed that it made my hand warm. "What do you think would cause that?"

PJ bit her lip. "I've no idea."

"I'd like you to have one of them."

"Oh, Kim, I couldn't. They're part of your Amazon artifacts ... your project."

I held up the two medallions. "Do you have any druthers?"

She gave me a dubious look. "I'll take the colder one, okay? I don't know what sort of magic might be at work in the other one."

I dropped it over PJ's head. "Wear it always." She nodded.

I placed the other one, which now felt cool to my touch, over my head and tucked it inside my sweatshirt. "Maybe I'm being foolish, caught up in the events of the past several weeks, but I take our discovery of these artifacts as yet another sign that we're forever connected to our Amazons. Marna and I shared the same soul, of that I'm sure. So who's to say she couldn't have intended we have these?"

"So, if you and Marna shared the same soul, you too were in love with Leeja."

"I expect so." I took a deep breath. "Everything that happened on the mountain has implications that we are unaware of as yet. Even the snakes were a sign."

PJ chuckled. "God, they scared me. Didn't they know we were there?"

"Rattlers are pit vipers. They locate prey by heat sensitivity and vibration. That's why I told you to be still."

"Then they must have been pretty stupid snakes because I was vibrating from head to foot."

"They knew we were there. That's why I believe there was more to it. They were telling us something."

"Like what?"

"I don't know. That it's over … for us anyway. The Amazons have told their story, now it's up to us to honor their memory by showing little girls they need not be second class citizens, that they too can grow up to be Amazons … warriors in the modern world of commerce, politics, and science. Nothing is beyond their reach. Our Amazons reached the New World. Our modern day Amazons will conquer time and space."

"Wow!" PJ fingered her medallion. "What a beautiful way to honor them."

"Wear it proudly," I said, getting up, but not before touching her medallion. "You've earned it."

Tears glistened in PJ's eyes. "I will, Kim. And I don't care what you say, I'm going to hug you."

She got up from the computer and put her arms around me. She felt good in my arms, as if she belonged there. I stepped back, afraid of my desires.

PJ looked at me with great sadness in her eyes. "Not ready yet, huh?"

"Don't rush me, PJ, please ... this is a serious step, one I won't take until I'm sure ... I don't want to be hurt again and I don't want to hurt or disappoint you."

"Okay, but going back to Leeja ... if you as Marna were in love with her, how does that leave me with Kim?"

"That was another time, PJ." I moved back to the sofa and started to tidy up the journals, which were scattered on the cushions and on the floor.

"I know you're being careful, Kim, and I understand, but don't wait until we're old and crotchety, okay?"

"Oh, I still have a little life left in me yet." To prove my point, I grabbed my damp hair towel, which I had left draped over the arm of the sofa, and slapped her across her rear end.

PJ raised an eyebrow. "I bet you do. But, Kim Blair, you'd better not be starting something you don't intend to finish."

Chapter Twenty-two

"Kim, you didn't *have* to come shopping with me, you know. I was quite capable of finding the Superstition Springs Mall on my own." I turned in a slow circle, checking the hem of a new pair of cargo pants in the three-way mirror outside the fitting room. "Dillard's has quite a good selection of sportswear, don't you think?"

"Very nice," Kim replied. She was slumped in a chair outside of the fitting room, surrounded by shopping bags.

"Is the hem too long, do you think?"

She stared at my feet. "Looks fine to me."

"Kim?" I waited for her to raise her sights.

"Mm?"

"You aren't having much fun are you?"

"Sure I am. Watching you try on tons of clothes... why it... uh... it..." A yawn threatened to crack her jaw. "Sorry. Didn't get much sleep last night."

"This was a bad idea, Kim."

"No, now wait. You needed to... *we both* needed a break from work. And you needed cheering up after that trip to the hotel." Her eyes warmed to the color of milk chocolate. "I'm really sorry there was so little left of your things after the fire."

I crouched beside her and gave her thigh a squeeze. She made sure we were alone before covering my hand with hers.

"And I'm really sorry you're miserable here waiting for me. I really do appreciate your support, though." When she smiled I could see the tension and fatigue fade away and only tiny laugh lines remained at the corners of her eyes. "Correct me if I'm wrong, but I think shopping, for you, must be like having a root canal without anesthesia."

"Marginally better, but yes, that's true."

Then, I'd better stop torturing you.

I stood up. "Why don't we get out of here…go get a snack or something?"

Kim straightened her back and folded her arms. "Wait. Hold on. You were looking at swimsuits over there on the sale rack a minute ago." She inclined her head toward a display of microscopic bikinis and sleek, one-piece, racing tanks. "Aren't you going to try any of them on?"

I followed her gaze and hesitated. *Uh…huh. I know what your game is and I'm very flattered, but…* "Nope. I don't really need to replace the one that got burned up. I've got plenty back in Boston."

Kim pouted. "Damn. I was looking forward to seeing you model a couple of those."

I'll bet. I shook my head. "Sorry. I won't force you to stay here a minute longer than necessary."

I changed back into my old clothes and carried the new shirts, jeans and shorts to the counter. "I'll take these, please." The clerk smiled and rang up my purchases.

While the register hummed, I peeked at Kim. She rose in deliberate increments and stretched, groaning to celebrate her release from captivity. With mathematical precision, she assembled my items into manageable bundles and staggered over to me in time to add my most recent purchases to the collection. "Just how many weeks did you think you'd be staying?" she asked.

I laughed and started ticking chores off on my fingers. "Well, you know it depends on the final reports, the insurance claim forms, the professors at the University of Arizona…and …uh…" I wiggled my pinkie while giving her a pointed look. "…a few more personal things. But, I can always use these in Boston next spring."

We took the stairs down to the lower level, as the escalator was out of commission. Parts of the mall had been closed while construction engineers made tests and evaluated possible earthquake damage to walls and foundations.

Bright Christmas lights were strung from each storefront and giant candy canes arched over the miniature Toyland set aside for Santa's Workshop.

A delightful carousel stood silently waiting for clearance to resume its spinning. Several children pressed up against the barriers surrounding the glassed-in rotunda, urging it back to life.

I admired the attractive terra cotta and pastel hues of the floors and walls as we strolled along. "This is such a beautiful mall, Kim." It had two stories that expanded into quadrants filled with airy sunshine. "Do you know what these geometric patterns on the floor represent?"

She shrugged. "I haven't a clue. I've only been here a few times and that was usually a quick trip into Dillard's from the outside entrance. I do know that it's been here about ten years." She chuckled. "And I read somewhere that when it first opened, they planted bamboo in the center area. But it grew at the rate of three inches a day, so they had to take it out. I see they have other trees planted along the sides now and, during this festive season, colorful Christmas lights hung from the branches."

We stopped at the center area in question where the main attraction was a thriving cactus garden. "Well, anyway, I'm impressed with the place and I admire bold and daring experiments, even if they fail sometimes. Where would we be if you had listened to the skeptics who discounted your theories on the Amazon women?"

"Touché," Kim muttered.

You're so patient with me...and my need to shop. I scanned the storefronts for a way to reward her.

"Kim, why don't we take these bags to the car and come back in for a milkshake at the Cold Stone Creamery or the Dairy Queen? My treat."

Her expression brightened. "We've been here so long, I may need something more substantial. How about a sandwich or salad at Ruby Tuesday?"

I stared at her, shaking my head. "Would you listen to us? I, the former 'health nut,' suggest a sugar-filled, calorie-laden treat, and you, 'Miss-I-can-eat-anything-fattening-and-not-gainan-ounce,' make a counter offer of salad. What's wrong with this picture?"

Kim smirked. "Maybe we've rubbed off on each other."

Oh, I'd like to rub off on you...don't tempt me.

I sighed. "Maybe so. C'mon, give me some of those." I took several bags and she redistributed her load. "Your shoulder just started mending. We don't need to tax it to the limit."

We found the minivan, dumped my purchases, and compromised with the Ruby Tuesday Salad Bar and a small hot fudge sundae at the Dairy Queen for dessert.

"Do you remember that cute tee shirt with the wolf on the front and the paw prints wrapping around the chest?" I asked Kim, as we climbed into the car after our feast. "We saw them in Sears."

"It was all pretty much a blur, why?" She adjusted the rear view mirror and buckled her seatbelt, then popped a peanut butter cup into her mouth and chewed. Our final stop had been The Sweet Factory for cashews, gummy bears and peanut butter cups.

"Well, I got one and I liked it so much I bought another one for you." I bit my lower lip. "I hope you don't mind."

"That really wasn't necessary, PJ, but thank you."

Kim started the car and we drove toward the supermarket. We had to buy food for our grand finale dinner with the students. Even though we weren't sure when it would be, Kim believed in being prepared.

"I do like wolves, as you know, one in particular, anyway." She exhaled. "Poor Pup. I hope he can hold on a bit longer. We've been gone for hours."

I spotted a Best Buy on the way out of the mall and was only half-listening.

"Sorry Kim. I guess we could go back to the motor home first, and come back later for the food."

She laughed. "PJ, I was just kidding you. He'll be fine. You can take him out for a long walk when we get back and I'm sure he'll forgive our neglect."

"Oh well, good. Um... Kim, would you mind if we split up for a little bit? I remembered something I need at Best Buy. Drive to the market so I know where it is and let me use the car, okay? I'll come back and find you before you're finished. You know about raw meat and all that sort of thing anyway."

She gave me a puzzled look. "You make me sound like a cave woman. Okay. We might as well do it all in one afternoon."

I dropped Kim in front of Albertson's, list and coupons in hand, prepared to make her assault as a modern day hunter-gatherer, and drove back to the electronics store. Several eager sales clerks helped me find just what I needed in less than twenty minutes.

Traffic along Power Road was horrendous. I did my best, but it was another ten minutes before I found a parking place at the supermarket and entered the store.

"Hey, there," I said, a bit breathless, when I caught up to Kim. She was scrutinizing heads of iceberg lettuce. I took charge of pushing the cart as we worked our way through the aisles.

The store was jammed with people; women with young children, teenagers in pairs, single adults, and clusters of senior citizens, all yanking things from the shelves with grim-faced urgency, tossing them into carts and careening off to the next aisle. "Is it always this busy?"

Kim shrugged. "I usually go early or late to avoid crowds. It looks like everyone is afraid of being caught in another quake without milk, bread or toilet paper."

I laughed. "It's the same way back east, only it happens when they predict a blizzard."

Kim hauled some packages of meat from the depths of her cart, handing them to me. "I got a couple of sirloin steaks and three pounds of ground beef. If we buy chicken, too, do you think it will be enough?"

I hefted the steaks and returned them to her. "I guess. You know how those guys eat.... like vultures. Remember those weekly dinners at Missus O'Brien's place? I guess if we add lots of salad and chips we can manage."

She nodded, thinking. "Drinks?"

277

We turned into the beverage aisle. I pointed to the rows of soda. "How about cans of soft drinks and bottles of water? We can buy a few foam coolers and ice it all down."

"Okay, but I'd like to get a bottle of wine or maybe sparkling cider...for a farewell toast."

I grabbed several twelve-packs of colas and a case of bottled water, while Kim found the cider. We checked her list and matched coupons. I offered to finance the deal, but she rejected all but a fifty-fifty split.

Since Kim knew the route back with all the detours, I let her drive, using my free time to review our master list of chores.

"Are you sure you aren't adding things to this list?" I asked her. "It doesn't seem to get any shorter."

"Haven't touched it, I swear." Kim made a 'crossing of her heart' gesture and smiled at me.

"How are you coming with the UA professors?"

Her eyes returned to the road. "I spoke with Professor Crandall and Doctor Bentz. Under the circumstances, they will accept data and reports from up until the day of the quake. If our people did a good enough job, they'll get credit for three quarters of a semester of fieldwork." Kim gave me a grin. "It's only fair; they worked their tails off."

I nodded. "You saw to that. There's no doubt in my mind that they fulfilled the requirements. But, what about the rest of the semester?"

Kim took a wide turn and came into her lot from the rear. "Ah, some more good news. In the three weeks remaining of this term, they will have two choices to complete their sessions. There's an ongoing project of Apache and Pueblo mapping sites in Silver Creek...that's in east central Arizona, or they can find openings with the Marana Mound work just north of Tucson. They'd need to do classifications and analysis of various Hohokam artifacts for the Museum at UA, but they can stay in their campus housing and commute by the university's van."

"Great. I'd be tempted by that second project myself. I imagine it'll be right up Laine's alley...maybe Mike's too."

"I think all of them could be happy with either project."

When the minivan pulled to a stop beside her motor home, I put my hand on her arm. "You know Kim, they were really devastated by this sudden end to our work. We all were."

Kim patted my hand. "I know and I'm very thankful to have had such a dedicated team."

"You seem to be the only one of us at peace with the situation."

She sighed. "It's odd, I know. I should be the one most destroyed, but I think it all somehow happened for a reason...the way it was meant to be. I'm not yet certain what it means, but I'm going to be patient and wait for it to unfold. Just knowing that my calculations and research panned out and that we actually located them, however briefly, is success enough for me."

I gave her hand a squeeze and unclasped my seatbelt. "You're incredible Kim. You've been a shining example to all of us. I'm so lucky to have worked with you on this project."

We grabbed armloads of groceries and climbed the steps into the motor home. "I hope it doesn't stop with this project, PJ." Kim placed her bags on the kitchen counter and looked at me for several seconds. "Whatever comes of this soul-searching I'm doing, I want us to continue to be friends and work together. Would you be able to do that?"

The sensitive nature of the subject caught me off guard. I bit down on my lower lip, feeling the sting of tears.

Is this it, then? Are you going to deny this thing we have for each other and reject me? Can I back away and remain friends, if that's all you want from me?

"I don't know, Kim. You're my best friend right now, so yes, I want to go on working with you for as long as possible. But, it won't be easy. You know that you're more than just a friend to me." I blinked and took a couple of calming breaths. "I'll try to give you all the time you need, if you keep considering your options."

She nodded with a shy smile. "That sounds fair...and very honest. I'm not deliberately trying to hurt you, PJ. It's taking me a long time to sort everything out and make everything better for all of us. Right now, I'm just glad that we found other work options for the crew."

I was relieved to have the conversation back on less personal ground. "Those choices should make them happy. They won't lose any credit hours or time. Will it pay as well as their work with the foundation?"

Kim frowned as she stuffed meat into the freezer. "I don't know, but I doubt it. Your father is a very generous employer."

I paused just inside the door, ready to return to the van for a second load. "Yeah...he is at that." I shook my head. "It's so weird not to be griping about him. I wasted so many years of bitterness...all that fighting and rebelling."

"You both have a lot of fence-mending to do."

I smiled as she followed me down the steps. "I'm looking forward to that."

We made several trips from the car to the motor home with our purchases, collapsing on the sofa when the final bag was piled on the floor beside me. "Whew! I'm bushed," I said. "Where in the world are we going to put all this stuff?"

Kim laughed. "*Now*, you worry about it! I've been fussing at you all afternoon about my lack of space."

"Wait, I don't mean my new clothing. That can go back to the car if necessary. I'm worried about the food. Where will it go?"

"Well, it depends on when we can have the dinner. If we schedule it soon, most of it can stay in the refrigerator." She stood up and peered at the answering machine, which was blinking. "Four messages. Maybe one of those is from Mike."

While Kim was busy with the machine, I leashed Pup and took him for a walk around the park. The air quality seemed better so we took a path around the outside, probably half a mile in distance. His tongue was hanging out when we returned and mine wasn't far from doing the same. I poured fresh water into his bowl and cracked open a bottle of Arrowhead, cold and fresh from the refrigerator.

"I'm going to hop in the shower and put my new things away," I told Kim.

"Clean towels in the cabinet next to the sink. Help yourself."

"Thanks." Whistling a few snatches of an old Beatles song that was a favorite of my mother's, I looked back at Kim as I slid the bathroom door open. She was stretched out on the sofa with a cold Coors Light in one hand, the television remote in the other.

"Why don't you try some of your new things on and have a fashion show. Pup and I will be your audience, won't we fella?" Pup gave an enthusiastic whine from his spot on the floor at her side.

"I figured you had your fill of that at the mall," I said, grinning at her from the bathroom.

"That's because I wasn't comfortable at the mall. Now, I am. So, bring it on, woman."

"Okay. Let me get cleaned up first." I took my shower and hurried into a pair of gray cargo shorts and the wolf tee shirt. Carrying her shirt in one hand, I strolled through the kitchen, swiveling my hips in imitation of a Vogue model, ending in a pirouette in front of her. I dropped her shirt into her lap. "Well, whatcha think?"

Her appreciative wolf whistle brought Pup to his feet growling.

"So you both approve?" I asked.

"I can't speak for him, but I love it, PJ." Kim accepted her gift. "Thank you so much for buying me one, too." She pulled me close to kiss the top of my head. "Yours looks fantastic. I'm going to try mine on." She dashed off to the bathroom with her shirt.

The deep turquoise made her tan appear darker and enhanced the silver highlights in her dark hair.

"Wow! It looks fantastic on you, Kim. I'm not kidding." She grinned and color rose in her cheeks. "I won't whistle because Pup would only start barking again.... but...really..."

You look so sexy, Kim. My eyes are glued to those embossed paw prints and their winding path over the hills and valley of your chest. I'd better look away or you're going to see me drool.

"PJ?"

It was my turn to blush. "Sorry, my mind was elsewhere. What did you say?"

She continued to grin, her eyes lingering on my paw prints. "I think I know where your mind was just now, but I'm not about to demand an explanation."

"Whew! Yes. Let's change the subject before... Oh, wait! I forgot. Something else to show you." I dashed out to the minivan and pulled the blanket off my purchase from Best Buy. With a grin, I bounded up the steps and into the motor home.

"Take a look at this, Kim." I unpacked a brand new HP Pavilion Notebook. "What do you think of it?"

Kim opened the case to examine the keyboard and extra wide screen. "Wow! It's a beauty...top of the line... plenty of power and memory. It'll more than make up for the one that you lost in the fire."

I gave her a delighted grin. "Oh, it isn't for me."

She looked puzzled. "It isn't?"

"I got it for *you*, to replace the one that was crushed by the landslide."

"Oh, PJ, you didn't need to do--"

I held up my hand. "Yes, I did. Consider it a thank you for letting me stay here with you. The insurance money would allow you to buy a new one anyway. This just gets it to you sooner, when you can really use it."

Kim's brow wrinkled. "It's too much, PJ. I can't let you do it."

Gawd, you are too stubborn for your own good. I chewed on my lip for a few seconds, trying for a compromise.

"How about, you pay me for this one when you get the insurance money?"

She pondered that possibility, tracing the edges of the case with her fingertips. Her eyes were already glazing over. "Yes, I can't deny it would help right now. Okay, that will work. But, you needed one, too."

I laughed. "And I got one just like it! It's still out in the van."

Kim chuckled. "Well, what are you waiting for? Go get it! We'll have a 'geek girls only' evening...setting things up together."

Once we had explored the features on the new laptops, we settled down to some serious report gathering, summarizing of daily field notes with analysis, budget tallies, chart making and all the little details required for the completion of a project that ended prematurely. Kim took calls from Boston, Tucson and Denver. The last was our wayward student, Mike, reporting in with the news that he had found a ride to Phoenix and would be able to join us the day after tomorrow. So our dinner was set for the same afternoon.

Thursday at noon, all of us will meet for the last time as members of the Superstition Mountain Expedition. Just the thought makes my heart ache...

I feel nervous...so very nervous about the future. Will you and I go on this way, or with something more?

How does that old saying go? 'I need patience...and I need it right now!'

We enjoyed a late night supper of crusty, multi-grain bread, sliced ham, havarti cheese and a fruit salad. Kim put a CD in her player and subdued piano and orchestra music enhanced the mood. She pulled the front drapes for privacy and we eased back on the sofa, propping our bare feet on a small hassock. Kim drank her water straight from the bottle and I sipped a glass of iced tea.

Sandy's call interrupted our tranquility, but we were happy to hear from him. He told us that his mother insisted on making a cake for our special dinner.

"That's so sweet of her," Kim told him. "Be sure to thank her for us."

"She's going to make her specialty...red velvet cake," she said after hanging up the phone. "We should get a gallon of vanilla ice cream to go with that."

"Yum. I'll add it to the list." I found a pen and moved to the refrigerator door where we had posted our menu and last minute shopping needs.

"A party with the kids." I sighed when I sat back down beside Kim. "Seems right, somehow, doesn't it?"

Kim poked my foot with her big toe. "Yeah, Ma, we've had enough ups and downs with 'them thar young'uns' during this project, but I guess it's only fittin' that we should end it on a happy note."

Right. But, will it be a happy note for us?

There was a long silence broken only by strident pounding on several pianos as Kim's CD reached its finale.

"Kim, I don't think I've ever heard that piece before."

"It's Schubert's *Fantasia* in C major, also called 'Wanderer Fantasy.'

"Oh..." *How appropriate.*

Kim turned off her player and returned to the sofa.

The alternating loud and soft piano notes had made my stomach tighten. I pondered the 'ups and downs' of our project and what might happen on Thursday.

You might not have made your decision by then. No news is still good news. Maybe we can just toddle along like we are for a few more weeks.

No, I'd never survive...and you wouldn't make me suffer any longer than necessary.

My vision blurred and I looked away...staring out into the evening sky, searching for a star to wish upon.

I've waited my whole life for someone like you. I hope I have the strength to accept your decision.

"Everything okay, PJ?" Kim put her empty bottle on the side table and picked up the remote, switching on the news.

"I'm fine." I swiped at my eyes. "Just tired.... It's been a long day."

"That it has." Kim shifted and slid her arm along the back of the sofa behind my neck.

We watched a bit of local news about the recovery and clean up of areas damaged by the earthquake. "Looks like we're getting out from under things." Kim muted the sound as the broadcast went to a commercial.

"Speaking of recovery operations, do you think we'll be finished by Thursday?" I winced at my possible double entendre. "With our project, I mean."

She stretched. "Well, let's see, I believe there's a bit to do on the desktop using that National Archaeological Data Base program and then we need to proofread everything and run-off several copies of the whole report."

"That should finish the project."

"Should, yes. Our menu for the big feast is all set. Josie and Laine called earlier and said they want to bring some coleslaw and bean salad. I told them it would be fine."

"Sure."

"We'll need ice cream and ice but that can wait until Thursday morning. I'll make the potato salad tomorrow afternoon. You can make up the hamburger patties tomorrow night."

"Okay. I'm getting pretty good at that."

Kim smiled. "I'll even let you whip up that mustard and salsa stuff you tried last time. It looked weird, but tasted surprisingly good."

I chuckled. "Gee, a compliment. You just like it when I yell, 'Bam!' each time I add some."

Kim gave my shoulder a squeeze. "Yes, I enjoy your 'Emeril Live' impression. Anyway, the burgers can go on the grill after the boneless chicken browns."

She frowned as the news broadcast returned with the weather portion. "I sure hope the air quality keeps improving. I'd like us to be able to eat outside or at least walk around out there a bit."

I pointed to the television. "There's the chart now. What does 'fair' mean?"

Kim laughed. "Not a whole lot, actually. Well, I guess it could be worse, but you stay inside as much as you can tomorrow. Your sinuses will thank you for it."

"Yes, ma'am," I said. "I thought Arizona had clean, clear air with no allergy or sinus problems. That's what all the ads used to say. What's up with that?"

"People brought plants and allergy producing stuff with them when they moved here...and dust storms coat so much of the place with dirt that I think a lot of Nevada and California got dumped on the state. I haven't been in this area very long, though, so I just repeat what the locals say."

I nodded. "That's right. You have that ranch in New Mexico. Is that your real home?"

The news ended and Kim turned off the television. "I think it will be once I get it renovated."

She took my empty glass to the kitchen and rinsed it, leaving it to dry in the dish rack overnight. The empty water bottle clinked as it fell into the recycling bin under the sink. I patted the seat beside me on the sofa when she returned. "Tell me more about your ranch, that is …if you're not too tired."

Kim sat close enough to me that our shoulders and hips rubbed. I relished the contact and I looked forward to this time of the day with Kim…the unwinding after long, arduous work sessions. It reminded me of our quiet campfires up on the mountain, just before we climbed into our sleeping bags for the night.

Kim cleared her throat. "Well, the owner was about to go bankrupt, so I got it for a song. Jasper, he's the caretaker who watches the place for me, said the guy had no business sense at all and would never have made a good rancher."

"How many acres is it?"

"About a thousand, but a lot of that is wooded and mountainous. It's northwest of Santa Fe in an area called Happy Valley. There's a ranch house, a huge barn, a home for Jasper and his wife, and several other outbuildings I haven't even investigated yet. The view is beautiful. Those Sangre de Cristo Mountains seem so vivid and imposing out the picture window. There's a huge fireplace in the living room…one of those kiva types that New Mexico is famous for…"

"It sounds fantastic, Kim."

"You should see it sometime. I think you'd enjoy it…'course it needs fixing up."

I smiled at her, resting my hand on her leg. When she put her hand on top of mine, we unconsciously laced our fingers together. "I'm sure I would love it, Kim. If…well…if it's meant to be…. then I will see it."

She squeezed my hand. "It's probably time to turn in, don't you think?"

"Yeah." I gave her a brief smile. "Guess you'd better get off my bed, then."

Each time I used the shower in the motor home, I removed the medallion Kim had given me. I was afraid the thin leather strand would break if too much hot water soaked it. I also didn't like the smell of the wet leather. Kim had said to wear it always, though, so I always replaced it right afterward. I wore it with pride. It was a symbol of our journey together in search of the lost Amazon women... a time I would never forget.

Tonight, as I snuggled into my sleeping bag on the sofa bed, I tucked my hand through the leather strip and rubbed the smooth metal surface between my thumb and finger. As I drifted off to sleep, I felt the presence of a familiar spirit touching my cheek and neck. This vague presence had disturbed me before, on the night I first wore the medallion, but nothing more sinister had happened, so I had learned to accept its occurrence at bedtime.

Tonight, the spirit was bolder, more imposing.

"Who are you?" I demanded of it, surprised to feel no fear. For a brief moment, I thought Kim had come to me for comfort and my body warmed at the thought. But, it wasn't Kim.

"Little One, be calm," a woman's voice told me. "You have taken up the Medal of Valor. You profess a love for our Protected One. You must be deemed worthy."

Sweat formed on my neck and between my breasts. "Gawd, you've never spoken to me before. I'm sorry...I didn't know. If I'm breaking some sort of code, then you can have the damn thing back."

The spirit woman chuckled. "It's not that easy, Little One. Your love is pledged to the Protected One, is it not?"

"Well, if you mean Kim... when you say Protected One...then yes."

"She is the one most favored, the one called Marna in our world."

My throat felt parched. "You...you're an Amazon, then?"

The spirit's hand pulled my cover back and lifted my chin. "It matters not, Little One. I have my orders. You will be silent

287

now and I will know your heart and your thoughts. If they are worthy, you will find your answers in due time."

"Wait." I felt more sweat now, under my arms and across my back. My thin, cotton, nightshirt felt clammy. "Um...you can't just--"

"Hush!" Her hand closed over my mouth. I gulped and remained silent. "Roll onto your back and do not move or speak. Do you understand? Just nod your head."

I nodded and turned onto my back. My nightshirt twisted underneath me, but I made no move to fix it.

She unfastened the top button on my nightshirt and took the medallion into her hand. It was too dark in the motor home for me to see her face clearly, but I sensed that she wore a mask over her eyes and nose. I could tell that she had thick, full lips and her jaw was firm. There was a power in her body that belied her ghostly state. I resolved to obey her commands and pray that she would release me to a more relaxed dream state as soon as possible.

There was a tickling sensation at my neck as she fingered the medallion and mumbled an incantation of sorts. I held my breath when she dropped the necklace and touched my collarbone, muttering more chants.

Amazon or no Amazon...you lay a hand on my breast and I'm screaming bloody murder!

"Steady, now, Little One. This is going to be difficult for you. I will make it quick. I promise you it will not hurt." She opened two more buttons and put one hand between my breasts. My breath released in a gasp as cold air struck my bare skin.

"I know. You are embarrassed, but this is how it must be. I am going to see and feel what is in your heart."

The hand on my chest felt strong and warm. I bit down on my lower lip, containing my panic, and listened to the magnified thumping of my heart.

It was as if she held a stethoscope to my ears. How can that be?

"Ah...I see," is all she said before pulling my shirt closed. She sighed and chanted some more. The top layer of my sleeping bag was replaced and her hands moved to my face and forehead.

"This is the final test," she murmured. "Look at me, Little One. Do not be afraid."

"Easy for you to say," I whispered, feeling a little more like myself now that my chest was covered.

She smiled. "We were told you had spirit inside you. Now, I know it is true."

"Is that a good thing?" I asked, almost afraid to hear her answer.

"Usually," she said. "Now, be--"

"I know the drill. Shut up and look at you."

"Yes, I am almost finished." She placed her hands on either side of my head. I felt a slight tightness above my eyebrows, but nothing more intense than a mild sinus headache. Then, she put one thumb above my nose and slid it up and down and back and forth. In a religious ceremony it might have been the sign of the cross, but I couldn't imagine what the Amazon equivalent was.

"Goddess Bless me!" she cried and pulled away. "I have never...in all my...so amazing..."

"What is it? Can I speak now?" I started to sit up.

"Relax, Little One." She pushed me down. "I am finished and I must make my report. You will sleep now."

Fat chance.

She faded from my sight. "But... what about my... Am I worthy? Do I get to wear the medallion? More importantly, do I get to live my life with Kim?"

Her response came from right above me. "You will know the answers to those questions soon enough. I can only tell you that I have never seen a love so strong in any of my examinations. You do great honor to the medal you wear. Your heart is strong and full of purpose. You will see great adventure, Little One."

"Please... Before you go... You make lots of these exams?"

She laughed. "Yes, of course. It is necessary for the continuation of the Amazon Nation."

"Please don't be offended, but you sure have bizarre initiation rites."

She laughed again. "It is necessary. These are uncertain times."

I wasn't sure what times she meant. "Can't you tell me anything about ...you know...my worthiness with Kim?"

"I'm sorry, I have my orders. I was to make the tests and file a report. You will know soon, however. And you must abide by the final decision. Even possessing as much spirit as you do, it will not help you to fight against the results. They are already written in the scrolls of eternity."

She was gone, then. I lay awake, certain I could never sleep after such a vivid dream.

I don't know what I ate to bring that on, but I'm never having it again.

A feeling of calm stole over me, though, and I was able to drift off.

Though I was filled with sketchy memories of my strange dream when I woke up on Wednesday, I decided to keep the thoughts to myself and concentrate on current duties. Our deadlines approached. Real life called and I had to answer.

Kim and I stood in the motor home kitchen, consulting the list. "I'll clean the place when you leave to take Pup on his walk. Don't stay out too long, the air is getting clearer, but you need to play it safe."

I saluted her. "Yes, General Doc, ma'am."

She laughed. "No need for such formality. A simple, 'Your Highness' will do."

"Okay," I replied, wrinkling my nose at her. I went to the table and picked through the pages of our assembled report. "Let's finish proofreading this and I can drive over to the copy center and get that finished this morning. I think there's a Federal Express place near there, too, so I can mail it right out."

Kim leaned over my shoulder. "Good idea. How many copies do we need?"

"Hmm." I did some mental arithmetic. "About six should do it."

We each took five of the remaining ten pages of the final draft and settled down at the table to read for errors. Pup gave me a soft whine and an anxious look.

"It'll be ready in just a second, sweetie." He snuffled and sat down with his nose on my thigh, waiting and watching.

We made corrections, which Kim entered into the computer. Corrected pages were printed.

I sighed as Kim put our finished document into a manila envelope. "Two hundred and twenty pages. Is that a lot for three months work? It doesn't seem like much."

"Hard to say, Kim. To quote Winston Churchill, a lot of our 'blood, toil, tears and sweat' went into that report. There's no way to account for that properly."

I stood up and located my purse and Pup's leash. He dashed to the door in anticipation of a great adventure.

"Anyway, if it isn't in there now, it didn't happen." Kim said as a final pronouncement.

Pup was nudging me along to the door in noisy fashion. "Easy, fella. I'm coming." I left my purse on top of the report and Pup and I took our walk.

"Ya know, I could do a lot better cleaning job if you could keep Pup away from here a bit longer," Kim said, when we returned.

"I'll take him with me in the minivan when I do the copying."

"You're an angel, PJ."

I headed to the bathroom for a quick shower and a change of clothes. "I'm a lot of things," I called back, "but angel isn't one of them." I looked down at the medallion as I pulled it over my head.

Am I worthy? Who knows? Anyway, it was all a crazy dream.

The motor home sparkled when Pup and I returned. Kim sat at the table sipping a mug of tea, munching on a fresh muffin. She got up and poured a mug for me, while I phoned Dad about the delivery of our report.

"They'll be on your desk by tomorrow afternoon, Dad. That's a promise."

"Fine, Princess. I'll make sure the board members get copies for the next meeting."

We wished each other well and I hung up.

There was a print out of an email on the table in front of Kim when I slid into my seat.

I poured milk into my tea, stirred in two spoonfuls of sugar and broke open a hot muffin. "Just what I needed," I said after breaking off a bite and sipping my beverage. "My mission is accomplished. Your copy of the report is on the sofa."

"Good." Her face looked tense.

"How's everything else on the home front?"

Kim slid the message across to me. "It was going just peachy until this popped up on my computer."

I scanned the message and the return address. "Shit. What are we going to do about the media? Specifically, what do we do about Fritz Green?"

Kim grimaced. "Well, he's one of your old drinking pals from the Oasis, isn't he?"

I choked on a mouthful of muffin. "That is so not funny, Kim. He's a pain in the neck and I'd just as soon--"

"I know, I know. He's been a thorn in my side ever since I came to Apache Junction." She paused, tapping her fingers on the tabletop. "Your father promised his station an exclusive...or at least a chance to make a documentary of the discovery. Now, there isn't anything to see. You'd think Green would give up."

"You'd think." I reached for another muffin. Kim slid the butter and jam closer to me. "Thanks, these are delicious, by the way."

Kim popped the last of hers into her mouth and chewed. "Mmm. They are. Albertson's has a great bakery. These are banana walnut, but the cranberry ones are good, too."

I licked my fingers to eliminate excess jam. "So, about Fritz..."

"We both have too much going on right now to worry about him. Let's see if your father can put a muzzle on him. Even from across the country, I'll bet Frederick can squelch the phone calls and emails."

"You've had phone calls? Why didn't you tell me?"

"Just a couple. I let the answering machine pick them up."

I shook my head. The nagging tightness in my sinuses threatened to return. "Why don't you talk with Dad? Or do you want me to call him again?"

"Why don't we both do it? We can present a united front."

I raised my mug to clink against hers. "To a united front against the Fritz Greens of the world!"

"There ya go!"

We finished our snack and made a second call to my dad.

"Wow! Twice in one day," he said with a laugh, when he heard my voice. He was delighted to flex his parental muscle from far across the country.

"Don't you worry about it," he told us. "I'll handle it with the station. They can demand all they want, but any interviews we grant them will be at your discretion. I'll have the foundation send them some data sheets and press releases.... maybe a few carefully chosen pictures from your reports."

He mused for a few seconds. Through the phone line I could hear papers shuffle and the tap of his pen. My mind flashed back to my childhood and the huge, leather chair he used to sit in when Mom would bring me in for a visit. I loved how it creaked when I'd climb onto his lap and bang on his intercom and phone. I recalled the spicy fragrance of his cologne, and his strong hands gripping my waist as I leaned too far onto the desk, in an effort to pile up all his important files.

"Thanks, Dad. I know we can count on you to handle things."

"Thank you, Frederick, it will be a great help to us," Kim added when it was her turn to speak with him.

We put that problem behind us and forged ahead with the schedule for the rest of the day. Our supper consisted of sandwiches and salad, which we ate at our laptops. The meat for our cookout was wrapped and sat ready in the refrigerator. Kim made the potato salad and divided it into two bowls for better storage. I lined up the paper plates, napkins, plastic utensils and cups in stacks on the kitchen counter.

In the morning, air quality permitting, we'd cover the picnic table outside with a checkered cloth. The park manager allowed us to borrow a second table for temporary use. We'd have plenty of room to eat and enjoy our last session together.

Okay so far.

Condiments? I opened the refrigerator and looked at the bottles and jars. *Better make a note to chop that onion. I can get more ketchup when we go for the ice and ice cream.*

What else?

Check the computer for emails. See if anybody needs a ride over here.

Kim and I worked on our laptops, sitting across from each other at the table, sharing online time. Darkness settled around us in the motor home. Pup stretched out on the floor at Kim's feet with a hefty sigh. As the hours passed, my back and neck grew stiff with tension and fatigue. I could feel the 'mother of all headaches' building behind my eyeballs.

If I don't quit soon, I'll have nausea to worry about.

Damn. There are still a few things to do.

And that nagging dream keeps intruding into my thoughts at the worst times. Now I know how Kim felt when she had her dreams.

I powered down my computer and eased upright, stretching to align my spine. "I'm sorry, Kim. I've got to give it a rest." I rubbed my eyes, keeping them closed for several seconds. "There's too much going on in my brain right now."

"Goodness, where did the time go? It's after ten." She moved to my side, touching my cheek. "What is it? Your sinuses again?"

I nodded, hissing at the resulting dizziness. "Ow. Too much tension I guess...or dust...eyestrain... something."

"You're exhausted from everything that's happened in the last few days. You aren't Super Woman, you know."

I gave her a weak grin. "I'm not?"

"No, little one, you're not. Sit on the sofa." She walked through to the bathroom and I heard a cabinet open. "I'll get some Extra Strength Tylenol into you pronto." The door shut and the faucet switched on. In a few seconds she was back with me. "Take these." Two pills dropped into my right hand. She pressed a cup of water into my left.

"Let me turn off my computer and some lights so--"

"Kim, you can keep working, if you need to." I swallowed the pills and settled into the sofa. "There's still the thank you notes to the lab at UA to do."

She sat down next to me, gently guiding my head to her shoulder. "Time for a rest, PJ. I can wrap up the last of the work in the morning."

Her chin grazed my forehead and her lips pressed against my bangs. I felt her right arm slide across my back, moving in slow circles, creating a pleasant friction of warmth through the fabric of my shirt.

The embrace was clumsy, but effective. Kim concentrated on my aching head. I couldn't suppress a moan when she stroked my temple and brushed her fingers through my hair, then back across my forehead.

Gawd, that feels wonderful. Don't stop...ever.

"Relax, PJ. Let the medicine work." She kept a gentle pressure on my eyelids and forehead, working her fingers and lips over my skin. I fought hard, but another moan escaped.

"Am I hurting you?"

"No," I murmured, "but you're making me ache in a different spot."

Kim chuckled and continued her gentle assault on my face, rubbing my temples, then reversing direction to include my eyebrows, eyelids and cheekbones.

"Sorry." Her voice was husky. "One ache at a time."

I breathed a deep sigh, feeling heat suffuse my cheeks. Kim's fingers combed through my hair, lifting my bangs. She kissed the top of my head.

"Your fingers are so strong, but your touch is so tender," I whispered, growing drowsy. I closed my eyes and felt her warm breath against my eyelids.

"So beautiful," she murmured, kissing the tip of my nose, making me giggle.

I opened my eyes to find her smiling down at me. "You're kinda easy on the eyes, yourself, Kim."

She touched my cheek with the back of her hand. "You're so warm. Do you have a fever?"

Yes, a fever in my blood that only you can cure.

I sighed. "Uh...uh. You're kissing me, Kim. I'm getting warm all over. Can't be helped." I sat up and looked into her eyes.

She swallowed.

Seconds spiraled away, dissolving into missed opportunities, never to return. I could feel my heart pounding, the heat in my face building, my mouth going dry at the sight of her intense eyes and soft, luscious lips, just a passionate gasp away.

We sat frozen with indecision, gripped by some mysterious force that neither propelled us apart, nor pulled us closer together. Kim finally gave an anguished sigh and dipped her head toward me. Her lips brushed against mine with feathery touches at first, then with force and conviction, leaving me in a state of blissful paralysis.

Oh my God...My poor head. What a kisser, you are. I'm positively giddy. If I died right now, I'd have the biggest smile on my face.

I regained my senses enough to return her kiss with all the love I possessed.

"Gawd, I've wanted to do that for ages," Kim said with a shaky laugh.

"I know the feeling."

She sat up a bit straighter and pushed me to one side. "Here, let me stretch out my legs." She grabbed a sofa cushion and placed it on her lap. "Now you lie down and put your head on the pillow." I did as she said. "Good. Now, I can continue to work on your head and see you at the same time."

"Are you sure this is what you want to be doing right now, Kim? I mean, it feels wonderful, but--"

"Shh... Little One. Relax. We need to talk a bit more, anyway. I think I owe you a progress report."

"Oh? I'm not sure I want that now...this feels too good."

She continued to stroke my eyelids and forehead, knowing just how hard to press for maximum relief. The painkillers kicked in and I grew sleepy. I wondered if the Amazon woman would return again tonight.

Kim was talking and I had missed her first few words.

"...so the dream made me think of Terry and you and all that has happened to me up until now. One of the things I'm looking for in a relationship is faithfulness."

"Okay," I murmured. "That makes sense."

"Someone who will make a promise to me and keep it. I thought I had that with Terry. She promised to love me and stay with me, but one day I came back to our apartment and found her in bed with another woman."

"Oh, Kim."

She took a ragged breath. "So, one of my needs is someone who will keep her promise." She stroked my cheek. "You've already demonstrated that to me by staying here and not demanding a quick decision."

I took her hand. "It hasn't been easy, let me tell you."

"I know. But, you said you wouldn't pressure me... that you'd wait patiently... and you have. I love you for that, PJ."

I turned her hand over and kissed her palm. "I love you too, but I think you know that already."

She smiled at me. "I do. I think you are the bravest woman I have ever met to be able to say that without knowing if I can give you my full love in return. I'm so sorry to have put you in that position."

My voice was strained with emotion. "It's okay, really. I know it's more complicated for us. And I know that sometimes lovers start out a little unbalanced in their devotion to each other."

"Unbalanced?" Kim started to laugh despite the seriousness of my words.

"Well, maybe that wasn't the right word. Sometimes, one person in a loving relationship has to be bold and make the commitment well ahead of the other person."

Kim nodded. "I see." Her eyes were shining. "PJ...the bold...the brave...the incredibly beautiful."

I swallowed hard against the lump in my throat. *Don't cry now. Tell her more.*

"It's not so bold or brave, Kim. I see it as my future. It's laid out for me...for us. As improbable as it sounds, I think we're meant for each other. It's our destiny to be partners...to love each other. Whether you permit a physical relationship or not, we'll share a lasting friendship. We'll work together, and our bond will be so strong it will last forever...always and forever."

Kim's eyes welled with tears. "Oh, PJ, that was so beautiful. How can you know that? Can you see into my heart and head?"

I yawned, feeling suddenly exhausted by my emotional revelation. "I think I dreamed it last night. An Amazon woman touched my chest and head, and my heart swelled with such emotion...such love...I don't know...I just seemed to see it all in my mind. I hope it comes true..." I yawned, feeling so warm and drowsy.

"Oh, Little One," Kim murmured from far off, "We're even sharing Amazon dreams now."

I fought to stay awake, but it was a losing battle. Some time later, in the midst of the most pleasant dream, I was certain that a strong Amazon Warrior had carried me to her soft, comfortable bed, where she kissed me on the lips and told me she loved me with all her heart.

And I smiled because she kissed just like Kim.

Chapter Twenty-three

"All right, lazy bones, up and at 'em."

I opened one eye. PJ was standing beside the bed with a mug of tea in hand.

"I thought some English Breakfast blend would help you wake up," she said.

I opened my second eye and focused on my surroundings and the lovely woman who had awakened me. Even to my sleep-laden eyes, she looked as fresh as a spring morning.

She put the mug down on the bedside cabinet. "Today is Thursday ... remember ... our farewell dinner."

"Geez!" I sat up, shaking my head to clear it and send my desire for further sleep packing. "What time is it?"

"It's just seven-thirty. No need to panic." PJ sat on the edge of the bed. She handed me my tea. "Drink up."

I took the mug from her, wrapping my hands around its warmth. As I sipped the hot tea, I peered at her over the top of the mug. "You're a sight to wake up to."

"I hope that was intended as a compliment."

"It was." A ripple of desire spread down my spine and settled in the vicinity of my groin. I took another sip of tea. I recalled that when I was with Terry, my urges were always strongest in the morning.

PJ cocked her head to one side. "What?"

"What do you mean, what?"

"You were miles away."

"No I wasn't. I was closer than you think."

She smiled. "Care to tell me where you were?"

I raised an eyebrow and handed her my almost empty mug.

"Are you going to tell me or do I have to wrestle it out of you?"

299

"I have to get up and get showered."

PJ put the mug down on the bedside cabinet and leaned over to kiss me. I turned my head. "Not now ... morning breath, you know."

She giggled. Then with a lightning fast move, she caught me full on the mouth. "Smells like rose petals to me," she said, straightening up.

"Girl, you are sick. Now go, I have to clean up."

She stood there with a 'come hither' expression on her face.

It happened so fast that I don't remember even thinking about it. I grabbed her and pulled her onto the bed. We roughhoused for a minute or so. PJ was squealing with delight. Then she stopped, and I stopped. I was lying on top of her, my legs straddling her hips. I was holding her arms down, our lips almost touching. We remained frozen in that position for several seconds.

"I'm sorry," I whispered, lifting myself off her. "I'm sorry."

"I'm not." PJ's voice was husky.

I wasn't sure if her eyes were shining from tears or from need. *Gawd, I want you, too, PJ, but not this way.* I was aware of a tingle between my legs. *It's been a long time for me and I'm eager, but this doesn't feel right ... it's not the time.*

"Please, PJ, not now."

"Then when?"

"I don't know." I got up off the bed. "I just know not now."

PJ stood up, reached for my empty cup, and went through the bathroom and into the kitchen. She slammed the door into its frame with a clunk that reverberated through the soles of my bare feet.

I leaned forward, cradling my head in my hands. "Shit!"

Several minutes passed. *Gawd, why am I handling this so badly?*

I pulled myself together, threw my sleep scrubs on the bed, and went into the bathroom. I squinted at the spotlight of sunshine beaming through the skylight as I stepped into the shower stall.

The cool water cascaded off my body, taking my mind off its sexual demands. *Damn it all, PJ, I don't want to hurt you.* I sighed. *Why did you have to fall in love with me anyway?*

Twenty minutes later, showered, and dressed in clean jeans and a fresh, long sleeved, checkered shirt, I joined PJ in the living area. She was sitting at the table nursing a cup of tea and staring out the window.

I slipped in beside her. "PJ, I--"

She held up her hand. "Please, don't say anything... There's nothing *to* say."

I put my hand under her chin and turned her face toward me. She'd been crying. "PJ, bear with me a little longer, okay?"

She took a deep breath and nodded. "Have you looked outside?"

"Just up ... through the skylight."

"It's a lovely day ... sunshine and blue sky, no wind, and no dust. It's warm ... perfect for the cookout."

I smiled. "Then we'd better get to work hadn't we?"

"Yes, but first, I'll run Pup."

"Okay." I leaned forward, intending to drop light kisses on PJ's eyes and lips. She pulled away.

"I'm sorry Kim. That's not a good idea. If we're going to work together as friends from here on out, then we'd better keep it platonic." Tears welled up in her eyes. "I just can't turn my emotions on and off like a faucet." She tried to stand. "C'mon, let me out of here so I can take Pup for his run. We've got to get going or the team will be here and we won't be ready for them."

I got up and moved out of her way.

She pulled Pup's leash from its hook just inside the front door and was gone. I followed her, down the three inside stairs and the two outside steps and watched her jog off down the road with Pup bounding along beside her.

"Damn!" I turned and punched the side of the motor home with my fist, cutting my knuckle on a sharp piece of metal. "Damn, double damn!"

I hurried inside to the bathroom sink, letting the water run over what was a small but nasty cut. Then, I drizzled antiseptic over it and covered it with a large Band Aid. The cut was in an awkward place so I ran two strips of tape across the Band Aid to keep it in place, one between my index and big fingers and the other between my middle fingers.

"What happened to you?" PJ asked when she returned, breathless, with Pup.

I shrugged. "Nothing."

"Well, it looks like a pretty painful nothing."

"I wasn't looking at what I was doing and caught my hand on a piece of metal on the siding."

"Yeah...and then you beat the shit out of the piece of metal, accounting for that bruise."

I glanced down at my knuckle, which had turned quite dark. "It'll be okay."

PJ slammed Pup's leash onto its hook and turned the sink's faucet on full force, splashing water into his bowl and onto the counter before banging it down on the floor. "I'm sure it will be." She raised her head and glared at me. "You're the iron maiden, after all." She stood up and grabbed a cloth for the spilled water. "You don't need any help ... won't let anyone get close. You don't know how to need anyone or feel for--"

"Don't start with me, PJ."

She stood at the sink with her back to me, squeezing out the cloth. "I'm not starting anything, Kim, more like I'm finishing..."

I took a step toward her, forced to converse with the back of her head and a set of tense shoulders. "What about our friendship?"

She whirled around to face me. "What about it? Do you need my friendship? Do you need *anyone* for any reason?"

Pup whined and rubbed up against my leg. I dropped my hand and buried it in his ruff.

"I'm surprised you even let *him* in your life." PJ pushed me aside and moved to the sofa, where she picked up each pillow and gave it a punch before arranging it.

"You know, you might want to leave a bit of stuffing in those," I said, trying to lighten the mood.

"I'm fluffing the pillows." PJ's words came through clenched teeth.

"Oh."

She stood up and folded her arms across her chest. "Let's get on with what we have to do here, okay? The sooner today is behind us, the better."

Her words stung.

Preparing the food, setting the picnic tables, and getting everything ready for the barbecue was a choreographed dance as we both tried to stay out of each other's way ... hard to do in the small confines of the motor home. Our only verbal communication had to do with preparation of food and setting up the tables.

I slipped some CDs into the player and allowed the music to fill the silence that hung like fog between us. To outsiders we would have looked like polite mannequins performing the minuet.

"Hey, Doc, look who we found at the bus station," Sandy said, sticking his head around our open door. "Laine, Josie, and I met him at the depot."

I wiped my hands on the dishtowel I'd tucked into my belt while mixing the ingredients for deviled eggs. "Our long lost Mike?"

Sandy stepped aside so Mike could take his place in the doorway.

"Hi Doc. Guess I missed all the excitement, huh?"

"If you want to call it that."

"I'm so sorry about the Amazons. Sandy and the girls filled me in on everything. We've lost it all, huh? We had 'em and they were stolen from us by a damned earthquake." Mike's brown eyes filled ... his lower lip quivered.

I know you're sensitive, but don't you dare start crying on me. "It's okay, Mike. We found them, they shared their secrets, and now they're resting in peace."

He sniffed. "Yeah, but they were your life ... how can you be so forgiving of circumstances?"

"Because that's all I can be, anything else is beyond my control, beyond anyone's control, except perhaps the Fates."

Mike stepped up into the motor home. "Doc, I want to shake your hand ... you're an incredible woman."

We shook hands. I saw a tear escape his brimming eyes and make its way down his cheek and breaking up in his scrawny excuse for a mustache. I pulled him into a hug.

"You're a good fellow, Mike, and you have a grand career ahead of you."

PJ appeared in the doorway after taking Pup for a last minute, leisurely stroll around the park before everyone arrived. I released Mike. "Go now, join the others."

"Welcome back," PJ said, when he turned around to face her. Pup gave Mike a lick on his hand.

"Yeah thanks." He kept his head down, patting Pup. I wondered if he was embarrassed to have been caught with his sensitivity showing. "I was just telling Doc here how sorry I am about the project."

"We all are," PJ said, glancing from him to me.

Mike turned in my direction. "Can I help with something?"

"Nothing in here, but you can see if Sandy needs help firing up the barbecues." We had borrowed one from Sandy's mom and one from the manager of the RV park.

"So," PJ said, as she hung Pup's leash, "you shared another one of your precious hugs. Better watch out, Kim, folks will think you really care."

"I'm seeing a side of you that I do not like, but it's good that you're showing it now and not later, after we..." I turned my attention back to the deviled egg mix. I heard another car drive up.

"After we what?"

I spun around. "It's not important, PJ. Save it for later."

"What later? There isn't going to be--"

Josie stuck her head around the door and snapped a picture of us with her flash camera, catching us glaring at each other. "Oops! Um...everyone's here."

"Thank you, Josie." I wiped my hands on the dishtowel. "I see you still have a patch on your forehead. Are you healing okay?"

"Yes, thank you, Doc. I'm fine." She looked hard at PJ and then at me. "Uh ... I think Sandy's ready for the meat and chicken."

PJ opened the refrigerator and pulled out two large, foil-covered plates. "Here, you take the chicken. I'll bring the meat."

She turned just as she was about ready to go out the door. "I apologize, Kim. My remarks were uncalled for ... I was way out of line."

I turned back to the counter and the deviled eggs. I was not in a party mood, but I was not going to allow the interaction between PJ and me to spoil it for the others.

When she returned for the condiments, I pulled her aside. "Listen, I don't care what you do afterwards, but we're going to put on a good face this afternoon ... for the sake of our people, okay?"

She nodded and reached out to touch my hand. When I pulled back, she dipped her finger into the deviled egg mix and licked it. "Mmm, good stuff." She winked and I was unable to suppress a smile.

Outside, the fellows had pushed two picnic tables together end to end making one long table. They insisted that I sit at the head of the table and set up a folding chair there for me. Sandy directed PJ to sit on the bench at my right hand.

"What is this," PJ asked, "The Last Supper?"

Everyone snickered.

Sandy sat on my left. Then, after much shuffling and scraping of benches, the rest of the crew settled onto whatever bench space was closest to them.

PJ and I were close enough together that we were forced to interact to affect the appearance of normality.

There were toasts to be made. "Laine, will you do the honors and pour the Sparkling Cider?"

"Sure, Doc." She opened two of the three bottles which, when she pried off the tops, popped like champagne corks.

"Got fizz, will travel," Mike said as he picked up the filled glasses and passed them around.

When everyone was served, Sandy stood and tapped his plastic cider glass with a plastic fork. I smiled because it sounded like a woodpecker at a knothole.

"Here's to Doc Blair," Sandy said, raising his glass, "the crown jewel of the archaeological community."

The chorus of "Here, here..." could have been heard all the way to the highway. It was followed by cries of "Speech ... speech," equally as enthusiastic and equally as loud.

I stood and waited for the applause to die down.

"Unaccustomed as I am to public speaking..." My words were received with loud guffaws. "Listen, guys and gals," I said when the group settled down. "First, how are you all doing? Lewis, how is that leg?"

He grinned. "This may be overkill," he said, tapping his air splint, "but I do have a hairline fracture and I'm babying it."

"Good idea. And the rest of you ... I still see some bruises."

"And we're proud of 'em," Dewey said, "and wear them like badges of courage."

Everyone snickered.

"Okay, well, down to business." I sipped some water. "I couldn't have accomplished what I did here without your help. You were all one hundred percent part of the Lost Tribe Project and you gave your all for it. The fact it ended the way it did was in many respects unfortunate, but if you look at it in terms of the Amazons themselves, it could have ended no other way. I don't think I could have lived with myself if they had been removed, separated, and stored away in some dusty museum vault or in glass cases for the world to peer at them."

More applause.

I silenced the enthusiastic outbreak with a downward motion of my hands. "I believe we all felt a very real connection to our Warrior Women and the journey they undertook so long ago. Their paths and ours crossed in our time and provided closure to their story. The fact that we as archaeologists have lost them now is of no consequence. We can be proud of our place in their lives."

Everyone stood and applauded.

"I have just one more thing to add ... two things actually. First, PJ will be talking to you about completing your sessions at U of A."

"Thanks, Doc," Lewis, said. "We were wondering where we go from here and how this situation affects our status."

"Well, not to worry."

"And the other thing?" Laine asked. "You mentioned you had two things to talk about."

"Yes." I took another swallow of cider. "I want to thank PJ." I reached out and squeezed her shoulder. "Without her I doubt I'd have made it through these past few weeks. She was there when I most needed her. And if you want to see a damned fine archaeologist, look no farther than to my right. She's the best and I'm proud to call her my friend."

A chorus of "PJ ... PJ ... PJ," sent the nearby Cactus Wrens fluttering into the air.

PJ stood to acknowledge the ovation.

Josie whipped out her camera and snapped a picture of PJ and me. "Now stand a bit closer together." She waited until PJ and I were standing shoulder to shoulder. "That's good. Now, smile and say 'Amazons.'" We all laughed.

The group called for a speech from PJ and she remained standing. She looked at me through watery eyes.

"Geez, people, I'm in no condition to talk right now. I do want to say something a little later though, about some serious stuff ... your future and that sort of thing." A round of applause interrupted her.

She glanced in my direction. "Thank you, Kim ... and thank you all for letting me join your tight-knit group. This expedition has been the high point of my professional career to date. Not only did it give me the opportunity to work with one of the legends in the archaeological community..." She turned to me and applauded, triggering another outbreak from the group. "...but it gave my life direction and purpose, something that was sorely lacking. Okay, I'll have a longer, more polished speech to make later, but right now, I suggest we get back to the important business of eating."

There were more cheers as PJ sat down. She covered my hand with hers and kept her voice low. "Thank you for filling as much of my life as you were able to do."

"It's not over, you know."

"Yeah, well..." She heaved a sigh and turned her attention to her meal.

Conversation was sporadic as we dug into the feast in front of us. I studied the assembled students. Soon there would be nothing left but empty plates, crumbled paper napkins, squashed soda cans, and empty water bottles. The voices, the discussion, the good-natured bantering of the team would be in the past, part of the 'I remember when' chapter. I wished for time to stand still so that our last meal together could continue forever.

James and Laine broke into my thoughts as they tossed a coin for the one remaining deviled egg. Laine won. She bit off half and handed James the other half.

He grinned. "Aw, thanks ... I think I'll marry you."

"Not in this lifetime," she said.

"Then I shall hang myself from that old Saguaro over there."

"That would be hard to do but I'll be glad to help pull the chair out from under you."

The barbecue, I felt, had given us all a false sense of continuation. *We are, after all, the seekers of the Lost Tribe of Amazons and that will never end, will it? We will always be The Seekers, won't we?*

But we had to seek no longer ... for we had sought and found The Lost Tribe. And now, they were sleeping forever in their caves in a tiny canyon, a canyon that was no longer there, on a mountainside that had undergone violent change. It was time for The Seekers to walk away and leave the Lost Tribe to their rest.

I scanned the group. The conversation was subdued. It was as if they all were very much aware that soon now, very soon, we'd be saying our good byes.

Gawd, you guys are the nearest to family I've ever known. Where do you all go from here? Where do I go, and where, PJ, do you go?

I was overcome by a deep sense of sadness, but as Director, I didn't dare show it. *Am I carrying this idiotic sense of aloofness too far? Will I never learn to be just a human being? I've put my personal life on hold for so long. When do I start to live again?*

I gathered up a stack of used paper plates and cups and was dumping them into the trashcan behind the motor home when Josie approached.

"Do you have a moment to talk?"

"Sure. What do you have on your mind?"

"Something off the record and kinda personal."

I took a deep breath and slid my hands in my pockets. "Okay, what's the problem?"

"You."

I frowned. "What?"

Josie held her ground. "You are. Walk with me, will you?" She headed off my motor home space and onto the driveway, which circled the Recreational Vehicle Park and led eventually to the entrance and the highway beyond.

Pup picked his head up when he saw me follow Josie. "No Pup, you stay." He rested his muzzle on his paws but kept his eye on me.

Josie waited until we were out of hearing range before she spoke. She wasted no time coming to the point. "What are you going to do about PJ?"

I felt my heart rise into my throat. "Stop right here." I turned to face Josie. "What about PJ?" *Who knows about me...us? Worse yet, is it something bad or sad I should know about PJ?*

"Don't dance around this, Doc." Her gray eyes met and held mine. "She's in love with you. Don't you know that?"

"She told you?"

"No, but you only have to see the way she looks at you. She adores the ground you walk on and if you don't know that then you're as blind as the proverbial bat."

"Josie, this is *none* of your business."

"I know that, Doc, but I'm making it my business because I care about you and PJ."

"Obviously you know I'm gay?"

She nodded.

"How? Sandy must have told you, or PJ. Did they tell you and the others about the night my ex showed up here?"

Josie puckered her forehead, wincing in the process. That cut was obviously still sore. "What are you talking about? No one has spoken to me about anything."

"But you said you knew."

"I've known almost since the beginning, when I came to work for you. There were rumors, Doc. Besides, I've been around gay people ... I have gay friends."

"And you?"

"I'm straight." She put her hand on my arm and smiled. "Look, Doc, I'm not trying to get into your personal life ... it's just that I admire you and I think PJ is great. Laine and I have been concerned about you for a long time. You seem so lonely."

"It's not--"

"And then when PJ arrived, she had you talking and laughing ... relaxing. She is so good for you, Kim. Don't you see that?"

"Josie, it's more complicated than--"

"Anyway, I'm not playing Cupid ... I just wanted you to know how PJ feels about you ... just in case you have any feelings for her."

"I see." I scuffed the ground with the toe of my hiking boot. "Your candor is refreshing, Josie." I reached for and lightly touched the patch on her forehead.

She gave me a bewildered look. "But--"

"I think we'd better get back to the others."

She started to say something, but closed her mouth instead. "Yeah, I guess."

We strolled back toward the motor home and the group who had assembled into chairs around PJ.

"'Bout time you guys got back," PJ said, handing us both a piece of Mrs. Arnold's red velvet cake. She looked from one to the other of us. "What was so interesting anyway?"

Josie and I exchanged glances. "Josie had some data to share with me."

"Yeah," Josie added. "Doc is going to process it."

I wasn't sure our explanation had satisfied her curiosity.

"I'll help you process your data, Josie," Mike said with a grin.

Josie stuck her tongue out at him and wrinkled her nose.

"All right, people, settle down." PJ's tone was authoritative.

I was so proud of her. She had grown so much as an archaeologist. She had come to me with the knowledge but during her time with us, she had gained presence. She was director material and would be a voice to be reckoned with in scientific circles.

"Okay," PJ said, silencing the chatter. "Take the weight off … I have two pieces of paper for you all, but first I'm going to make that speech."

A chorus of groans greeted her opening salvo.

PJ stood up and smiled. "All right guys and gals, let's just settle down, okay. You're going to hear me out anyway so you might as well accept the punishment. The sooner you let me have my say the sooner you can all go home."

"You have our attention," Sandy said.

PJ produced a large manila envelope and opened it, making a big deal of clearing her throat.

"You'd better give up those cigarettes," Mike said.

PJ grinned. "Thank you, Mike, for that unsolicited piece of advice."

She cleared her throat again, an action that triggered a chorus of 'Get on with it.'

"Okay, here goes. When I arrived here I had a reputation as a spoiled, rich playgirl who couldn't keep her hands off a man." She tugged at James's shirt, only because he was sitting closest to where she was standing. He turned beet red. "While there was probably some truth to that, I learned a lot working on this project. I looked upon Kim as my mentor and she taught me plenty."

She was interrupted by applause and smiled at me while waiting for the group to settle down.

I smiled back. *And you, my dear, taught me more.*

"But I learned a lot from all of you, too. Working alongside you has been a pleasure." She smiled at the young faces that for the moment had eyes only for her. "Here is the first piece of paper." She took several sheets out of the envelope and

311

handed them to James. "They're all the same. Just take one and pass the rest along."

"Is this a quiz, PJ?" Donny asked with a grin.

PJ wrinkled her nose at him. "Yes…and your semester grades depend on it."

"Oh, God," Lewis and Dewey cried in unison.

"Take it easy, guys. It's the information we have on two possible programs that you can join for the remainder of your term."

"This is great." Josie scanned the printed document.

"What a relief." Donny fanned his face with the paper. "I was afraid I'd be wandering the streets with nothing to do for three weeks."

PJ waved her hand for silence. "Pick one or the other and after you have finished those three weeks, you'll get full credit for the semester."

Sandy was reading his sheet. "That's cool, PJ. Thanks."

She looked at me. "Doc and I made some calls. We didn't want you all to lose out on anything because of the quake."

"Well, then, thanks to both of you."

The others murmured their appreciation.

"No problem," PJ assured them. "Now, as you are no doubt aware, I'm heir to Curtis Enterprises and The Curtis Foundation. There's an obscene amount of money in those two organizations. It makes me nervous because I don't always agree on how the money is spent. What good is all of it if it can't be put to productive use?" She patted her manila envelope. "I'm going to change that today, by spending some of it wisely." She slid out several sealed business sized envelopes. "Here, Sandy, see that they go to the right person, okay?"

Sandy matched the names on the envelopes with the right team member.

PJ folded the empty envelope. "Now, I'd appreciate it if you'd wait until everyone has his or hers before you open them."

Donny laughed. "This feels like Christmas."

"Either that or midterm grades," Mike said.

The group gave a collective nervous laugh.

"Relax, it won't hurt a bit." PJ smiled. "I promise." She cleared her throat again, grinning at the groans. "It gives me great pleasure to present each of you with a check from The Curtis Foundation to help you with your future studies. You may open your envelopes."

"My God!" Laine shouted. "Twenty Thousand smacker-oonies!" She kissed the piece of paper.

"I don't believe it!" James murmured.

"I was right. It *is* Christmas." Donny's smile was expansive.

There were more gasps as the significance of PJ's words sank in.

"With dedicated young people like you working hard in this field, archaeology and its related sciences will be well-served. Kim and I are so proud of all you accomplished on this project and we look forward to watching you succeed in future endeavors."

They cheered and applauded. They stood and mobbed PJ, giving her enthusiastic hugs and kisses, which she returned with warmth and genuine affection.

I was blown away by PJ's generosity and flicked a tear from the corner of my eye. Then, the party wore down until there was nothing else to do but bid each other farewell.

And while the final disbanding of the group was sad, there was hope too, in the snippets of conversation that reached my ears as I was saying my goodbyes and hugging first one and then another. "Hey, we'll keep in touch," James was saying to Josie.

"I'll email you," someone said.

"Listen," Sandy said, raising his voice, "next May Laine and I earn our doctorates. I've asked Doc to assist me at the hooding ceremony. I'd like to invite all of you to come and attend, if you can."

"That's a wonderful idea, Sandy." Laine looked around at all of us. "And I wish I'd thought to ask Doc sooner." She thought for a second. "Hey, Arnold comes way before Watkins. Could you just stay on the dais and do my hooding too, Doc?"

I smiled at her resourcefulness. "Well, Laine, it is a small group, as I recall ... maybe a half dozen doctorates and the same amount of masters. I'll do my best. Okay?"

Laine grinned. "That's great. And everyone else, come if you possibly can." She looked at PJ. "Can you be with us, PJ? We'd love to have you attend."

PJ cast a brief glance at me before she answered. "I'll do my very best to be there, Laine."

"Fantastic!" Donny clapped his hands once. "I can hang around until then." He looked at the others. "How about it? Can the rest of you make it? We'll have an Amazon Hunters reunion next spring."

The idea took shape. Sad voices grew cheerful again. The gloomy prospect of our disbanding was tempered with the possibility of a reunion in the spring.

I was hugging Lewis when I heard Laine's voice. She was speaking to Donny who was teary eyed. "Hey, we're all family here, Doc, PJ, the rest of us ... we may not be together but we will not be apart." That, in my humble opinion said it all.

"I hope I wasn't out of line," Josie said when we gave each other final hugs. "I just wanted to ... well, you know...."

"Yes, I know, and thanks." From the corner of my eye, I caught sight of PJ watching us. I couldn't read her thoughts but I knew that she had been curious since Josie and I had walked away from the group.

Sandy threw his arms around me and wrapped me in a bear hug. I punched him playfully on the chin. "Get outta here. I hate seeing grown men cry."

He kissed me on the cheek. "You're the best, Doc. I'll stay in touch, don't you worry."

"You'd better," I told him.

He turned to PJ. "Do you still want me to take the minivan now?"

She pulled the keys from her pocket. "This is as good a time as any, Cowboy. I sure appreciated having it during our project."

"Walk me to the van, would you? I'd like to ask you something before I leave."

Knowing they were good friends, I moved away.

I watched them stroll to the vehicle and continue talking for a few moments, her arm around his waist, his around her shoulder. When they reached the car, Sandy dipped his head and gave her a quick kiss on the lips. PJ smiled and gave his nose a playful tweak.

After everyone had left, PJ and I stood facing each other across the narrow floor space of the motor home. Silence wrapped itself around us like a cocoon, preventing us, I thought, from grieving the immediate emptiness created by the absence of colleagues.

"They've gone," she said, tears leaving shiny tracks down her cheeks. "They've gone and it's really, *really* over."

I nodded.

"Well, can't you say something? Don't you feel anything?"

I listened as the final vehicle left the area. "Yes, they've gone, and I'll miss them." I turned my attention back to PJ. "I've worked with many people in my time, students, graduate students, fellow scientists, but Sandy, Laine, Josie, and the others ... well, they were special, dedicated individuals. They're made from the right stuff and we'll hear more of them in the years ahead, you'll see."

"And what about you, Kim?" PJ sat down on the far end of the sofa. "You've closed the door on your project. Any last words on that?"

"Have patience with me, PJ. I have feelings... way too many to put into words right now."

She nodded, biting her lip. "That introvert thing again, right?" She shook her head. "I can't seem to stop this bitchy attitude I've got going here." Her head dipped and I heard a sniffle. "I'm sorry, Kim... I just hate to lose."

I closed the door against the cool breeze that was starting up. Then I sat down at the opposite end of the sofa from PJ. I turned to face her, my left knee bent and resting on the sofa, my ankle hooked under my right knee.

"I know something about loss. I've spent most of my professional life searching for the Lost Tribe. I found them and now they've been taken from me. That's disappointing, despite my knowing it ended the way it should have and that they are where they should be ... together."

"And now?" She stared me down.

What do you want from me, PJ? Don't you understand that I need time to absorb all that has happened these last few days.

I traced the outline of the medallion hanging around my neck, under my shirt. "I'm empty ... inside."

"That makes two of us." PJ sighed. "Have you thought at all about your professional future?"

"When do you suppose I've had time to do that?" I immediately regretted my snappish tone. "I have to work because that's what makes me who I am. Not knowing where my profession will take me from here does bother me ... a great deal."

"As a fellow archaeologist, I can understand that," PJ said.

"What about you?" I kicked off my shoes and shifted enough to ease the cramp that was forming in my left leg. "Have you given any thought to your professional future?"

PJ caught my gaze and held it. "No. Not really. I've been a little busy with personal matters ... where I fit in with you, for example." She exhaled and raked her fingers through her hair. "But I'm not blind ... I see the handwriting on the wall. It's pretty obvious that you don't have room for me in your future." She sat up and tapped her thighs. "So, it's time for me to get the hell outta here."

"Would you like a small glass of wine, some Sherry perhaps, or Port?"

PJ laughed. "You know, Kim, you're an expert at changing the subject. The conversation gets serious and you trivialize it."

"I'm not changing the subject nor trivializing it ... I just thought that ... well, that we ... It might help if we had a drink... Damn it, PJ, I want a glass of wine. Do you want to join me or not?"

PJ eyed me suspiciously. "I haven't had any alcohol since that awful night when Sandy dumped me here on your doorstep. I wanted to avoid any repeat performances of public drunkenness and so far, I have." She smiled. "You know, I never forgave Sandy for bringing me here."

I chuckled. "Well, I don't think a small glass of wine will undo the good you've done for yourself. And we should, you know, toast our Amazon friends."

She shook her head. "It's all about the Amazons isn't it?"

"Face it, PJ, they're part of our lives ... yours and mine. No matter what happens here tonight, we'll never be the same again because of them."

"Okay, fine. I'll have a drink with you ... in fact I'll do the honors." She was on her feet in an instant, retrieving two plastic goblets from the cabinet above the kitchen sink. "Where do you keep the wine?"

"In the cabinet under the counter ... the one on the left."

"Sherry?"

"That'll do just fine."

I watched as she pulled the cork and inhaled the fragrance. "Mm-mm good."

"Sorry, I don't have crystal wine glasses in the motor home," I said, when she handed me my drink, "this being a special occasion and all."

PJ returned to her place on the other end of the sofa. "Special ... or sad?"

"Sad, we've had, so let's go with special."

Her eyebrows arched.

"Cheers." We leaned forward and clinked glasses.

She giggled. "Doesn't have the ring of crystal, does it?"

"More like a muffled thud." We both laughed.

We sipped in silence, savoring the rich flavor of the wine.

"Wow," PJ's eyes widened. "I'd forgotten how warm a good sherry feels going down."

"By the way," she said, after a moment of silence, "what did you and Josie talk about?"

"She had a question. That was all."

"You're not going to tell me, are you?"

"Perhaps Josie doesn't want you to know."

"Humph."

There was a prolonged silence as we looked at each other.

I exhaled. "If you must know, she wanted to be sure I knew that you were in love with me."

PJ's eyes opened like saucers. "You're kidding?"

I shook my head. "That's one very perceptive young woman. Apparently she's known about me from the beginning … when she first came to work for me."

"Well, I'll be...."

"That's what I said, or thought anyway."

I stared into my glass of amber liquid. *Well, this is my moment of truth so I may as well get on with it.*

"PJ, I've given us a lot of thought."

She stiffened, her green eyes darkening. "Kim, I've already figured that…"

I leaned forward and put my glass on the table before sliding toward her.

"What... are you…"

I took her glass and set it down.

"Kim?"

I put my left arm around her shoulder and leaned in to her, lifting her face with my right hand and kissing her full on the mouth.

Her breath released with a rush. "Wow…"

I felt desire course through my body when she moaned against my lips.

We broke apart long enough to take a shaky breath.

"You don't know how often I've wished you would do that." PJ murmured, touching my cheek. "How often I've dreamed about it."

She shifted onto her knees. Her arms snaked around my body and we embraced. This time our kiss was longer, more passionate. Her fragrance and the sweetness of her tongue excited me to distraction.

"Kim, I'm … uh … a bit confused here." PJ continued to caress my face and neck, curling her fingers through my hair. "I was so sure that…" She paused and started again. "But I don't know what you want… or what I should do to please you. I don't want to make any mistakes. I do want to please you."

318

"There are no mistakes, PJ, and you're doing just fine, just fine."

Oh gawd, are you ever ... I don't want to scare you by rushing things, but I want to make mad passionate love to you.

"Wait," I whispered as PJ managed somehow to get her leg wrapped around my left hip. I laughed. "You're going to tie yourself in knots."

I untangled myself and stood up, taking her by the hand and pulling her up to me. We kissed again. I was aware that while my right arm held her to me, my left hand rested on her firm buttock.

"Watch it, Kim, you're squashing my shamrock."

"I want to see it ... will you let me look at it?"

"Jesus! For weeks you can't make a commitment. Now, you can't wait to get my pants off me..." She giggled.

"I love you, PJ."

"I love you, too, but you've known that for some time, haven't you?"

"Yes, I have ... and now you know that I love you, too."

PJ reached across me to turn off the light switch. As she did so, her hand, either intentionally or accidentally brushed my breast. It was like an electric shock.

We kissed our way into the bedroom, managing to pull apart long enough to turn down the bed covers. I started to unbutton PJ's blouse.

"No! Wait a second! This has to be just right." She dashed out to the dinette and took the candle from the table, lit it, and placed it on the bedside stand. I waited while she collected our wine glasses and added a little more to each. When she came back into the bedroom, she handed me my goblet, which I placed on my bedside stand. She put hers on the other side. The flickering light of the candle created a golden, lantern-like glow in the room and in the wine.

We came together again at the foot of the bed. PJ's eyes sparkled in the candlelight. "Now, Amazon Woman, you may do with me what you will."

I hugged her to me. "Gawd, I love you so much...and what I will is...to make the sweetest love with you that either of us has ever known. We will take our time. I promise you, I will be gentle..."

"I know you will, Kim." She squeezed my waist. "I trust you completely."

Gawd, give me self-control. Right now!

My lips left a trail of warm, moist kisses down her neck. I unbuttoned her blouse and slid it from her shoulders. She leaned her head back, granting me fuller access to her lovely throat. Her arms dropped allowing the silky material to glide all the way to the floor.

"You are so beautiful," I whispered.

"You're kind of easy on the eyes yourself." PJ's voice was husky.

Her sculptured shoulders reminded me of a bust I'd seen once, an artist's likeness of an Egyptian Queen. My gaze lingered on her luscious breasts, still partially hidden within the constraints of her rose-colored, lace bra.

Need coursed through my body like a river in flood. I unbuckled her belt and loosened the top button on her cargo shorts. *Be gentle, remember.*

"Hold up, Doc." PJ covered my hand with hers. "Isn't it *my turn* to admire the scenery?" She tugged at my shirt and kissed me while fumbling with the buttons. "I seem to be all thumbs. Sorry."

"That's okay, little one. It isn't a race." *I am getting close to the breaking point, however.*

PJ stripped off my shirt and let it fall. "This is a new experience for me, Kim." She stared at my breasts for several seconds. "Loving a woman, I mean." She wet her lips. "I think I could get to like it, though ... with enough practice."

I chuckled. "That's good to hear. Just do what feels natural to you, okay. I'll show you what I like and you can do the same."

"Right now, I really like the kissing part."

"Then, by all means..." With my arms around her, I responded to her kisses while releasing her bra and freeing her lovely breasts. I cupped one sweet mound with my right hand, feeling the hardening nub beneath my palm.

A pleasurable groan escaped PJ's lips. Her hands were in my hair, her tongue exploring. With my free hand, I pushed her shorts down off her hips.

Well, well. Matching rose-colored panties.

PJ whimpered. She unbuckled my belt and unzipped my pants. Her little moans were driving me to distraction. I wanted so much to just take her, but I needed to slow down ... to make it special. I kicked off my jeans and together we fell onto the bed.

We hastily finished undressing each other and slipped between the sheets. PJ reached out to stroke my breasts.

I smiled at her hesitancy. "You can do it harder if you like. They won't break."

"It's just ... I'm not used to..." Her fingers continued their arousing exploration. When they flicked across my nipples, bringing them to rigid attention, I gasped with delight.

PJ giggled. "Wow. This is so different. But good."

"Indeed it is." I squeezed her breasts while she caressed mine. "One of the many benefits of loving a woman."

"I've so much to learn, Kim. You'll have to be patient with me."

"Oh, I have every confidence--"

She leaned in to put her mouth where her fingers had been.

I moaned. "Gawd, you learn fast."

She grinned up at me. "You make the subject so pleasurable, Doctor Blair."

I rolled her over onto her back and covered her with my body. A thin film of sweat glistened on our skin. Her spicy scent filled my nostrils, arousing me further. I could feel the eager beating of her heart keeping time with my own.

"The subject is love, Doctor Curtis," I growled into the hollow of her throat. "And, my beloved, you have only just begun to realize the pleasure. Ready for another lesson?"

"Oh yeah." PJ pulled my fingers to her mouth, sucking on each one, before releasing it. "And I want you to know that I'll stay after class for extra tutoring if necessary."

I slid my wet fingers across her belly. "Somehow, I doubt that you'll need tutoring. I think *I'm* the one who's going to need help."

She laughed. "C'mon, Doc. Less talk, more action."

I don't remember much on the conscious plane after that. I know PJ lit a fire inside me. It was like rainbow colored lightning and spring rains as the salty sweet smell of passion took the last of my senses. I was aware only of our bodies touching, tightening, and tingling with the love we shared. Again and again, we rode waves of intense pleasure as orgasm after orgasm brought us to exquisite heights and then released us.

Finally, we lay together in sweaty exhaustion. I smiled into PJ's half-closed eyes. *This is where I belong.*

"Where have you been all my life, Kim?" She turned to me and slid her hand across my stomach. "I've wasted so much precious time with all the wrong..." Her hands moved upward. "Because it was never ... like this." She leaned in and kissed my breast. "Never! Not even close." Her tongue left a wet circle around my nipple. I groaned and pulled her against me, encouraging her breasts to warm my own.

"I know. I've never felt anything like this before either." I kissed her neck, licking the hollow of her collarbone, making her smile.

She stretched and rolled onto her stomach. I admired the tiny tattoo on her buttock, touching it with my fingertip. Then, I leaned over to kiss it. "Whoa, that's a turn-on."

"Enough of that," PJ whispered. "Or, I'll have to do a little butt-kissing of my own."

"Promises, promises."

She rose up to kiss me before pushing me onto my back, moving down my body, leaving a trail of sweet kisses along the way.

I was in pure ecstasy, every nerve ending in a heightened state of excitement. It was just the two of us alone in the Universe. I could hear myself moaning, crying out for more, begging her not to stop. It was then that I lost all control. I could only respond physically to what she was doing to me.

And this woman thought she needed lessons.

My body arched off the bed. I gasped for breath and hung on to PJ for dear life. "Oh, gawd, please ... don't stop ... not now ... please not now." Then it was as if my whole being relaxed and I was in her arms and she was smothering my face with kisses.

"Wow, Kim, that was amazing!"

"I don't know what all you were doing, PJ, but I know I'll never be the same again."

She giggled. "Me either."

It was morning when I opened my eyes to find PJ lying beside me, looking at me. The faint scent of passion lingered around our bed.

"Morning, darling."

"G'Morning." I detected some sadness in her eyes.

I sat up and rested myself on my elbow. "Something's bothering you, I can tell."

Her eyes filled with tears.

"Tell me, what is it? Are you sorry we...?"

"Oh, dear God, no!"

"Then what?"

"We made love, Kim, just as I was preparing to give my goodbye speech. It happened so suddenly and now I'm afraid." She stroked my bed-tousled hair back from my forehead. "I know you're not into one night stands, but I worry ... I'm not rushing you for commitment, nothing like that, but we did make love and if you're not into one night stands ... then what?"

"Darling, it means that I love you more than I ever thought possible. I want us to be together forever."

"Oh, Kimmy." She pulled me closer. "That's what I want, too." Her kisses were fervent, demanding.

We made love again; it was a fire devouring us like an inferno.

"You know, darling," I whispered afterwards, "I'm not as young as I used to be. You're going to wear me out."

PJ giggled. "Sorry, honey. I just got carried away."

"Gawd, woman, I'm going to die...but what a way to go."

We slept, then, together with arms and legs entwined.

"And what a lovely morning it is," PJ said hours later when we re-awakened. "The sun is shining, the sky is clear, and there's no dust."

"I love you, PJ. I want us to be together forever."

"I love you, too, Kim. I will forever love you."

I rolled over and straddled her hips.

"Oh, Kim, I like that."

She pulled me down to her and kissed me, probing for my tongue with hers.

Later, much later, in the fog of passion spent, I thought about the future, our future and all the delicious possibilities and the significant milestones that lay ahead. Sometime in the next few days, we'll travel to Boston so PJ can begin her reconciliation with Frederick and introduce me as her partner in life as well as work.

If that news doesn't deter you, Frederick, nothing will.

It's a leap, PJ, from financier of an archaeological project to father-in-law of its director, especially when that director is of the same sex. You must understand and know what you are doing by telling him about us. The choice is yours to make, but be sure to know that the new beginning you're experiencing with your father may be short lived. Unfortunately, loss of friends and family is the price we have to pay sometimes for being different. I sighed. *I hope you don't experience that kind of hurt, PJ, because it cuts to the heart.*

But, if all goes well, we'll spend Christmas in New England before going to my ranch in New Mexico. You're going to love it there, PJ. We can start on the restoration, a little at a time. It'll be a lot of work but it'll be fun doing it together ... making it livable for us as a couple ... making the house a home and filling it with our combined personalities.

We must decide, too, what we're going to do professionally. We're too young to retire. Besides, I don't believe either one of us is ready to be put out to pasture. I could teach, of course, and write, but what of you, PJ? What are your thoughts about your professional future? We have so much to talk about, you and I. So one of these days we'll have to get up...

For now, the immediate present, and for the rest of the day, in fact ... my lover and I will stay right where we felt most comfortable...in bed.

K.C. West and Victoria Welsh met online several years ago when they joined a fan club forum for Xena: Warrior Princess. Despite living practically on opposite coasts of the United States, they found plenty of common ground in their love of the show's characters and their interest in writing.

K.C. lives in the east with her husband and two daughters.

Victoria (photo inset) is a poet and writer. She and her life partner reside in the Southwestern United States.

The authors are hard at work on the second book in the 'Shadow' series.

Order These Great Books Directly From Limitless, Dare 2 Dream Publishing

The Amazon Queen by L M Townsend	15.00	
Define Destiny by J M Dragon	15.00	The one that started it all…
Desert Hawk, revised by Katherine E. Standelll	16.00	Many new scenes
Golden Gate by Erin Jennifer Mar	16.00	
The Brass Ring by Mavis Applewater	16.00	HOT
Haunting Shadows by J M Dragon	17.00	
Spirit Harvest by Trish Shields	12.00	
PWP: Plot? What Plot? by Mavis Applewater	18.00	HOT
Journeys by Anne Azel	18.00	NEW
Memories Kill by S. B. Zarben	16.00	
Up The River, revised by Sam Ruskin	16.00	New scenes & more
	Total	

South Carolina residents add 5% sales tax.
Domestic shipping is $3.50 per book

Visit our website at: http://limitlessd2d.net

Please mail orders with credit card info, check or money order to:

Limitless, Dare 2 Dream Publishing
100 Pin Oak Ct.
Lexington, SC 29073-7911

Please make checks or money orders payable to **Limitless**.

Order More Great Books Directly From Limitless, Dare 2 Dream Publishing

Daughters of Artemis by L M Townsend	16.00	
Connecting Hearts by Val Brown and MJ Walker	16.00	
Mysti: Mistress of Dreams by Sam Ruskin	16.00	HOT
Family Connections by Val Brown & MJ Walker	16.00	Sequel to Connecting Hearts
Under the Fig Tree **by Emily Reed**	16.00	
The Amazon Nation by C. Osborne	15.00	Great for research
Poetry from the Featherbed by pinfeather	16.00	If you think you hate poetry, you haven't read this.
None So Blind, 3rd Edition by LJ Maas	16.00	NEW
A Saving Solace by DS Bauden	17.00	NEW
Return of the Warrior by Katherine E. Standell	16.00	Sequel to Desert Hawk
Journey's End by LJ Maas	16.00	NEW
	Total	

South Carolina residents add 5% sales tax.
Domestic shipping is $3.50 per book
Please mail orders with credit card info, check or money order to:

Limitless, Dare 2 Dream Publishing
100 Pin Oak Ct.
Lexington, SC 29073-7911

Please make checks or money orders payable to **<u>Limitless</u>**.

Order These Great Books Directly From Limitless, Dare 2 Dream Publishing

Title	Price	Status
Queen's Lane by I. Christie	17.00	HOT
The Fifth Stage by Margaret A. Helms	15.00	
Caution: Under Construction by T J Vertigo	18.00	HOT-NEW
A Sacrifice for Friendship Revised Edition by DS Bauden	17.00	NEW
My Sister's Keeper by Mavis Applewater	17.00	HOT-NEW
In Pursuit of Dreams by J M Dragon	17.00	Destiny Book 3-NEW
The Fellowship by K Darblyne	17.00	
PWP: Plot? What Plot? Book II by Mavis Applewater	18.00	HOT-NEW
Encounters, Book I by Anne Azel	15.00	
Encounters, Book II by Anne Azel	15.00	
Hunter's Pursuit by Kim Baldwin	16.00	NEW
	Total	

South Carolina residents add 5% sales tax.
Domestic shipping is $3.50 per book

Visit our website at: http://limitlessd2d.net

Please mail orders with credit card info, check or money order to:

**Limitless, Dare 2 Dream Publishing
100 Pin Oak Ct.
Lexington, SC 29073-7911**

Please make checks or money orders payable to **Limitless**.

Order More Great Books Directly From Limitless, Dare 2 Dream Publishing

Shattering Rainbows by L. Ocean	15.00	
Black's Magic by Val Brown and MJ Walker	17.00	
Spitfire by g. glass	16.00	NEW
Undeniable by K M	17.00	NEW
A Thousand Shades of Feeling by Carolyn McBride	15.00	
Omega's Folly by C. Osborne	12.00	
Considerable Appeal by K M	17.00	sequel to Undeniable- NEW
Nurturing Souls by DS Bauden	16.00	NEW
Superstition Shadows by KC West and Victoria Welsh	17.00	NEW
Encounters, Revised by Anne Azel	21.95	OneHuge Volume - NEW
For the Love of a Woman by S. Anne Gardner	16.00	NEW
	Total	

South Carolina residents add 5% sales tax.
Domestic shipping is $3.50 per book
Please mail orders with credit card info, check or money order to:

Limitless, Dare 2 Dream Publishing
100 Pin Oak Ct.
Lexington, SC 29073-7911

Please make checks or money orders payable to **Limitless**.

Order These Great Books Directly From Limitless, Dare 2 Dream Publishing

Humanz **by Richard Ellis**	17.00	SciFi-NEW
Pirate Justice:Kara's Story **by j. taylor Anderson**	17.00	Adventure-NEW
Poetry from the Featherbed **by pinfeather**	17.00	Poetry
A Woman's Ring **by Rea Frey**	16.00	NEW
Sweet Melody **by Liana M. Scott**	16.00	NEW
Still Life **by Tracy Haisley**	17.00	NEW
Walnut Hearts **by Jackie Glover**	17.00	NEW
Soldiers Now **by Dean Krystek**	16.00	November 2004
Sins of the Innocent **by Deborah E. Warr**	18.00	Mystery-NEW
Guardians of the Stone **by Josiah Lebowitz**	17.00	SciFi/Adventure NEW
Where Love is Not **by Deborah E. Warr**	16.00	Ellen Richardson Mystery-NEW
		Total

South Carolina residents add 5% sales tax.
Domestic shipping is $3.50 per book

Visit our website at: http://limitlessd2d.net

Please mail orders with credit card info, check or money order to:

Limitless, Dare 2 Dream Publishing
100 Pin Oak Ct.
Lexington, SC 29073-7911

Please make checks or money orders payable to **Limitless**..

Printed in the United States
24292LVS00001B/229